Other Books by Sharon Marcus
from The Sufi Press

My Years With The *Qutb:* A Walk In Paradise
Five Times Of Prayer
Sufi
Adam's Story
A Traveller's Notebook
The Sufi Experience
The Stradivarius Poems

THE BOATMAN'S HOLIDAY

A FABLE

SHARON MARCUS

Printed in Canada

FIN 24 02 09

Library and Archives Canada Cataloguing in Publication

Marcus, Sharon, 1934-
    The boatman's holiday : a fable / Sharon Marcus.

ISBN 978-0-9737534-7-9

    I. Title.

PS8626.A744B63 2009   C813'.6   C2008-907518-8

THE SUFI PRESS
Toronto, Ontario, Canada

It is a dusty street rising almost accidentally from the squat red buildings hunched on the north shore of the lake. Curving in a fine line for three or four miles it expires like a spent arrow in a bus loop. The slender grey cathedral which gives the street its name languishes there helplessly displaced a mile north of the lake. For the next two miles corrupted rooming houses glower in bleached silence, the unstrung arcades of solitude, monuments to desolation. *Le silence défile, musique en tête, dans les rues de Chirico.* Blackened shop fronts decorate a building here and there.

August. It is morning. By ten o'clock the heat and light locked in that hazy corridor articulate their promise, dust and sorrow. A cellar door inserted at street level between two debauched houses opens carefully, a padlock released, a chain slid back. The heat folds about Thomas Archer (Steele), a shapeless figure already wrapped in layer after layer of decomposing garments, his raincoat which yields to all weather, a jacket broadly stuffed at the shoulders, a rust colored sweater with a dirty white vee at the neck exposing a blemished undershirt, and sagging, loose trousers which lope carelessly against his bare ankles, slapping now and again at the unlaced canvas running shoes.

He fixes the padlock to the door from the outside, pauses a moment and removes it, thrusting the lock instead into one of several pockets all in constant use. They are crammed with certain necessities: a micrometer, a meteoric stone, a handful of tonka beans, some broken charcoal sticks, a compass, a stiletto, a cat's eye, a tiny bronze figurine, an old *Fate* magazine, a small vial of neroli, a microphone, a reel of tape, pencils, crayons, graph paper, tracing paper, *The Birth Of Tragedy*, two boxes of Italian wax matches, a surgical knife and a detailed horoscope, his own. Born with the sun in Sagittarius and the moon in Libra. The zodiacal sign of Scorpio was ascending on the horizon at the time of your birth, with Mars, the ruler, in position at the eleventh house. Scorpio, the eighth sign on the belt is represented by the glyph of the eagle and serpent. Sun, nine degrees of Sagittarius; ascendant, twenty degrees of Scorpio; moon, fifteen degrees of Libra; Venus, twelve degrees of Sagittarius; Mercury, twenty-three degrees of Scorpio; Mars, twenty-five degrees of Aquarius; Neptune, fourteen degrees of Virgo; Uranus, twenty-eight degrees of Aries; Pluto, twenty-five degrees of Cancer.

Sunday. It is quiet. A meticulous examination of the street. Up. Down. Then over there, across the intersection — nothing but a sabbatarian cat stalking birds and a shuffling old man stooped beneath the weight of his own decay. Archer pushes one hand through the wiry hair dyed to orange streaks and pulls at his thin, straggling mustache. The pale flesh is slightly edemic, the features sharp, pointed, and the eyes, O the eyes. *L' attitude maudite a fait du maudit un privilégié, un protégé.* Quickly, still facing the street, he pokes his arm behind the door again and retrieves a canvas, carefully stretched, six feet by four in

2

dimension, paint clinging in viscous globules. It portrays a large, intricate machine, one which could even have been designed by Spohr, lying on its side half buried in desert sand. In the background a fixed green sun, round and sticky, emits spasms of light. A man's shadow, implicitly grotesque in flight spreads a pattern across the foreground. He calls the painting Mithras Perplexed.

While Archer gallops nervously up the street abruptly inspecting from right to left a venerable black limousine follows him, just out of sight. It is an extraordinary vehicle, a ludicrous, antique hearse ornamented at the corners with gilt angels holding fluted instruments to their lips. A black crown lifts a large cross aloft at the center point of the roof, gold fringe hangs uniformly in the windows. Beneath those windows carved black wreaths are draped in perpetual mourning. It moves without noise carrying an empty box, patiently, expectantly. The chauffeur and his companion are silent.

Filth. What unspeakable filth. They are undeterred.

That summer I lived in the open. At peace. Free. To use these words knowing their meaning has eluded me causes not so much pain as confusion. Now there is only fear, the fear which excludes everything outside itself, the fear which is my barricade, my prison wall, and there is no safety here. Back when time was a lyric in the hot summer wind, unencumbered waves rolling endlessly across the lake, and a frail girl whose long stripes of blond hair held me day to day, back then we bound ourselves with the waves, a salty stillness of the shore, the high summer growth, heat, the moonlit grass on a quiet night. Quiet, that penetrating quiet, and her green eyes smiling. For a time in that lucid summer we were alive, enchanted, we felt free. No voices demanding, no ugliness intruding on the simple rhythmic tick of day succeeding day, each complete, neither past nor future, only the present made explicit. Our language had no word for necessity, thought shaped itself along the grain of our senses, time was a concept outside experience and we found ourselves united by the cool grass on our bare feet, by the hot sun on our bodies, limb encircling nights, peace, an unqualified repose of the mind. All our pleasure was defined by that innocence. We had nothing to measure our understanding and no wisdom to preserve, it would have defeated our awareness, our proximity to a natural cycle which moved us both so deeply. In the strangeness, the remoteness touching this experience, in each other we found everything we had always known, and familiarity was unexpectedly the answer to longings which possessed us. The intimacy of that landscape taught us to see as though the spectrum were new, we learned the intricate harmonies, the prismatic touch of a single blade of grass. This recognition came to us when we were young, too young — why does it happen when we are too young? By the time our lives had unwound, by the time we could examine the thread of consequence we had lost that innocence. What a paradox, to be so loved, to be so damned.

Spohr and Nella live in a rambling grey stucco cottage somewhat submerged by the taller brick houses on either side. Its somber exterior exposes a scarcely visible patch of uncovered lathe, one cavity in this mortal facade, and a single window carefully widened by some previous tenant, now half masted with a yellow shade hovering above an old Christmas candle lost in glitter. To the right the door rises directly from its foundation without a front porch, just a single step, the door clinging to the house on two deliberately perilous hinges, although Spohr does not discourage casual visits now. The garden at the back is a slightly dusty compound, including as it does, his workshop and a large plot of grass scattered with his inventions, his designs. Every instrument or mechanical contrivance, apparently cast out, is precisely covered, maintained in working order; he is a fastidious man in a few ways and dislikes waste, his sole, enduring concept of sin. The knock at the door is about to be repeated as he appears, opening cautiously to preserve the inventive hinges. Spohr seems, all in all, a blonde but beady man, angelically plump, his pale, myopic eyes stalking out behind round, steel framed glasses over which he frequently glances sideways then up, like a fat white bird. His face is round and bland but marked with a deep double groove across the forehead. A wide, spreading belly protrudes unaffectedly from his half buttoned shirt.

- Good morning Archer, what brings you out so early?
- A dispute among the gods. Can *you* still tell the difference between right and wrong?

5

The question is not moral and Spohr recognizes its importance immediately, with only the faintest breath of alarm. Nella comes in shaking the sleep from her long fair hair and smiling eyes. She watches him take the padlock from his pocket, unlock it, snap it into place behind their door. A hand touches his.

- Tom, hello. What is it?
- Bad, very bad. Jews are persecuting blacks, interplanetary violence is imminent, I am in exile, Nietzsche is dead, a tricky Buddha is leading a revolt among the gods. Someone has been following me for three days.

They consider this intelligence carefully.

- What's to be done?
- You keep my painting Spohr, it's material evidence. They won't find it here, the jackals, and just when I was starting to like it. What do you think? It's quite verbal, another few days and I could have had that machine speaking unmistakable blasphemy.

He leans the painting against a wall as the three of them peer into it like tourists.

- Why do they always choose moments like this to get at you?
- Nella, some coffee, quick, and lots of glucose in Tom's. His blood chemistry needs changing.
- Carbolic acid in Spohr's, he has no blood.

He hurls the stiletto at the frame of his painting.

- Now do you have any doubt?

Schradieck enters as usual, climbing in through the kitchen window at the back.

- What's up Nella?
- Only Archer going out of his mind again.
- Christ. Make coffee for me too, I've got time to kill until the decent people get out of church. I have a hangover that would honor the devil.
- Wretched man, did you steal anything?

He leers.

- Answer me.
- O a purse, a few odds and ends. It was so simple, really, I'm still laughing.
- I don't want to hear any more, just make sure you don't come asking me to get you a lawyer. Go drive your taxi.
- I want to see Archer. I have to tell him something, a message from some Chink.
- You can't see him now, I think it's serious this time. He's really not fit to be seen, he looks wild.
- He's never fit to be seen.
- What message?
- Well last night I picked up this fare, a huge Chink —
- Stop using that word.

- Anyhow, it threw me when he started to speak very, very correct English with the kind of accent, you know, they get from fancy schools, you know, the real thing. He said, 'You are Thomas Archer's friend.' Well Tom isn't the sort of guy you admit to knowing, not to just anyone and especially not to a goddam Chink. So I said I didn't know him. I wanted to ask why but he never stopped, 'Tell him I'm waiting to speak to him,' gave me a fiver and got out.

- I don't trust Schradieck, I think he's in on it.
- Now Archer we need some facts, something to go on. What have you been doing the last few days?
- Facts Spohr, you always want facts when I give you my word. I repudiate facts, accept the experience, don't ask for it sliced up. Wait until you huddle night after night, day after day, alone in the dark chambers of your skull. Save those cold hallelujas for moments of intuition and frenzy, then see how they work. If you can't figure it out by yourself make a deal with the gods, but don't pester me for facts Spohr, I have none. *Nella, you bleak hearted witch, why did you leave me?*
- Just a minute now, listen to me, this is a bit of a problem but I think we can work it out. Everything seems to depend on Schradieck for the moment. If he knows anything he has two choices, either he can tell me or keep quiet. If he knows something he'll probably tell me, then again, perhaps not. After all, he doesn't like me, so why shouldn't he hold out? If he is in on something sinister he probably won't tell me, unless of course I can force him to speak. But you can't even be sure of that because he's such a buffoon, and not a very trustworthy

one come to think of it. If he does know anything either he will try to conceal that he does or he won't bother. This would give him an opportunity to tease me, to torment me a little as he would no doubt see it, and he'd like that, poor fellow. If he can conceal what he knows, from my point of view it would amount to the same thing as not knowing, unless I can bring some pressure to bear. But then if I can't make him say anything it still adds up to the same thing whether he knows something or knows nothing. Now suppose he actually knows nothing and pretends to know, it's much the same as knowing in one sense. Or suppose he knows without knowing that he knows, this is something I have to find out, and either I will or I won't. If he doesn't in fact, know anything but thinks he knows, he'll either tell me or he won't, and if he doesn't tell me anything I won't know whether he knows or doesn't know, or thinks he knows and doesn't know. And then again, if he tells me anything I won't know whether he actually does not know and is making the whole thing up, or whether he does know and is telling the truth, or knows and lies. If he pretends to know and doesn't tell me what he pretends to know, I won't know whether he knows or doesn't know or pretends to know. The points are quite simple themselves, does he know or doesn't he, how will I know whether he knows or doesn't know, how will I know whether he doesn't know or merely pretends to know, how will I know whether he knows or merely pretends not to know? If I can't know whether he knows or doesn't know, or pretends to know and doesn't know, or pretends not to know and knows, I'll do whatever is necessary, and if I have to I'll administer some form of

9

persuasion to be sure, and to be sure I'm sure. That's what I'll do. Now what do you think?

- You leave me gasping. My God Spohr, I may be half mad but you are something. What do you say Nella?

- You know Spohr would never lay a finger on anyone. Schradieck won't lie to me Tom.

- And why not, he lies to everyone. For that matter, everyone lies to everyone. In any case, whether he lies or not is irrelevant.

- Please don't go off and have a fight with him.

- What difference can it make, do you like him? Do you care a little bit, just a little bit too much about him, is that what it is? Do you fancy him with his shifty eyes and his grossly carved up face? Is that the truth? Come now, be open with us. I was your beloved once too you might remember.

- O for God's sake!

- Do you know what I think? It's me he loves, me, not you, and that's why he'd lie to you. You're wrong Nella, Schradieck is mine.

Searching for Schradieck, assaulted by wave after wave of celestial fire, the midday sun. He sheds a few outer garments like skins, the remainder impact themselves densely about his body now wet with fear and the pulsing sun. *Homage to thee, 0 Ra, who wakest life from slumber!* With one hand he counts the little tonka beans over and over, with the other he caresses the stiletto, stopping to stare at the sky and groan through tightly clenched teeth, 'You! You!' A legion of good, stately women pass him on the street, carefully sweeping to one side, recognizing at a glance the unbearable contagion his sickness contains. They flow past him in gauze-like dresses, flowered blues and pinks, films of whites, creams, mauves, yellows and greens. Their freckled, varicosed feet are squeezed into walking pumps, blanched hands pressed into frothy nylon gloves, and pearls fall across their parched skin haunting the memory of some distant time in glory. Sagging faces variously dotted with warts, wens, tumors and pale liverish spots sprout thick sprigs of hair from lip and chin, a fearless profusion. Occasionally a tame but withered spouse follows in their wake, carrying a Bible and a cane, an umbrella, sweating politely beneath palm hats into grey tropical suits or striped seersucker jackets. At last the streets ring like a desert, hollow, empty.

Hand braced against the point of the stiletto he pushes, pierces through skin, flesh and sinews to the bone. The pain holds him erect against the knock, the knell behind his burning eyes.

This, yes, this is how it is. This finally is what I know, the truth. I stagger in the streets wrapped about my self-inflicted pain, my own, self-imposed, and I affront the gods, I take my strength from them, my pain from their affliction. I take their wounds upon myself knowing that pain is only pain, suffering only suffering, a grim, pointless invention. I deny them, I defy them and they are obliged to yield, to leap down screaming from their sacred circle, submit and bury themselves in the lie. You impersonators of destruction, you lie, you cheat. Come down I say, come down. Descend from your doomed cathedrals, learn to echo in simple quarters, learn to curse, to reason, to swear by me. Look now, up there, see, see the sky! It splits the gold mosaic crust and every little square of light hurls its beam on me. I win Mithras! I win Siva! I win Marduk and Ra! Bring fire! Bring fire! O, O they live, they still live and I am deserted. They pave these thoughts for my destruction, they have distracted me. Schradieck, I have to find Schradieck. Where is he? Where in this god illumined town can he hide? He won't help me, he can't, he's on their side, he's in on it. And then there's Nella, he wants Nella. But he can't have her, she's mine, that silky witch. She won't escape again, this time I'll tie her down, I'll tie her hands, I'll bind her feet. So lost, so marooned, why did they leave me, why did they go away? Not even the wind to carry me to heaven. Where does it blow now? Do you hear the rustling, the toads of night? Somewhere innocence prevails. Hear the sparrows cry. Why does the sun disappear in the bright noon sky? Where is wisdom, where is goodness, where is mercy, where is that gentle wind? But I don't suppose they let you die of it, I don't suppose they let the bees rot and buzz in your skull. They take you off these gold infested streets, lure you to a dungeon where you howl in slime and filth, their unspeakable filth, hold you down against a dirty floor and hands that claw rip out your eyes, tear off your flesh and throw the pieces to the wind.

He lies face down in the dusty street. The chauffeur and his companion fling a body into the box in their ornate, ludicrous vehicle and drive off.

When Archer disappeared Schradieck came to Spohr's house more often than before, but now he came to confide in Spohr and not to make love to Nella. Of course Spohr tried to find Archer after he vanished without a trace, and Schradieck for that reason acquired a sudden importance. He did know something as it turned out, and he was made to tell his story again and again. It began on a hot Saturday night cruising in his taxi, searching for a fare, stopping instead at a bar, then another and another to fill in the long slow hours. He wasn't sure how much time passed this way, picking up a few passengers once or twice. It was August, the dense heat and noise of Saturday night assailed him, he felt he could no longer endure the rush, the hilarity, he didn't mind so little business coming his way that night. The crowds of revelers melted away on either side like ghosts, or perhaps he was the phantasm passing invisibly among them. With each stop and each drink he felt less interested in the night's work. It seemed more and more as though he had embarked upon some private celebration, a holiday of his own as he toured the bars. Schradieck recognized an acquaintance here and there, not talking to anyone, merely savoring the relief of being alone, for once not worrying about the trivial domestic afflictions, the minor legal embattlements, the financial hopelessness that haunted his days and soured his nights. He dammed up the whole stream, the petty difficulties which taken together meant a life of torment, and let them swell quietly in an underground lake while he took off in a small euphoric craft, destination oblivion. His funds exhausted, Schradieck cashed a cheque with the friendly manager at The Embassy and was heading out towards the Danforth where he knew a pleasant bar or two when quite unexpectedly, he was hailed by a man at the subway entrance. In a drunken leisurely way . . .

- Sorry, I have a fare.

He drove past, then on an impulse, perhaps remorse for the night's wages, he made an abrupt U turn and circled back. Spohr listened to the tale of that night many times, always returning to this moment, this impulse, as Schradieck called it.

- What was going through your mind, what were you thinking at the moment you decided to pick him up?
- I wasn't thinking anything, except possibly that Lisa would be upset. About the money I mean.
- Is that why you turned back?
- Hell no, if I had to worry about Lisa being upset . . . I had a funny feeling, you know, like a premonition, you know, only different, it's hard to say.
- Can you describe it?
- I don't know, it was a kind of restless feeling, a hesitation, uncertainty. It's hard to remember and harder to explain

because I was half cut to begin with; now going back over it I can't be sure how much I'm exaggerating.

Spohr pursues his unexpected candor tactfully, with persistence.

- I know this is difficult, but concentrate on that moment. Try to forget you've ever mentioned it or even thought about it, pretend you're telling me this for the first time. Let's wait a few minutes, there's no hurry, think about something else. Good, now do a little playacting. Let the recollection flood back on you, let it rush in suddenly and check every corner to see what comes in with the tide. There is something here and I don't know what it is, I'm not too sure what we're talking about yet, are you? Had you in fact, seen the man who hailed you?
- I don't think so because I remember how surprised I was when I looked at him.
- Why was the feeling you had so unnerving?
- I thought there was something I was supposed to do, absolutely had to do, only I'd been drinking and couldn't imagine what it was or recall anything about it. Like a sudden flash of having been somewhere before, having done exactly the same thing, when everything looks and feels too familiar and you know it must have happened before, like that. Something bothered me when I drove on, you know, and there I was slowing down and turning around. I had to do it.
- Do what?
- Turn back.
- Why?
- Well to pick that man up of course.

15

- You already told him you couldn't take him.
- But I lied. O God this is silly, maybe I just changed my mind. It's useless trying to remember what I did when I was so juiced, let alone why.
- Listen, it might be a clue, it could be important even if it doesn't tell us exactly what we want to know. Do you see what I mean?
- This is too much. How are we ever going to find him? Spohr, this might sound silly, but have you thought about getting the . . . ah police, you know, the cops?

Spohr laughed, unusual but not improbable in his dealings with Schradieck, a deprecating, lascivious laugh that began in his inner depths and ended at the back of his head.

- Did the queer feeling go away when you turned back?
- I don't remember.
- What were you thinking?
- I don't know, nothing.
- What were you feeling?
- Uneasy.
- How?

O haunted, followed, betrayed.

- I don't know, I can't describe it.
- Just as you couldn't describe the rest?
- I am telling the truth.

Again the humiliating laugh.

- You must be nervous.
- Leave me alone Spohr, I can't remember any more.
- Well let's go on to the man, tell me about him.

He was carved of translucent jade.

- He was an eyeful, hard to believe even looking straight at him, weird, a big man, huge in fact, rolling fat chins, enormous gut, tall, actually very tall, well-dressed, completely bald . . . and Chinese.
- Chinese?
- Chinese. Why do you keep asking the same questions, that was the first thing I told you about him and you don't seem to believe it. What's so amazing about that? There are lots of Chinks in this town, you know.
- Do many of them look like that?
- How do I know, they all look alike to me.
- Did he?
- Did he what?
- Look like the others.
- No, not really, not in the least.
- How was he different then?
- Well he was bigger.
- Is that it?
- No.
- What else?
- He had an English accent.

17

- Begin again.
- Where?
- The beginning.

There was a crescent scar curving down Schradieck's face from his thick, succulent lips to his chin. Whenever Lisa asked how it had happened his face spread in an unctuous smile, his profession of good humor, and although he never did convey any details, by swagger alone he managed to conjure a glorious but scarred conqueror of the streets. He described fights he had been in with relish, especially when it made her squirm with apprehension and distaste. He liked the rhythmic satisfaction he took swinging his arms, the shock ransacking his body on impact, the collision of fist and flesh, he liked the physical release even going down in defeat. She accepted this about him as she accepted everything, the pregnancies, his occasional incarceration for despicably petty larceny, the frequent dilations of drunkenness, the infidelities, the poverty. Lisa's passion was undivided, without compromise. Absorbing him whole, she faithfully tried to please him, to make him comfortable while he bit his fingernails to the quick, laughed his shifty, evasive laugh, lied and was desperate, always desperate. The final declaration of her Yorkshire ancestry, Lisa resembled a small sprite, emanating intensity, darkness, something perhaps like a gypsy in her wild crest of wiry hair and the deep ringing voice locked within her mute, prolific body. Their children, all female, a gnome-like brood with long bulbous noses, had inherited something corrupt from both of them. During periods of self-rehabilitation which manifested now and then in a repentent uxoriousness, Schradieck would search for more or less legitimate employment and invariably fell prey to unscrupulous employers: he sold heavy blocks of ice from a truck for more than fifteen hours a day one intensely hot summer and was arbitrarily dismissed when an unexpected cold snap set in; he was briefly a blackleg longshoreman, unloading cargo from a decrepit ferry which caught fire and sank to the bottom of the bay; as doorman for an unsavory downtown bar he was severely beaten by several ill-disposed patrons; sometimes he would line up for day labor outside a Salvation Army hostel; but when his license was not under suspension he drove one of a fleet of taxis painted orange and black. During all the years preceding Archer's disappearance, soon after she had married Spohr, Nella contracted a special friendship with Lisa, through Schradieck of course, a friendship which overtook them like some disease with long periods of remission but inevitable progress. It was too deeply entrenched to cut away by the time they discovered their affinity late one wintry night lost in certain confidences. They had learned to enjoy each other's company outside ordinary affection, in part because gradations of feeling were unknown to Lisa who seemed to feel little between indifference and the overmastering passion for her husband and children, and in part because Nella usually preferred the company of men to women. But she took cool pleasure in being a friend when there was trouble. When Schradieck's misadventures ended in legal difficulties Nella could always find a lawyer and money for bail from assorted reluctant friends. For that alone Lisa was grateful, and in any case, she knew nothing about her husband's obsessive interest in Nella. Neither did Spohr for that matter. Schradieck's gloomy passion for Nella had been transformed one dull afternoon when tired of talking, she suggested going to bed together instead. His appetite for her taut blonde body was kept sharp by her apparent lack of desire for him, her friendship with his wife, and of course, Archer's persistent dreams.

All those years ago when I was young, when I was Spohr's bride and my hair hung down in long gold streaks, when Archer worshiped obliquely under Spohr's dispassionate gaze and Schradieck screamed like an eagle, the days were ripe with deliverance from mortality. Those were my summery years, united to Spohr, devoted to Archer, longing for Schradieck. I had come to Spohr quite simply for knowledge, and he taught me everything in his inexhaustible way. He taught me to conjugate Latin verbs, to solve quadratic equations, he taught me Aristotelian logic, linguistic analysis, atomic weights, the genus and species of hundreds of plants, the classification of animals, and in a practical way so that I could help with his work, he taught me to operate any number of machines: a surface grinder, a punch press, a metal band saw, a south bend lathe, an air compressor, a multi-roll straightening cradle, an arc welder, a spot welder, a double end brinder, an electric chain hoist, a power hacksaw, an endless collection of useful tools. Can you imagine it? But I never acquired an intuitive familiarity, a sympathy for his instruments, and often I failed to grasp the point of his refinements, his playful application of immensely complicated functions to trivial tasks. I lacked, he would say, the artistic mode, and that was true. It was a particularly important point. To be an artist in the twentieth century, he would also say, was supremely irrelevant. As he understood it, art had ceased to function, had been exhausted, was clinically dead every way except financially, and that ironic distortion logged in history's footnotes never failed to amuse him, to evoke his detached, humorless laughter. Nevertheless, he expected me to bring a sense of artistry, some secret, a gift to the service of his technology which, he claimed, had supplanted the dead limb. He was an unrelenting tutor determined to use every available technique to make me learn, teaching fundamentals by rote, by memory, repetition, tricks, understanding, and even by a careful exploitation of intuition. Learning was an orderly process set in motion by amassing and memorizing simple components, his logical atoms, and then by combining them with increasing dexterity. For him knowledge as well as the wisdom that accumulated inseparably was an upside down pyramid, each particle interlocking with whatever came before and after. He insisted on economy, on simplicity. When I married him everyone was surprised; they assumed his love, his desire for me, and found themselves puzzled, unable to understand why I wanted to marry him. They were wrong about Spohr, we shared the same bed infrequently, he was oblivious to my occasional infidelity, he didn't want children, he certainly didn't expect me to be his housekeeper, to keep order for him; nor did he want me as an ornament, an amulet against his latent ugliness. He seemed to want me as his wife, quite arbitrarily. But how can I account for the changes which swelled with tidal inevitability over our days and nights? During the five long years between Archer's disappearance and Spohr's sudden death, my husband underwent a change which even he wouldn't have described as merely glandular. He suffered with increasing frequency and intensity from hallucinations, or so it seemed, in which Archer appeared to interpret his own tumultous, inner life. Looking back down the long corridors which separate then from now, I see how adroitly Sevcik played his part in our lives. It was Sevcik who persuaded Spohr that he needed a wife, and Sevcik who persuaded me to be that wife. I don't remember how or when this man first appeared, he always seemed to have been there, an insistent presence, a powerful image which had to be accounted for, even appeased. It was not as though we needed him or even trusted him, yet he managed to slip into the folds of our existence, to maneuver for his own quiet purposes. He was not a carnal man, his appetites were not of the flesh and he was undoubtedly no materialist, but he hungered, you might say, to dominate the lives of others. You would never have suspected this from observing that ungainly flux which constituted his movement, the lurch which was his walk or the sudden catalepsis bringing him to a standstill. However, if you looked carefully into his face where a few whiskers erupted in barren places, you would have recognized the *siddha* who was not to be trifled with. Even Archer held him in sardonic respect, asking about him often, curious and amused. Sevcik was actually very kind, he never seemed formidable in anything he said or did, still, he always appeared to be lying in wait, deploying secret forces which urged our destinies upon us. He was like an obstacle along the way which ought to have been circumvented, bypassed, but he fascinated us and we stopped to be entertained, to be distracted. Why can't we see these things, why is it impossible to read the signs? Why can we never, with all our science, our astrology, our divination, foretell the obvious? Are we afraid to know, are we incapable of knowing or not permitted to know? The vengeance of days. Questions, answers, look at me. My face is slack and dim, my neck is wrinkled and my hair has lost its color, its brightness. Is this a sacrifice to time, is it reward or punishment? *Be merciful my God, be merciful.*

The Boatman's Holiday

The Meeting

The Boatman's Holiday

When Spohr died everything changed. It wasn't just that Nella's perception altered, the whole world was different, transformed by a slight variation, a shift in the polestar which occurs only once every twenty-eight thousand years giving rise to rearranging particles, realigning energies. The rational, logical episode in the dream of the world began to subside. Allegiance to the verbal, the phenomenal, to proof itself, faded with the reawakened belief in Thomas Archer's gods. Art and the institutes of religion died of natural causes although their minor deities were unexpectedly much in demand. During Spohr's time wit, intelligence and good will had been considered adequate for survival, and then survival itself was discovered to be inadequate. There was a thirst for life after death, a genetic suspicion the truth tables lied; all the little gods were coaxed back, lured from quasi-retirement into the thick of it, along with jinns, fairies, demons and dark powers. But no true secrets were revealed to them. And Nella drifted like a ship without a course, without a pilot. Life as she understood it from Spohr's perspective had failed her, she knew nothing, hoped for nothing. Breathlessly, she allowed herself to be carried along by the tides and currents in an unkempt sea. Her frail, precarious craft, the sallow body poised on a slender waist became thinner and darker, her green eyes glowed against greenish skin. That enervated, emaciated body attracted eager suitors, perhaps the attraction was nothing more than availability and the obvious need to be cared for, yet she sailed away instead on a dark, uncharted sea.

Although Spohr died some five years after Archer disappeared the two events were linked, twin disasters in Nella's life, one depriving her of the alchemy which lit up certain elliptic moments, the other removing her rational frame. During the interval between these events, a time of waiting, a time of change, Monty Wells bore down upon their lives with occasional drunken fury. B. Montgomery Wells he liked to sign the letters he addressed to *The Globe And Mail* on issues of local or national importance, and also the precise papers he wrote in the field of molecular biology. When he wasn't drinking, that is ordinarily, he was content to live quietly with his wife and a dark haired daughter in their suburban townhouse, to conduct himself with the necessarily undocumented reserve required of a comparatively junior researcher, to wear tweeds, a crisp white shirt and a well-knotted tie. The thin bloodless lips remained tightly pressed together, the eyes were warm behind rimless glasses, the complexion very pale. His dry, attenuated body had arched prematurely in an elderly stoop, and although he laughed often, his laughter rang false. His greatest pleasure was to play Chopin while having fantasies involving a girl, almost any girl, a remote island, a sleek concert grand and himself, whimsical maestro, beloved hero. Two or three times a year something began to roar inside him and for a few days he would leave his wife to engage in self-abusive bouts of alcohol and metaphysical speculation. His appearance, always neat, never betrayed him; he didn't manifest the classical symptoms of drunkenness in the way he walked or talked, but his behavior became obsessive, bizarre. Once when he was drinking with a few students in a bar whose pretensions of another day were brought to mind by the rotting gilt satin interior and crusty chandeliers, he insisted upon flicking the waiter's tie into the poor man's face as he served them. At last, white with indignation, and believing himself to be the victim of a conspiracy whose outcome he could not begin to predict, the waiter had them removed from the premises. Not the slightest inconvenienced, Wells proceeded alone to Spohr's beckoning house.

- B. Montgomery Wells, madam, your faithful servant, he greeted Nella.
- Monty, surely to God you're not drinking?
- You dear, beautiful creature, surely to God I'm not, he replied waving the bottle above her head in the direction of Spohr who appeared in the doorway behind her.
- Don't let the bastard in!
- Don't let the bastard out!
- O come in!
- Spohr, began Wells quickly, have I complimented you on your wife's friendly sexual orifice? Have I told you how she soothed my unraveled appetites for a few insatiable nights with her darling crevice, her fertile hips?
- Yes, I'd have to say you have insinuated, you have implied and you have even announced unmistakably that this strange

intimacy took place, said Spohr blandly, accustomed to specific themes which recurred during Monty's drunkenness.
- God curse you Spohr, you are an evil man!

Alfred Spohr, fair haired, smooth, round, triumphant, always in command, always in control. Was there mercy for you?

This lull, this lingering interlude before Spohr's death was their middle age. Nella glided aimlessly in the wake of her husband, cool, untouched by the revolutions which erupted continentally on all sides, and Spohr pursued his own inspiration, designing, inventing extravagant devices to execute the most ordinary tasks, a laser to open and close doors, different versions of a computerized mechanism to handle his meager correspondence, his stocktaking, to play games and operate remotely powered toys. Nothing was trivial and nothing had any meaning for him beyond the substantive, formal power to solve problems. He was friendly, expansive, entertaining, benevolent, not what you would call kind but the best, most solid person in any emergency. Nella believed during their first few years together he was never angry; later she saw, once or twice, something dark in the depths of his eyes. All through this time he engaged most fervently in those marital deceptions which scarred and seared her love for him beyond repair. It was not as though he didn't engineer his affairs with scrupulous attention to deluding his wife, but this he always managed in such a way that she could only avoid knowing by deliberately not knowing. A certain artfulness in accounting for pink lace undergarments in the pocket of his overcoat, an inadvertent gonorrheal infection, letters, his failure to return home one night, mysterious telegrams and importunate telephone calls showed the careless hand of a master so sure of his ability to sway, to deter, he was prepared to risk everything for nothing. He was always casually and systematically ready to glut his appetites. Was this why Monty Wells who admired his intellect, who was astonished by his inventions and championed his resourcefulness, was this why Monty detested him? O those listless years. Nothing happened, whole worlds exploded and yet nothing ever happened. How calmly they navigated those troubled years, impervious, aloof. Perhaps because they were fundamentally unattached to life, careless of its value, Spohr if not Nella, grew fat with indifference. The two long haired black cats who traveled everywhere with them in a wicker hamper grew fat too. Geoffrey, the male, had been emasculated and was unaffected by Isobel's tender purrs and desperate wooing. Spohr studied them with interest, comparing their delicate complexity to his computers. When Isobel's frenzy made her yowl and scream, hurtling from one side of the room to the other, one day he inserted the blunt end of a ballpoint pen into her delicate aperture, manipulating it until she sprang away across the room, the howling stopped for awhile at last. Staring over his steel rimmed glasses he watched

31

her lick her paws with satisfaction. Spohr laughed and laughed. Nella did not approve, still, it would never have occurred to her that she might interfere, not from mere supineness but a deep conviction which respected the right of another to behave with whatever indiscretion his folly or passion might bring him to. She would make no comment, she felt no impulse to reject what she could not condone. This enraged Monty who tried to move her with detailed descriptions of some old infidelity committed by Spohr. Such information she would store in an icy way, and at the right moment thaw a few particles to hurl at him with contempt. There was time enough for contempt in that bleak November of nights, time enough when lives hung from their fingertips in a starless void.

Sometimes Monty brought along a young Englishman, Edwin Knight, a tall, rugged looking man whom they privately and pleasantly called the philosopher, this because he had the habit of groping for answers in a stylish, syllogistic way. Unfortunately he also tended towards inarticulateness when he drank too much — rather often — but he was a friendly, handsome man and his friends overlooked these excesses. Others, not so kindly disposed towards him, were offended by the automatic responses of an English gentleman, mistrusted the intuitive support of class, wealth and station. In his younger days such matters did not weigh heavily upon him, as he matured however, in the way these things do, they became increasingly important. A mutual acquaintance, it was Charlie Cohen, years later informed Nella with horror and distaste that on a certain occasion when a strike threatened in a theatre

32

where Knight was working, he said coolly with sympathy for the owners, some distant family connection, 'O come on fellows, let's just forget all this nonsense and get on with it.' To Charlie this was both incomprehensible and unforgivable. Knight's beautiful wife had been sent back to England for the birth of their child; he had been expected to follow soon after. They corresponded infrequently but affectionately, and on her side with growing surprise as it became apparent he was reluctant, even unwilling to return home. Meanwhile he lived in straitened circumstances with the prospect of great wealth to be inherited upon his father's death, or sooner if the lawyers succeeded in setting aside the trust his grandfather had established against the profligacy of his heirs. Until that prosperity should be upon him Edwin found it preferable to remain abroad, less conspicuous in employment beneath his expectations for himself, and beyond the range of his wife's breathless sibilance. He worked in the theatrical arts as a stagehand, then somewhat later abandoning this promising way of life, he began to study philosophy at the university, ardently, under the tutelage of Wells and the guidance of Spohr. Gradually Spohr became the architect of his experience, teaching him in a good humored, thoroughly Socratic way, imparting his values, his knowledge and his immense gift for reason without compassion. In those years Spohr was the master. Now at this time Nella also cared for Edwin who appeared to be quite uncomplicated, undemanding. Aside from a habit of occasionally regurgitating without restraint when he drank too much, an admittedly rather frequent occurrence, he seemed a charming, sensitive man. Indeed she found him attractive enough, and perhaps a few years later, wearied by Spohr's relentless infidelities, Nella might have taken him for herself. She turned instead to Sandy Burns, a passionate and gifted actor several years her junior. *When Spohr died a thin stream of blood spurted from his lips.* Edwin called Nella my dear lady, and found comfort in the arms of thoughtful young women who lived in hope of a triumph in the theatre, a triumph in their lives, and the inevitably consequent triumph in the world. They found the accent in conjunction with his ascot useful props for their aspirations, while he acquired an unfounded reputation for amatory excellence. But when Edwin made it increasingly evident he regarded himself as Spohr's disciple, his principal disciple at that, Nella began to tire of him, finding his long visits tedious, inevitably taking refuge in sleep when they embarked on their drunken exploration of the universe. They spent one long winter debating natural law. Spohr cunningly maintained that a statement describing an invariable function in nature was correctly called a natural law; Edwin insisted the very word 'law' meant a thing had to be so because it was decreed, and such legislation entailed the existence of a lawmaker, which was of course, unacceptable. If Boswell rushed to the bedside of the dying Hume to observe that great sceptic's death, what might he have felt beside these two? The stalemate which unfolded between them, a ball endlessly passed for the sake of the throw and the catch, was usually resolved when the younger man succumbed to the drink and passed into a stupor beyond reason, in accordance with its own laws. Frequently the next day found them caring for their hangovers with ice-cold beer, judiciously picking up the threads of the previous night's dialogue. They laughed a lot, found humor in the most unlikely propositions and rejoiced in their mind's pleasure. The tower of intellect is a tower of darkness.

On an early autumn afternoon when the trees were still green although a little dry and pale, when leaves on the maples and chestnuts had just begun to curl and the curving grey sky was whitened with cool, slanting rain, Nella raised the window blind habitually lowered against the people who passed no more than a few yards away in the street. Thunder, a collision of memory and longing, mute filaments curling towards her from the past and the future. The lightning snaked across the sky bringing her abruptly back to the year she had spent on Ward's Island with Thomas Archer. Together they lived in a dilapidated, sagging house considerably more ruined than the one she was to share with Spohr, a shack open and vulnerable to the wind and rain that fell in the still silent summer not so long ago. And now as the rain stopped the birds began to sing, a chorus she had learned in that brief summer, luminous and free. It was, they sang, a place beyond reckoning where there was neither before nor after, where beginning and end had disappeared in a slow accretion of awareness pointing to a faroff but accessible truth. Archer painted furiously in those days, stunned by the flexibility he found in the paints, the knife, the brushes, spattering his boards and canvases with oblique joy. He dragged the muddy depths within himself and began the cycle of paintings called The Sound Of Darkness. Rolling in his madness he emerged covered with precious gems, the darkness gilded, the disorder assuaged. *Les peintres qui se soulagent.* Nella watched him paint, both brimming over in his ecstasy. When he wasn't painting they played games together, talked a little, sang songs, lay down in the sand on the beach and washed in the waves of the lake. Time was their guardian, letting them slip out between its shining gaps where neither memory nor desire held them. Several times Tom started a portrait of Nella, trying to rivet some record to the canvas, but he was stopped by his inability to catch her likeness in a way that satisfied him. He had few technical reserves, his genius confined to specific conditions, limits he recognized and obeyed. In the past he had tried occasionally to expand his resources by taking lessons from an odd assortment of teachers when their interest and his inclination coincided, although it was never any use, he could only paint what he knew intuitively, and for that reason his work remained more or less private, shared by a few friends, a steadfast nucleus of enlightened observers. But his approaching eclipse in the darkness which bubbled continually beneath the surface was clear to him even then, and he would shake with the terror of what he saw, what he knew lay ahead. Damnation they say, is less than a hair's breadth from salvation. That summer was the last time the angels sang sweetly to him. When the bad times came, when the terror was strong Nella was helpless, she could neither dispel the darkness nor dissuade the demons. Sometimes Spohr — he came frequently to the Island that year —

was able to calm him by administering vitamins and practical solicitude, a tough, efficient nursing which was effective when the fear and frenzy were not too acute. Nella hardly noticed him, except to acknowledge his usefulness with gratitude, as Spohr quietly pursued his own ends, patiently. Joy and pain in Tom and Nella's world were so intense, nothing, no one could penetrate it. They were careless of their surroundings, their physical well-being, living in such chaos that Spohr once commented, 'My word, don't you ever clean up?' They hadn't noticed the encrusted spaghetti plates, the dirty clothes, the unmade beds, the dried up Christmas tree; they lived only for what they sought, the power of an emotional aesthetic enhanced by personal rituals. This lured Archer into ever more esoteric practices and studies of magic. Then he began his investigation of ancient religions, of the kabbala, of alchemy and the hermetic mysteries, he recited mantras, chants, formulas and looked at worlds within worlds, percolating with madness and the desire to conquer galaxies. His good angel wept. One day a little boy died, he fell off the pier on the bay side where he was playing and drowned before anyone missed him. Wracked by some inner sorrow Tom mourned the lost child, this death, as though the boy had been his own. The hooting whistles of the police boats coursing across the harbor awakened such horror in his mind he couldn't shake himself free. That whooping, haunting sound rang and rang in his ears for days, unleashing the terror, blinding him, holding him down in a dark pit. He cringed in the corner playing with matches, unable to find his way back. He lit the matches in ones, twos, threes and finally whole books at a time, watching the paper blacken, curl, crumple and drift away. 'It is my life, it is my life.' He snapped his fingers in protective circles around his head. Schradieck happened to visit on the fifth day of this; he and Nella whispered together wondering whether to send him to the hospital. He had been there before and each time he came back something was burned from his memory, whole circuits of wit, delight, fantasy and knowledge erased in the battle to save what his doctors valued. Nella and Schradieck felt unwilling to let them continue their experiments. When a few more days had passed however, the terror slowly began to subside and Tom started painting again, relieved and silent, without laughter, driven now by the whips of time. In a few weeks he was calm again. Their stay in paradise was over, and even though they sang and played once more like children, they were children damned forever. God the protector of us all has granted this power even to the worms which stalk us in paradise.

There was a narrow brick house several doors south of Spohr's on Bellair Street, a house subsequently torn down to make a parking lot for a fashionable restaurant when the neighborhood spiraled dizzily upwards, after Spohr died. That house, Spohr's and several others nearby were owned by an elderly broker, a lady who appeared unannounced in the doorway, tightly corseted, clad in grey Persian lamb and ambiguous hats. Mrs. Hurst had a lucky instinct for property values, and although she was said to be inflexible about the rent, her prices were fair, she was tolerant of the artistic semisqualor in that latter day bohemian community which was now about to capitulate, to be submerged in a new wave, the intoxication of a modish, middle class chic. Its adherents sampled drugs like connoisseurs, bought paintings, listened to the Stones and went to parties where their hosts laid out dishes of multicolored pills. But that was later. The last tenants to occupy the narrow brick house before it was demolished were Jan and Marguerite Mundt, young, Dutch, sickly in an unspecified way and prodigiously Anglo-Catholic. They barely managed to scrape by on their combined incomes, he as an odd job man and carpenter, she as an artist's model, sitting for life drawing classes at the College of Art and for a few Latvian painters who shared a loft on King Street. Jan and Marguerite rented several rooms in their house to passing musicians, students, aspiring actresses, dancers, and on a more permanent basis, to a commercial artist and to a poet who earned her keep at the university bookstore. Nella and Marguerite had become friends, Edwin had fallen in love with Marguerite, Marguerite had fallen in love with Bollard, the commercial artist who loved only himself but was valiant in bed. Marguerite's slender breasts and the squarish body she herself was dedicated to induced a condition of erotic thoughtfulness in Bollard. For a few years they deceived Jan in his own home, but never, it must be observed, in his own bed, until at last their passion wore them out. When Jan left to work at a jewelry store in Hamilton, Marguerite and Bollard discovered they didn't much care for each other after all. On dark winter afternoons, especially in their deceiving first year, Marguerite plucked the flowers of her passion petal by petal, displaying them for Nella who was amazed by her lovely, brown eyed splendor. Spohr could not discern the basis of their friendship; Edwin sometimes trailed along to listen. 'I would give this arm,' he would say later, 'Up to here,' chopping dramatically at his elbow, 'For one night, just one night.' And then he'd laugh at himself, sensitive to his absurdity, nevertheless suffering the predicament. Nella smoked endless cigarettes and listened, awed by Marguerite's poised sexuality, by her devotion to Jesus and Mary, and to her innately aesthetic response to flowers, books and music. Marguerite and Nella continued their exchange of secrets during the long winter months when time fell like the snow all around them, indifferent to the clamor of life and the stillness of death.

Annie March lived alone in the comfortable second floor room overlooking Bellair Street in that narrow brick house. On Wednesday afternoons when she finished work at the bookstore Annie went to visit her aging mother, the only living relative she had. Although that parent was now quite deaf they maintained a conversation by shouting, intuition and deep affection for each other. 'Mother,' Annie announced in a loud, clear voice, 'I started three new poems last week.' 'How nice dear,' she replied smiling happily at her bright eyed daughter, the hair already laced with grey, lips unnaturally red beneath a shocking lipstick which made her bloodless face appear ghostly. 'A flower that fell too soon, my child, my child,' her mother thought. And then later at the mission the old men would say to her, 'Miss Annie, yuh know I haven't been into the drink, now don't cha?' 'Bill, you old coot,' she'd say, 'I think you lie worse'n you play checkers, look at this,' jumping over three vanquished pieces. Then back in her room lying on the narrow bed with the blankets folded double, staring into the unlit room, she felt the waves of the black, the red and the silver oceans break beneath her, while beyond and above an ocean of light showered its radiant bliss upon her, wave after wave, pure light carrying her away to far places. 'Is there any way to understand this, will my body tolerate it, will my mind? If it is too much to be borne let me be swept away, let me die. I will not relinquish this clarity, this illumination.' Her pale body hung in a cocoon suspended from a thread in time.

No theory was adequate to account for the abrupt, mysterious manner of Thomas Archer's disappearance. Schradieck refused to talk to anyone once Spohr finished questioning him. He particularly declined to speak to Sevcik who pursued him diligently, or at any rate as much as a man like Sevcik would pursue anyone, but it must be remembered he was a *siddhayogi*, no one was prepared to take him lightly. It was just at this time certain photographs came into Schradieck's possession showing Sevcik in unmistakable levitation off the earth's surface, photographs demonstrating he had set aside the consequences of gravity and risen some eight to twelve inches, cross-legged above the place where he sat. Schradieck was overwhelmed, he didn't know what to think or how to think for that matter, having nothing other than neurosis and superstition at the core of his apparently down-to-earth attitude, the sham straightforwardness. As always when he felt troubled or confused the crescent scar on his chin became brighter, he sucked moistly on unfiltered cigarettes until they were streaked with brown, his speech was erratic and sweat began to stud the line around his slicked down hair. Examining the photographs he was stunned, it did not occur to him for a moment that this might be some trick. What he saw he believed was literally true, Sevcik had levitated. 'O God, if there is a God, what does it mean, how can he levitate? What on earth was Archer up to? Why was he so angry, what happened to him, who was that incredible man?' He continued to be evasive with Sevcik, allowing himself to appear intimidated, and Sevcik was reluctant to press him. But he remained convinced Schradieck did know something about Archer's disappearance. Like all those whose lives had been touched one way or another by Tom, and because he realized Tom had become something like a priest of the esoteric to his friends, Sevcik felt it was imperative to establish what had happened, to find out how, what, anything. As he understood it, Archer was their key, their witness. In the days before his bejeweled madness overreached him there had been a holiness about him, about his poverty, his directness, his concentration, his devotion to the madness and artistry which, while never resulting in any paintings that were

42

indisputable masterpieces, nevertheless promised something extraordinary, something about to be delivered, about to be revealed. Those who knew him, except perhaps for Sevcik and Spohr, hungered to have him produce a miracle for their sake, for themselves, as proof of their perception, as proof of their longing. And he hadn't done that yet. They clung to this hope expecting him to clarify the past and permit an unscathed voyage into the future where they would be deposited together on a distant shore, comfortable and yielding, their life's work done, minds intact and spirits refreshed.

Tell me friend, is it like that?

At first there had been talk of calling in the police, but since no one favored such an oddly uncomfortable proposal the idea was quickly dropped, with some relief. You don't, after all, ask the police to look for someone whose greatest fear is the police will take him, Nella observed. For awhile there was some hope he had gone to visit friends in remoter areas of the province, Wellington County, the Bruce peninsula, Haliburton, Parry Sound. Long past the time when the landlord had confiscated his few possessions in the subterranean room on Church Street, his friends concluded he was not coming back. If Sevcik looked upon Tom as an adversary or rival who continually maneuvered to claim ascendance, even outright mastery over his friends, he also felt a genuine not entirely inconvenient concern. Therefore he took a decision to act, and with Marguerite's help invited everyone to a meeting at his wife's studio. The assumption was that by exchanging and piecing together the available information they might find a way to help him. Schradieck of course, would feel obliged to take part in such a symposium, tell what he knew. But he didn't. Instead he sent his wife Lisa, her bulbous nose gleaming, while he drove remorsefully away in his taxi, off in a northwesterly direction to haunt some deserted part of town. He drove around by himself, puffing on the wet cigarette in his mouth, breathing heavily. Tom and his rituals, his powers, not that great if he couldn't protect himself, couldn't prevent the danger he walked straight into. He was convinced his friend had been trapped somehow and plunged into hopeless disaster. Echoes of the C.I.A. and international espionage rang through his head until he remembered how unlikely a person Tom was for that sort of thing. And then a new note sounded, reminding him Tom always survived, always had a little cash in his pocket, his friends didn't give him money, he didn't live on welfare, yet he always managed. His tramp-like appearance was a matter of choice or possibly just an accident of disposition. Carl Schradieck sighed, what information could a man like Tom possibly collect, for whom, who would trust such a wild if not demented source? Was he a courier of some sort? Speeded up fantasies, comic book burlesques spun across his mind. He laughed out loud and sighed again deeply, it made no sense. Then why did Sevcik pursue Tom so closely, was he involved too? That remained to be seen. When he could endure no more an elderly woman coming from a small apartment building signaled him, putting an end to the disquieting speculations which the night's assembly urged upon him.

Birgitte Meintz welcomed the guests to her large studio with friendliness, with dignity. She was short in stature, an unpredictable number of years older than Paul Sevcik and devoted to him. The product of severe German theatrical discipline from its zenith, the purest expressionism, Birgitte had brought a small school of dance into existence. These dancers of hers she trained, coaxed, encouraged, bullied and inspired. *Tänzerin: O du Verlegung alles Vergehens in Gang.* She choreographed their dances insisting upon disciplined improvisation, designed the sets which were geographically brutal, then begged musicians to play for them, to improvise with them. The ensemble performed publicly twice a year, brave in the face of supreme audience indifference. It was not within her nature to be discouraged, but her face acquired a quietly ruined quality, with excessively reddish cheeks and a network of red threads bursting on the wings of her nose. Altogether though, it was a face remarkably unlined when you considered Birgitte had been born at the turn of the century. She customarily brought such vigor to her teaching, such strength to the dancing, rumors of her advanced age were scarcely believed until the day President Kennedy was assassinated and Annie March found her wandering aimlessly through the studio building, moaning, weeping, wringing her hands in fluttering, futile gestures. She spoke darkly about the day the Duke had been assassinated. 'It was like this, a terrible time, the people suffering his tragic death, and then suddenly, I was just a young girl but I see it so clearly now, while the news was still on everyone's lips, while they were saying the Duke is dead, the Duke has been murdered, assassinated, the shooting began, our world came to an end. It will happen again, it will happen again, those murderous

45

days have come again.' Bewildered at first, Annie finally understood Birgitte was talking about the Archduke Francis Ferdinand, and her own sense of loss, her distress occasioned by Kennedy's death went skewing off in an almost comic feeling as she grappled with the half century mingled in Birgitte's grief.

From the Notebooks of Annie March (1963)

August. The prose elegy: destroyed. It haunts me still; feel it imperative not to write if I cannot discover a new form, find a new language, a new experience. And I can't carve out my passage to that innovative place; have decided therefore, not to try the Archer story cycle. The original is not particularly inventive, but that I undertook to see if I could at least do something conventional. Also as a distraction from The Sound Of Darkness when the poem was going so badly. Think there is no choice but to abandon prose completely, leave it for now; later, much later, perhaps again. In any case, I might have to abandon poetry too. Not only do I find myself without the language, the right verbal construct, but lacking in *matière* as well, and this is most surprising, most disconcerting. What remains, what persists is a sense of form, so powerful, so crafted, so unoccupied. How can I reduce the flowing duality, *le néant* elaborated by time and experience to an individual, a situation, a single word?

October 21st. S. in town for his sister's wedding. He irritated by me and I bored by him. He condemns, although he does not say it, what he sees as my perpetual solitude. I condemn only my perpetual inactivity. Self-castigation does not produce results in words. Still rereading Proust: he continually lamenting, for more than 2,000 pages, that he cannot seem to write.

November 29th. 2 staccato compositions in word elements, structures, archaisms, sounds, tones. Exploring the new word-sound-meaning: my dictionary obbligato. Is it possible to make patterns of words without direct reference to their meanings and still convey some overriding or undermining sense? Preoccupied with dissonance in words: the difficulty lies in establishing patterns which fulfill expectation in a purely harmonic sense, and then detonating that expectation with the words themselves. Rhythm and meaning will flow in different directions. It seems impossible to define sensual patterns except rhythmically or musically, certainly not in form alone. Feel obliged as always, to invent my language, nurture the seed, study the root and watch it sprout. *Wit wat witten waste.* Perhaps I should learn to think in Latin or some other dead language and put an end to it all.

Feel compelled to note this down: Kennedy was shot, assassinated last week. So much emotion pouring forth, true and accurate, and so much what's Hecuba to him of the imagination — mine, that is. Among others, even Marten Bender, never before observed to notice anything unrelated to music, makes statements resounding with sentiment. The proseurs, the journalists grind out copy endlessly. And I? And I? That's not it, not at all why this needs to be written down, it was the most disruptive, the most shocking event in the world, out there, since the end of WWII. And that's not it either. This in purely personal terms, I experience it.

From *The Cloud Of Unknowing* we learn that our whole life must be one of longing, the longing to achieve perfection, oneness with God. This longing must exist in our innermost depths, awakened by God in response to us as we consent. We must turn our back on His creation and turn instead to Him. What the soul does in its search for God is what pleases Him most. His saints and angels delight in our search for truth and eagerly help us on the path.

Guests arrive slowly at first, the *andante,* the slow and stately opening. Jan, Marguerite and Bollard enter bringing Annie and the ubiquitous Charlie Cohen who has lurked astutely in the shadow of the house next door, waiting for someone to escort him inside. They sit in silence awkwardly, on chairs placed around the edge of the large room. Neither Birgitte nor Sevcik makes any attempt to encourage conversation. Charlie Cohen apologizes profusely and with customary good humor for his unsolicited presence. Enter next Sam Docherty and Harry Bell, a pair of reckless Bobbsey twins. They're not Archer's friends but they know him, they are journalists and someone must take note of the proceedings. Instantly determining there will be nothing to drink they withdraw to The Pilot, there to strengthen both nerves and resolution. They will return somewhat later, impaired but improved. As they depart they cross the path of a few new arrivals, Claudette and Pavel Robichaud, two half starved mendicant artists from New Brunswick, a rather tall young woman unknown to either of them, two biology students accompanying Monty Wells, a handsome faggot and his friend from the house next door, then a lull, no others in sight.

<u>Sam</u>: Whew.
<u>Harry</u>: Hm.
<u>Sam</u>: Well I guess you can say the fat is in the fire now, well and truly in the fire.
<u>Harry</u>: Yes indeed. *[Long pause]* Just what does that mean?
<u>Sam</u>: Thinking actually about Archer, you see.
<u>Harry</u>: So . . .
<u>Sam</u>: Suppose for a minute he is engaged in some secret work, I mean all these people coming together like this can't do anything but hurt him ultimately, in the long run. Sevcik was ill-advised.
<u>Harry</u>: Do you think there's a particle of truth in that undercover agent theory? He's bonkers for one thing, and the most naturally conspicuous creature on this earth for another. Maybe he's just in jail, maybe he went right off his rocker, maybe they've clapped him in the slammer for beating someone up.
<u>Sam</u>: They say he's never violent, even when he's flipped out.
<u>Harry</u>: I'm told the opposite. Anyhow, he could be in the bin somewhere, raving out of his skull, lunatic, unbefriended.

Sam: Let's have a couple more, doubles let's say, and then get back.

Harry: Well don't rush, I'll need a little more noise if there's nothing to drink. Nice to have you home.

Sam: This is a terrible town, I hate it here.

Harry: Does that mean you're going to leave again?

Sam: Don't really know, CP offered my old job back. I swore I'd die before doing it again, you know, but look at me, actually considering it. Must be the old death wish speaking. What to do?

Harry: Good God, at least cheer up old man, you can't go through the rest of your life being so gloomy. Just decide firmly that everything will get better, stick to it and you'll be surprised how much things improve.

Sam: Ha, you haven't changed you optimist, you abominable opportunist.

Harry: That's more like it, as long as you're abusing me it's not all lost. A drink to diplomacy and the slow deterioration of moral values. O there you are, doubles please. The trouble with you Sam, is you drink too much, you have to watch it or you'll end up like me.

Sam: And the trouble with you Harry, is you're so damn insensitive. Can't you tell the difference between the real thing and acting? Did you think it would be like this, did you ever for one minute think it would be like this? *[Long pause while they drink.]*

Harry: Maybe not old friend, maybe not.

[Exeunt]

The tempo begins to accelerate as the dynamic range increases. Hypnotically Monty approaches the tall girl, 'I'm Montgomery Wells,' he announces. 'O that's very nice,' she replies walking away. Marguerite and Lisa exchange greetings, Lisa's deep, resonant voice travels out into space landing nowhere, blue snow on a cold mountain, 'The children are fine thank you, they're so well-behaved. I'd like to go home for a visit. My father died, my mother is all alone, she has no one, no one but me and I'm thousands of miles away. I want her to come here so much, you know, just for awhile. Schradieck won't hear of it though.' 'Won't he let you go there?' 'No money.' The Robichauds describe the series of Archer's paintings called The Sound Of Darkness in great detail, their French accents a dominant voice gathering up a knot of interested people: a musician, not Marten Bender, he isn't here yet, but a short intense man, Jock Carogna, home from a long tour in the States, his lined and dreaming face draped with a flowing blond mustache; a rather fat, elderly lady rocking nervously from foot to foot — it was her mother who had been so kind to Tom during the few years she had known him; a man who is believed to be a stockbroker but is in fact, a friend of the faggot next door; another more sober journalist and two impecunious actors who work at Eaton's; and the faggot next door. They are clearly impressed. 'These canvases by God, they have true beauty, his colors are so clean, so new, and if you place them in a circle around you, if you stand in the middle the sound will actually come from them. You can follow it from picture to picture, a terrible sound which haunts you under the skin, *nel'orecchie me*

51

percosse un duolo, a sound to waken the dead, the color of despair, the sound of despair that makes you clench your teeth to keep the screams from rushing out. No one else paints like that today Claudette, no one.' She continues where Pavel leaves off, *'Il peint les nuances de la forme.'* Assorted dancers from Birgitte's school and a few yoga students join the group, glad there is something to do, uncertain what is supposed to happen or why they are there. Birgitte serves a particularly vicious herbal tea in paper cups at one end of the room. 'He is so gifted and not just as a painter, his power is not just as a painter, he is a magician too.' There is a sudden lull as ears bend to catch the sound, and Claudette, aware that everyone is listening stops, self-conscious, not daring to say more in the presence of so many people. The pause falls awkwardly, reaching out to all four corners of the somber, paneled room, the guests immobilized in glaring spots of light. Activity at the doorway pops the silence like a bubble as Spohr, Nella and Knight come in with Sam and Harry, returning from their brief sequestration. They are accosted at once by Charlie Cohen's routine but not rhetorical inquiry, 'Where's the party, do you know where the party is?' They ignore him and move cautiously into the studio which now seems quite crowded although nervously restrained, submissive. Nella, wondering if it will be a party or a wake appears in loose, liquid white silk trousers and a flowing shirt, both decorated with her long blonde hair. The tall girl in jeans towers over her inquiring, 'Who the hell are you, Little Bo-Peep?' Delighted, Nella bursts into laughter, her green eyes bright. 'Spohr,' still laughing, 'Offer the girl a

52

drink.' He proffers a chromium plated flask filled with bourbon. 'I'm Sally Reger.' 'Ah yes,' said Nella, 'I've heard Tom rhapsodize about you, how nice. You've been away?' 'Yes, for three years, just back a few months from Europe and still feeling pulled in both directions. Do I stay, do I go back?' They understand each other perfectly from the first moment and the pleasure of recognition spreading like light between them overflows to include the people close by. Soon everyone there in the room succumbs quite willingly to the unaccountable gaiety. 'No, not Nellie, Nella, short for Campanella, my mother was Italian, my father is Rumanian.' 'My mother's parents were Rumanian.' Edwin Knight observes them from a far corner of the studio, watching as a large shaggy man, his face like a ghoul's, lumpy and disproportionate, separates himself from the others then comes towards them. 'Nella,' he bellows, he does not speak, 'I miss you.' Neither his face, his diction nor his reeking armpits proclaim him poet, but that he is. Subsequently famous for a collection of poems called *The Taste Of My Tongue,* declaimed in squalling recitations at coffee houses across the country, Myron Bridgewater is known to have hated, to have threatened Archer, 'I'll kill him, I'll kill the bastard if I find him,' for, as he supposed, stealing his lovely young wife. In fact, she had tired of playing beauty to his beast and merely used Archer, a pretext to escape, now a long time ago. 'Nella,' he trumpets, 'I'm so miserable.' Sally drifts gracefully away, saying very clearly to no one in particular, 'There is a straight line running through the universe between God and each one of us.'

Sam: Did you hear what I heard?
Harry: I think I did.
Sam: What do you make of that?
Harry: I don't have the equipment to make anything of it. Do you think she's a little crazy?
Sam: A little? She has incredible eyes. Did you notice the size of her pupils? I think she's on something.
Harry: You mean . . .?
Sam: Yes, I do.

'Blazing rockets in the night, we hurl ourselves upon our destinies. We are free and responsible or determined and bound. If we find our origins in a place of freedom we are obliged to return, if we are chained to the sound of darkness we are subjugated by passions, we are the victims, the objects of desire. His paintings say that.' Sevcik speaking now to the little forum in the room. Then Birgitte, 'But we pursue the truth or else we live and die like animals, don't you see? There is a truth for our bodies, a truth for our minds and a truth for our exalted spirit. That is why we dance, why we celebrate, to discover these truths and live more precisely.' She is solemn now, correct and serious as she speaks. The little puff of curls on her forehead bounces up and down while she nods with conviction, her face puckered, the elastic, aging body coiled around her own mortality. 'Now this good man here,' indicating her husband, 'Has spent so much of his life in contemplation, in meditation, but the world ignores him. That is the way it is, why should they care? They don't need art or wisdom, they only need to gratify their hunger and lust.' She continues to expound at length on the natural indifference of untalented, ordinary men, a speech which she has delivered from time to time in the past. After awhile Spohr, who is courteous and tactful, interrupts when Birgitte pauses to emphasize a point, her unforgiving disquisition obviously not concluded. The interruption is occasioned not so much by impoliteness as concern for the speaker and her auditors. 'Just let me break in here a moment, let me tell you a story. I'd like to tell everyone a story, would that be all right, okay?' A laugh, a murmur, a gratified buzz around the room, and he begins.

A very wise man set off one morning to climb a tall mountain and think things over. 'There is no need for others to fear my asceticism, I am not without compassion,' he thought.

As he left the flat plain and began to climb, easily, quickly at first, heart and body light with anticipation, with notions of pure ascension, he reflected tranquilly on the people, the circumstances which had brought him either pain or joy. He felt quite detached, satisfied to study the pleasures and difficulties in his life from a great distance. Any lingering sorrow was wiped out by the moving muscles, the sensation of lungs, and he saw, dispassionately, how on this and that instance he had erred in confidence, been betrayed by presumption.

'Yes, yes, I see now how it all worked out, why I was inevitably injured or injurious; there is no error in the universal order, everything led to that separation, to this misunderstanding. Things are as they are, they cannot be disturbed or altered by wailing, by exhorting myself or anyone else. Rejoice when you can, do not look for reasons in between.'

And he climbed on, pleased with his strong, solid wisdom, the peace he felt. On and on he climbed, up and up, higher and higher, willing himself forward. The movement which had pleased him some hours before bore no relation to the winding ache of shoulders and legs, the frailty in his chest. Whereas earlier he had paused only to admire the sea stretched out behind him, to praise the red poppies burning in hot white fields, now he stopped often, flinging himself down under the shade of a tree, looking neither up nor down, feeling the rough earth on his skin, the blazing sun beating down through the gaps between sparse branches. On and on he climbed, up and up, higher and higher, willing himself forward. Now there were no thoughts of friends, reflections on treachery, no speculation about freedom, now there was only the moment described by exhaustion. And he climbed higher, concentrating, energetic but beyond ideas unrelated to the articulation of limbs. Thought had fled outstripping emotion in its eagerness to escape. His body continued the upward climb only because it had been set in motion, because it lacked the ability to give new instructions, correct the course. Nothing could turn him back now.

At last night descended upon him, he knew he must sleep, try to recover, but sleep on that night was fragmented while morning brought nothing other than the impetus to continue. On and on he climbed, up and up, higher and higher, willing himself forward. Late afternoon, blind and dumb with fatigue he arrived at his destination, the journey of his life accomplished. He fell to the ground, unmoved by triumph or elation, unconcerned about anything except the relief of muscles.

The wise man stayed on the mountain for many years until he decided it was time to return, then he descended happily and easily, with no doubt that the things he had learned would benefit everyone, family, friends, colleagues, neighbors, his fellow countrymen, the whole world. Confidently he strode back along the plain, but just as he was approaching his hometown, a gang of thieves fell upon him and beat him to death, enraged by his empty pockets.

After a long pause the friend of the faggot next door comments, 'Science is as inscrutable as art these days.' Someone else calls out, 'But what does it mean?' 'Yes Spohr,' adds one of Monty Wells' students, 'What does it mean?' 'Shut up you imbecile,' a growl from Wells. Nella, uneasy that Spohr's story might be construed as insulting to Sevcik, inquires carefully, 'Anyone want some tea?' She detests it herself, but drifts down to the tea urn, a shifting cloud of white. Several others follow her, shaking loose the troublesome anxiety which for a moment, seemed imminent. Spohr vanishes somewhere pursued by Charlie Cohen. 'My dear Nella.' It is Marten Bender at last, the infamous Hungarian, a thoughtful but quietly scandalous man who always appears to be hastening to or from some orgy, some unspeakably salacious episode which he will describe in full detail; nevertheless, he plays Scriabin so exquisitely it is hard to believe his indecencies. His wife Trudy, a voluptuous, clamoring lady never accompanies him in public, whether because Bender does not permit it or because, as he claims, she is afraid to leave her house, Nella has never been sure. 'Why have we been summoned here?' His greying, dignified goatee juts around the room as he notes who is present, who absent, this to project the length of his stay. 'We have come together to consider Thomas Archer's mysterious, his inexplicable disappearance,' announces Sam, his tongue loosened by another quick visit to The Pilot. There he has lost Harry to a mutual acquaintance whose intoxication is a little more predictable than Sam's. 'Ah Docherty, I didn't know he was your friend too,' says Bender. 'Not really, I've met him occasionally; Nella talks about him frequently.' From this Bender deduces correctly, with a single glance, that the two have, as he would put it, in golden dalliance met. Nella notices the observation but trusts his discretion. More than a little tight and in any case, unaware of that exchange, Sam extends an imaginary microphone, 'Well now sir, just speak right into the mike if you wouldn't mind, what can you tell us about his last days among us?' The *allegro* commences. 'You know, curiously enough, I have been thinking about that because I did see him rather often just before he left.' They note his verb. 'We had been meeting, apparently by chance at first and then by arrangement, to go for long walks near the lake, beyond the Beaches and into the wilds of Scarborough along the bluffs. Very tiring for me I assure you because, like Baudelaire, I detest the vegetable world. Archer's stamina on the other hand is amazing, he has a kind of rubbery resilience, he bounces. Well he had talked about going up north, and when I didn't see him or hear from him I assumed he had gone. Sevcik and Schradieck insisted he did no such thing, I hardly knew what to make of this, but, you know, I didn't attach any importance to it until a few days ago. On Tuesday I received a hand delivered letter, no postmark, no stamp, no return address. The letter was from him, from Archer.' A few hover around and move in closer to listen. Cecily Turnbull, the fat, nervous old lady who rocks from side to side keeps saying, 'Excuse me, excuse me,' pushing her way up next to Bender, Nella, Bridgewater and Sam, 'Did you say you received a letter from young Tom?' she asks puzzled. 'Yes,' replies Marten politely, 'I did.' 'Well my stars and garters, what's *all* the fuss about then?' 'It is, I'm rather sorry to say Miss Turnbull, a mysterious, even an ominous letter, if I may use that word.' 'What on earth do you mean?' 'Let me tell you this, I doubt if he wrote it of his own free will.' 'But how could you possibly know that?' interrupts Nella who is well-acquainted with Bender's talent for the macabre. She has already had an account of this letter which, in her opinion, is probably of no consequence. 'Because he says nothing, absolutely nothing. And why should he write a letter about nothing to me, from nowhere as far as I can tell, with no explanation, nothing to account for where he is, how the letter came to me, why the letter came to me, except if someone insisted that a letter be written, a letter be sent, who knows why, as an evasive tactic, a placating gesture to reassure his friends? It's all very disquieting. Let me tell you I hadn't given his absence a moment's thought until this letter came.' Annie March speaks a bit acidly, 'Can we see it then?' 'Yes, see it of course, but I don't have it with me, in fact I'm not sure whether I still have it at all.' 'O bother!' Annie's strongest exclamation erupts from her, 'Does that mean you've lost it?' 'It's hard to say, I was quite certain I had left it on a pile of paper but it's not there now. Perhaps it got mixed up with some music, I'll search again. Still, it is odd because I can't tolerate disorder, especially when I'm writing. I need to keep everything in the right place or it discomposes me, so to speak, like our friend Spohr here.' Smiles and peers around the room for Spohr who is not to be seen. Conversation about the missing letter spreads in slow waves, ripples from group to group, building in importance as the news travels. Monty Wells somewhat later, trying to engage Sally Reger's attention, overhears Charlie Cohen tell Bollard and Claudette Robichaud that a document providing conclusive evidence Archer is being detained against his will was stolen from Bender's personal files. 'Is it you again?' Sally's clear, piercing voice rings across the room and falls with a sweet, seductive note in Knight's ear. He studies her obliquely, she is a delicate girl, although quite tall. A shower of light pours from her dark blue eyes, 'Professor Wells, is it? Well, well, I've heard about you, I've been told to be a little wary of you.' 'What have you heard?' 'I've been told you like to brush casually against a girl when she crosses your path, that you scurry in search of adventure when your wife is away, you endure much and inflict more.' 'Do they say that? How wonderful, then you know everything, wouldn't you like to spend the night with me you precious beauty?' 'I can't decide whether you're very silly or very smart, which is it?' 'Both, I'm afraid my dear, both. Now look, please talk to me, tell me about yourself. Archer used to babble about you, but he's such a damned liar I didn't believe a word he said.' 'And what did he say?' 'O that you're beautiful for one thing, that he admired you, and your brother shot himself. I'm sorry, this slipped out on purpose I guess.' 'Do you really want to know, do you care one way or another? My life is open, I'll tell you anything. I have no secrets, do you want to know, do you think you can bear the details? Here, take it.' She speaks quietly now, looking beyond Monty at some obscure point visible to herself.

SALLY REGER'S PERSONAL MONOLOGUE
(1)

I am not who I am, I shall never be who I was. The night destroys me, nothing can hold me now, you see. I was born on a frosty winter morning, fast, dropped like a slicked beast without fuss. A colicy baby, I screamed for the first few months and that put them off right from the beginning. My sister hadn't cried, my brother didn't cry, he was a good boy they said, his head crowned with curly black hair. He would tickle and pinch until he made me yell. We were Siamese twins, joined at the heart from the moment of my birth. I discovered at once there was no way back, obliged to remain a period of time. If I could have learned to put up with it I would have, but I didn't know how, you see. There's nothing much beyond immobility to recall from the first fifteen years. Nothing ever seemed to happen until by chance one day, I learned something about making love. Coincidentally, I stopped sucking my thumb, that's how it began. My brother stopped teasing me, my sister left home, my mother who was always angry cried a lot and grew fat. My father's blood pressure rose and rose until one fine summer day he told me unequivocally to leave his house, my home, and I left, fast. That summer I fell in love with a homosexual poet, although I liked making love more than anything. It was time to figure this out; I found a job in a small factory, oddly enough in Yorkville, a small manufacturing concern which produced dress patterns. I picked out the completed patterns from rows and rows stacked by number on shelves that reached from the floor to the ceiling. They gave me a small green card with a list of numbers for each order. I bent and stooped, stretched and climbed up a ladder, made a note of the ones which were out of stock, tied the others tightly together with a white cord and dropped them into a box. Then I started on the next green card. There were a dozen girls who were much better, much faster at it than I was. One was especially fast, a stumpy legged girl who wore her blouse hanging outside her skirt, but she was fast. She never spoke to me, no one spoke to me; so I spent my time between green cards trying to figure things out, nothing made any sense. One day the poet I was in love with said we ought to get married. That was a breathless disaster which left me gasping, and I still had nothing figured out. The wind changed, I went back to school and fell in love again, this time with a rather effeminate professor who gave me an endless list of books to read. I began to speak with a funny accent, but, you know, I still liked making love better than anything. It seemed important to figure things out. My professor used to take me for long walks in outlying parts of the city. One day we got lost in Willowdale, surrounded by fog which rolled up quickly in a deserted pasture. 'Don't worry,' he said, 'I know this place like the back of my hand.' And he did. Going to school was pleasant, they left me alone and I didn't have to sit in on the classes more than I cared to. I liked to hang around or tour the art galleries looking at paintings, how I first met Thomas Archer. I was madly in love with art, with painting in particular, although I have to admit I don't care that much for it now. One day my professor suggested we should be married. This was an even quicker disaster than the first marriage, but it didn't bother me that much because I was starting to figure things out. By then it was the right time to leave for Europe. There was a Russian girl, a ballet dancer who was supposed to go with me — it turned out she was so messed up she had to go to the hospital on Queen Street instead. I went alone, in London I saw Lawrence Olivier play Titus Andronicus, in Florence I studied Michelangelo's slaves at the Accademia, and in Paris I spent every day for three months reading at the Bibliothèque Nationale. One night, blitzed on applejack, I made love to a tall, blonde Dutch vagabond who had a flat bottomed barge anchored on the Seine at the foot of the Eiffel Tower. Eventually it occurred to me I didn't need any more of that and went back to London. What shall I tell you now? There was a loosening, an unraveling as I began to recognize whole sequences of change. My head was so crammed with useless stuff there was no room to think, but sometimes at night I would hear a voice, a familiar voice calling me, calling my name across the night. That summons waking me from my shattered dream of sleep was terrifying; someone, I thought, was trying to get in touch with me, trying to get hold of me. I didn't know what was wrong, didn't know what to do. Finally I went back to the university there in London, just for awhile. Sometime later I met a dusky skinned Catholic from the Middle East who taught at a girl's school in Wales, and we would amuse each other in his strange foreign car until one day he sobbed, 'I don't think we should do this unless we're married.' He meant he wanted to marry me, not that we shouldn't do the things we were doing. He had to return to his school, but six months later he sent me red roses on Valentine's Day, an odd thing to do, don't you think? During the Easter vacation we celebrated with a party at my tiny flat in Flood Street. All my friends came and somehow it went on for two years, in other people's flats up and down Chelsea, on the Embankment, in Tite Street, Rossetti Gardens, or else perhaps in Lancaster Gate, in Kensington, Ladbroke Grove, anywhere people didn't mind if the police came. During the day we often met at the Churchill Arms, an inconspicuous, rather dour pub in Kensington, and on Sunday mornings at the Catharine Wheel, in the very footprints of the poet, there to read the Sunday papers, all of them, and sip dark frothy pints of Guinness on draft. By that time I had quit the university altogether, too busy, too frightened and dazed, perhaps even too euphoric while searching for a solitary glimpse, an illuminating flicker which now and then preceded the collapse, the crumple into drunkenness. I felt continually as though something important was about to happen and didn't care to know what it was. The remedy was to get wrecked, stay stoned and go to bed with whoever was with me longest, sometimes at my place, sometimes wherever we found ourselves. One cold night we crossed into oblivion a bit off our usual beat, a room in Knightsbridge where a silent, phlegmatic and rather distant acquaintance lived. When we walked there from Kensington it seemed like miles and miles on that freezing winter night. Later, asleep or passed out on the floor, I awakened without having the slightest recollection of where we were. Staggering down a dark unlit hallway I arbitrarily opened the first door I came to, blazing lights were instantly switched on and a woman with fat curlers all over her head sat bolt upright in bed screaming. 'Please don't be frightened madam, I'm looking for the lavatory,' I explained as matter-of-factly as I could. But poor thing, she looked so ridiculous and wouldn't stop yelling. I retreated in haste, closed that door and found the one at the back which led to a tiny garden. There I remained by myself, blissful among the loose, falling flakes of wet snow. In the morning we took our host's last one pound note, more than adequate for the taxi back to Chelsea, found some money and carried on. It was a good day, a happy day full of laughter, how we laughed that day. Gradually things began to clear, the party stopped or at least it went on without me, then my professor husband who had come to England tried a little marriage with me again. I started all over, from the beginning, when I came home. My brother shot himself while I was away. *I will offer any part of my body to save you. I will offer any part of my body to save you.*

Bollard, pretending to be in conversation with Marguerite and Claudette but listening instead to every word from Sally,

65

exhales softly. Wells smiles, wondering about the ratio of accuracy to narrative. And Sally, moved by her own recital, concludes waving her hand lightly as she does to emphasize a point, 'It's not easy to unwind your own navel cord, the only thing left now is to make a choice between the rational and the nonrational; so far the nonrational seems worth more. There's my story, how do you like it so far?' Spohr reappears in a knot of people which includes a slight, fair haired girl, Brenda MacIntyre, whom he has just engaged in a sexual act, discreetly, in a washroom on the third floor; George Hassan, a decidedly corpulent Copt from Alexandria with a dubious past; Brenda's husband Jim, a Bay Street lawyer sniffing suspiciously at his wife; John Adolph, the friend of the faggot next door who looks like a stockbroker; and the two unemployed actors. 'This is a very tricky matter, let me be the first to assure you of that, because when Nasser's agents pursued and hounded me out of England, as they did, there's no doubt on that point,' glancing around the studio, 'They endowed me with a sensitivity to a certain danger, and Thomas Archer reeked of it, let me assure you on that point.' He rocks on his heels with some authority. 'Come now Hassan,' Spohr says affably, 'What are you trying to insinuate, that our friend Archer is some kind of cloak and dagger man?' 'No, not that, not that at all, let me assure you not that at all, merely that something clings to him, something which I, representing another, a foreign culture, can spot very quickly, and I don't mean his strange dress or the artistic atmosphere he exudes. I mean something else, and it is precisely that something which has brought him into danger, serious danger I have no doubt. He will be lucky to escape with his life, he has been unfaithful to his gods.' Hassan crosses himself fervently, theatrically.

From the Notebooks of Annie March (1962)

Dis-
connections:

I am I
you are you
they are they

Well what did you expect?

John Adolph is walking down the street, a silly but satisfied grin on his face. He does have an English accent, he does wear tweeds, he is a Rhodes scholar, his disposition is vitriolic, he drinks too much, he considers himself a founding member of the Royal Society for the Return of the Dauphin to the Throne of France. There is a letter in his pocket addressed to Sally in Flood Street containing an unused contraceptive device which is stuffed with a number of dried rose petals. The dead flowers were a present, living, from his crippled father to his dying mother. In Vancouver. Now his mother is dead. He has been fired from a succession of hopelessly trivial jobs for irresponsibility, alcoholism, an inability to hold his tongue in the presence of his employers, and for reasons which even his sometime employers prefer not to disclose.

Sally walks along the Embankment at about ten o'clock at night. Crying. Well what did you expect?

Thomas Archer (Steele) does not exist, never did; he is a mythological character, the hero who mysteriously disappears. Never to reappear?

George Hassan, a pesky Arab; remote; does he suffer some attenuated paranoia or were Nasser's agents really a step behind him when he crept aboard a ship in Liverpool bound for Canada?

Myron Bridgewater one day commented, 'Haven't read Shakespeare but think my poems are better.'

Cecily Turnbull is walking down Avenue Road wearing a snood, carrying two shopping bags, one in each hand. A byproduct of life talking loudly to herself, 'O dear, O dear, he didn't even notice my blue eyes. I do have lovely eyes, they are my best feature even with my spectacles on.'

Nella.

Jock Carogna, short, very short, the supple guitarist of a jazz band with a surprising reputation in Paris, although unknown, utterly, at home. Bleached blonde hair, high heeled boots, menace on his face. He exudes sex in a rather underprivileged way.

I don't know whether this is a story with a happy ending or whether it's even a story at all. It resembles a time bomb with the timer set against the big bang. Well that's common enough. What do you make of my friends? They're not much but they're all I have. Who would have thought life would end like this, sitting at a desk bored out of my mind day after day. It hardly seems worthwhile trying to grapple with the past or the present: the future is inconsolable.

John Adolph is bored all the time too. His adventures, *la chasse* he calls it. The Baron de Charlus, only not so fancy.

Con-
nections

I am you
you are me
they are us
we are them

Well what did you expect?

Who can help Thomas Archer now?

A child lies here whom the Greeks feared and slew.

Cecily Turnbull quotes copiously from *Reader's Digest,* including this, God grant me the wisdom to tell right from wrong. Well the truth is everywhere after all, you only need to know and look. A dark wind howls through my life. Thoughts come too rapidly to exclude. Boredom is paralysis, life a frustrating burden of days.

Nella sees Spohr with Brenda MacIntyre and makes no inference, but talks instead to Jim MacIntyre, steadying herself behind the devastation of her understanding. 'Schradieck it seems,' she said, 'Was the last to see him, that much he admits freely. At first he talked to Spohr and then something like panic settled over him, now he refuses to say anything more. Part of his story hinges on an oddly elusive Chinese man, a diplomat perhaps from the way he was dressed, a man with a strong English accent who appeared in a limousine driven by an Asian driver. I've been a close friend of Tom's for a long time, very close, and I really have to say it, this makes no sense except possibly in terms of his whole life.' 'What do you mean?' 'Well I'm sure you must know this, everyone does, he has involved himself in so many esoteric practices, at least since I've known him. He never refuses to investigate any occult source, any dark terrain however perverse or diabolical it may be, his pursuit of personal power leads him everywhere. You can't invoke those forces for nothing, free, they always exact payment one way or another — from your body, your mind, your soul. That's no secret.' Jim listens almost holding his breath, he has never heard anyone talk this way before, doesn't know what to make of it. Nella speaks quite openly, assuming her view of the world is no different from anyone else's. And there is something else, angered in a quiet, subtle place by what she will not let herself suspect the connection between Spohr and Brenda might be, she finds a need to speak energetically, accusingly, on the unnerving darkness in the human heart. If for her own reasons she will not find fault with Spohr she still seeks redress, compensation for the dagger pointed at her heart. Jim soothes his bristling mustache, calculating as he surveys her why a smart fellow like Spohr would have such a peculiar wife. Nella smiles, realizing he doesn't understand what she is talking about, 'Never mind Jim, let's go listen to what Sevcik has to say, he seems ready at last to speak.' 'My dear friends,' he begins, 'I have been listening to your comments and speculation all evening, and I must say I do find this merging, this pooling of resources instructive.' *Nel cerchio secondo s'annida ipocrisía.* 'Good lord,' says Spohr, 'He's a politician, will you just listen to that?' 'However, I don't think anything new has been added to the sum total of what we know, and I do feel Thomas Archer's friends have a special responsibility to look further.' *It is better for a man to speak well of the gods; he is less to blame.* Sam Docherty leans down and whispers cheerfully to Spohr, 'My only fear is that this pleasant evening will end in the nomination of a committee to pursue our ever receding friend.' Spohr looks over his glasses at Sam, perceiving with amusement how his intelligence has been undervalued. He smiles, 'You may be

71

right, you may be right at that, it is entirely possible Sevcik is simply manipulating us, how interesting indeed. He is quite capable of that.' Sam, baffled, says nothing, earning points for his silence. 'Does anyone have any suggestions?' asks Sevcik. 'Let's just all mind our own bloody business,' murmurs Sam to Spohr. 'But what can we do?' asks Miss Turnbull, rolling her large blue eyes, pursing dry lips meaningfully, shuffling her feet in a nervous two-step, 'They say we can't report him as a missing *person.'*

A burst of talk spreads in all directions. 'No, we can't make any public inquiry.' 'Why not hire a detective?' 'O God, this isn't the movies, you know, it's the real thing.' 'Where *do* you get your lines?' 'What does he mean?' 'What do you want?' 'Let's not waste time!' 'What else is there to waste?' 'But what can we do for him anyhow?' 'Surely we have to do something.' 'Our hands are tied.' 'We don't even know what would be helpful, doing something or doing nothing.' 'How can we be sure?' 'This is too silly. If we ourselves can do something . . .' 'This is ridiculous!' 'Can't we just speak one at a time?' 'We have to be a bit more organized.' 'This isn't going to work.' 'Now what?'

Sevcik moves slowly once more, gliding along invisible grid lines to the center, orchestrating the talk with his nodding presence, leading them gently to the *adagio* and *finale.* Does he give Birgitte a covert signal? Slowly, with a deliberate air of patient consideration, sighing she begins in her firm accent, born in the north of France, cooled in some Bavarian village and finally, steeled in the heart of Berlin. 'My dear friends, we are obliged as artists to protect what is sacred to our art, we are obliged as human beings to protect what we value as men and women, to shape our civilization in this hostile universe. How can we permit the loss of anyone among us to go unnoticed, unaccounted for? How can we tolerate the possibility that someone so dear to us all may be in trouble, may be detained at this moment against his will? Will anyone forgive us for this neglect, for this failure to a fellow artist? And let us think a moment, he is not just any artist, this is Archer himself. To abandon him seems not only absurd but fainthearted. Come now, let a few of us get together, investigate this quietly with whatever means we can muster, we'll need your monetary support, then we'll be in touch with you again.'

A Fragment: From the Notebooks of Annie March (undated)

The Boatman's Holiday
— A Prose Elegy —

A parallelogram. The boatman came to visit.

And there among the recent dead she came, still hurt and limping.

- You have been asking for me.
- I have some questions. Will you submit to me?

- Possibly yes and probably no.
- Which of the three worlds do you come from?
- Not the midwest and not the land of Canaan, but some contiguous state I am not free to discuss.
- Do you have a professed avocation?
- I am professor of logic to the unblessed. My living, such as it is, however mean, is efficient and true. I cultivate an incapacity for desire and spread it when I can, where I can, like disease. You are my best infection.
- Tell me boatman, is life a benediction or an affliction? Am I striving to be wise or unwise? Do I just betray myself or do I entrap others too? Is time incurable? Can distance be annihilated?
- Suffer the consequences of yes and no. Do not burden me with what passes for your conscience. I can only dictate in terms of what will not be. So don't listen to me for signals, I won't give any. Fortitude is holiness; no life is reprehensible; invent what you cannot destroy. Submit or revile, it's all the same to me, your senses are not accurate. Therefore, be misled willfully if you choose. Do what you must and howl when the reverberations penetrate or rebound on you.
- Boatman, who is wise?
- A dedicated fool.
- Boatman, who is good?
- A consistent malefactor.
- Boatman, what is evil?
- Betrayal.
- Then how can I discover what I need to know?
- Experience all deception and treachery, and perish.

- But I have rejoiced boatman, I have seen joy naked in the dark and I swear it is true.
- You have rejoiced in your own foolishness and despaired in your wisdom. There is no separation of lies from what you say. *E io, che di mirare stava inteso, vidi gente langose.*

I felt the terrible accumulation of events and knelt weeping at his feet.

- Take me with you.
- Not yet, remember our next voyage is the last. You are not ready, I shall come for you again.

Myron Bridgewater in a booming voice tries to persuade Spohr and Nella to go with him to a fellow poet's, and while they hesitate Charlie Cohen interrupts, 'O yes, what a good idea. Let's go, we'll all fit into my car.' Spohr laughs, Nella looks away and then laughs too. 'What about Jim and Brenda?' she asks, 'They might like to come.' Spohr thinks, 'Damn, she knows,' and they leave together in a stream of laughter. Monty's students go on to The Embassy while he returns home to his wife and dark haired daughter. Harry Bell comes back to look for Sam, together they leave with Marten Bender and a nubile practitioner of the yogic arts. Several stay behind in earnest conversation with Sevcik. Edwin Knight takes Sally Reger by the hand and leads her away as John Adolph kisses the other one in farewell. The Robichauds decide to sleep on the floor in Birgitte's studio, having previously declined Marguerite's invitation to sleep on the floor at Bellair Street. Annie has already departed inconspicuously; so Bollard, Jan and Marguerite go home without her; John Adolph hurries off down Yonge Street in pursuit of male carnal ecstasy; Lisa waits for Schradieck. Singly and in groups the devotees aim their arrows at diverging targets in the night.

A Parallel Affair

The Boatman's Holiday

From the Notebooks of Annie March (1960)

There is a contradictory but parallel experience of time, the first is that time is short, running out, and the other is an endless sense of days marked off, time's nerve in vinegar the poet said, wasted days one by one in faultless succession, waiting, waiting, for what, for whom? And there is fear of boredom, but not, I console myself, as long as there are books and music. Then that thing insinuates itself, and what if you come to the end of books and music, what then, what then will hold back the night? Either everything is standing still or it's happening so quickly nothing can be reckoned with. The daily accumulation of nothing.

A dream that we were back in Florence, but the colors were wrong, the light was wrong and I couldn't see the Duomo anywhere. We must have been on the other side of the Arno at first, high up, at the Piazzale perhaps, looking down over the city spread like a contour map beneath us. Why was everything so dun colored? *Sixty-six is the number of apothecaries and grocer shops.* Where were all the pinks and greens, where was the dazzling light with the erotic, hard edged clarity that makes frescos leap off the walls? Then the scene changed and it was Easter Sunday in what I took to be the Piazza della Signoría where we had come to watch the ceremony, bumping elbows with confused English ladies, 'O where can I get a *billy-etto?*' 'Do we need a *billy-etto* for this?' We didn't dare speak to them. If it had been that Piazza we would have been standing near the Loggia, in the company of Cellini, but instead we were on a little hilltop some distance from the church I recall identifying for S. as the Baptistry, which isn't in that square anyhow. Very cold for April; everything glittered and sparkled. I remember explaining, to S. or to my mother who had been in a preceding dream, in the afternoon we would see the ceremony of the dove, but that would be at the Duomo. Then I saw the falcon perched on a leather gauntlet held aloft by some minor official. It was wrapped in a light red garment with long black leggings to protect its slender limbs. A thick silver chain was wound several times around the bird's body. As soon as the creature was released it soared straight up then plummeted down and alighted directly on the back of my right hand, twisting the skin with its beak, pinching me sharply. There was no blood, but a complex knot of red lines appeared just below the surface. 'A son,' the Florentines cheered, 'A son as strong and true as this falcon.' It means my writing I thought, and tears streamed down my face.

Happy wakening; told the dream while half inside it, 'Ah, you wished we were back in time and everything had worked out well.' It was not what I meant at all. That elation, that enlarged sense of destiny, of optimism, lasted until the mail was delivered and I received the poem back, rejected. I was more surprised than disappointed. Dream protection. Fierce, unrelenting need to write.

How could I have imagined I was preserving, that it was not an act of destruction, throwing away the notebook? Not just another notebook, any notebook, the prose elegy. A spontaneous impulse — it seemed the only way to dismantle my life without prejudice, to examine my expectations, the whole ringing apparatus, a blind gesture. For that suspended moment I needed to rid myself of the one thing I have guarded, have carried everywhere with me. And I did it, just like that. Naturally I learned nothing, all it did was slit open a new vein of loss, a deep new channel through which to grieve, to regret. What can I do? What's lost is lost, Proust wasn't taken seriously even though he was writing seven hundred pages a year. Perhaps that record of weeping days and insomniac nights is well lost after all.

Solitude and introspection on the one hand, and on the other that paranoia which dares not look at the spot right beside itself. S. and I together, a paradigm of double paranoia, his a desperate feeling of never being alone, and mine a desperate feeling of always being alone. We frustrate, we persecute, we overwhelm each other. I do not feel alone when I write; he discovers the solitude he craves when he writes. How sad that we should both so completely lack discipline. Although the hare has all the talent the tortoise is rewarded by the gods for his persistence.

How can we break the cycle, the pattern built on emotion, relation and expectation? How can we preserve what we need and at the same time destroy the destructive? The profound despair we've both felt in the last few weeks culminates as usual in the separation motif. There is a terrible sense of loss, the uncertainty, the longing and the need, always the need. Even if I could find or devise an adequate language, what guarantee is there I would learn to speak it, let alone dance and sing it? This may be the biggest red herring so far, or is it just that the most despairing moments inevitably trail a jetstream of futility? It becomes impossible to do anything, even write this down.

And I do nothing, nothing. This is the greatest torment, the fear I can't do anything. The only thing that sustains me is the conviction I must, even if I can't I must. Illusion run wild over fancy. S. asked once with such bitterness, 'Why do I always get stuck with you?' More dreams evoking betrayal, the many forms of delusion, dreams centering on the shattered house, a barn-like building, or is it possibly a library, with burned bodies like sculpture fixed in niches all around the outside. They move, they come to life again, and they are all black, such courageous black men and women.

Perhaps if I weren't so many years older than S., if he hadn't acquired the habit of deference and respect for intellectual rather than personal reasons, if either of us had been more normal, if he didn't drink so much, perhaps if we could stop cataloguing each other's faults, if we didn't both have so many impossible, contradictory conditions . . .

Nearly Christmas. I dreamt last night someone wanted to publish the prose elegy. It was very real, the dream syndrome not present . . . much relief, elation. Awoke between laughing and crying, I tore it up months ago. How it clings to me and I to it.

Now to fill in the solitude before death or empty it beyond fear and expectation. Feel perpetually close to a great word pouring forth and strain towards that place as though it held the answer to every question, every anxiety, every dilemma. A form of worship I suppose. Is this expectation a frequent delusion? And if I were to do something, complete anything which satisfied me, what would I do then? I have no idea how to obliterate the 'so what?' reverberations ringing from any act. If that is relevant, appropriate, then nothing remains but the question. Answering would be a contradiction, but to act in spite of the question, or interpret the question as a function of this state of mind? Or as a conscience maker for mere inactivity?

Imagine being chained in the corner of a large empty room, inside a large empty house, in a desert: for eternity.

It is perplexing to mind not having anyone to be friends with in an easy, casual way, to mind not being able to talk quietly, intimately, about important and unimportant things. If I leave the house it is only to go for a walk, if I speak it is only to myself now. Most of the time I prefer this, I think I'll wither into spinsterhood.

And despair. Is it not better to abandon oneself completely?

Spohr and Nella had a farm some miles south of Highway 89 and considerably east of Mount Forest. It was a small farm which they chose not to work but kept instead as a buffer between themselves and the rest of the world. Originally it had belonged to Nella's mother who left it to them when she died, not because of any special affection for her daughter, merely to keep it from her husband's hands. This natural enmity between her parents Nella had always regarded as an irreversible geological fault which did not touch her directly, like a volcano erupting on another planet or an exploding star in some distant galaxy; neither parent thought to confide in their daughter. There had never been any special grievance between them, nothing more than the old antipathy between a rather peevish woman and her sullen, indifferent spouse. They had left each other almost accidentally, certainly without reluctance when Nella was not quite grown up. After her mother's death Nella considered this unhappy parent frequently, wondering how she had filled in the slow, sad years, what she thought about, what feelings and recollections she kept locked away inside. She had spent nearly forty years in a desolate old house, hidden away in the poor Italian section of Hamilton, rarely going out, almost never leaving home except to go to church. When her work around the house was finished she sat at the living room window in a painted chair, rocking very carefully, very slowly, arms folded across her overflowing body, back and forth on the grooved and worn linoleum. She would sigh from time to time, stroking her curled, dyed hair where the grey showed through in thin patches on the crown and at the temples. Oddly enough, her mother had not only abjured the traditional black dress of the Italian peasant but had also forsworn her charismatic Catholicism for a succession of Evangelical sects, settling finally on a Pentecostal faith for her salvation. She studied the heretical Bible every evening, memorizing texts in a language she barely spoke and comprehended even less. There was no actual antagonism between mother and daughter, it was just that Nella had grown away from her while she was still a child. Like a flower taking root at a distance from the parent plant she developed a separate stance, a calculated independence in the privacy of her own life, besides which she felt little for the strange, foreign woman who seemed in turn, uninterested in that child, her daughter. For the most part they left each other carefully, even politely alone, although the mother might occasionally chastise and the daughter might occasionally dissent. There were rare visits from the father arriving unannounced every once in awhile, laden down with baskets of fruit and armloads of vegetables; he would scarcely intrude upon their even landscape. The fruit he brought turned moldy and rotted away on the kitchen floor weeks after the gloomy Rumanian had departed. Even though he seldom bothered to address his wife directly, he took care to be cheerful with Nella, eager to offer the secret lore accumulated in random, unaccounted for ways. Somewhere in his past he had become interested in yoga, astrology, theosophy and Mme Blavatsky, in vegetarianism and herbal medicine. He made a point of providing alternatives to aspirin and penicillin which she gratefully accepted, locking the knowledge he proffered into her understanding of right and wrong, her idea of the universe. The inherited mistrust of doctors and medicine was permanent, the unorthodox turn of mind unshakable. From time to time her father would remove the heavy black horn rimmed glasses he wore, and using them as a baton, conduct himself in lengthy astrological discourses, explaining the different sun and moon signs, characterizing his family and acquaintances according to their ruling star's disposition. This was the origin of Nella's implicit belief, and nothing Spohr ever taught her could dislodge it. 'Come now,' he would say, 'You know this isn't scientific.' 'I'm not so sure,' she'd counter, 'After all, it's based on data accumulated over thousands of years.' 'But it's not falsifiable,' he'd announce playing his ultimate card. 'So what?' she'd say, throwing his learning to the winds. This sense of inherent power in diverging natural forces gave Nella a generous, forgiving disposition. 'Ah,' she might say, 'Of course he would do that, he's a Pisces,' casually, automatically. She once told Marguerite she wouldn't want to have a Scorpio baby and was particularly careful at the appropriate time to avoid that difficulty. Or she would say, 'But he's a Gemini, he can't help himself.' Her belief in a destiny shaped by the stars included an awareness there are interwoven lines of chance which, taken all together, gave her a comfortable view of the universe and her own place in it. Something within her was solid; no matter what calamity threatened she could usually measure out a remedy or comfort or an explanation to soothe the feelings of injustice and self-pity which so often accompany misfortune. Her friends relied on her. As for her parents, she was never able to regard them as other than enigmatic strangers with whom she had a fortuitous connection. When she found herself thinking about her mother she speculated, without regret, why they had never managed to be friendly, to be affectionate with each other. She wondered what buried secrets united them now across the grave, what had occupied her attention, her thoughts day after day, rocking endlessly like a small craft on the waves of the sea. Had she seen something, had she known something? Once, abruptly, she asked her father, 'Did you two ever love each other?' she inquired hesitantly. 'Ah yes,' he sighed, 'But that was long ago, so long ago.' 'Well what happened?' 'What do you mean, what happened?' 'Why did it change?' 'Nothing happened,' he said, 'Nothing happened at all,' and then began to speak about the specific healing properties of comfrey. Marriage is not commonly unhappy observed Dr. Johnson, otherwise than as life is unhappy. The image of her silent mother rocking through life was there in her reckoning, an image Nella found herself referring to more and more as the years dropped their weight upon her.

Every once in awhile Spohr and Nella would visit their rural paradise, Spohr talking politics, farming and even religion with a few old-timers, drinking whiskey all night and sleeping all day, Nella talking to no one, tramping around the countryside during the day and sleeping all night. She liked the winters best because they were so quiet, so private. Days when the snow blew up hard, circling, swirling, clogging the roads again right behind the snow plough, forcing them closed, these were obscure gifts offered to Nella alone, no one could touch her then, the world stood still. The urgent necessities, the compulsions which proceeded without interruption in the life of the city were obedient to all the natural forces out there where sunrise and sunset were still important events in the day, where the direction of the wind, the massing and movement of clouds, the precious rain, all counted for more than business, timetables and philosophy. A strong feeling of being in touch with something rhythmic and cyclical in the world satisfied her deeply, set an understanding in motion which she had never been able to identify before, that recognition of the elements in her own body, that sense of being not different, not separate from anything else. She had no desire to discuss the feeling or to analyze it, and certainly not with Spohr who seemed to have no such awareness himself. This was something she wanted to keep intact and feared he might tamper with it. So she kept all that to herself, protecting it from his scrutiny, his inquiring need to examine the axioms of her feelings, the way she perceived life. There was an aspect of Spohr which made her a prisoner, which interrupted her responses, her reactions, made her submit them to him for approval. Nella felt constrained even as she denied it, even as she deliberately tried to refuse it access. And so although she had never capitulated, he cut off her intuitive investigation of mystery and the nonrational. Pleasure, that is the feeding of appetite, desire and the senses, was not only permitted it was encouraged, while the study of more private, inner matters was subtly forbidden in ways that Nella could never quite account for, but which made themselves explicitly, directly understood. When they left the city behind and went to the country she no longer felt imprisoned; there was nothing the truth tables could do with feelings too penetrating to be altered, too rooted to be driven out. The peaceful, rolling countryside around the farm was neither deserted nor overly populated, and on a luminous January day Nella was happy to camouflage herself like a jackrabbit, march up and down the packed, crusty roads with purposefulness, examining the tracks through a recently established pine forest, skirting around the frozen marsh sometimes, watching out for an occasional doe or buck. Walking past Walt Jackson's place, always interested in his loose, ramshackle style of farming, she'd stop to play with Lady, their old dog whose tail was matted into thick braids of burrs acquired over the years spent roaming, then be overcome by the maple lanes lining the roads and running deeply back to the farmhouse set a couple of hundred yards from the road. She might stop again farther up the road and look down into the cradle where old man Henderson's farm lay on one side, then up towards the crest of the hill at the Jeffrey's place directly opposite where the soft brick, weatherworn house stood. The fields and pastures were etched by lines of stubble interlaced with snow, by the sagging rail fences and an occasional stone hedge, by an arc of elm as it shot up suddenly over a hill like an arrow, or by the slowly undulating waves of hills rolling from crest to crest. Nothing spectacular, just the ordinary miracles of creation which hold you forever. Over at the glittering, frozen stream before the crossroad she could scramble down to look for places where the sun and moving water had punched out holes in the ice, there to catch the slickering movement of unchained fish. And up above in the open sky the sun glowed, icy, no warmth, only a brittle shower of light. An exquisite mourning dove might appear on the telephone wire and then the other wintering birds would scream their mad choir of bliss, exploding crescendos which rang like crystal through the clear, high space. At the crossroad she might continue uphill a little way, and following the road drop quickly down to the marsh, fringed and plumed with snapping reeds, then walk across the ice to the islands where they said a herd of deer could be found, only she never did see them. Sometimes instead she'd turn north to the highway even though the road didn't go through there. To reach it she would have to turn west again at the next concession line, going north once more on the main graveled road, center sideroad it was called. By that time she'd be too cold or it would be too late, long past time to head back to the farm where Spohr would be up and about, chortling as he fed too much wood into the stove, making lavish tuna fish and mayonnaise sandwiches, a diet which, if supplemented with beer or whiskey, could sustain him indefinitely. Nella's mother had seen to it that the old farmhouse was stuccoed before she died; it stood there perched impractically on top of a windy hill, white and neat against the sky, so unlike their city home. Whenever she approached, no matter the direction she came from, Nella always stopped a moment to look at the house, to observe it standing there in the blowing wind high among the trees and rolling hills, offering thanks to her mother, the curious stranger who had kept this for her. What other secrets had she kept?

The winter following Thomas Archer's disappearance was bitterly cold with unrelenting intervals of temperature well below zero on the Fahrenheit scale, but it was also one of the first years the snow plough was used to keep the small sideroads open. Spohr and Nella came often to the farm that winter. Now it would be incorrect to think Spohr was untouched by their time in the country. If he customarily displayed ease and equilibrium imagine the repose when he relaxed, when he loosened and unfettered himself, surrendering to the total absence of demands, imagined or actual, which city life imposed. Not that he was ambitious in the ordinary way — for him success meant his own instrument, a tool forged in the furnace of his talent and offered back to him by a multitude who were not so much to be conquered as won, dazzled by his gift to them. Out there he had nothing to give and nothing to take, and so on a Saturday night he could stop for hours at the general store, leaning his elbow on the glass display case talking to Fred and Janie Wardle, the old couple who farmed a little and owned the store, or to the farmers who might come in for tobacco and a ball of twine, or nails, a loaf of bread and rambling conversation. They might blaspheme against the government in Ottawa, mildly but deliberately cursing those poor fellows up there who hadn't a grain of sense among them, and certainly not the slightest notion of what it takes to spend your life on the farm. They'd talk about crops and the weather, local politics, prices, keeping the hazardous farm machinery going. Or they might plan to work on old man Henderson's binder to see if they could keep it in active service a spell longer, lay the sins of the world at the

Liberals' feet, think about going to euchre or the church social, reminding each other without saying so how mutually dependent they were. Walt Jackson told Spohr of a saying they had, you can do without your friends but you can't do without your neighbors. Sometimes Reverend McDougall, the Evangelical preacher with a small following in Luther, a village nearly eight miles away, sometimes he would drop by for a few supplies if he was working in the area. He ordinarily made his living as a handyman even though a combined lack of skill and patience made him maladroit, casually slipshod. 'For a preacher,' Spohr told Nella, 'He sure has a murderous light in his eye.' 'What do you mean, how can you tell?' 'Well he likes to shoot, likes to hunt, and when he talks about taking aim, getting a bead on the target as he puts it, holding an imaginary gun at eye level, you can see the steel glinting in his eyes. I wouldn't want to cross that man.' Then Walt Jackson might arrive with his half dozen children and Spohr, frugal in principle if not always in practice, would buy ice cream for the little ones, offering the older boys a cigarette under the half amused stare of their father. Country folk usually did not take much to strangers, but for reasons which were never clear to either Spohr or Nella they were accepted and made welcome, much as if they had been local people who had moved on to the city but came home for a visit now and then. The men who liked to take a drink against the long winter's night were pleased to come in for a quick one when Spohr's light was on, and sometimes they brought their own, talking and drinking until hours later. They would stagger back into the icy darkness clutching the precarious remains of a bottle wrapped in brown paper, counting on the stars, the moon and the snow to light their way home. Once when Nella remained in the city they brought the local whore with them, to Spohr's profound delight. Having been raised in a quiet farm town himself, he was at home there, as content as a man like Spohr could be. *Spohr, Spohr, that was all for the world. When he died a thin stream of blood froze to his lips.*

Touched by Sally Reger's grief which gushed from her in an unspoken stream Nella offered friendship, numberless cups of tea and finally in that galactic January a few days in the country, hoping somehow to ease her pain. 'I don't really care much for the country,' Sally commented thoughtlessly as they drove along, 'I wouldn't know how to survive without concrete floors and steel girders around me on all sides. I think I need the neutrality of concert halls, the anonymity of libraries and theatres. Even so I did leave London, but only occasionally. Cambridge was beautiful with its green river, rolling lawns and colleges like castles in a dream. I went once to Ilfracombe in Devonshire and twice to Swansea in Wales, although London was really England for me. If Paris is a jewel burning distantly in the background, London is frontal and luminous, it heats you up while Paris cools you down. Paris was nothing to me, I was lost there, a foreigner, and if you think the English hate strangers you can't begin to imagine the open space a Frenchman can slip in between you and himself. I didn't speak to a soul for a couple of months until I received a cable from a friend, an Englishman who knew a thing or two, urging me to telephone his former wife, also a foreigner, and after that I would meet a circle of expatriates at the café before dinner, at Le Select in Montparnasse. We were Hungarians in exile, an American painter, an elderly American poet and translator of French surrealist verse, an elfin woman with no discernible nationality or means of support who claimed to be American, except she drank *un tilleul* every day and that seemed uncharacteristic, a student from South America, Argentina I think, frequently insisting that he too, was American, a German photographer, probably an illegal resident, an aspiring writer or two, O and sometimes a painter from British Columbia who seemed equally foreign to me. Other friendly foreigners drifted through looking for someone to have a drink with, wanting to talk or just to make love. When I finally settled in London I was at home, several kind English friends took me immediately to their hearts. I also fell in with a few ardent Welsh nationalists, journalists for the most part who were friendly to me, their compatriot in colonialism. Their wit was always amusing, the petty rivalries, the disputes which tore at their fraternity devastating. I made a great effort to complete everything I could salvage of what had passed for my education, London however, all of it, was my finishing school. I warmed myself by the generous fires burning brightly in that cold place. I think I should go back there soon, maybe finish my degree, I don't know, I don't know.' And she wandered back to the heart of her sorrow. 'It's funny,' she said, her attention returning as she stared out the window at the 401, 'It wasn't until this moment driving along our absurdly multiple highways that I feel for the first time how small England is, how like a dwarf to this roaring child of the giant.' Spohr grinned, hoping the old DeSoto was up to the journey there and back. It was late and snowing heavily by the time they reached the farm, they turned up the heat, lit a fire, drank beer and listened to old 78s on an almost worn out phonograph. They played an incalculable mixture, famous Italian arias left by Nella's mother, some old Leadbelly blues, Maggie Teyte singing French *chansons,* Gabriel Fauré and Paul Verlaine, a gift from John Adolph many years before which Sally brought along, and the Mozart Clarinet Concerto forgotten by some unknown guest. They didn't talk much but there was laughter; Nella was glad her friend's eyes stayed clear and bright all that evening. While Spohr wallowed in bed next morning the women rose early, drank their tea and set off in a northerly direction, staying close to the road because of the loose, drifting snow. The sky darkened and began to close in rapidly, hurling its white legions in swirling formations down upon them. Sally was gasping and panting, 'I'm not used to this cold, but it's so beautiful I don't want to go back. Did you ever read the story of the Snow Queen when you were young? I can't remember whether she was a good queen or not, I remember a feeling like this, the magic, the crystalline delicacy, the whiteness, the blinding purity of this whiteness, my God, as if all the filth could be frozen and picked off particle by particle, as if each gust of snow could blow away your past, blow away your sins, make retribution for all the clumsiness and bungling. Nella, do you think I'll survive? Do you die just because they've taken your heart, cut it into little pieces and fed it to the dogs?' They walked in silence again as the sun appeared briefly in the sky, light but not warm, a quivering green spasm, malevolent. 'Let's go back now,' suggested Nella, 'It's very cold today and I think a real storm is going to blow up soon.' 'I'd like to stay out in this, I'd like to be part of the howling white madness.' 'Well how about getting the car then?' They stopped at the farm long enough to make a thermos of tea, find blankets and a shovel in case they got stuck and set off again, north, to the highway, driving slowly in the center of the road as they do in the country, watching for rabbits, astounded by their snow wrapped world. At the highway they turned west towards Mount Forest and it suddenly became quite dark, *e già le notte al mezzo dì sen vanno,* black clouds dropping like bombs all around them. The windshield wipers barely managed to scrape a patch clean enough to peer through. The headlights, turned on although it was high noon, were stopped by the swirling, twisting snow receding before them, luring them on. Both sides of the road disappeared and nothing remained but a funnel sucking them into its vortex. They were crusted with diamonds on the passenger side as the wind reared back and gathered its forces. Whips of wood slapped against the car urging them on, urging them on. Abruptly, the face of an old man in a black hat with a wide brim, the lines engraved deeply across his forehead and sunken cheeks, this face came into focus through the slashing snow, then his body, just above the level of the car roof, this too became visible. Dressed in a formless black coat drawn up around his ears he was seated on what appeared to be a bench, a blanket on his lap. Beside him sat his twin looking equally grim, and beside him was his twin, and beside him his, and another and another, six in all. Sitting facing them in identical clothes, posture and expression were six more, all twelve poised in the delirium of the snow, fixed by a single streak of light. The benches they sat on were fastened to a wooden wagon moving along on four enormous wheels traced with iron, a long, rough cart with nothing to hang onto but the bench itself. They sat high up in the storm, looking straight ahead, not speaking, not touching. And then the horses came into view, two fine, surprisingly light creatures to draw such a load. They lifted their legs high in curving arcs, very rhythmically, dancing across the snow towing those mute, unnerving figures, colossi from another age carved in darkness, transported by some noiseless furnace of time. The two women in the car overtook them and drove slowly past looking back, not daring to breathe, not daring to believe they had seen what they had seen. Later when they returned to the farm neither of them spoke of the incident. 'Eddy Knight phoned,' Spohr told them, 'Surprised as all get out to find us here. When I mentioned that Sally was with us he acquired a need to consult me about an essay he's writing on philosophy and science. He'll be here soon, if he makes it before the roads close. People who will drive around in this weather . . .' He looked over at them severely with a hopelessly ambivalent expression on his round, cheerful face, his eyes smiling, his mouth pinched. Nella went to the kitchen, disliking to be told what to do no matter how indirectly, while Sally was unaware anything out of the ordinary had been conveyed. As Nella pretended to be busy in the kitchen Spohr undertook a little groundwork on behalf of his friend, 'Edwin is a handsome, lusty young man, good taste, good manners. You could do worse, you could do worse.' Soon they heard the red MG rattling up the drive, more toy than car as it bumped along the snow encrusted laneway. Young Knight, his nose shining with the cold that always managed to creep in under the convertible's top, bounded from the car and came roaring into the house, hooting, howling and waving a bottle like the flag at the top of a mast in a stiff breeze. He stood there shivering in his heavy, faded red and blue workman's shirt worn on top of a silky white one, a blue ascot knotted loosely at his throat, pale grey Mexican trousers stuffed into the tops of irontoed boots, a maroon corduroy cap and immaculate black leather driving gloves, buttoned down across the backs of his large, bony hands.

- Well I never, lord what a drive, damn near didn't make it. Now where's Nella got to? Sally, Sally my girl, what I've come through to find you, yippee! Here my good man, have a drink of this excellent stuff, it'll curl your toes all the way back to Christmas. My God what a drive, snow coming at me from every direction. Spohr, how d'you manage it? I do declare it'd fry my boots to drive about in this too often. Now where's Nella? Nella, come have a swig of screech dear lady, it'll warm your heart, it'll fan your fires, make a new woman of you — not that the old one is so bad.
- Eddy, how many stops did you make on the way up?
- Just two Nella, just two, but good ones. Man O man was I freezing. First one was the irresistible Dewdrop Inn back down there at Little Orange, and next your inestimably fine local, the commercial hotel in downtown Luther.
- Well I guess it's a miracle you got here at all.

- Now, now, he's a grown man and fully responsible.
- Fully irresponsible you mean.

Sally moved away from the noise, the bustle and banter, settling herself on a sofa near the fire in a far corner of the room, watching them carefully. Edwin knelt suddenly in front of her dropping his head on her lap, kissing her knees, kissing her thighs. 'I love you,' he whispered quite soberly, 'I love you.' Startled, she jumped up to join the others.

- Let's have some music Spohr, put a damn record on man, will you?
- Okay, what'll you have, blues, Dixieland?
- Knight, here, put this in your rum, hot water, lemon and cloves, it will get rid of the chill.
- That's a right fine woman you have here Spohr, a right fine woman.

A loud honkytonk blues poured from the phonograph, surrounding them, suffusing the air, hiding the moderate knock when it came some time later. Finally Reverend Allen Norman put his head inside the door, he was vicar of the Anglican church, one of the ten religious institutions represented in Luther, population fifteen hundred. Religion was the favorite pastime there, with politics a respectable but definite second.

- Anyone home?
- Allen, come in, come in. Good, I see the snow's let up.

He was a plump, elderly white haired man who looked sixty-five, although probably younger. The slightly rosy cast to his cheeks was no doubt due, at least in part, to extra communion wine — he stemmed from a low church tradition which did not entirely meet his needs — and for the rest he seemed very much like a poor English country parson. Fond of Spohr he came to visit often, happy to chat about his intricate doctrinal difficulties and the trilogy of plays on the life of Jesus he had been writing for years. Spohr the unbeliever was obliging, sympathetic and altogether liberal on the question of alcohol. Having clearly established years before that he rejected every premise governing Reverend Norman's existence, he was quite happy to engage in disputation involving hair's breadth subtleties on matters which were of no consequence to himself. They maintained a warm friendship.

- Now you haven't met Sally Reger here, but you probably remember this young ne'er-do-well.
- Howdy preacher, good to see you again, good to see you.
- Well now then Edwin, how are your studies coming along? I hope you haven't fallen into frivolous ways. My own son has I think.
- Allen, don't think that for a moment, why this is a serious young man. Travelled up all the way from Toronto for help in elucidating a small philosophical point. How's that for the pursuit of knowledge?
- I don't know, young people don't seem to care very much about the old truths anymore, for loyalty, honor and trust, being concerned about others. They appear a little shallow, unthinking,

100

they only seem to care for themselves. It's as if we've raised a generation of vipers whose answer to every difficulty is the deadly sting. I can barely understand what my children's friends say, let alone grasp their meaning. What I find hardest to endure is the callous way they use each other. What about you Edwin, don't you have a cast-off wife and babe tucked away somewhere? You seem to be a good fellow, how can you just let them go their way while you go yours?

- Well now, all that sounds like so much social varnish to me, and with all due respect to your age and calling sir, I'm afraid I find myself obliged to inquire into your assumptions. I challenge you directly with one assertion, one unquenchable fact: desire. Desire and loyalty do not live equally in the same house, this isn't a matter of choice, this isn't a matter of reason, the one simply purges the other. Desire corrupts with a sweet and subtle joy, can't you remember that? Personify grief and pleasure unexpectedly leaps into the void; invert pleasure and the light expires. Now then sir, even though you are a man of conscience I will not tolerate lectures, nor is it the moment to dictate terms and arrange conditions. Abuse, abuse, I say it is time to destroy what has no genesis in desire, no culmination in desire. — God, sometimes I do feel sickened by the sound of my own voice. — Do you know anything about the imperative for change and the reaching, the searching for something, what is it, casual or brutal, disease or a sense of clarity, treachery or its opposite? That so-called responsibility, that thing you call loyalty, that word and its world must be wiped clean. They will never get me, I repudiate virtue and all claims made against desire. Crave and satisfy, gorge and vomit, desecrate, that is purity, that is the meaning of purity. Well so much for social varnish. Exile and disfigurement have their own rewards. For God's sake Spohr, why don't you pour us all a bloody drink?

- Hm, you sound like a revolution my friend.
- O it's talk, talk, you know it's all damn talk. Sorry preacher, you touched on a sore spot, please don't take what I said personally. It was meant for that damn world out there, not a decent chap like you. I don't know what to do with myself these days.'

Sally had been listening carefully to every word and she came up to him now.

- Yes, that's something all right, that's something to pay attention to. Desire. *I will offer any part of my body to save him. I will offer any part of my body to save him.*
- Ha, you youngsters, you haven't learned anything beyond sensual gratification. Love is natural, but you must love within bounds, talk to me again when you're over forty then you'll have a perspective on that charnel house. All flesh is mortal, and still you cling to the expectation that a few acts of pure lust will change the world, the irony of it. Now Eddy please forgive me too, I've had my own parental agony today because my boy, God he's a man not a boy, he's nearly your age, my son has behaved with appalling thoughtlessness to a young lady. His mother and I were aghast when she came to us with a tale of woe. Now we feel responsible you see,

because he is our son, we raised him. How are we to recompense the world for his errors? The children's sins are visited upon the father. *What shocks the virtuous philosopher, delights the camelion Poet.*

Spohr intervened at this point.
- Well, well everyone, I feel one of my stories coming on, a charming fable for our time. Are you ready for this?
- O lord Spohr, do we have a choice, do we really have a choice? Well keep it short, keep it simple, and try not to be too mysterious old man, all right?

With that mockery from Edwin as his introduction Spohr began vigorously, calling up the elements in his repertoire, embellishing the details with incidental gestures while the story rolled off his tongue.

Tarzan, the survivor of an ancient, highly skilled race of giants pushed away a rock hiding the entrance to his cave, crawled out, studied the shadow he cast and stretched as he examined the world from treetop perspective, 'Master,' he spoke aloud, 'Which of the true ways should I follow today?' He listened for the answer which came like a voice on the wind, 'The way of the undivided spirit.' Satisfied, he returned to the cave then bathed in the widest of three streams running behind it, all three glistening softly in the dim light. As he washed the water darkened and it occurred to him he had been guilty of impure thoughts. He prayed to be forgiven until eventually the water ran clear again. Hungry, he inspected the food stores which were pitiably low because he spent so much time improving his mind and wrestling with his soul when he ought perhaps, to have been providing for the needs of his body. He sighed, swallowed a red powdery substance and chewed on a blackish green root. In five minutes he had reduced himself to the size of an ordinary man, now there was enough for many large meals, enough to feed dozens and dozens of people. He disliked being small because he found himself subject to constant minor indignities which of course, could not touch him in his original, his true form. Still, refreshed by the meal he set off through the jungle, now a considerable obstacle to his journey; he felt pleased with himself and happy about his way of life. After walking for many hours he stopped to rest under a huge oak tree, tired by his exertions. In a little while he saw a man approaching from the north, calling out to him with great friendliness, 'Hey dwarf, hello there!' 'And just whom do you think you're calling dwarf, we seem to be about the same size.' 'Ah my little friend, if you had eyes to see you'd hide yourself before making such a bold speech to me.' 'You're a very self-possessed individual, why so much bravado, you don't look particularly strong to me. Let's fight it out and see who wins.' With that the tricky dwarf fell upon Tarzan with a hatchet and hacked off his head.

Soon an old woman, it was actually Jane in her dotage, came stumbling across the head which lay there on the ground a significant distance from his body. You can imagine her surprise when she heard speech coming from the lips of the severed head. 'Old woman, old woman, do as I ask and I will grant you many favors.' The old woman, in need of this and that, decided she would help and shoved the two parts together, with considerable repugnance it must be admitted, sprinkling the place where they met with a yellowy brown powder, then sealing the wound with a sticky, green liquid. She placed her left foot on his belly, as he had instructed, chanting *ti ratana, tri ratana, ratana-ttaya, ratana-ttaya,* over and over, cupping her right hand on her left breast all the while. Body and head were thereby reunited.

Tarzan was very grateful, 'Here, eat this,' he said immediately, 'It will make you young and beautiful.' Jane had not had that particular favor in mind, so time does warp our inclination, but she decided it was a good idea in any case. She ate, becoming young once more and beautiful for the first time. 'Very nice,' observed Tarzan, 'I think I'll call you Jane, now come stay with me awhile.' However, he realized soon enough what he had fed her was not capable of changing shrewish thoughts or cranky ways; he decided he would have to pay the woman off to get rid of her. 'What would you like me to give you as a farewell present?' he inquired one day, expecting her to ask for money and a good property settlement. 'I don't think I'll be ready to leave until you can answer this question,' she replied, 'What is the truth that makes us free?' 'Blessed gods, how am I supposed to find that out?' 'Search, search until you find the answer dummy! I'll wait in the Hilton just outside the jungle for your answer. Remember,' she warned, 'You won't be rid of me until you bring the answer.'

Cursing his human size he hurried off to seek the wise men in the city who might help him if he could win their patronage.

When he got there several days later people were all talking about a sum of money large enough to satisfy a potentate, a prize offered by the wise men to anyone who could level the Ominous Rocky Mountain obscuring their view of the seashore and setting sun. Tarzan rushed to offer his services, not for the money he explained, but the answer to a very important question he would put to them. Confident of their wisdom and delighted with the saving they agreed to the proposal, including his unusual condition: for one day and one night all the people in the city or within a ten mile radius were to stay in their homes, the doors tightly closed, the windows shuttered. During that time they were to fast, to remain pure in thought and deed. 'At the end of this short period of time,' he promised, 'The Ominous Rocky Mountain will be gone and in its place will be flat meadowland.' Since the wise men protected those people they were inclined to indulge their whims, and when the appointed time arrived not a soul was to be seen for ten miles in every direction.

Tarzan stood at the edge of town facing the Ominous Rocky Mountain, swallowed a blackened green powder then chewed a red root. In five minutes he had expanded to fill out his original giant form and set about leveling the mountain. His labor was complete in one day and one night; however, just as dawn was breaking on the second day he discovered he was being watched by one of the wise men whose curiosity had overcome his prudence. Tarzan laid hold of him, pulled out his tongue and bound him tightly shouting, 'This is the curse of the sword, the stone and the book!' He assumed human size, presenting himself to the wise men as he flung their trussed up comrade among them, 'The Ominous Rocky Mountain god demands the sacrifice of this creature because he nurtured immoderate desires. Now here is my question: what is the truth that makes us free? When I have the answer to this question I can get the old lady off my back and continue on my way.' 'Imbecile!' they roared, 'The truth shall make you free.' 'I don't think I take your meaning,' he replied. 'No, you wouldn't, the answer to the question is the question, the asking. Now shove off, go home. We no longer believe in our wisdom, we abdicate.'

So what could the poor fellow do? He went back to Jane, married her, took her to the cave and lived the rest of his life according to the story with which we are all by now, well-acquainted.

- Most amusing, thank you to be sure, most amusing.
- My word Spohr, what's the point?
- O ho, don't you know? Let's have a drink. A little more rum toddy for you Allen?
- Dear no, I've had my limit, I'll be running along now. Don't fuss, I'll just slip out quietly, as I came. Goodbye Sally, goodbye all.
- I wonder what drove him away so soon. Nella, tell me if I was unforgivably rude to the poor fellow. He's a nice enough man, I know he doesn't mean any harm, but when he starts talking about the good old values he puts my back up. Shall we have some music now?

Edwin sat on the sofa beside Sally, close to the fire, holding her hand thoughtfully for a long time.

- Sally, I'm going to take you to bed now.
- No.
- No?
- No, I'm done with routine love affairs, I've had my limit too. Good night to everyone.
- How did I mess that one up Spohr?
- Do you expect them to fall into your hands just like that, like ripe apples dropping from a tree?

After another day of polite nonstop drinking the blowing snow subsided, and Sally went back to town with Eddy in his bouncing little MG. They saw each other in the weeks that followed, at the library, at Spohr's, near a busy, windy intersection at midday once, but never alone, never in the privacy administered by Edwin's explicit hunger, never in the corridor where his dreams held her with the strength of his longing alone. She felt the trap laid by his desire and surveyed it from a distance, enticed by his need, cooled by the certainty of that need. She calculated nothing, did only what she felt like doing; for six or eight weeks as winter's muscled arm lost its might, she played out an interlude with Sandy Burns, the handsome young actor who in later years was Nella's companion. Still very boyish, like a child in many ways although gifted and ambitious, Sandy was given to frequent recitations of The Love Song Of J. Alfred Prufrock. He performed with bitter zest, a groaning Prince Hamlet, until Sally pointed out how inappropriate that youthful passion was. Considerably younger than Sally, he took routine pleasure in reminding her of this and she in provocation. 'Ah right,' she might say, 'I didn't like that when I was your age either.' And he would respond, 'I hope I still won't if I ever reach your age.' They were two mindless pups rolling over on each other, biting, playing, nipping, yowling. Once they made love in his mother's sitting room while that abstracted lady and her two daughters had afternoon tea in the dining room, almost within range of their gasps and moans. Sally was continually aware that Eddy circled nervously about their terrain, never intruding, never quite disappearing. He would phone occasionally leaving messages which needed no reply. He told Nella to say he had been asking for her, always leaving his scent, marking a trail. This seemed only to intensify the pleasure she took with Sandy, Knight's presence like a catalyst, an erotic sketch.

It was during this time Sally first noticed Spohr appeared to know something about Thomas Archer he had not divulged. She arrived at Bellair Street one day when Sevcik was there, a great honking laugh inside the house betraying his presence from the street. As she walked in he leaned forward, laughter bending the tall, gaunt form, then he rocked back on his heels, apparently in some danger of falling over the other way. Spohr didn't seem to notice and Sally made no comment. She was pleased to find him there because he had spoken so kindly to her that night at Birgitte's; furthermore, she had heard he was an unusual man, that he had certain powers, and having this in mind she lingered to hear his conversation with Spohr. They looked like comedians, Sevick tall and hollow, Spohr short and round. It seemed appropriate to find them laughing, although she didn't understand what they were laughing about. They had been trading suggestions, Spohr advising Sevcik to use his divinatory gifts, Sevcik proposing that Spohr's scientific methods be pressed into service, both clearly intending more than their words conveyed. Sally kept quiet, the two men were guarded, almost uneasy, and it occurred to her they might prefer it if she left. That thought made her more uncomfortable as the room began to ring with dissonance, each one eyeing the other two awkwardly, helplessly. Finally Spohr said, 'Well Sally, Sevcik's on his rounds, checking up on all of us. Have you had any word?' 'From Tom you mean?' 'Yes.' 'Why no, I didn't know anyone had, is there news?' 'Not really, Marten Bender received a communication from Archer all right.' 'I had heard that too of course, but no one knew what to make of it. What happened to the people who were going to investigate, did they uncover anything?' 'Yes and no, we've met frequently and undertaken to check Bender's story, but what is puzzling us for example, is we know Schradieck has information,' Sevcik glanced at Spohr, 'Which no one has been able to get from him. He seems troubled about something or other, hard to know what's worrying him, he's a little furtive. A good man no doubt, but it's difficult, very difficult.' Then he changed the subject. 'Have I mentioned there has been a surprising increase in the number of people coming to me for instruction? I've just rented my own studio because I needed space Birgitte could not spare, and a suitable place on the second floor overlooking the ravine fell vacant. It's charming, now do visit when you can, both of you. There are changes in store for us, we would be ill-advised to ignore the signs. Not even you Spohr, can afford to be indifferent, they are strong, very strong. Something I think is imminent, such opportunities are too rare to pass up.' Spohr scoffed happily, 'I'm certainly pleased to hear that.' Sevcik smiled, 'One day my friend, one day.' Sally interrupted, 'I dreamt about him last week only I had forgotten.' Sevcik was immediately interested, 'Tell us the dream.' 'It's hard to assemble the recollection, such as it is. No light, there is no light, only darkness and no continuity, just images, a series of pictures. I remember one quite vividly now, Tom is stretched out on something, is it a rock? He is tied or chained down somehow with his arms over his head. *Di qua, di là, su per lo sasso tetro.* I see him at an angle, as if the slab or table or whatever he is lying on had been raised to a forty-five degree angle, for the viewer's sake it occurs to me, and he is still, he doesn't move but his eyes are open, sad, deep with sorrow, not pain, just sorrow. He seems isolated there in a dark red pit. What is it trying to break into the circle of visibility? Some animal thing cutting at the darkness, only Tom doesn't see it. I do, I see it standing there watching. I always dream about fear, that is the subject of my dreams. There are other images, not really clear . . . a strange building, I tell myself it must be an oriental palace. It crumbles to dust, literally a little heap of powder, and some odd characters I can't identify. Sorry, this is all that comes back to me now.' She stopped speaking as she realized the dream meant something she could not convey to them. Sevcik thought she was withholding her clarification, he would have to pursue that point. 'We're keeping a record,' he said, 'I'll make a note of this, stop by one day to make sure what I write down is accurate. And thank you Sally, we have to keep track of everything, no matter how we come by it, no matter how strange the information might seem to our friend Spohr.' 'Information!' exclaimed Spohr, for a moment dislodged from his imperturbability, 'You call that information?' He restrained himself, determined not to interfere, 'Well Sevcik,' he laughed, 'This takes us back to our original point, you have your methods and I have mine.' Spohr laughed and laughed until the others were caught by his spasm of laughter, the three of them clutching their sides. *Let them laugh a little; much will they weep.*

Before Archer, before Spohr, all those years ago, there was another day like this, a day in late February after a long bitter winter, a day when unspecified gentleness fell upon the earth and it became warm, unaccountably, unseasonably. I came by bus from Hamilton, not for the first time, I knew the city well enough by then, yet in a sense it was the first time, my awareness was so different on that day it still flowers in the bed of recollection, memory's season. There are a few days when the light, the very taste of the air, the moisture and wind on the face, the feeling of happiness and some inner private bliss stay with us forever. *And the rest Soon break, soon wither, soon forgotten.* Why should I remember one day among how many thousands and thousands on which nothing special happened? Why should I remember with such poignant accuracy how I looked, how I felt, how absurdly confident I was? Why was the sense of being uncontained so plainly etched I can study it, look at it again today? Outwardly almost nothing happened, I walked down Yonge Street in the bright sunlight thinking I wanted violets, I had never seen violets but I had that idea. How much is born of illusion, how many fables are realized in fantasies, fed on the expectations bred by stories or books or ideas, expectations which become the substratum of our experience. In the flowershop they said it was too early for violets, and so I had to be content with a single white carnation pinned to a spray of green fern. I fastened the flower to my coat completing the telescopic perception of myself, the long happy streets, the wind, the light and the city, then I walked slowly on looking at the shops, feasting with every step, never for a moment thinking such pleasure comes once or twice a lifetime, and only if we are lucky, never for a moment doubting life would be like that, a series of bright images lit by the sun, never for a moment suspecting we walk for the most part on the other side, the left, the unlit side where the sun never shines, where its light is filtered through the slanting shadows cast by tall buildings and passing clouds. The resonance of that day rang and rang so sweetly, a pure clear bell, its note reverberating, echoing in the unvoiced score which seemed to be my life. Then to come upon the same note again, to hear the note once more nearly thirty years later, knowing what I knew then, and still rejoice with the sound of every sparrow as I strolled, walking in the footsteps imprinted by the girl who was

113

once myself, conscious of an illuminated present and past, tasting innocent delight on the palate of experience, that was a dream in perpetual springtime, paradise given and not yet taken away. Now those two days ring in unison, one note, their vibrations interlocked forever, and I cannot look at one without the other chiming the correct response on its separate clock. I walk this particular corridor in time, a transient limping between the past and the distant past. On that first day, the day of my innocence, I slipped casually into the afternoon smiling at no one in particular, disregarding the bitter forces crouched behind an intersection of March, certain life would be kind, as it can be for those with the gift to receive it that way. And on the other day, the one which came some thirty years later, after I had encountered everything, had done everything, had known everything, I could give it all back in exchange for the memory and receive it as if for the first time, only knowing, this time knowing. Now, today, having sailed into the future and beyond, I know it doesn't really matter whether life was kind or not. Well then, how did it work out, how did it end, how could it, that rare and innocent day, except in a ludicrous paradigm of romance? North of Dundas two crumbling movie theatres nearly as disreputable then as now used to show old films. There I felt attracted by a name, the beauty, the sadness of a place name heroically linked with a not very distant war, Casablanca. How I sank into this illusory Casablanca, how moved I was by Bogart's stony immobility, Bergman's melting, languid passion, the unimaginable suffering of Henreid. Not for the first time I looked betrayal straight in the eye, incorporating it at once into the dream of bliss, the worm

114

that gnaws in paradise. Nothing is given, nothing is taken away.

Sally hurried from Spohr's house, restless, uncertain, haunted by a bad dream, haunted by the roar of a bullet exploding in her brother's brain, its bloody echo in her own skull. She was disoriented, scattered, and just when she felt she might be blown into a thousand irreducible fragments she stopped, her aberration halted by the appearance of a squat, solid figure in bright blue. It was Miss Turnbull, Miss Cecily Turnbull, a shopping bag over each arm, the expression on her face carved in the stone of anxiety and remorse, tears rolling down her fat cheeks behind the rimless glasses, sighs, moans and gasps in a pathetic chorus bubbling from her lips, 'O dear, O dear, O dear!' She was about to sail blindly past when Sally forced herself to speak, 'Miss Turnbull, Cecily, what's wrong, is anything the matter, can I help?' 'O they're too strict, they're simply too strict, I can't be held responsible for this. I'm not to blame, I didn't have anything to do with it, you know, I absolutely did not have the slightest bit to do with it.' 'Now Cecily, who would ever blame you, what's the matter?' 'Really I won't do it again, this time I promise, I give my word.' 'I don't understand.' 'Now they say they are going to fetch the police and what can I do?' 'Why don't you tell me what happened.' 'Nothing's gone right since mother left, well she didn't leave, she died, you know, and when a person dies they live on in your memory. I know that of course, but it's not like having her here, all the same. Now my friend Harriet, you understand she's a witch, a white witch, a good witch, a perfectly good witch, well they've arrested her at the tearoom, at least they said they were going to get the police, then I know they'll come for me. O dear, O dear, it's all so unfair, I only served the tea. I mean it's five dollars a cup and rather expensive to be sure, but I only served it. What *are* we going to do?' The tears came faster than ever, 'There, there,' said Sally, 'Now don't be upset, at the worst it'll be a fine for your friend and I'm sure no one will worry about you. They won't now, will they? Come on, let me walk you home, you'll see, it'll be all right, please don't cry.' Something like an unused gate, almost inoperable, swung open in the hollows of her mind as she tried to comfort the sobbing, sighing woman, something that recoiled from the recognition she was talking to someone who might well be herself in a few years' time. She pushed away her own panic with the thought, 'No, I will not be that person, I will not be that person.' The walls of her imprisonment could be breached then, clearly there were not only entrances there were exits as well. Sally scrutinized Miss Turnbull carefully now, studying her like an actress at a mirror, examining each gesture, each word of a role she deliberately turned down, refused to play. She realized there was no point trying to establish what had happened to Cecily. She would tell the story again and again over the weeks and months, over the years, details would become all too familiar.

'I mean when you think about it, there is nothing wrong, well not really wrong like killing or stealing or rape for heaven's

sake, in serving a *simple little* cup of tea. Now what harm is
there, I ask you, in a cup of tea, and if Harriet has the gift, well
everyone knows she has, she does only good with it, never bad,
only good, so what harm can there possibly be? O dear, O dear,
do you think the police will come for me, will I have to go to
court, will they put me in jail?' Tears flowed copiously. 'Cecily,
please stop worrying, I know this is terrible for you but I can't
believe they'll be too severe, if anyone takes any notice at all.
Come on now, how would it be if I bought us some ice cream?'
The tears stopped and Cecily prattled on in a new direction for
a few minutes, then as the thoughts she could not control
bounced up again she returned to that woe. Sally abruptly
considered the precipice at her own feet, acknowledging how
easily she could slip over the edge, end up a half demented old
lady, like Cecily. It was the first intimation that unhappiness is
reversible, she was free to save herself, to be quite sane if she
chose, but the recognition came and went. Sally had never
considered herself particularly strange until she caught the
shadow of her own portrait in Cecily, realizing that the
neurosis, the uneasiness which she had valued and in some
ways encouraged might, with time, culminate in nothing more
than a harassed old woman barely competent to navigate the
rough waters of life. She looked at that and found it worthless,
a hollow, shifting grave. The two women walked along
together, Sally composed now as she contemplated this city
which had been her home, this city with much of her short,
unhappy life embossed upon it. She did not want that history
reprinted, once again inflicting its savagely peopled memories.
She longed to be out of reach, out of touch, never to come back

no matter what. She wanted to find herself beyond the claims of necessity and passion, beyond the obligations which snared her in the line of her own traps. 'Let us repudiate promises,' she thought, 'First preserve ourselves, be ruthless with those who burden us, who lie. All promises made without desire or lapsed in desire are lies and therefore void, there are no obligations but desire which makes itself known without speculation.' She thought briefly of Edwin's tirade against the preacher and smiled, 'He's right, of course he's right.' Then she turned to Cecily whose bright turquoise snood had slipped off her head while she licked at the ice cream. Sandy Burns was not at home when she phoned him. Without hesitation or reflection Sally dialed Edwin's number, 'Hi, would you like to do something?'

From the Notebooks of Annie March (1965)

One word, she said it all hinged on one word. He uttered one word at the right time, in the right place, and her life dissolved around it.

A callow youth, to me at any rate, but to her — a tall blonde god of burnished beauty all wreathed in sunlight. Immortal. We fall in love with our idea of a person, not the person himself. (S. and I.) Sally told me, 'I felt safe as long as he was searching for me. Once he felt safe I was finished, it was over. I knew it would be like that.' Retribution.

Reading Blake as if for the first time, the prophetic books in chronological order, trying to separate Blake from Frye but I cannot. Want to get him (Blake) straight once and for all. Am I becoming superstitious or only pretending to be?

I want to be in constant exultation.

Today the feeling, very strong, of having already absented myself from the world. No longer feel able to deal with the simplicities of nine to five at the bookstore, relations with mother, with all the anonymous, the harmful and harmless people who surround me. My head aches. Want to write, all the time, and I do not write or practise as say a violinist does, for hours every day. So what am I doing? Painful to extract this when I want only to be ecstatic. Thoughts like these make me realize it could be desperate; I'm not.

Long conversation the other day with Spohr and Wells. Tried to convey the conflict between poetic statement and rational discourse, Spohr of course maintaining, 'An apple is an apple,' Monty looking metaphysical and helpless. A touch of the romantic there — all that Chopin. I need to postulate another understanding, another description.

Thinking back on what Sally said; it occurs to me that master Proust was right, there is no equilibrium in the business of human love. It is always a teeter-totter, when one is up the other is down. What you have is not what you want, what you want is what you can't have. Why? S. and I: he hung around and hung around, specific about what he pretended not to know he wanted. When I gave it, all of it, it was too much and he ran away.

That slick, sophisticated empiricism has been so deeply embedded in my thinking, the habits of my mind, I am imprisoned by it, imprisoned to such an extent that when I wander from my jail, I long for the jailer, I can't function, can't evaluate, have no way of knowing whether two plus two equals four and whether or not it matters. Difficulty lies in the belief itself and attachment to the belief when I want to make such fantastic statements, utter paradoxes of pure, misleading impossibility.

What happened that night, that early spring night when the sky itself celebrated with a false orange half moon hanging inverted, close to the horizon at first, then rising quickly like a balloon, what happened was the roads were slippery with winter's oily accretion, a thin sludge which ringed the rim of the tires like iron, binding them, sending the front wheels careening on a separate course, their own route, while the back ones spun around and around, and finally the grand arabesque of disaster uniting them forever in an incident which would have been too commonplace to describe, except that they were to be greatly, you might even say heroically, in love. The little red MG, half toy, half car, crumpled with exhaustion after whirling like a dervish through the deep curve on South Drive, just north of the bridge on Sherbourne Street. As the car landed on its side the driver moaned to his passenger now pressed against him as he always knew she would be, 'O baby, are you all right?' No one had used that word, had ever called her that. Something split and gave way with a crack so violent, so wrenching to the heart she thought her veins might open spontaneously and drench them both in blood. They stayed there squeezed against each other, not daring, not caring to move until a couple of benevolent passersby reached in to pull them out and right the car. Abandoning it they walked slowly away clasped tightly to each other, joined at the hip and thigh by a cement which oozed from both of them, not speaking, stunned by the accident which interlocked their passion with a snap that sealed their fate. Abruptly terrified, they hid beneath the verandah of a house they happened to be passing, until they could stop shaking, until the street seemed quiet and deserted, until the world seemed safe, and they set off walking south again towards Bloor Street. A police cruiser roared up behind them, bells clanging, lights flashing, tires rocking to a comic book stop. Two huge figures in blue leaped around them with agility and speed, surrounding them, confronting them, blocking even the thought of escape. 'Mr. Knight?' his name was on a parking sticker fixed to the car, 'Mr. Knight, we want to ask you some questions, you'll have to come with us. The lady can go home.' 'No, I'll come too.' Forlornly comforting each other, they sat on a long wooden bench at the station on Jarvis Street, waiting for they knew not what terror to clap him behind bars. There was a little detail, a mushrooming cloud obscuring every aspect of their landscape, Edwin could not produce a driver's license, didn't have one. Whole continents were erupting, galaxies were forming, stars were disintegrating, but they inhabited a universe whose polestar pulsed one signal, the inability to present a driver's license. Yet they were pardoned this indiscretion, it was forgotten in the confusion. He was asked to show his ownership papers, the rough sergeant at the station not knowing the arresting officer had omitted that detail when he stopped Eddy some distance from the car. 'Now then Edwin, you're at the university I'm told, you must learn to take a little more care. You've left us no choice but to charge you with failing to remain and failing to report. You'll be informed of the date of your trial.' They might have missed the license, but how could they have overlooked the alcohol he had consumed, was it the intimidatingly correct accent? Eddy ground his teeth suppressing rage and relief at the same time, then he and Sally hurried off to find Spohr.

Eddy had moved recently into the small room at the back of Spohr's spacious cottage, this in part to satisfy his need for Spohr's companionship. He looked to Spohr as his principal tutor, although the university had offered the best in disciplines for the mind. Spohr and Nella received him there graciously, this in part because they had entered upon a period which was close to financial ruin, although their friends were not permitted to deduce that. Spohr occasionally received trifling research grants, consultant's fees and small sums from the sale of certain patents. Nella was incapable of working — the idea rarely occurred to her. She had an unquestionable sense of helplessness in matters relating to her own survival, always dependent on someone else to sustain her. For the most part her material requirements were few, she had none of the taste for alcohol her friends had, drugs were not interesting, she did not mind what sort of disarray she lived in, she had no need for books and little for music. All in all, Nella presented a very thin edge to the world. Her life was internal, enacted within, only peripherally along the glancing rim of the world, in the gardens and offerings of civilization which devour us day by day. She felt concern for her friends, suffered when they did, was happy when they were, but remained essentially unrooted. Even during her years with Spohr Nella was like a bird ready for spontaneous flight across a street, a continent or across unimaginable spaces to a distant planet. In the country she kept more or less outside, in the city the streets could not claim her. She stayed indoors, her back turned to whatever went on out there, little concerned with politics, national events, society, the exploration of space, business, war, sports and the other acceptable forms of human mockery. Not particularly self-analytic until later, much later, Nella merely looked in rather than out. She hungered abstractly for the truth, and perhaps it was that appetite which kept the attachment to his wife alive in Spohr, persisting through every flirtation and infatuation, through the multitude of minor love affairs which only seemed to deepen and enhance his attachment in a way. Years and years later, looking back on Spohr's habitual, casual infidelity, long after her love for him had withered and died, long after his death, long after she had stopped trying to unravel the man she felt certain no one had known better than she herself did, and she didn't know what to make of him, Nella would still feel a tremor of distress when new information came, however inadvertently, about his old adventures in the flesh, the amatory exercises in which he polished his desires more or less as he polished his mind, with all those stratagems, plans, inventions and philosophies. She could summon up a clear picture of him, slightly overweight, fair haired, icy blue eyes smiling behind steel framed spectacles, all affability, his left leg frequently extended straight out, propped up on a stool or chair because of an old knee injury, pale blue pullover, shirt, tie and white trousers, his outmoded but customary dress, friendly to everyone, open, never happier than to talk and have a quiet drink or two, except that some details never fell into place. He seemed to have no scruples whatsoever about money or how he acquired it; after a time he made no attempt to find work, even the kind which by his own admission he thought he might enjoy, he preferred to drift in an almost derelict state of impecunity rather than be saddled with anyone who might eventually dictate rather than consult. *What would it pleasure me to have my throat cut with diamonds?* He had no need to impose himself on anyone and a powerful aversion to the possibility someone might try that on him. Physically lazy, he did not care to move unless it was unavoidable, his mental energy however, seemed without limits. It was his occupation and his amusement to examine every knot of understanding no matter how securely and ingeniously tied. Years and years later looking back at that time, she could never reconcile herself to the memory of a situation which came up often enough, Spohr wanted, needed something. As she pointed out there was no money he would flash with implacability, 'Well get some, damn you!' 'But where, how?' 'I don't care, just get it.' She always did find a secret reserve or beg a little cash from one of her parents, occasionally even from his, but never from their friends. If he had been an artist failing to sell his canvases or a writer unable to find a publisher she would have understood and forgiven him, but because he cared only to offer an imponderable array of gadgets, toys and exotically unnecessary devices in exchange for his keep, she did not consider this adequate for the system of barter whereby, in return for your life, the world grants you a living. He had a variety of alternatives, 'Let's live on your mother's farm and raise ducks,' he would say. This might precipitate weeks of casual and then increasingly precise data on the economics of duck farming, the required investment, operating costs, production needs, expected returns, until finally the idea was exhausted. Then it might be replaced by another plan, say the manufacture, right there in the house on Bellair Street, of any one of his patents which might appeal to the masses. While these proposals blossomed like the short-lived flowers in spring, they were regularly supported by a tiny monthly sum Nella's patient father had borrowed on their behalf. When Eddy moved into the room which had once been Spohr's office Nella felt a measure of relief, aside from which he had stayed there so frequently it hardly made any difference. She was used to his presence in their lives, used to his friendliness and the somewhat idolatrous admiration for her husband. He looked to Spohr as though he held the keys to the universe locked in his brain, and Edwin hoped to pick that lock or learn the combination for himself. During the years when other young

125

men were schooling themselves for a profession Eddy had run away to sea, this to escape the painful drama of his parents' divorce. Sentimentally attached to his mother from whom he had acquired a certain sweetness of disposition, that parent being unwilling or unable to keep him, and repelled by his father from whom he had acquired a brittleness, that parent being indifferent to him, at the age of fourteen Eddy turned his back on investments and industry, his father's side, and the arts, his mother's side, to embark instead on a career in the Royal Navy. When he first met Spohr some ten years later he had spent a few not entirely miserable years in the merchant navy — he fled the academy before being commissioned — from which he promoted himself to cub reporter on a small newspaper in northern Ontario, from there to a few minor jobs in theatre and television. For years he felt nakedly uneducated and happily took the advice of Spohr and Monty Wells to complete his studies, but he had kept an arrogance of class, clinging to his gentlemanly disdain for the world and its ways. In Spohr he recognized the tutor who would train his mind, discount his weaknesses, support his vanity and encourage him to become the skilled, even scholarly man of leisure he yearned to be. He and Spohr shared a half serious, half amused belief in their future, something well beyond the common man whom Eddy had learned to call, thanks to Mr. Eliot, abstractly and with pleasant contempt, Sweeney. 'I can assure you, Sweeney does not want to live the way we do,' or 'Sweeney has never, to my knowledge, manifested any interest in the arts,' and 'Sweeney, above all, wants to be left alone, drink a pint, bang the wife and go to the flicks. That's it.' Spohr himself was not the sort of man to find fault with others. His analytic gift was never turned against those who fell within his range, he might study them, penetrate their secrets, understand their motives, their idiosyncrasies, but they were never rejected and were never without interest. He would pursue what concerned his friends until their difficulties had been resolved or their attention was exhausted. He understood his friends well. 'I think I am completely amoral,' Sally once remarked. He replied after a slight pause, he weighed what he said, 'No, I don't think so, you measure your actions against a scale of values, sometimes you make a little noise scampering up and down that scale but you never let go. Why do you suppose you do that?' His questions were not to be understood as interpretive in the psychological manner, he had no use for what he looked upon as the bastards of science, those schools whose axioms and suppositions he found either laughable or misleading. When he set about examining behavior his mood was always quantitative never qualitative. With Eddy he acknowledged his friend's willingness to accept the instruction he was prepared to offer; for his own sake however, as well as for the younger man's, he would hold him off slightly, obliging them both to examine what they wanted from each other, what they could expect. 'Don't ever depend on me,' Spohr said, 'I'm not reliable. O I'll do what I can for you, help you write a paper on Kant if that's what you want, tell you what to say to your wife's lawyer if that's what you want, but don't count on me to be here whenever you think you need me. Still, I am your friend, always on your side no matter the odds, I will never violate your interests except of course, in the unlikely event they should happen to conflict with mine. And I more or less expect you to return the compliment, but I don't require it. Something to think about though, there are poisons which infect the bloodstream when we are young, sometimes genetically. If we don't filter them out, those charming idiosyncrasies so amusing, so entertaining, those minor imperfections may harden on our backs like the shell of a turtle. They can be a refuge but they may also become a burden, eventually even a torment. Look at Bender, better still at Archer, an extreme example I admit. He wanted to examine the idea of madness, well I think he has let himself go mad completely. Who's in charge now? Select your weaknesses, your foibles if you must, with circumspection because they dominate you in the end. At some point a transition must be made, if you don't assert yourself, the ascendance of your own mind, be prepared to submerge who you are in a trough at which every passing creature is free to snuffle, leaving its trail of filth on you. There is a master in any situation. Be that master, a prince must know perfectly how to act like a beast and like a man. It's all right to take what you want if you take it with good manners and adequate concern for others, they inhabit your world after all. Make them comfortable, then they won't dump their discontent on you. What do you think?' Nella rarely listened to these conversations, they made her restless, irritable. She preferred Spohr's inventions to those ideas of his which circumscribed the possible with judicious deliberation. That was another reason she was pleased when Eddy moved in, it relieved her of listening to Spohr work out his ideas, she was quite ready to entrust that to Edwin. And he was delighted, the unending conversation spun from the same threads every day was what he wanted, a carefully executed background, the well-wrought figured bass for his daily life. He basked happily in Spohr's tuition unaware that what he needed was a guide to the inner chambers, the inaccessible avenues of his leaden heart. Spohr's fundamental egalitarianism was so deeply engrained he was as happy to pass the time with Fred Wardle at the general store as with his most sophisticated friends in the city; for Eddy however, he observed there was something else, there were differences. Although he might follow Spohr's lead in most things, he sometimes made references to standards he found appropriate for a gentleman, to what might be acceptable in this country that he did not permit himself at home. All this thought Spohr, was the shadow of his father, a ponderous Englishman filled with conviction and prejudice. His son had sipped a few drops of that corrosive dribble from his lips.

That night, that early spring night when the air was loose and soft and sweet, when Edwin and Sally spun out on the slick, oiled wheels of misfortune, landing sideways and sprawled out on each other, that night had disaster coiled around its heart. From the police station Eddy ran to Spohr with Sally, the prize he had plucked from the darkness on his arm, the woeful tale ready on his lips, 'I tell you Spohr, the bloody steering must have given out, I can't account for the way she behaved. There was no control, nothing, I don't believe my driving could have been at fault, it must have been some damn mechanical failure. And my word we were badly rattled, it could have had a much nastier conclusion, we might have both been smashed up, you know. Lord, we were shaking so much we didn't know what to do, because of all the booze and not having that cursed license, and do you know what we did, will you believe it? We hid, we hid like two scared rabbits under someone's verandah, crouching there, two desperate criminals in the night.' Overcome by their unheroic conduct and the sheer imbecility of what they had done, Sally began to laugh, 'Spohr, we behaved like morons, we expected to be led off in chains to who knows what horror story, but when the police came screaming up behind us, around us, all over us, they were actually quite decent. They were instant father figures, chastising, remonstrating. "Mr. Knight," one of them says, "There is a university parking sticker on your car. Uh, does that mean you are a student there now?" "Yes, I'm afraid it does," replies our friend here, "Well then," says the great beast, "Uh, Mr. Knight, you really should know better." It was too much, I mean really too much, that kind of anticlimax.' She was laughing as Eddy continued, ' "Uh, Mr. Knight, you youngsters, what is your first name by the way?" "Edwin." "Well Ed, you youngsters are going to be the leaders of this country one fine day, you can't drive around knocking cars over in this reckless way. And you young lady, what will your mother think about this, what will your father have to say to young Edwin here?" They went on like that all the way to the police station. God, by that time we didn't know what to think. Then alas, we saw our two friendly cops talking to a tough looking sergeant and we were done for. They left us sitting there on a bench in the corridor, it seemed like hours, and I was convinced we should make a break for it, head for Mexico or the States, anywhere out of their reach. They had

130

us sweating again, man I tell you it was tense, but silly, lord it was silly. And listen to her now. You're right Sally, you're absolutely right,' concluded Eddy laughing hysterically himself now that he had a few more drinks inside him, the blissful feeling of being safe, unassailable at last. He smiled at Sally, sitting close to her, touching her shoulder, her knee, her hair, while she smiled back at him, seeing only the innocent boy, fair haired, loving, eager. 'I must call for Nella,' said Spohr, 'I'm sure you two can find some way to amuse each other.' Then off he went to spend an hour or two with Brenda MacIntyre.

And there she sat, her long, straight brown hair uncombed, soft brown eyes staring without blinking beneath flat bangs, perched on the dining room table swinging her legs, the essence of casual carnality. Bollard the lover, sitting across the room under a somewhat oblique scrutiny by the husband, felt himself flush as he studied the line where her dress ended, far up her pale thighs. Jan left the room, unable to endure the sexuality he felt emanating from his wife and flowing out to another man. 'I must do some work in the basement,' he said. Bollard groaned, 'Damn, he knows, I think he knows.' 'So what?' replied Marguerite coolly, 'If he minded he'd do something but he's never said a word, never, and he's seen us together, once even sitting on your bed. What a man!' 'Don't Marguerite, don't talk like that, I can't bear this, it doesn't seem decent.' 'Listen to him Nella, listen to him. If you can't put up with the way I talk then you'd better go too.' 'Look love I'm sorry, sometimes it gets to me, you know,' placatingly, 'Having you so close, looking like that and not even able to put a hand on you.' 'Poor bollocksey Bollard, it is hard for you darling, isn't it?' 'O the bitch,' he thought to himself, 'The bitch.' Then he smiled, 'But I do have to leave, there's an early morning deadline at the agency and a lot to finish up.' He came close to her and whispered, 'Slip into my bed tomorrow morning after Jan leaves, there's a good girl, please don't forget.' He left and Marguerite flung her arms up over her head laughing exhuberantly, 'Isn't it wonderful Nella, isn't it simply amazing?' Nella smiled as she bent her head to light a cigarette, 'Is it?' 'Tell the truth now, are you really bored with sex, Edwin said you told him that.' 'Marguerite, I didn't say that, at any rate it's not what I meant, he must have misunderstood. I was only trying to explain why there's no need to attach so much importance to it, for me, why I don't find myself being lead around by a single passion. This doesn't mean the desire has gone, I merely find it less compulsive, less imperative, but you know it's there, very much so.' 'You have every right to whatever you like, it belongs to you. Listen, I started doing things to myself when I was, O two years old or so, and it was mine, no one could take that away from me, not even my mother, and did she ever try! Do you know she threatened to break my arm if I didn't stop. If she suspected anything she'd start hitting me, I think she enjoyed being brutal, and if she didn't catch me I'd run from the room, out the back or down the lane, anywhere. I like it, still do it. Sometimes I think that's the best even with a beast like Bollard around, and he is something. Do you know I feel orgasms now in parts of my body where I never have before? Did you know they have been classified according to where you feel it? With Jan, if anything happens at all, very uninteresting routine stuff, but with Bollard, my God he slams me around the bed and makes the whole house shake, he screams and yells a lot too. Sometimes I have to laugh, I can't help myself, it's so funny to hear him moan like that. But I've never gone with another woman. Have you? I never have, I'm not sure whether I want to or not, sometimes I think I'd like to. That dancer friend of Sally's said any woman worth her salt has to have a little of that. I might once, just to see what it's like. A woman's body is more beautiful than a man's. I can't believe you'd be ready to give all this up Nella. Come on now, admit it, you still like it, don't you, don't you?' Nella started to laugh, 'Marguerite, you make the whole thing sound like banana splits, sure I like it, who doesn't? But not that much, let's leave this. Is it cold in here?' Nella was pacing up and down drawing deeply on her cigarette, 'Would you mind if I opened one of the doors? I find the room claustrophobic with both doors shut.' The small box-like dining room had a high ceiling with loops of painted over plaster flowers high up the walls. There was one narrow window looking onto a broken cement walkway and two doors, one connecting the room to the kitchen, the other to the hallway and front door of the house. With both doors closed the room became a vertical casket sealed off from the rest of the house. 'I just don't feel the way you do Marguerite, although I guess I used to. This is a lot easier to live with, you know.' 'I have no doubt of that, I am actually frustrated in each cell of my body if I don't make love every day. Is that so strange?'

SALLY REGER'S PERSONAL MONOLOGUE (II)

What I said before was my song, a lyric for myself, a riddle, my private joke. Although it had all the turmoil of a lie this was in fact, the truth. If you stop to think about it you'll see my life can be described that way; essentially it was the truth. Those things all happened more or less as I said they did, the lie however, may be sought and found within, it didn't feel that way. You have to see what was happening inwardly all that time. *I was a flower with a spiny stem growing from the wound in my brother's flesh. Every thorn scoured and seared his body, every point of my life was a spear thrust into his. Together we are now as rooted in death as once we were bled into life.* It is true I had a few savage encounters with certain individuals who devoured me, swallowed me whole, but I didn't disintegrate and I couldn't be digested. I wriggled and wriggled like a fish on a hook, or better still, the bait engorged without being chewed. Eventually I was either spat back or I squirmed my way free. In any case, don't forget I found myself changed by each misadventure. It was a double process, they ravaged me as I infected them, the pustulous inflammation in their bodies. I wasn't a mindless, inert thing waiting to be enveloped by

passing disaster, there was something I needed, something I
wanted and went burrowing inside my tormentors without
conscience, without remorse; I used them as a nesting ground,
a feeding place. Don't ask what there was to be found right
down in the belly of my assailants, I don't know, I'm still
looking. Who can tell me, who can say what it is? When I stand
back and look at myself, life seems like a crazy kind of snakes
and ladders played out on a board with secret rules. I know it
has rules because I keep feeling their weight, only I can't
penetrate the meaning, I don't seem to have a key that
deciphers the code. Once I did something, it seemed trivial
enough at the time, which has required such fierce recompense
I find myself paying for it to this day. If you take anything that
doesn't belong to you, isn't yours, if you deny what is
rightfully another's, if you try to add or subtract a single detail,
the balance must be made good, has to be restored. Knowing
this isn't enough, you have to do it, be the source of restoration.
You have to know forgiveness before the rule stops knocking
you down at the end of each round. I'm sure of it, sure there is
a law of hurt and retribution, a universal account you withdraw
from that you pay back again and again. What I've seen so far
doesn't amount to much, what I've learned doesn't amount to
anything, everything is still to come. Can I live through it, will
I survive? And the other aspect of the lie, nothing happened
quite the way I described it, nothing like that at all. Only what
occurred inwardly was true, everything else was faked, a crude
illusion to gratify the requirements of the sensory game, the
intractable plan. There was no professor who taught me,
tutored me and then obligingly walked offstage in a cloud of

ambiguous sexuality, although there might have been. Nothing was casual or insignificant, it was merely not the truth. *Qu'on ne m' attende jamais à mes rendezvous illusoires.* Even so every lie must be penetrated, every diversion has to be weighed, recognized so that the straight, true line buried beneath an avalanche of mistakes and misconceptions can be known at last. Every time you walk away from that line you become so entangled you lose the fact of its existence, the remembrance, and I have lost it. When I am swallowed by some predator on my path I acquiesce because I have an idea the way back lies through the greatest danger, the greatest sorrow. *Like my brother who followed the bullet's path to oblivion.* And don't for a moment think this isn't a lie: it seems that way today, yesterday was different, tomorrow will be something else. You can always manipulate events, tell a good story, make it sound like the truth. The difficulty is not knowing exactly what the line represents, not knowing whether you are already suspended from it, battered in a night of pain or whether you only imagined it. And don't think this isn't the truth: don't barter your understanding for a moment of bliss, don't cash in on the costly lies. What else is there except to hang on, hang onto anything that will bear your weight even for a moment, keep going. *My brother, my brother, did he fall into the endless night?* Bloody hell! We really don't know how to tell right from wrong, true from false, don't you think I'd tell the truth if I could? What is it after all, some ancient hieroglyph carved from whole dynasties, the private romance of bird, sceptre and sandal, the penetration of the sun's secrets, the quiet evaporation of the moon? Listen to the sound of a solitary bird in mid-afternoon, that bird knows exactly what it needs to know and proceeds with a perfect sense of destiny even though it entails thousands upon thousands of miles across bleak oceans, hostile continents. And how many times does a bird make that journey in one lifetime? Never faltering it keeps flying, true to a destination, always departing and arriving on time according to an inexplicable schedule, instinctively with the little it possesses, the tiny bit that it knows, doing exactly what is right, looking after itself, its mate and their young, caring, feeding, protecting. The tiny bird soaring up there flies into the teeth of time and never makes a mistake, never creates mischief, never loses its place and never knows grief. Flying high on the currents above earth and water, sometimes even against the winds in the sky, aloft on the curve of the sun, the moon, it never slips from that fine line bound like an intuition of gravity, a girdle about its waist. Then look at us as we stumble under the weight, the burden of our knowledge, falling, flailing, queasy, desperate. O it's a comic enough opera, make no mistake about that, as our Egyptian Hassan would say, make no mistake about that. Only it's not funny, it's awful. The dead pharoahs who lived like kings and died like gods, whose graves were robbed even so, they kept their secrets. Thieves and robbers can steal nothing more than the gold, the treasure and the lie, while truth lies bleeding, buried away inside carved blocks of stone, inside those great pyramidal jests, themselves hoodwinked by the thief of time. What's a few thousand years of cosmic bliss worth? Let me describe a touching thing, let me tell you how we are preserved beyond these jokes which time and misery and death foist upon us. I saw them first as an island, golden, laughing silence, a midday revelation right there on the crowded street. No one else could see them, they were invisible, two angels on a personal excursion hiding out in street clothes, their robes of time. I don't know who they were, those two cavorting and laughing in a silent capsule devised by the sun, but I thought it was Archer with Pavel Robichaud, a long time ago. Walking along Bloor on a cloudy summer day as the office workers started spilling out at noon, on the other side of the street, across the parked cars, across two lanes of traffic each way and the streetcars in between, slamming and clanging on their rocketing steel tracks, I saw two unkempt, ragged men, one short and dark, the other tall and fair. They flung their arms up laughing ecstatically, enveloped in a light separating them from the crowd which parted in dark waves as they slipped through, a shower of gold. They seemed to be in little more than rags, and there was something about those emblems of poverty which filtered the dust of the world from their shoulders, which promised abstention from frivolity, the obsessive triviality flowing around them, away from them. Whatever it was that occupied their attention, they evidently were in touch with a world unavailable to those who walked past, unaware of their presence. And it made me happy, briefly, because I knew then that something worth more than everything the street scene implied would one day be made known. I've never forgotten that intimation, the promise, and I haven't understood it either. Do you think I will ever know that secret, do you think I can find comfort in the clatter of this world, do you think I will be able to distinguish illusion from illusion in time? Archer was preoccupied with it, sometimes when he was starting to drift out into his fear, when that madness set his body on fire he was haunted by it, he would ask himself over and over again, but do you, do *you* know the difference between right and wrong? Only once did I catch a glimpse inside another life, and that one died playing with the weapons of his destiny. *I travelled with a bullet exploding the chambers of blood in his brain. I will offer any part of my body to save you. I will offer any part of my body to save you.*

During the hot spring days that followed, Edwin and Sally enacted their paradise of the senses, unconcerned that a coiled serpent lay inside the garden. They lived together in Spohr's expansive cottage sharing the room which had been his office, where once the walls had been lined with shelves from the floor to the ceiling, holding tools, plans, spare parts, unfinished toys, microscopes, telescopes, meters, wave generators, transistors, components, circuits, modules, models, the proliferation of instruments Spohr used to measure the universe, now kept instead in tidy collections throughout the house. While Eddy finished his studies for the year, working when the occasional opportunity presented itself, Sally found a clerical job at the university. The salary was despicable, the work was mean, the people who hired her humorless and dedicated to their bulging empire of paper. Sally accepted her tedious position with self-deprecation, amusement. 'Miss

Euphemia Birtwhistle, that is indeed her name although close friends are permitted to call her Birtie out of office hours, well Miss B. is in fact, in love with Mr. George Haldimand, the Director of Extension,' she informed Annie March one morning as they walked to work together, 'But he has a tenacious mother and it's a rather dicey affair. Euphemia must be well and truly beyond fifty, her hair is dyed purple, and I think the good Director has to be a few years her junior, maybe more. I once caught them holding hands during lunch hour — he was annoyed I observed this breach of decorum, he seemed embarrassed. I think rumors have reached them that I live in sin and they can't stand it, poor darlings. What *are* they going to do about me?' 'I think,' said Annie, 'You'd better stop being late, stop taking such long lunch hours or they'll fire you for sure.' 'That place is so polite I doubt whether anyone has ever been fired, I have to give them grounds because they clearly don't know how to do it. When I asked to leave early once a week to take a class, of course I promised to make up the time, they tried every way they could to stop me until I cornered Mr. Haldimand, suggesting his stance would appear ludicrous to other faculty members, he had to give in. They all line up to watch me leave early on Wednesday afternoon, it's a funny place.' Annie smiled and said nothing. 'Anyhow, it's a dreadful job, they'd be doing me a terrific favor if they fired me. I can't decently quit with neither of us having a penny to our name. How well do you know John Adolph? He phoned yesterday and said he has to see me; I wonder what he wants.' Sally continued without waiting for any comment from Annie, 'I've known him a long time, we went to school together in fact,

140

although he's older than I am. He was kept back several years, a sickly child, but he's quite brilliant, perverted and brilliant. Strange man, he inhabits a totally contradictory world, all glitter and brilliance on the surface, all misery beneath. His social life, going to the right parties, seeing the right plays, the right films, knowing the right people, living at the right address, that kind of thing is unspeakably important to him. It's hard to believe anyone so clever can be ruled by such nonessentials, a hint of M. Proust perhaps. There is a line from William Cowper he used to chant obsessively when he was drinking, "I was a stricken deer that left the herd." He would repeat the line until it became unbearable. Do you know what he said to me once? He said God made him queer because he's such a poor, weak specimen He had to ensure there would be no more like him, that he would be the last of his strain. I guess if you think you're weak, in fact you are. I tried to tell him that but he refused to accept any share of the burden, he wanted God alone, whom he doesn't quite believe in, to be responsible for all his failures as a human being. With that vicious, acid tongue, the excessive drinking and his genius for setting friends against each other a lot of his circle have given him up. We used to be close at one time, but the tides and the winds have carried us in different directions over the years. I am looking forward to seeing him; still, I wonder what he wants. Eddy will be working and just as well, I don't think they liked each other. I hope Spohr won't be around, can you imagine the two of them together?' 'They do know each other.' 'So they do.' She looked at her watch, moaned theatrically, waved and hurried off down St. George. Annie had become fond of Sally

141

in the short time since she moved in with Eddy; now however, she was glad to spend a few minutes alone before going into the bookstore, a few minutes to sun in the light of her labor, the poems she found herself caught up in. 'It's funny, sometimes the stuff just keeps pouring out of you, like toothpaste after you've stopped squeezing the tube.' The analogy took her fancy as she laughed out loud a little, 'The boatman theme again, he won't leave me alone . . . first the elegy and now this, there must be something there. I like the ballad, imagine writing a ballad . . . and the boatman, the figure of the boatman has changed. In the elegy he was the emperor of logic chopping off my head, only now he's more like a dirty old man. A fisherman? O God, how he hungers for life, my life, will he eat my life? His knowledge is mysterious, indispensable I suppose. The Egyptians thought you had to travel across chaos to became immortal, the waters of chaos which are the waters of creation. I like the ballad and the poor bewitched bride. Her husband, who is the husband sad and gentle? The boatman is the lover, the other man. Is he death or knowledge? Both, either. It's good, it's so good.'

Saturday afternoon Sevcik and Marten Bender arrived within a half hour of each other at Spohr's house on Bellair Street. Sally groaned with the expectation of John Adolph's visit. The day had begun badly, she felt numb, a heaviness that amounted to confusion, she couldn't think, was nervous about the visit which obscurely promised something unpleasant, and when the mail came it brought a letter from her ex-husband. She hadn't thought about him in months, suddenly he was right there in a witty, erotic letter replete with the loving declarations she had waited to hear throughout their hopeless married episodes. Now she felt trapped by arrows aimed from the different corners of her life. She was lethargic, even dizzy, fearing the darkness behind her eyes would burst in a fugue of blood. Bender, who arrived first, talked to her while he waited for Spohr, offering a drink of cheap cognac which she drank quickly. Increasingly she felt isolated, speaking with difficulty. Marten did not observe her distraction at first, so preoccupied with his own interests he barely seemed to notice her. Sipping the cognac slowly he savored it as though it were a costly liquor, stroking the little grey goatee on his chin thoughtfully, ceremonially, 'Music is the only form of expression I know. Did you ever hear my sinfonia or the partita? You haven't? Too bad my dear, too bad, they are excellent I think, but the new concerto, what an intricate work, full of surprises even for myself, this concerto will put my name on the map, I'm sure of that.' Sally filled her little glass again, wondering what on earth he was talking about as he began to describe the orchestration in detail. He looked at her again slowly, speculatively, 'Come to my studio sometime and let me play Scriabin for you, the secrets of the human soul will be unlocked.' In his peculiar way Bender came to a sensitive understanding of the people he encountered, expressed however, only in terms compatible with his own interests. Once when he hadn't seen Spohr for more than a year he greeted him, 'Ah Spohr, here you are, look at this manuscript will you, can you imagine a more perfect resolution? It even looks good on the page, and listen to it, listen.' He sang, hummed and waved his hand across a shower of notes. Spohr nodded, accepting that his unaffected self-absorption was not simply a raw, clamoring ego, although that was undoubtedly there, but a devotion to his music, an instinct for perfection which left no room for triflers. His own concentration was so much the standard he didn't notice anything less, it failed to ignite his attention. Spohr came in, 'How much of that stuff have you consumed girl?' he asked with indifferent severity, peering at her above the steel rimmed glasses. 'Not enough, not enough,' she answered pouring herself another drink. The tall, swan-like form of Sevcik filled the doorway, his spindly frame telescoping a little to enter the room. 'What a coincidence,' said Spohr blandly, 'Welcome my friend, welcome. Will you have a drink with us?' 'Thank you no, I don't take alcohol, as I believe you know.' 'Ah quite so, quite so.' 'Well Sally, how are you?' Sevcik's attempts to be polite inevitably reduced him to a posture only slightly resembling what might have been a salutation, the decaying memory of some minor court in Europe, an opera cloak over his shoulders. Spohr marveled that a man who seemed so awkward, so like a strung puppet in motion could flow into those liquid feats of yoga he had watched from time to time. Sally, dazed by the arrival of yet another actor, found herself unable to speak. Slightly hysterical now, she escaped to the kitchen where she remained, drinking cognac, staring bleakly at her hands. The three men hardly noticed she had left. 'Marten,' began Sevcik without pause, 'Have you had any further communication with Archer?' '*With* Archer? That's a curious way to put it, how the devil would I know where he is?' 'Then you have no new ideas about the letter?' 'All I know is that someone delivered it when no one was around, difficult enough with my neurotic wife watching the street every minute of the day. She may not like to go out herself but she watches the street continually, especially when my son is away. Actually, she must know the secrets of our neighborhood, a remarkable woman, I'm sure you'd agree if you knew her.' Sevcik nodded. Spohr recalled the only time he had seen her, one summer evening years before, he had intended to call for Bender at home, finding him instead several blocks away, walking quickly, puffing at his pipe and not glancing back. Trailing a short distance behind was a rather swollen looking woman in a brightly colored oriental wrapper and bedroom slippers, calling Marten, Marten, in a gurgling, heavily accented voice. He jumped into Spohr's car without comment as neither of them referred to the incident. 'Perhaps I should come to see her.' 'If you like, please do, she doesn't have many visitors. She'd be interested to meet you.' 'MacIntyre has agreed to be our legal representative if we need to take action.' 'Are you considering that?' 'It may come up.' 'In what context?' 'Well investigating the rights of the disturbed, for example.' 'So you think he's being held then, would you really drag Archer through something like that?' 'We would have to be circumspect.' 'Then you won't get anywhere, besides I wouldn't support anything which suggests Thomas Archer is abnormal, however extranormal he may happen to be. What do you think Spohr?' 'I think Marten, I'd be inclined to agree. Reputation is a fragile thing, and it wouldn't take much to deduce the subject of any such inquiry; it could harm him in the long run.' 'Actually Spohr, my objections are rather more aesthetic than practical, I have a strong aversion to providing ammunition for the art as psychosis doctrine.' 'But,' interrupted Sevcik, 'You know what our friend was more or less deliberately doing with his life?' 'Yes I do, of course I do, nevertheless it seems to me that whatever Archer pursues every artist investigates one way or another,' said Bender. 'The basis of his art is the basis of his life, we hunger to identify, to locate the source, the meaning, and I don't think this is only true for the artist. There isn't a real man who doesn't sooner or later have to think in terms of laying his life on the line, if he won't he's an amateur who will never amount to anything, be his own master.' 'What do you mean?' asked Sevcik, 'Isn't that just a manner of speaking, a metaphor?' 'No, I mean it literally, and this is what the true artist clarifies. Look at Scriabin, look at Beethoven, the great Johann Sebastian Bach serving his soul up piece by piece in unequaled music every Sunday morning, in between as well. No, this is what it is. For mastery we are obliged to serve, it's the only way we have. A self-effacing paradox, we do uniquely what we do so that everyone can taste the experience. Who on earth would live like this if it could be avoided? Do you know what it's like to serve something, I mean form, even formlessness, something you never fully understand, never knowing how much is enough or whether your best is adequate, obliged to invent, to trick, to amuse, to glorify, be happy and witty, be sad and moving, obliged to espouse the secrets in a way that preserves the mystery and lets

146

the meaning be known? We're damned if we do and damned if we don't. In the classic manner we walk an incredibly fine line; this is what Archer is trying to do, he's not mad, he's merely trying to discover the limits of his authority. He has the clarity he needs.' Bender stopped abruptly. Spohr said, 'Go on, go on, this is interesting, I don't agree with what you're saying because I can't see how you are anymore subjugated by whatever motivates your music than I am by science. It's true that I like my work and respect the techniques which advance it towards more complete understanding, but science is not my god, I don't feel as if I have contracted a duty or obligation beyond my capacity. This is what I do, I am a scientist, Archer is a painter, that is what he does. Tell me what you think the difference is.' Sevcik commented, 'You do however, have a coolness which might not be shared by all your colleagues, you may not see this science of yours as a god, but you might treat it that way anyhow. In any case, I don't think you would consider your soul to be a servant of science.' 'Well that's true enough, then of course, I don't actually believe I have a soul.' 'Only because you can't admit it if science is incapable of showing it to you, right?' said Bender, 'But consider your great hero Einstein.' 'The reason he's such a hero,' laughed Spohr, 'Is because his mysteries have been verified in natural terms.' 'Perhaps then, we should wait to see about the soul?' asked Sevcik. 'Maybe so,' replied Spohr diplomatically, 'Maybe so. Do go on Marten.' 'Well Sevcik will understand this, no matter how bizarre a stance the artist takes he operates from the fulcrum, the point of understanding on the axis of a particular experience. Initially he may look in the wrong direction or choose the wrong instrument, the wrong technique even, like a scientist, but he refines his vision as he keeps practising, his capacity to penetrate becomes more subtle until eventually he arrives at the heart of it. Each act of self-discovery is unique, no one path is ever walked again. He preserves and hands down what needs to be preserved, at the same time protecting what needs to be protected.' 'I understand what you're saying,' said Sevcik, 'Only it occurs to me the opposite may be true, to be essentially human you don't want to be separate from other men, you want to identify yourself with them, eliminate whatever makes you different, focusing on whatever produces identification.' 'But that won't make an artist,' responded Bender quickly, 'He has to be separate to perceive, he needs distance to understand his relations with others, the world they inhabit together. He must be free to look up to God, out towards other men, then in upon himself and his personal deity.' 'Why not say the same thing about the scientist, the businessman, the shopkeeper, the factory worker then?' 'Because they don't see themselves in that light, they don't live that way. Did you know, in Memphis, the ancient Egyptian capital, a high priest designed the great public buildings? Artisans had jobs which were hereditary, like kings, they were supported by the people in return for their service. There must be understanding between the artist and his community. It may take time to establish because the artist has to see farther around the curve into the future as it comes charging down, farther than most men, and that's why he may sometimes look out of place, he is; he is farther along, everyone else needs to catch up. That's why Shelley proclaimed poets the unacknowledged legislators of the human race, that's why Picasso draws people who look sideways and forwards simultaneously, that's why they howled at Stravinsky, at Tchaikovsky and Beethoven for their indecent sounds. Hard to believe, isn't it? This is not new you see, why do we have to keep going over old ground again?' 'Well Bender,' said Spohr, 'You are eloquent but I can't buy it.' 'Tell me Spohr, what has made you such a chronic unbeliever?' 'I like the style of your question but I doubt whether there's a simple answer.' 'No one can expect Thomas Archer to look normal, there's no standard for what he does. What he discovers is for himself, he can give it form, pass it along so the rest of us will understand, and I have to say this again, no one else can do exactly what he does, each route is unique, exhausted by a single traveller. He can point the way, others however, can't follow precisely in his footsteps without betraying themselves. No ordinary person is expected to do that, partially because he doesn't have the capacity, the determination or the gift, partially because he doesn't want to, and partially because he won't dare take the risks. It's a terrific gamble, you can spend your whole life in a crazy pursuit which ends nowhere, in a cul-de-sac or a place which is so inconsequential it wasn't worth the trouble getting there. If you succeed you are forgiven for everything. They will pardon Paul Claudel said Auden, pardon him for writing well, just as they will pardon Tom for running berserk in the streets dressed like a rag-and-bone man with his hair dyed orange. Who will care what eccentricity he lived out in the flesh when they see his paintings? His life is exclusively in his paintings, mine in my music. *Socrate n' était pas surréaliste.* I don't give much thought to anything else, why should I? Someone else has to take that on.' He finished almost brutally, biting the end of his pipe, looking gloomily at his two friends. 'It's not a job you can take or quit, give up or change, if you are called you have to come, there is no choice. As I said, you're cursed if you do and doubly cursed if you don't, the classic double bind. You should enjoy that one Spohr.' 'Yes, yes, I do find it interesting Bender, I just wouldn't put it that way, the bitter, romantic emphasis on a lonely traveller, the inflexible duty to some absolute, unknowable standard. I wouldn't want to deal in absolutes here.' 'That's why you design toys and mechanical devices instead of sculpture.' 'I wonder if that's so,' said Sevcik, 'You can look at the absolute in anything.' 'I won't exclude that,' answered Bender, 'I mean the artist has a continuing preoccupation with form.' 'Tell me Bender,' said Spohr, 'Don't you think a scientist has to look around the corners into the future too, how do you think I know people will be playing with computer toys in the next ten years?' 'It's not the same, that's a purely material consideration. Dada Dada have a drink of water. I'm talking about the conceptualization the artist has to make, he must project the totality of man's experience so that his work will fall naturally into place in a world to come.' 'That's what I'm saying science does too.' 'I can't accept that; science gets thrown out when we're done with it.' 'Sure, to a certain extent, but it's more likely to be preserved as the cornerstone, even the foundation of what happens next. I think you will have to accept that one day, you just haven't seen it yet. I don't know how to put it any more tactfully than this: in some ways your ideas seem to me in

150

danger of being defunct, obsolete. Our public monuments are found in technology today, not in buildings. Art no longer has a public function, I'm not so sure it ever did. Today art survives primarily as an investment for the business man, a negotiable commodity exchanged in terms of market fluctuations, and that, I think you'll agree, has nothing to do with what you call the soul.' 'I don't really see the point. Perhaps science is the guardian of another gate, and in that case I suppose this pathway is closed to all except its own initiates too, but the artist resembles conscience, a discriminating preserver or a reckless destroyer. Sometimes he's a hot radical purging what he cannot contain, what he does not value, at other times he's a cool, seductive conserver sweeping everything up in a loving embrace. Now that's an interesting idea, isn't it? You might even study the history of civilization with that, don't you think? Or has some bold creature done it already? Well science can talk about natural law with authority I suppose, but the artist penetrates the heart. You do admit the human heart into your scheme of things, don't you Spohr? Granted that art which passes into the businessman's jurisdiction, even the state's for that matter, is institutionalized and must function another way. This however, is a social failure not an artistic one, this is a national conscience failure not unlike the failure of a great religion, founded in memory of a wholly illuminated prophet but without his understanding. Say something Sevcik, you occult practitioner.' Sevcik laughed, 'O I'm a practical man, studying the obvious and assuming responsibility where I can. It's not that I'm uninterested in your theories, I prefer the harmony extracted from the conjunction of art and science, electronic music for example. I don't search for conflict, I try to find resolutions. It would be good to rescue Thomas Archer from danger, otherwise there's no need to worry about him. Society protects what it imagines to be its own best interests and invariably chooses incorrectly. There isn't much you can do about that except be as explicitly honest as possible, study yourself and help others with compassion, with integrity. Spohr and Nella are the only people Tom seems to have trusted without reservation. His paintings are here, he comes to this house like a homing bird when he's in trouble, since they of course, are not strangers to the art of survival. From their early days Nella has had a special sympathy for him, and Spohr knows how to help when the darkness prevails. I have always looked upon Archer as more necessary than all the politicians, the lawyers, the professors and doctors because he cares only for the truth no matter where it takes him. I admire his paintings, his constant struggle to know. I'm not sure it's wise to summon up certain powers in this struggle — it can be dangerous even for a great magician to seize a tiger by the tail. It's probably safer not to name some powers, let alone try to call them to you. Archer once decided to spend a week alone in Georgian Bay. The island he chose was one he believed the Indians used for sun dances, for certain other practices associated with worship of the sun. He took food for a week, there was nothing much on the island except rocks and grass, then paid an Indian to paddle him in. The old man promised to come for him in seven days, but when he hadn't shown up by the ninth day Tom realized he would have to get himself off somehow. He was weak by then because he had been almost without food for two days, eating sparsely before that, and he knew he would have to swim for it. He made slow, exhausting progress in a huge curve, resting on rocks, on little islands, plotting a course from refuge to refuge, finally making it back to the mainland. He never found the old man again, couldn't discover whether he had forgotten about him or deliberately left him there to die. Tom looked upon the whole thing as a test he couldn't say whether he passed or failed, couldn't decide if it had been carefully prepared for him or he had just fallen into it, accidentally. Perhaps this was the only possible conclusion to the things he had been experimenting with that week. Some aspects of the situation made him nervous although it also made him laugh, the irony that the great test of his powers arrived as a swimming marathon. Who knows how to interpret the latest episode? We can't be sure what he is pitted against or what form the contest may take.' Bender smiled recalling Archer's version of the same story, with Sevcik the protagonist. 'Birgitte thinks we should pray for him and perhaps we should. I wonder if it's possible to put yourself in a position which automatically precludes God's help. Is anyone ever beyond God's help? What do you think Spohr?' 'Now then if folks want to pray that's their privilege, but you obviously don't expect me to do anything so outlandish, do you?' 'No, no of course not, Birgitte thought it was important.' 'You know Spohr,' interrupted Bender, 'I've been trying to remember incidents from Archer's past, anything which might explain some of this, and it's interesting, I realize how little we know about him, about the ordinary events in his life. Where was he born for instance, where did he grow up, does he have any family? I've known him casually for years, recently we spent all that time together, hours and hours walking and talking, but I know nothing except his ideas about art, some pseudoscientific notions, others might call it science fiction, which he adheres adamantly to, that's it, nothing much to reconstruct a man's life around.' 'Curious,' remarked Spohr, 'We seem to know less and less as time passes, besides which our assessment of Archer's work has undergone a considerable change over the last few months. Have you noticed, either of you, when people refer to his paintings they talk about them with respect, some even with reverence, although last year I doubt if anyone would have described them as much more than interesting, competent. I mean when he is weighed on the same scale with giants like Rembrandt or da Vinci he's an insignificant painter, yet somehow he has laid claim to a response beyond anything we might have expected. Now I find that worth thinking about, don't you?' 'Yes, true enough,' Bender said without much interest, 'But the personality, the physical presence of an artist can sometimes be an intrusion, a hindrance almost, to an accurate perception of his work. Who can look at Tom, except a few friends who see through his tramp's disguise, and accept his paintings? He's too peculiar, too much of an aberration for most people to tolerate; even among ourselves when he's sick, who can handle that? This is approximately what I meant when I said his life is in his paintings, everything else is a distraction. Now we find it necessary to look at the distraction and turn away from the point, that's a bit unnerving. Do you know where he was born, can you stare down that avenue back into the past, find some ordinary answers?' 'O,' said Spohr matter-of-factly, 'He was born right here in this city, went to public school with Schradieck in fact, they've known each other that long. According to him Archer looked more or less like anyone else until he was about fourteen or fifteen. Schradieck says he was quiet as a boy, although different in some ways, when he spoke he was witty, he was great with puns, he seemed to know things other boys had no idea of, became interested in space travel when most people believed it was nothing more than a fantasy, but you can ask Schradieck about this yourself.' 'He's become a slippery fellow lately, I can never get hold of him,' Sevcik put in, 'He's been more than usually troubled since Tom disappeared.' 'What about his family, does he have anyone?' 'He has an aunt,' said Sevcik, 'Whom I've heard him talk about now and again with great distaste, he calls her the Countess Goathead. I did of course, check with her and she knows nothing, I doubt if she's even aware he's missing.' 'Well there's his father,' said Spohr. 'His father!' the other two shouted in unison. 'Actually his stepfather, he was married to Tom's mother for about ten years. To say that Tom hates him is describing his feelings as pleasantly as possible. Who knows why, he's probably a decent man, but Tom apparently never liked him from the beginning, then when his mother was so ill he held the fellow responsible for her wretched condition. I doubt if he'd know anything, Tom has avoided the man all these years. No, I suspect what Marten said is true, this routine business is no use. To understand what happened to Archer we have to look at him, understand what he was doing with his life, then calculate the importance of the sacrifices he was prepared to make, O not in terms of family, home, job or material things, he didn't have that, didn't want that. It's beside the point to talk about giving up or trading in something you've never had or wanted. The only thing Tom had to speculate with was his own life, whatever gave it impetus, his aesthetic, his idea of himself as an artist, his conviction that art purifies, it absolves, that the artist is apart from other men, above them, therefore entitled, even empowered to engage in activity not permissible for the ordinary man. He dabbled with fire, he was prepared to be burned, be consumed to a fine ash in exchange for what he wanted, and that one thing was to paint, to create. His studies of magic from an increasingly esoteric point of view made him ready to disappear if he had to for the trick to succeed, only the trick was his life and it seems he hadn't mastered it. Now this is easy enough to say, it's easy enough to be clever about someone else's life, but no one can cut the knots on our behalf, that is clearly reserved for each one to look after for himself. We can stand by, offer encouragement, moral support, friendship, enthusiasm, it's about all we can do. We'd each be willing to help Archer out of a difficult spot if that were the problem. My point is, this is not an isolated episode, this is the core of his life which we can't snatch away from him. If he needs rescuing, no matter where he is, no matter what's happened to him I doubt that very much, then we do what we can, it's like helping someone meet his mortgage payment, but what we can't do is presume to interfere with the arrangements he has committed himself to. This is his contract, he has to honor it, alter the thing or default on it. So in my opinion it's up to him to work that out for himself, we have no

156

right to interfere, as I see it.' Bender interjected, 'There are social forces, there are economic pressures which hold a man or an entire class of men in their grip.' 'That is doubtless true as long as men are prepared to function merely as social animals, to behave as though they were unable to respond individually to their plight, they are to that extent imprisoned. No thinking man is a slave, no rational man is incapable of exerting relative control over his existence, but he can't in any sense be an animal, he can't view himself as an object if he is to extricate himself, he must be absolutely clear about what is required. He can't be a fool, he can't grovel; no man is a slave to any master he hasn't imposed upon himself.'

Sally sat in the kitchen waiting for some horror to explode around her, the cognac swelling like a bad dream in her brain. While Spohr, Sevcik and Bender talked on and on about art and destiny she thought, 'If it were possible to be good, purely, without deviating, it would put an end to all that talk. Why doesn't someone tell them?' When the afternoon had finally worn its way into evening John Adolph arrived, hours late, with a large bottle of scotch. As he bustled into the kitchen his stiff red beard bristled with amused and righteous anger. Marshaling well-disciplined invective, he directed his scorn initially against the principal of the school where he taught French to heedless young women. His scurrilous employer, he indicated, had caught the alcoholic scent on several occasions, but he had never been incapable of conducting his classes. Now however, neither his dignity nor his wit could save him; his days were numbered and few. Slowly, methodically, like a beast of prey stalking its victim the vituperative circles drew closer. From the opening fire directed against his principal he turned a bursting fusillade on the three in the front room. 'Spohr, ah yes, the man of science who fraternizes with Einstein in his dreams. I came here one afternoon not so long ago and found him lolling on his bed in a gold silk dressing gown, staring at the television set like a beached whale. Do you know how our eminent man of science regularly spends his afternoons? Let me tell you darling, watching the soaps, the bloody soaps if you can believe it. While we're out there among the pigs in wonderland he's at home with Dr. Kildare and As The World Turns. What an amusing life this is. Now don't try to defend him, you've been living in this house long enough to have noticed something fishy, haven't you? He's all brain and no heart, none whatsoever, nothing inside all that blubber which beats with love or passion or pain from time to time, nothing but that neat set of cells computing the odds. Still and all, not as weird as our beloved Sevcik. My God, when I hear him laugh I know it's not human.' Over the years Sally had become used to his wit speeding like an arrow from target to target, so accustomed to his tongue etching disgrace with every syllable she noticed nothing. What will deter the hissing cobra? 'I had lunch with Birgitte last week, an extraordinary woman, you know, we talked about the Bauhaus. It's really too bad, buried here all these years where no one, absolutely no one has any idea what she's trying to do. An outcast, an exile like myself, stricken from the company of men, but so brave, almost absurdly optimistic, carrying on in that bleak studio of hers, working with anyone who comes in to grind a little fat off

158

the thighs. Still, a lot better off than I am teaching those comic opera young ladies to write *Je vous remercie d'avantage,* can you imagine it? When Birgitte speaks she's always in deadly earnest. Have you noticed she rarely laughs or smiles? There beats the overwhelming Germanic heart, all sentiment, no feeling. Marriage to the great, gangling Sevcik must be something though, what do you think? I wonder if they . . . no, no, I mustn't indulge such crass speculation. Sevcik and Bender make a strange enough pair, Sevcik so straight and Bender so bent. I've heard stories my dear,' and here his chin stuck out, his beard parallel to the ground, 'That would, I'm sure, curl your hair. But I must get to the point. No, first I absolutely must tell you this delicious little tidbit about Bender. He's impotent my dear, im-po-tent. Do you doubt it, how do I know? I was with him in the company of a young lady who did everything she could for him. Nothing my dear, nothing. As I have heard it said by a dear old lady from Barbados, everybody bake his bread different, but Bender dear girl, has apparently tried everything to get the bread to rise. God, the noise around here is terrific, where is that jackhammer? It sounds as if it's next door. I guess you're used to it; even the birds don't seem to mind anymore. I've never been able to adjust my ears, there's no end to it. A building is scarcely up before they start to pull it down, the road is fixed then they dig it up to improve something else, most amusing.' And all the while sip, sip at the bottle of scotch. Sally listened, her own darkness bubbling up through the confusion. The cobra at last spread its hood, turning a subtle face upon her, never deterred. 'Look, there's something I have to tell you, have to warn you about, it's your sister and her husband.' Startled she asked, 'What do you mean, what are you talking about?' 'I saw them when I was in Montreal last week. Your sister and her squeamish spouse, my erstwhile chum I admit, told me you roared in there on a drunken joyride at two in the morning rousing the whole neighborhood. As far as they are concerned, if you ever come back again, drunk or bleeding, desperate, whatever, they'll dispatch you to the Sally Ann. They said you're squalid, a nuisance, a pest, an irritation they would disown if they could.' Sally stared at John Adolph thinking for a moment he had gone mad. 'What on earth are you talking about? I drove through Montreal a couple of weeks ago and felt guilty that I didn't even phone them.' She tried to assemble her thoughts, 'I know what it is, they must have been talking about something that happened more than three years ago, before I went to England.' 'Are you sure, they made it sound like last week.' 'Anyhow I was not drunk, what is all this about?' 'You should know they were vicious my dear, they snarled your name like beasts. Tell me what happened.' 'It was such a long time ago, let me think, O yes, a beautiful night, I do remember now. Some of us had been out drinking, you know, the usual crowd. More or less on impulse, not a very drunken one at that, Pavel Robichaud and I decided to drive to Montreal. Claudette happened to be there, they weren't married yet, he wanted to see her and I wanted to see my sister before I left the country forever, as I thought then. We borrowed some money, rented a car and took off. It was a long, slow drive. We stopped to make love twice, passionately, without much thought, it was just part of the journey. When we

160

pulled the car into a field off the road near Kingston I remember the cows mooing somewhere close by, we laughed so much. Then we stopped again some place outside Montreal,' she waved her hand delicately, 'It was a dark night, O it was sweet, it was so sweet even if the whole thing meant little to either of us. I suppose it meant a lot too. There were no questions, no promises, just trust. I've never been afraid of dying, John Adolph, I've only been afraid of living. At five o'clock in the morning we arrived in Montreal where neither of us knew our way around. I sent him off to find Claudette while I sat in a cold, dismal restaurant waiting for morning. Finally, a little before seven I telephoned. My brother-in-law answered the phone sounding annoyed, I thought he was just sleepy, then my sister came to the phone, "How dare you call at this hour of the day?" Nearly a year since we had seen each other, that was her greeting. Apologizing I hung up, so angry I wanted to go back without seeing them, then it seemed silly to have come hundreds of miles and be driven off by ill-humor. So I waited, spent a few hours with them, and to complete their horror, borrowed ten dollars to buy gas for the return trip. That must be the visit they meant, only it was years ago, I don't understand.' 'Well dear girl, for them it happened yesterday. I wouldn't have anything to do with them if I were you, avoid them like the plague, they mean you no good.' 'You're probably right, *except for one who was tied to my heart with irreparable bonds of love,* they find it hard to admit how they feel about me. Their catechism doesn't include dislike of a daughter, a sister, yet that seems to be it. They're afraid to think I bleed their blood; I don't look like them, I don't act like them,

161

I don't think like them. They're so busy amassing things to protect themselves from the horrors in life they have forgotten that nothing will protect us from death. I don't accumulate possessions, I've never wanted anything from the world, perhaps that's why they are shocked by my freedom.' The hood of the cobra spread once more, 'They are offended because you give away what you have.' 'They are equally offended because I am ready to take what I want.' 'Sally it's true, I've seen you give handouts to anyone who asks.' 'What are you talking about? Anyhow, why shouldn't I?' 'Come now Sally, I'm not attacking you, why would I? As far as I'm concerned you are respectable, you have your own room here, don't you?' 'No, as a matter of fact I share Edwin's.' Nothing to protect, nothing to defend. The night closed upon her, jaws of steel swallowing her live and whole.

Spohr dies on a cold intercalary day beyond reckoning. *Le sang de mon vieux corps n' a fait qu' un jet vermeil.*

Thomas Archer is lost in the time zone between the notes.

Be merciful, be lenient in summer, the north will return.

The seas of open blood run their rivers through my head.

Beneath these mummy wrappings wear we bones: the violet end of the spectrum.

Annie March searches for bullets to blow holes in time.

Who will pick the flowers in hell?

Ride stranger, ride, ride out the cold night.

Of the twenty-eight letters in the body, one is the letter of darkness.

The sword of wisdom is a sword of light.

Never, never for a moment turn your back on the light.

The woman who strewed thorns on the prophet's path recovered in a fever of love.

The crippling letter from her ex-husband creased in the back pocket of her jeans. Why should those untimely declarations come now? When John Adolph left Sally's distress compacted itself about that letter, a tangible point in the heaving sea, a concrete thing to examine. 'I have to be close to Edwin for peace of mind, I need his presence in my life, I know that, even so I cannot say with total conviction, "I love." There is so much I find strange, such isolation, a sense of being separate, divided from myself. How critically I examine my feelings, always searching for constancy, the passionate conviction of knowing. And how can you be sure, how can you be certain you love if you are not tuned to that awful pitch which comes only with its denial, its deprivation? When I don't feel that I think perhaps this is not love. Why do I suspend myself from this man as if my life depended on him? Maybe it does. Sometimes I want to live through him, sometimes I feel more intensely through him, I can be joyous, even ecstatic; now this letter with such love, for the first time. It's what I wanted to hear, what I convinced myself I wanted to hear and that amounts to the same thing. Suppose I were with him now, would Eddy be obliterated as easily as he was blotted out? Why do I stay with him? At first it seemed the violence of his emotions would inspire the same response in me, now I don't know, I really don't know. I feel tied to him, not only by the accident and the trial he faces, by something else. Sometimes he feels my hesitation, only we don't talk about it. This wretched letter made me cry, it actually made me cry. What can I do with it, how can I answer him, say I'm living with someone else. Yet if I were to go back to him, would I love him too? Should I say I cannot come for this and that reason, or do I want to go? If my head would just stop aching.'

- Sally, who was here? Spohr said some chap came to see you. Who was it?
- Thank God you're back, I've had a dreadful, awful day. I've nearly gone out of my mind, thank God you're here.
- Well who was it?
- John Adolph, you've met him.
- I don't want other men coming to visit you here, I won't be made to look a fool in my own home.

- Don't be silly, he's a flaming faggot.

- I don't care what he is. Other people see a man coming here and draw their own conclusions, I won't have that.

- Please, I'm out of it, completely, exhausted. There's been crisis after crisis, a terrible letter came, my parents detest me, my sister wants to disown me and you come in raving, jealous of an old friend who happens to be as queer as the birds, a *faygelah*. If you don't want me here throw me out, don't invent stories about my friends or your friends. Do you think Spohr and Nella will question your manhood if I have a visit from a screaming faggot, for God's sake?

- You're drunk too.

- Maybe I am, I don't feel drunk but by God I feel marooned, by God I feel cut off, and you're no bloody help with your hypocritical comments on what this one sees and that one thinks.

- Look darling, I'm sorry. Is there any booze left or did you drink it all? Don't be upset, I just want you to understand I can't have my woman seeing other men, is that so unreasonable? Why are you hysterical, what's wrong?

- Here, read this letter. What do you know about it? I don't recognize you anymore. Here, read it.

- I've seen letters from him before, this one looks pretty much the same as the others. Why are you crying, what is it, what is it?

- Give it back to me, give it back. You can't read it, you can't touch it. Don't touch me.

- Sally, stop yelling, Spohr just put his head in to see if I was murdering you.

- Well you are damn it, you are. Don't you know that, can't you see what you've done? Don't look so hurt, don't look so innocent. Why should you be frightened?
- Sally if you want to go back to him, go, you don't have to kill me, go, just go. I can't endure this.
- Edwin there's a face at the window, I saw a face, O my God there's a face at the window!
- There's no one there, believe me, you're imagining it again.
- No, there's a face at the window!
- I'll go look outside, you'll see there's no one there.
- No, don't leave me, don't leave me alone.
- But who could it be? Why are you screaming? Stop it now, stop it.
- I can't, O God, I can't.

The face is my own.

Nothing, nothing could pierce the black cloud, the tears, as she sank slowly in a capsized craft wrecked on the shores of her sorrow. No comfort, nothing but the fragile flight of time could help her now. Yet she held on, she held onto one nail in one plank, tossing on the midnight sea. While she held fast she was buoyed up, something opened her lungs, her heart, brought moments of reprieve. Images tossed back from the depths: cups of coffee, the interlocking circles on the table a messy emblem; Edwin's sullen face, pinched and unhappy at first, then cruel, menacing; sitting alone in the kitchen, the crenelated knife pressed against the thin skin of her wrist, sitting for a long time, the blade of time held against chance, not yielding to death; the scar, a tiny nick one-quarter of an inch long; 'O I thought you sent me out to the kitchen to die;' a furious moment trying to pull the separating fragments together; talking, silence, long silence; victim and torturer changing roles — she can no more stop him than he can stop her; attempts to climb out, falling deeper instead. Later Edwin said, 'All that time you wanted to die.' 'Wrong,' she replied.

Finally the exhaustion, the hysteria left them both in a state beyond sleep. The next day she wanted only to let time build its web across the sickness, the degradation which clung to her like a garment of fire. When she slept at last the following night two dreams beset her. In the first there is a girl in a rough dress of dirty brown sackcloth, ripped and decomposing. Wild-eyed, her hair matted, she crouches like an animal in the corner of a cell. They catch her up in a filthy blanket, tossing her in the air again and again. She is mad. Sally thought, 'She is myself.' In the second she and Edwin sit in Spohr's kitchen, bare except for three chairs. With them is a stranger, a rather coarse, youngish man with a crew cut. He is tedious, his conversation has an obscure edge of criminality. Eddy is apparently absorbed in what he says while Sally thinks, 'He is bored with me, he's tired of having me around, he will not say who I am, he will not tell this odious creature what I mean to him, and this stranger, this filthy stranger looks at me wondering why I don't leave.' In her pocket she has a small parcel for Spohr, a pair of gold cufflinks and a set of shirt studs his father has sent him. Somehow, the stranger, the brute knows. Exasperated, unable to put up with it any longer she starts to leave and he speaks, addressing her as if he has concluded Sally is an unscrupulous whore, 'Say honey, you'd better leave those cufflinks with me.' She takes them from her pocket intending to throw the box straight at him, wondering if the tiny gold things will spatter across the floor. 'But they are Spohr's, aren't they?' she asks. Eddy intercedes, 'It's all right, let her have them.' When she awoke she thought, 'That's the way it is, he doesn't care for me any longer.' The next day he left for work early in the morning, when he came back late that night there was peace once more.

Looking back along time's empty corridors I recognize the inevitability of my destination, the pointless symmetry of each journey embarked upon. I can't help wondering about the parallels in our experience between life and death, I can't help wondering about the ignorance which betrays the rhapsodic intervals prescribed by youth and the despotic uniformness in maturity. The pressures of both transform us, diverting light into dark. As a child I found experience inconclusive, nothing was predictable, everything seemed open and possible, that was unquestionably true. As an old woman wrinkling back into the surface of the earth I found there was no escape, everything was fixed, a crooked race you had to run because you'd been entered for the grand prize, how willingly at first, how reluctantly when it became evident the prize had already been spoken for, secured by someone else. And that was true too.

There are no contradictions, only confirmations. What you expect is what you get, what you fear will attend you, what you long for will be deferred indefinitely. A flower which bursts into bloom like the day lily passes abruptly from existence to finality, a languid bloom which strays slowly into life lingers for a time, preserving its scent, preserving its color, then almost imperceptibly begins to lose its beauty. Does it look different from day to day? It wrinkles and dries softly, a withering death imposed by time and the natural decomposition of cells. Is there a choice between the two? They both lose their brightness, they lose their beauty, they die, they are thrown away. And yet a sweetness persists. In my time of reckless bliss with Archer, how could I have known the ancient history that bone falls heir to, the siege of flesh, how could I have known a secret is revealed only once? Carelessly we aimed our arrows, indifferent to the target, mindless of the direction and force governing the wind we soared on currents which might have dashed us to the rocks below. Later when we tried to ignite that bliss again the result was a mere flicker, an afterglow which became a painful reminder, and finally with a sigh as much of relief as disappointment it was done, finished, something to look back on, puzzling, relinquished. Time and distance which curve the shape of events as events themselves impose on time have their simplification, an arithmetic created by selectivity or cancellation. When we look back we see only the parallel curves glyphed on the staves of our individual preoccupations. Again and again we glided past, we dipped, we foundered, we crashed, only to take off once more. If God forgives us it will certainly be for our ignorance. In those enigmatic middle years with Spohr, while the rest of the world exploded with discoveries we had made for ourselves, while we idled on our inner energy, it was easy to avoid the truth, easy to ignore the obvious. Sevcik was merely treacherous, working against us all the time, Spohr was merely deceptive, the only one who knew where Archer was, Archer merely a pawn jailed in his own fantasy, and Schradieck the go-between, an unwilling messenger for all. What was the point? We arrive at the same place in our separate vehicles, then what? Today I see only similarities, yesterday I saw only differences. We all have access to the same routes, no one is excluded, nothing is withheld, yet we choose unwisely for our own entirely justifiable purposes. We have our carefully devised handicaps, our bodies, our minds, our indifference to the suffering of others, our failure, our inability to comfort each other. Annie March was the only one who deliberately changed her life, she stopped writing when she heard the truth reckoned out night after night and flew without deviating, directly into the heart of her understanding where she disappeared, not like Archer, but like an eclipsed sun leaving a shining ring of light in her place.

I sit quietly by myself now, like my mother years ago rocking herself from darkness to darkness, watching the birds circle and scream up there in the sky. The huge winged gulls are city birds now, their cries filling my ears with sorrow. We circle together on the same currents up in the air, crying the old complaints, bemoaning the passage of time, the wind, the sun and the rain. A morning in spring with the sun poised and balanced against wave after wave of darkening clouds is the same for them in their unsettled formations as it is for me, a sober spot on the darkening earth. Who will claim us, time's restless scavengers searching the unsorted debris, flying higher and higher, swooping lower and lower, feasting on the wounds of hell? I wonder if this is what my mother saw or whether I live this way because she failed to see, and I fail to see too. Then what can I say about Spohr who died beneath the burden of his knowledge before his fortieth birthday, what can anyone say about Sally, tall, beautiful Sally whose eyes strayed out of focus, who drifted in uncertainty until that springtime when she found a way to her own undoing, tablet by tablet, and all that remained was a waxy form, an image carved in tallow, bloodless, bereft? Edwin who sank like his own forbidding father, what can anyone say about these lights extinguished too soon, who can calculate the profit and loss, what do we reckon is owing to them? Is their passage through the fire discountable or are there not some particles, a fine dust, some precious grains adhering to the truth which can be sifted from the ash of their ruin? Do we not lie and lie, deceiving first ourselves, hiding behind that deception from the truth itself? Are we not warned against judging others? Must we not come stripped and humiliated to the ultimate place of judgment ourselves? Where will we go from there indeed? I feel old now, so old I hear the earth calling me back, reaching out with open, loving arms. One day soon I will vanish like a dark stain spreading evenly into the unblotted crust of soil. What remembrance will there be then, who will mourn the ones I've mourned? Who will take my place on the chain which linked our hearts for this lifetime and beyond? Who will ask my questions or hear my answers?

I know what it means to be sad, how to search out a point of grief even though I finally scrambled to a place which looks equally on joy and sorrow. I try not to deceive myself nor be confused by desire or expectation, the polished fruit of our youth which in age we discover to be hard, tasteless at the core. I try instead to celebrate the unvoiced beauty paralleled by our lives. Even Spohr would acknowledge that quiet acts of heroism in the face of all the disasters beleaguering us are declarations, an insistence upon the purity found at the heart of existence itself. There is so much to look back on, to reassess, so much that is merely forgotten, overlooked. There will never be time enough as I hurry along to the grave; let it be, what's past is past, all debts are canceled except my own. May I recognize my obligations, may I make restitution in full for the things I've done and the things I haven't done, without sentiment, without fear.

Even while I look down the length of my life I feel as if I never really knew Spohr, never understood him. With Archer there was always the esoteric frenzy to reckon with, the sheer madness, but there was also a bubbling delight, a clownish optimism which invited you in to laugh, sometimes to cry. Spohr always excluded you, kept you out. You could join his deliberations, play the game according to his rules, you could laugh, you could have fun, only he would never weep with you, never express regret, sorrow, disenchantment, disappointment. During the year we were separated before his death, even though he wanted me to return, tried everything to get me back, he was never disturbed, not even upset, first determined to ignore my departure, then confident I would yield to him sooner or later. In the end I probably would have, would have sought him out as a companion for old age and death, would have come back to that imperturbability, that undiagnosed, emotionless charm which was loving in its way but never moving. His mother told me once that something terrible happened to him when he was a boy, that he was never the same again afterwards. He didn't speak about it and I wouldn't ask. As the years went by he worked less and less, until nothing remained but the fiction that he labored at his latest, his most important invention, a device whose significance was to be as revolutionary as the microscope. It was to plug the brain's output directly into a network of circuits which would analyze and solve a problem before the mind itself had been able to grasp and solve the nature of the problem. Today his innovations sound either odd or old-fashioned, and I no longer care about these things, I care only to know how each one seeks the circuit of his own understanding, why some like Sally on a bright spring day abandon everything, why others like Archer, like Spohr, crave power or knowledge so acutely they offer their lives as bait to the gods, why Annie succeeds, why Edwin fails. One key unlocks all these puzzles. If I can pull back the right bolt the gates will open, even for Spohr's widow.

Not long after Sally had come to live with Edwin in Spohr's rather peculiar house, Schradieck stalked in one day trailed by the faithful Lisa. His tight black leather jacket was zipped up the front, up the sleeves and across four diagonal pockets, two on the chest, two at the waist. The zippers had silver clasps which rang to the crunch of the leather as he moved. The high heeled cowboy boots added a careless and slightly precarious touch to the familiar strut. Lisa glided noiselessly behind with one of their four children gathered in lightly under her arm. Schradieck sent out a noisy shout, 'Anybody home?' Eddy came from his room where he'd been studying, delighted to be interrupted, curious about Schradieck whom he knew only slightly. Spohr and Nella appeared waving a bottle of Spanish wine. Sally slipped quietly into the room, sitting in a dark corner surrounded on either side by the two black silky cats who had fecklessly attached themselves to her. The square shaped sitting room, scarcely inches above the surface of the earth, had been brightened considerably over the years with a few exotically refinished pieces of furniture, a carved wooden coffee table, an art deco side table, a hard, rose colored settee with a rigid back, a few decadent chairs, one actually comfortable which Spohr habitually occupied, an aging carpet whose original colors were long since muted to a modest softness, and a black, lacquered Chinese screen rescued along with the other things from different secondhand stores. Several of Archer's smaller paintings were tastefully framed and carefully hung on the walls. Everyone except Spohr lounged about on the floor listening to the music Eddy chose, a favorite Bessie Smith recording. There was laughing, joking, friendly conversation. It was Saturday afternoon, the weather was mild and bright, a happily in between moment when nothing was demanded except the benevolence easily enough forthcoming

174

on such a day, at such an hour. Schradieck brought his old guitar in from the car and Lisa sang, a resonant, throbbing, even surprisingly assertive voice, old blues which they all knew and eventually sang together, a ritual of friendship laced with memories. The wine was finished, another bottle was produced; by late afternoon as the light began to deepen like a great gilded shield they sat quietly, hardly talking. Sevcik with his gift of knowing where anyone was at a given moment walked in. 'Ah, here you all are,' he said with surprise as everyone laughed. Ignoring their laughter, sensitive at once to the mood he lurched across the room, standing beside Spohr. 'Well dear friends,' his voice dark with eastern European solemnity reverberated around the room, 'How is everyone? Lisa my dear, how nice to see you, and which one is that? Ah Henrietta of course, what a good girl to come out with your parents. Are your little sisters well?' A strange but apparently calculated misapplication of rhetoric clung to his remarks as he directed a question or comment to everyone in the room, then joined the silence. The golden light shafted obliquely into the room, parallel beams pouring a special grace and beauty through the window. That single instant perfected in a shower of unrestrained light bound them together, making the moment ineradicably important. The silence was long and deep, penetrated by the profound equilibrium mingled with light; now Sally spoke softly, her shyness dispersed at last, 'This is God's light which He sends spontaneously from time to time. If our sorrow and pain do not drag us to His feet perhaps the affirmation of His beauty will. Surely you must feel it too Spohr, surely you feel a loving presence in your life. He does

175

exist, a radiant light at the center of each soul, at the heart of the universe.' 'Darling,' said Eddie with concern, 'You read too much poetry.' Spohr merely smiled but there was a gleam in his eyes. Again no one spoke as the soft shadows became darker, the light grew taut for a final moment, a brief, surging tide of blood, then subsided. They began to talk and murmur among themselves, not entirely sober but not quite drunk either. Lisa said she ought to fetch the children while Nella encouraged her to stay, 'They'll be all right with Marguerite, she'll teach them how to draw or dance or sing, they'll have a wonderful time. Don't rush.' Lisa sank back with relief, and leaning against her husband's arm, thought how happy he seemed. Schradieck looked with kindness at his wife until Nella turned, her long fair hair obscuring Lisa's face. He sighed, regret contracted to a particle of sound in the dying light. They were still again, the mood unbroken, their harmony a bridge for the approaching dark. Finally they began to stir, talking quietly among themselves.

- Why can't it always be like this? asked Schradieck in the semidark, Why do we always screw up? Spohr, you're a smart man, you tell me.
- Wouldn't it be nice to know, laughed Spohr.
- I guess no one knows, Schradieck sighed.
- Men are ambitious, said Sevcik, Even if you establish your own peace with incredible care and luck, someone else's need will intrude. This makes us restless, in ten or twenty minutes I'm sure we'll have an inescapable reason to jump up or run around.

- Some women have a capacity for sitting still, said Sally, They don't seem very happy either.

- What do you think Sally? asked Eddy, Why doesn't our happiness last?

- Well for one thing, there's a difference between pleasure and happiness, I have no idea what happiness is, do you? Maybe it can come only from God, the rest is just pleasure, the gratitude of the senses.

- I think, said Schradieck, If we're meant to be happy no power on earth can change it, if we're meant to be unhappy no power on earth can do anything about that either.

- But Schradieck man, I don't see how you can find things so cut and dried, said Eddy. You leave little room to maneuver. I just don't feel as if I'm being controlled or manipulated that way, I feel as if I'm the one minding the shop.

- Well, he replied gloomily, I guess that's it; some things are concealed. Why should you expect to know everything?

Spohr laughed the laugh of innately sceptical delight.

- It's true, you know, Spohr, Lisa added, There are things to learn in wild places like the moors. Maybe you have to be born to it.

Her throaty voice lent weight to what she said.

- Hello folks, Annie March unexpectedly walked in with Lisa's three other children, We thought you might be wondering about these ladies and decided to come find out.

- Annie, how kind, thank you, what's happened to Marguerite?
- Bollard.

Everyone laughed as Lisa reluctantly stood up to take her children home.

- Lisa, said Nella, Make some sandwiches and let them play outside, it's a warm night.
- Hello Annie, Spohr greeted her, We haven't seen you for awhile, what have you been doing?
- Working away, how about you?
- O everything's normal here.
- That's a remarkable answer, she laughed.
- Is it now? Tell us what you're working on.
- Hard to describe especially while I'm still in the middle of it, a series of poems, all connected, all flocking around the same images.
- I'd like to see them.
- You will, but not until I'm finished.

She sat down and pulled a half bottle of scotch from her handbag with a flourish. Everyone cheered.

- Your timing, as usual, is perfect, announced Spohr, We've been talking about fate you see, and your arrival lends weight to what Schradieck says. We all wanted a drink more than anything. Cheers, you'll have to catch up, our destiny is fulfilled.
- You know, there are some things Spohr, said Lisa, You shouldn't make fun of.

- He certainly is a brave man, observed Sevcik, He knows how to be cautious, but I don't think he understands fear. Do you, have you ever been afraid in your life, I mean profoundly frightened?

- O once long ago; we needn't however, go into that.

- Why not, asked Sally, What happened?

- A man, said Eddy quite seriously, Doesn't want to have his past scrutinized, not even by his friends. Situations don't always bring out the best in a person, you may be driven to the kind of folly you'll never forgive yourself for. Everyone has a thing or two in the past well worth forgetting.

- That sounds like the opposite of what you were saying a few minutes ago, said Schradieck.

- Not so, it's entirely possible to find yourself hemmed in from time to time by ignorance or inability or sheer miscalculation without thinking you are the pawn in someone else's game.

- In any case, interrupted Spohr adroitly, It was nothing like that, I was reminded of something that frightened the pants off me when I was a wee fellow, no more than three or four years old. What do you think now? A bunch of us were playing out in the back lane when the kids all began to shout and scream, 'The witch is coming, the witch is coming. Hide, hide, everyone hide!' They were all so scared I had no doubt a witch was coming, even though I didn't know what a witch was. I ran to the back door of our house which was locked. I hammered on it yelling for my mother. She called out I'd have to wait, was anything wrong? At that moment I didn't know how to convey the fear I had caught from the others, because I was quite sure she didn't believe in witches, whatever they were. It's funny how you're aware of these things when you're only three. By this time the lane was clear, every child had disappeared and down the unpaved road a little old lady, I swear it, dressed in a long black dress with a lace collar, now how do you suppose I could have seen that, this little old lady bent over a cane, yes indeed, bent over a cane, began to hobble up the lane towards my house. By then I was ready to be struck down any moment. Now the house had a double door at the back, the outer one must have been a screen door for summertime. There was a narrow space between the two and I crouched down as far as I could, I was smaller then you see, waiting for the visitation. Curiously enough, what I remember most vividly, most distinctly is not the fear, in the midst of my fright I noticed a few reddish globules, congealed paint clinging to the inside door and I began to lick at them. They had a slightly metallic taste which still comes back to me this day. Frightened witless, yet I crouched there licking the little globs of paint on the door. When I peeked up behind the screen as the old lady passed the house beyond ours I felt safe. Gradually my heart stopped pounding, I calmed down, but I was fascinated by the paint. I crouched there licking it until my mother opened the door. In answer to your question Sevcik, I have been scared silly at least once, you see.

- Interesting, said Annie, The point about destiny though, I do find the idea possible, tempting. Equally tempting is the possibility we are all endowed with a special gift to outwit it. Sometimes I think that may be why I feel so driven, as though I have to write my way out of someone else's script or I'll be nothing more than a pawn in their game. It's the style of self-individuation which seems important to me. If I could believe there was another way to do it I would, but I've never come up with an alternative; so here I am, a condition laid on me that I don't mind yet I resent in some ways because I feel it's not my own choice. Do you know what I mean?

- Come now, said Eddy, Do you think Thomas Archer can paint his way out?

- In general yes, although I don't necessarily mean that in terms of a particular situation, like this one now for example.

- But the generality is only a series of particular situations, innumerable points making up the line, if you want to think about it that way, said Eddy.

- If you stand back from the picture and consider the composition, that's what I'm talking about, replied Annie smiling. Here, pour us another drink, I don't find this illuminating.

- Be a sport Annie, said Eddy, Don't back off now, it's just getting interesting.

- But this isn't sport for me, it's life and death, the bull and the matador. As you said, there are some things you don't care to scrutinize this way. Some things you have to work out privately, you may never be able to talk about them because they might be irrelevant or unintelligible or quite simply not true. I wouldn't want to propagate my errors.

- Spohr, come on now, are you going to let her get away with this? Can a scientific man endorse an attitude like that?

- Why not? Science is a flexible instrument. What matters more than the tool is the man who wields it, we can all rest comfortably under the shade of the same tree whether we sit, stand, lie, lean or flop down. I investigate in my own way, but I don't write poetry.

181

- You're generous tonight Spohr, commented Nella, We don't often find you willing to divide your universe.

- Keep the peace my dear lady, said Eddy, Keep the peace, we'll not have any of that now, it doesn't go with the whiskey. How about more music? Lisa, sing Shady Grove for me.

- We have to get my woman off this religious mania of hers, Eddy murmured to Spohr.

- But what about your poems? Sally whispered to Annie as Lisa sang.

- I don't know, said Annie quietly, You might not like these poems, I'm not sure if I can stand them myself.

- What do you mean?

- It's hard to say, they look at life from a moment which is not death and not life, not heaven and not hell, a moment when you can theoretically I guess, still save yourself, but I wonder if anyone does. It's a terrible perspective, gloomy and damned. Some part of my life, my understanding is embedded there, and I don't know whether I'm cultivating it or curing it.

- What you called self-individuation, isn't that what being born means, doesn't every soul affirm something unique? What more do you need?

Annie thought about that in silence, listening while Lisa's delicate song about a prostitute drained wrenching, ironic notes from the clear night. Abruptly everyone felt like singing as Schradieck plucked, strummed, stroked and beat the old guitar with pleasure, his face shining, the crescent scar on his chin barely visible while he accompanied the familiar songs. They sang, they hummed, they roared with comic gusto, they languished in tenderness through a repertoire of soaring old blues, rhythmic gospel tunes, familiar folk songs in several languages and a common stock gathered from nowhere in particular. They sang Michael Row The Boat Ashore, My Train's At The Station, St. Louis Woman, The M.T.A., The Wild Colonial Boy, Waltzing Matilda, Irene Goodnight, The Rock Island Line, The Midnight Special, Life Is Like A Mountain Railroad, Tom Dooley, Won't You Come Home Bill Bailey?, The Worried Man, I Never Will Marry, When The Saints Come Marching In, I Know Where I'm Going, In Norway Town, *À La Claire Fontaine,* The Rising Sun, Frankie And Johnny, Kookaberra, *Il Était Un Petit Navire, La Vie En Rose,* Ol' Riley Walked The Water, The Big Rock Candy Mountain, The Little Brown Jug, Go Tell Aunt Rhody, Galway Bay, Blue Moon. Spohr had a guitar with only four strings still on it and a saxophone left over from his college days which he brought out to vigorous applause. With this new accompaniment they went on to Careless Love, On Top Of Old Smokey, The Red River Valley, Walking Down St. Louis Street, Shenandoah, Down By The Riverside, Kalinka, *Eres Alta, Plaisir D'Amour, Vicin' Al Mare,* The Harlot Of Jerusalem, Take A Girl Like You, Jimmy Crack Corn, If Your House Catches On Fire, The Leaving Blues, I'm So Glad Jesus Lifted Me, *Et Là-bas Dort Le Coeur De Paris,* Barbara Allen, John Henry, You Are My Sunshine, Let My People Go, The Yellow Rose Of Texas, You Take The Highroad, It's Too Late, Too Late, Too Late. These were the songs they sang, the silly, the joyous, the sad, fiery old songs, the lost and lonely blues crying for another place, another time, another love. These

183

were the vessels they filled with their grief, their happiness, their unquenchable longing. It is the way of the world to seek old woes to staunch new wounds, and they went on singing without restraint until no one could remember any more, until the tide of their pleasure or their restless sorrow flowed back out to sea. They sat in silence once again, savoring the night, tasting the comfort in shared solitude.

Lisa and Schradieck assembled their children and went home, Sevcik had long since left, Annie drifted back down the street to her quiet room where she could dream her own dreams and Nella went to sleep. Spohr, Sally and Edwin found the few bottles of beer hidden at the back of the pantry for such occasions and sent out for some food. The bond among these three had been forged on other nights in the past and was deepened in the months to come. Their friendship was without limit, undemanding, there was nothing arbitrary in it, nothing treacherous. Spohr was not quite a father to the other two, yet he was more than a friend, his relations with them in no way intruded upon their relations with each other. Sally trusted Spohr more than she trusted anyone, possibly because he made it clear that his friendship did not include carrying her burdens, only perhaps from time to time noticing them and offering laughter turned against them, but never against herself. And Eddy, a devout believer in the efficacy of pure reason, remained convinced that Spohr's genius, his intellect would one day sweep away their difficulties, then they would live on indefinitely in a chain of rationally perfect moments. Spohr was in some ways disarmingly open, prepared to accept friendliness, what he called good will, wherever he found it, but the uncritical affection of his younger two friends supported something he had never wanted before. Their approval was sunlight, a warmth which unlocked frivolity when he felt like playing, when he wanted to be a child in a world that did not change. All this they offered each other, all this they bestowed upon each other without calculation, without reserve. Their reward was a faithfulness among them which lovers might envy, which outlived their friendship and travelled with Sally and Spohr to their dark, cold graves. Nella's kindness to Sally was apart from this, set aside without resentment. Although she would have been welcomed into the alliance she retreated as soon as it emerged, possibly because she didn't have the temperament for the long hours of drinking, possibly because she had no taste for the meticulous analysis, the procedural wrangles, the linguistic speculation which they amused themselves with and whiled away their time. Sally on the other hand had a natural curiosity about everything, an insatiable appetite for facts on any subject whether practical or aesthetic. She became interested in exploring her world on Spohr's terms. He offered a systematic analysis of experience which was new to her, which she had never been able to manage by herself. An intuitive philosopher, she could readily put aside her own convictions for the sake of a conversation, adopt rules for her understanding, be amused and entertaining while they wrestled with great concepts from the past, expecting to explore the present, to unravel the future. Spohr and Sally often continued their rambling discussions long after Eddy had capitulated to the quantity of alcohol, and when she discovered by chance that Spohr had never read the great classical poets she took to improvising dissertations on the Greek golden age, the European renaissance, the Italian baroque, until fainting with laughter, fatigue and the drink she would collapse leaving Spohr to a ceremonial solitude. This he customarily filled by swallowing the contents of any half empty glasses, humming to himself and contemplating his projects, the reflexive brain embellisher or holographic toys. Sally developed an intimacy with Spohr which Nella was never aware of and which would not have offended her had she known. She wanted to reserve for herself only the practical, an explicit version of moral loyalty in her marriage to Spohr, not the imaginary or the intellectual. She was quite happy to relinquish those to whoever would claim them. What Sally recognized in Spohr was a core of feeling, a specific emotional quality no one had found before. What Spohr released in Sally was a capacity to function normally. No one had helped her more, no one had drawn her closer to her own destruction, like a star whose polarity was the reverse of her own. And what about young Edwin, poor Knight who might have protected her, he failed to see what snapped and growled at his own heels, the very dogs whose desperate bite would sever his purpose in life.

As they ate from cardboard containers much later on that night of song and friendship, Sally asked Spohr questions about elementary particles. Her interest had been kindled by his understanding of these matters. And so he began with the conservation laws at the subatomic level, three laws relating to the creation or annihilation of particles and antiparticles. When a particle and its antiparticle collide, he explained, both are annihilated and other particles produced. In some cases this represents the total conversion of mass to energy. All particles belong to one of three groups and they cannot be destroyed except in pairs, one an ordinary particle and the other an antiparticle belonging to the same group. He went on to describe the link between the conservation laws and the basic symmetries in nature. The symmetry which is known as homogeneity of time entails the constancy of physical laws, and that in turn entails the conservation of energy. Then he accounted for the special conservation laws associated with space, time and charge, observing that although the three laws may not individually apply in all situations, their combination is considered to be a law itself. Accordingly, if a particular situation occurs a corresponding situation must also be possible in which particles are replaced by their antiparticles, reversing them in a mirror-like way and the situation itself in the opposite direction in time. He speculated that it might take the next thirty years to develop a theory which would treat all particles as one and see all force as aspects of a single underlying force. The conservation laws he concluded, offer us a key to the material basis of the universe. Sally was amazed at the similitude between the nonmaterial and the material, the one representing the in-breath of the universe, the other the out-breath. Spohr was not in the least evangelical, it would not have occurred to him to alter or influence Sally; he hoped only to elucidate a perspective and let clarity speak for itself. Eddy kept checking Sally's responses, watching her face for a change, and Spohr watched him with amusement. 'You have to be patient Eddy, you have to know how to wait if you're going to survive this mad spectacle. You can't be too eager, you can't run faster than the mind or the muscles will allow. Be moderate, be temperate and wise.' 'Especially temperate,' laughed Eddy opening another bottle. Sally was silent, preserving an immobility which conveyed nothing. As long as she retained the symmetry of the two views she was balanced, the pendulum moving easily from side to side without disharmony, without confusion. Such evenings made it seem possible she might survive, might live out her allotted time, the precipitate days and unyielding nights. She smiled at Edwin the charming, who would have protected her had he been able to, at least for a time. 'Eddy, for all you have given and for all you mean to me, my thanks, whatever happens I can never say I have not tasted it. We may live to grow old together and we may not, we may turn away from each other in time, but there will always be that place in my heart. Nothing can touch this love,' turning to Spohr, 'And nothing can tamper with this friendship. Together you have offered me a respite, even a reprieve.' She hugged them both. At last it was late and there was nothing left to drink. 'Before we say goodnight,' said Spohr, 'There's a story I've wanted to tell but the moment didn't present itself till now. Let me think for a moment, right, here we go.'

Once upon a time in a distant land that lay neither too close to the sea nor too far away, a profligate pair lived in marital bliss. Although he came from a solid old family he had managed to squander his patrimony in a few short years, and so now he relied on his wife's fortune to maintain him in a gentlemanly way. He was an amateur, a dabbler whose attention did not remain long on any one object. He delighted in tasting, sampling, and especially in throwing away. He was known as Waste. His wife was a tall, beautiful lady of ambiguous parentage but excessive wealth; her every whim was gratified immediately by servants and retainers. The name of his wife was Illusion. Neither his gambling, his carelessness nor his idea of luxury had been able to make a dent in her self-perpetuating fortune. There was one thing she ardently desired however, which all her wealth could not produce, that was a child, a child resembling mother and father in every detail, a child who would exemplify everything they believed in.

One day a seed began to sprout in her memory, a recollection which grew and grew until remembrance flowered. When she herself had been little more than a baby, oracles and fortunetellers had prophesied to her unlucky parents that their daughter's husband would never father a child, she would be the last of their line. There was an interesting proviso nevertheless, a codicil tacked on more or less as an afterthought. If she could master the techniques involved in phyloprogenesis she would have a child whose influence would last until the end of the world. This was exactly what Illusion had in mind as she industriously set herself the task of learning everything she could about autoreproduction. A day came when her fancy grew so big it crashed headlong into that desire itself, and in due course she delivered a sickly child. He was frail at first, pale and weak, requiring constant nourishment, dedicated care. He cried a lot and could only be appeased by his mother's tireless attentions. Her servants, a bizarre collection with such names as Anger, Lust, Greed, Falsehood, Envy, Fanaticism, all happily stood at her side, ready to help with this demanding child, the darling of everyone.

The initial, critical period passed, the child began to flourish and was named Sin. His parents as well as their friends considered the child miraculous, indulging and fondling him, granting every little thing he seemed to want, until at length, as he grew older, stronger and more inflexible, he became their master and master of all the people around, then of their children and their children's children, each generation capitulating enthusiastically to his gratification. Even the child's nominal father who evinced routine indifference to anything but his own pleasure found this growing lad a source of delight, undertaking to teach him everything he knew, to his mother's satisfaction. When it was time for this remarkable youth to go into the world he was better equipped than all the others in his peer group put together, establishing a success for himself that amounted to absolute triumph. His parents exulted when they saw whole worlds erupt, empires tremble and collapse, nations wither, families despair, individuals disintegrate and die. They observed the sanctuary their son had found in men's hearts, also recognizing his dominion at the shrines of the educated.

It so happened that a soothsayer with an international reputation came to visit, seeking an opportunity to speak privately to Illusion. 'Your son is doing well,' he commented, 'Sin is easier to accept than logic, therefore he prevails; but remind him please, that he exists only as a concept, a turn of phrase could eradicate him at any moment.' 'Never,' replied Illusion, 'Never, I have bewitched the people, my husband has enslaved them, my son will rule forever, as the prophecy indicated. We are the last great imperialists.' That distant land of long ago, lying not too close to the sea yet not too far away, still sends forth its conquering emissaries, and the nations, unaware that a single word could topple her son, still crumble at his feet.

- You ought to have been a bloody preacher Spohr, remarked Eddy with pleasure.
- I would like to know how it turns out, said Sally.
- So would I, responded Spohr, So would I.

And now the weeks which flowed at first like rivers, springtime rivers rushing eratically, overflowing the days and bypassing the hurdles of the night were curbed. The season which had begun with warm days and glowing nights cooled in mid-April leaving buds stranded in the path of the northwest wind, naked against the cold sky. The incubating leaves were locked in dreamless chambers, a legend to be deciphered in a mist of days to come, now mute, now folded in upon themselves. Will they die a secret death, will they live? There were also days when a biting wind blew in from the east and a precarious race to the zenith of the year slowed down, seemed to stop. Even the birds sang obliquely on cool, bitter mornings. The season had

191

established itself however, and although there was frost at night the days marked the direction of the sun as it moved higher and higher, an ascending no wind or frost or night could touch. When the freezing nights had run their course and the moon began to wane, the tension which had come with the cold withdrew to its Arctic source. The rain came, a black, murderous rain which fell equally on the good and the bad, a survivor's rain nevertheless. On such a day two old friends met in their last meeting place to resist the changes at the heart of the city, The Pilot Tavern, a rank, cavernous den which would not endure there much longer, but would rise again close by.

Harry: God, couldn't you be on time once, just once in all these years, even for your own farewell celebration?

Sam: Haven't we done this before?

Harry: True, we have marked a departure or two, but damn it man, it may well be the last time we see each other for years, I never know whether you're going for good.

Sam: I wish you were coming with me, I hate going alone.

Harry: Sorry, no, that kind of thing is not for me, once I did the grand tour after college I was finished with my travels. O I'll take a vacation in Puerta Angel or Nassau now and then, but I like it here, yes siree I don't see any reason to drag my butt across the face of the earth when right here suits me so admirably.

Sam: I'm not sure whether I'd trade places with you or not. I think you'd have found reasons to rejoice if you'd have been born on a dungheap.

Harry: I can't deny I'm contented here. My work is going reasonably well, I have to grub a bit, but so far I'm selling enough to get by nicely, and I haven't fallen into the clutches of the advertisers yet. You'd be good at this, why don't you try it out for awhile? I'll stake you if you need it, you know I would.

Sam: Thanks Bell, you're a good man and you've been a true friend in your way. It's not the work I'm afraid of, it's this city, it haunts me. Maybe if I had been born here like you I wouldn't notice it so much. Damn it, this place has always seemed so small town to me, you can't get away from people who know you, who know your family, who know you flunked out of school or got the wrong girl pregnant. There's no privacy here, I'm always running into someone I'd have ducked around the corner to avoid talking to. You're a sociable bastard, you love it, but I hate it, you know, and I'll never feel comfortable here. I need a big city, I need London or New York or L.A.

Harry: I hope you know what you're doing.

Sam: I've never known that. There is something that keeps me hopping, away from here at any rate.

Harry: You always seem to hop back.

Sam: True, that's the curse of it, easy enough to fall back on with parents here I guess.

Harry: And friends?

Sam: A mixed blessing, a very mixed blessing. I wouldn't mind so much if I didn't have the feeling that I owe someone something, or if I don't I ought to.

Harry: A moralist! What on earth do you expect with an attitude like that?

Sam: You know you're very cool about things, who would suspect your engagement was just broken off? I can't figure you out, don't you mind?

193

Harry: Of course I mind you idiot, and I'm not in any mood to discuss it. Shut up about that, will you?

Sam: Whoa, sorry old man, I didn't mean to offend you, it's just that you don't seem changed. This doesn't appear to make any difference, I find that peculiar.

Harry: When you and your old girl broke up you weren't upset either.

Sam: Well I ended it, she was the one trampled, and very, very hurt actually. She told me that the other day. She'd never mentioned it before, but it was rough for her, very rough. Another damn reason to clear out. What about you?

Harry: I'm all right.

Sam: Apparently.

Harry: I could wish her reasons had been different. She's been away for nearly a year, that's probably softened the blow. Still . . .

Sam: I know, a weird business. I mentioned it to Nella, I hope you don't mind, and she wasn't surprised at all. She seemed to know something about it.

Harry: Nella's an extraordinary woman. How did she know, or can women tell that about other women?

Sam: No, something happened at the party we had last year before Clara left for Oxford. At least she says something happened that didn't seem significant at the time. Now, in retrospect, it does.

Harry: What did she say?

Sam: Not much, Clara was going around saying goodbye to everyone. We were all so smashed you remember, and she took Nella by the hand, leading her out to the balcony. Do you really want to hear this?

Harry: Yes, you bastard, I do.

Sam: Clara took Nella's face in both her hands and kissed her, on the lips. Nella said she looked her straight in the eye, smiled a little secretively, held her face between her hands for a moment and kissed her, hard.

Harry: Jesus.

Sam: That was what happened, and she knew from this, or thought she suspected something from this. At any rate, she wasn't surprised.

Harry: I wish she had told me then.

Sam: She thought about it, only there didn't seem to be much point and it would have been difficult to convey. Before.

Harry: I guess so, I bloody guess so.

Sam: Look, this place is starting to fill up, do you want to stay or move on?

Harry: Stay here, it's all right here.

Sam: Are you sure? I believe I just caught a glimpse of Charlie Cohen.

Harry: The everpresent. No, it doesn't matter, we'll stay if you don't mind, but for God's sake, not a word about this in front of anyone else. It'll get around soon enough.

[Enter Charlie Cohen]

Charlie: Well, well, what a nice surprise. Docherty, I thought you'd left already. Put it there Harry, I heard your rotten news and I'm truly sorry. I must confess I find scholarly women attractive myself, but I'd never want to marry one. No sir, I want a nice soft woman who's never even heard of Voltaire, much less read him in the original and formed scrupulous opinions which are bound to be more perceptive than mine. I'm thinking of getting married too, you know, but I want a girl who'll have children and make me chicken soup. I'll find a mistress for intellectual companionship, thank you very much.

Harry: Thanks for your commiseration, don't ever let anyone underrate you. Sam, we are in the presence of a genuinely original man, this round is on me.

Sam: Your face is cold but your heart is warm. In this flyspecked universe Bell, you ring true. *[The following is accompanied by great mobility of face and abundant comic gestures.]* In a five and dime world however, you have certain extravagant tendencies which interfere with the revolution. I'm so sorry, but I'm afraid we'll have to terminate you for the good of the masses. Please take your place against this conveniently located wall, fold a hanky across your powder blew eyes and allow us sir, to pop you off with these antique Sten guns, or if you prefer we have solid, vintage machine guns at our disposal. Now don't trifle with us sir, we can't hold the revolution up much longer, what do you fancy? A firing squad! A whole firing squad for just one man, are you mad sir? This revolution is for the people not the individual.

Charlie: What's he talking about?

Harry: Don't you know, haven't you been recruited? Boy Blunder, I'm afraid we've bungled, this man's an agent, take cover. Code seventy-six.

Sam: Not seventy-six Moriarty, they've cracked that.

Charlie: Is it a game?

Sam: A game? Your life is in jeopardy and your country is at stake, what kind of liberal are you anyhow? Take this down Moriarty, we need evidence against all these Jewish intellectual

196

terrorists. Are you going to talk or must we resort to . . . torture, a little torture, just a teensy little bit of torture, for the boy's sake sir. I mean, he's all I've got and he has to learn sir. Can't we have a little torture, just to entertain the lads sir?

Charlie: You're nuts Docherty, plain nuts.

Harry: No you don't Blunder my boy, you won't get away with the old insanity plea this time. Now about your accomplice here, an intellectual with strong emotional attachments to the left, I take it. Speak up man, are you a faggot too?

Sam: Ah you've got him there Moriarty, right between the balls Bell. Round one.

Charlie: And what do you call this, Tiny Terror Time?

Sam: A hit, a palpable hit! Round two.

Charlie: Enough, enough, let's make a truce. The next round is on me, what do you say?

Harry: Fairly spoken, sometimes it's awfully hard work with tough guys like you Cohen. What've you been up to?

Charlie: Making too much money. What about you?

Harry: Well you seem to know all about us. We have no secrets, I'm disengaged and Sam is heading back out into the world once more. Why don't you take Charlie with you Sam? You'd inspire each other.

Charlie: Where are you going this time?

Sam: Not too sure where I'll end up. Going down to mosey around New York for awhile, maybe go west after that, L.A., San Francisco, who knows?

Charlie: Is there any word on Archer?

Harry: I heard that MacIntyre made discreet, very discreet inquiries at a few local health resorts and came up with a big fat negative, that's all I know. You hear anything?

Charlie: No, I ran into Sevcik the other day, but you can't ever get anything from him.

Harry: You do have to be circumspect with a *siddhayogi.*

Charlie: What's a *siddhayogi?*

Sam: A man of action.

Charlie: I don't get it.

Sam: Neither do I.

Charlie: Well what does it mean?

Harry: It means, as far as I can tell, that he's very accomplished, that he does what he does rather well, first class with a gold star.

Charlie: And just what does he do?

Sam: Why, he stands on his head of course.

Charlie: Docherty, you lack a few of the social graces, not all of them mind you, just a few crucial ones.

Sam: If it's any comfort to you, I've noticed that too. It doesn't seem to matter anymore, nobody minds, if you insult them I mean. Nobody seems to notice; so I say whatever I find coming out of my mouth. That's company policy if you want to work for us, you know. Sharp wits in a drowned out body, that's the answer these days. Gentlemen, shall we drink or shall we dabble?

Charlie: You're going to damage your liver.

Sam: Perhaps I value the damage.

Charlie: Well I'll wander around a bit, catch you later. Let me know if a party materializes.

[Exit]

Harry: I guarantee you'll be the first to know.

<u>Sam</u>: Are we awful to him or do I merely imagine we are? There's something about this man which invites a fist in the face. Pow! Just like that, right between the eyes, and I hate myself for it because I like him. He may be stingy but that doesn't seem like a fatal flaw, does it?

<u>Harry</u>: I don't know why he sets himself up, I can't believe he enjoys it, he's too smart and too sensitive.

<u>Sam</u>: Well he grovels and I can't stand grovelers. Who's buying, me or you?

<u>Harry</u>: Me, save yours for your travels. Why do you go if you don't like to be alone?

<u>Sam</u>: I don't know, recklessness, a choice of hatreds. When I'm alone I can curse the whole world, abstractly. When I'm here I have to direct it at someone, whup! *[Flattens an imaginary fly on the table.]* There doesn't seem to be any point in staying here. Then again, there isn't much point in leaving either. How do you find the point?

<u>Harry</u>: Don't you know better than to go on searching for the elusive, unimpeachable, almost certainly nonexistent point?

<u>Sam</u>: That's not a comforting answer, a lot of folks don't buy such stuff. Take Annie for example, she just smiles when we talk like that, she smiles because she knows something we don't, even if she won't talk about it, not to me at any rate.

<u>Harry</u>: If you don't mind my saying so, I like my world the way it is. Why don't you go easy, accept what you stumble across and stop busting your ass with worry? You don't have to be a lumpkin to enjoy all this, you can specialize in thrillers and expensive wine if you need to. Be decent to your family and loyal to your friends. Look at me, I know what you know, I do

what you do, I want what you want, at least I think I do, wife, house, kids, cars and something special, a private thing for the mind, for the ego. Let me think I'm making it a little better, a little different from the guy next door, not too different, just enough to remind me my standards are more sophisticated, my aesthetic requirements subtler, only not enough to hound me, to distract me from the good life.

Sam: I can't do it Harry, I can't do it. The politics of the ark — sink or swim and everybody knows you can't swim. Besides, what if the world and your good life just blow up? This whole thing will end in a poisoned mushroom anyhow.

Harry: At least you're cheerful! O look, there's Marguerite with Bollard. They might have brought Jan along for form's sake, or have they gone public?

Sam: I think she doesn't care, and he, I can't make anything out of him. He doesn't even behave nicely to her, very cold, he speaks coldly, abruptly to her. Do people do that to hide their feelings? I can't believe it's true. And how she looks at him, shifting from hip to hip, crossing one leg over the other like that. She asks for it, does she ever ask for it. I wouldn't mind a taste of that.

Harry: Well I've sampled it, you know.

Sam: You? You?

Harry: She was wearing a thin dress, cut low, front and back, in the middle of winter. Somehow or other we found ourselves drinking alone together, here in fact. It was during the day, late afternoon, she took me home with her and I remember thinking anyone could come in, find us there, but no one did. She's very soft. Wave, they've spotted us.

<u>Sam</u>: *[Mimes elaborate gestures of greeting.]* Halloo you Dutch treat, you and your priapic playmate make a splendid couple, but I have a fine and private bed too, you know. Let me dream of you, come to me with two lips my love, and leave your little friend whirling at the windmill. Shall we join them?
<u>Harry</u>: Why not?

[Exeunt]

From the Notebooks of Annie March (196-)

I like to be alone, I like the solitude as it grows dark on a long slow day, with children playing in the distance, their toys rumbling across the pavement, cries and yells spattering in the dusk. Comfortable to sit in this room as the darkness gathers, accumulating in every dusty corner and finally landing in my lap. I watch them reluctantly give up the last game of ball or hide-and-seek, hopscotch, roller skates or skipping, as they try to evade their mother's voice, perhaps it's an older sister, demanding, impatient. No one ever called for me, no one ever sent to find out why I did not come. The best time is early morning as the darkness breaks up, scattering bars of light across the sky, a few birds testing the night's last resonance. Their sound brings the silence, the quiet into focus, it is a wakening. Yet I have never adjusted to my permanent solitude; still seek the dissolution of personal locks & barriers. If I do not write I consider myself nothing, and I do not write. What fragments do *I* have shored against my ruin? A handful of short bad poems and one long bad poem. My thoughts keep turning to the Archer stories.

I would never have taken a rush at words and come up with say, a Shakespearean sonnet or things unattempted yet in prose or rhyme, but I might have eloped with metaphor and emotion, offered phrases, abstracted my own sound of darkness. The finger of reason has purified the language, the unbending scepticism has widowed the roots leaving them so lacking in spontaneity I scarcely find it possible to ask the ordinary questions about life and death, let alone the extraordinary ones. The point is that it is not possible to ask questions at all. An efficient scepticism arrests all talk, removes superstition and becomes the instrument of its own destruction. Finally reason, rationality itself must be doubted. Why shouldn't reason be destroyed by the weapon it forged to claim its own supremacy, why should reason be invulnerable? *But who will wield the sword?* In the end I suppose you close your mouth, sit and stare without reflection, without comment or thought or doubt. There's nothing left to do and no point mentioning a word about that to anyone. *But who will wield the sword?* It seems unnatural that the end of it all, reason, emotion, fear, argument, hope, knowledge, should be a self-imposed silence. Absolved from the possibility of question, the answer long since cast adrift, why do I find the need to ask persisting? Why is need not obliterated, what persists? Wait, I can't ask, all that remains is a mouthful of expletives it would be indecent and farcical to exercise. Beckett's old men — I understand them.

So if that insidious thing, that fair, calm, liberal reasonableness which has held me in its grip for so long does not work, abandon it. Can I, will *it* let go of me? Who is holding on, who is held?

April

Marguerite said, 'I'm bad and I like being bad, I don't want to be good. Anyone can be good, but I will be bad. I go to church and pray, I used to go to church, it's no use now. I don't know whom it is I pray to, I don't even know who it's supposed to be. And the people sitting there, do you think they know, do you think they have any idea who Jesus is, do you really think they know who God is? They play a game with loaded dice and hope the odds are in their favor. What a laugh, how can anyone take them seriously? If you go to a big church the noise made by the collection plate drowns any real prayer. Women wrapped in the furs of slaughtered creatures are barely able to move their lips in a smile. What prayers come from such lips, to whom can they be addressed? Does their god permit them to kill for their own pleasure, their own amusement? And if you go to a poor church and look, really look at the ignorance in the faces there, that tells you something even worse. They don't know, nobody knows. I don't know. Once I thought I did, I used to wear a big cross around my neck, a hat on my head and trip off to church holding Jan's hand. We would kneel there together feeling awfully pure. My God it makes me feel silly to remember how sweet it was. The deception! There's nobody there, don't you understand? There's nobody there.'

Good and evil: is it a battle, do we fight our way from one side to the other, do we cross the street casually, do we choose, are we chosen? And if I were free to ask the questions, how would I find the answers, how would I know?

When the boatman is on holiday we linger on the far shore of hell, sweat and study the terrain. We move, slow motion, a frieze of images projected by memory and desire, the ghosts haunting the past activated by the imminence of the future. The ancient boatman: rough; unyielding; sclerodermatic; hardened by the salt winds in the endless night through which he steers his craft; looking straight into the eyes of children, he pilots them to perpetual oblivion; not the hangman nor the angel of death; not vicious but undeterred, implacable; not the master, the servant of a dreadful master, the lord of the dead, he walks among our savage ghosts; contempt, he has contempt for human frailty which he himself was never subject to; not human, an animal who never had to choose between good and evil.

Forgetfulness, the Greco-Roman double edge, the comfort of nothingness, the desolation of nothingness. Spinoza said the temporal relation falls away in true knowledge. Einstein said gravity affects light and time but its grip on time diminishes as you rise above the earth. *The poet only bringeth his own stuff.*

Admiration for M. Grand in *La Peste,* the man who empties his life to pursue the perfect sentence. He believes he is writing a book, in fact he has only the opening sentence which he rewrites endlessly. When it's right they'll have to say hats off gentlemen, a masterpiece. That character and his sentence have bombarded me for years. He's the tramp, the Chaplin of my own experience, funny, serious, silly, tragic, futile in his pursuit of perfection. He dies in the plague, his sentence unfinished, the echo of emptiness.

In the fifties they said the novel is dead, the sonata is dead, a form comes into being, flourishes and dies. It occurs to me now that art, all of it, has flourished and died. Our society's secrets are encoded messages flashed subliminally on a television screen. Spohr may be right, technology is the mode which interprets and responds to this world, art is depleted. Too fragile to bear the weight of whole galaxies, it persists like a faithful servant with no place to go when the master dies. Well then, fetch me something while you're standing around doing nothing. Not a novel thank you very much, fiction doesn't interest me. I want to understand my experience, put together pieces of the present, the past and dreams; all this to confront the future. Give it your best M. Grand, and don't bring me any characters, just revelations. The word and the consequence of the word, that interests me. Don't however, for a moment think I'm not curious, voracious to observe, only it has to be perfect, they must be obliged to say hats off gentlemen, a masterpiece. Still, my thoughts turn to the Archer stories.

All this restless intellectual passion.

1964

Dreams, the preamble: a separate but compatible truth with laws comprehensible in its own perspective if nowhere else. Hard to reckon with in the waking world, some weigh so heavily upon you they cannot be ignored even there. A month after my father died I dreamt about him. He said, 'I didn't really die Annie darling, I just pretended to die. Look at me, aren't I here?' And he smiled in such an ordinary way I had no doubt it was true. The relief was immense, a stone rolled away from my heart and that buoyancy, that lightness continued for an uncircumvented period, out of time, in the dream. My first waking thought was for my mother, to tell her father was alive, we had been misinformed, misled for whatever reason about his death. The dream was so persuasive it did not dissipate significantly for moments, until other images, seeing his dead body, watching them lower his coffin into the ground, these fugitive recollections began to penetrate that other truth. All day I vacillated between the two, although I knew my waking perspective would prevail. And yet a certain feeling persisted, there was a sense of his being alive which was just as meaningful as the sense in which he was dead, and though the feeling began to fade, it stayed with me for days. When the contradicting images first began to usurp the other, I felt bitter, cheated because I was constrained to accept the waking version over the one my other awareness chose. Looking back I find the bitterness difficult to understand, not a predictable reaction. Disappointment yes, frustration perhaps, pain in the renewed sense of loss to be sure, but bitterness? It's not an emotion I have any familiarity with, I can't remember feeling quite like that before or since. Where did it come from?

When I was eighteen I had the first dream which was clearly not a dream in the ordinary sense, and which I think of today as a vision. Very few dreams have that quality. What distinguished this one from other night images was the clarity, the preciseness, its focus on the revelation, although I don't entirely understand it yet, and especially the persistence of the afterimage. For years I could recall the dream in detail, consult it like the faithful reproduction of a painting, it did resemble a painting, or perhaps it was more like stained glass because the images were translucent. There was a ruined, a shattered church, had it been bombed? What remained was a collection of spare parts, a nave, the remnants of an altar, an apse, a baptismal font, no roof, fragmented walls, but a composed arrangement suggesting they all belonged together. The air was filled with smokey sunlight, darkly, as though a roof had blocked the direct rays. There were a few blackened trees, perhaps the charred timbers of blasted walls, and a small rose window behind the altar, oddly enough without any glass, just the leaded frame. The slanting light came in through that window, dim streaks of a theatrical gel, unidentifiable, golden. It was very still, a proscenium stage with an observer, myself, placed in front where the audience would have been. There was a little sound off stage left which I followed. The sound like squirrels chittering led me to a door stained dark, dark brown. When I opened it I found a dirty spiral staircase, run-down, wretched, the walls painted a filthy pale green as if it were a public lavatory. It smelled, the paint and plaster had come off in large chunks and at the top of the staircase three small children huddled together in communal misery, dressed in dark, dirty rags, chattering, making the squirrel-like noises I had heard. It was a wrenching declaration of poverty and destitution before which I found myself paralyzed. I couldn't move to comfort them, couldn't understand what they were saying or whether they were using a human language. I was incapacitated by their suffering. 'Where is my sister?' In the dream I knew who she was. 'She'll know what to do, she has a conscience.' My 'sister,' a nun's hood on her head, appeared instantly at my side, her hands open in a gesture of sympathy. The children disappeared, the door disappeared, the staircase disappeared, my 'sister' disappeared, the stage disappeared, and I, the observer, remained in what would have been the center aisle, if there had been walls, if there had been a church. The light faded slowly, the vision ended and was enclosed within me where it persists, diminished now with the passing of years, but a reference point. About this time I stopped looking in the churches and started a more vigorous study of philosophy, both eastern and western, until finally, and this was a few years later, I realized that religions and philosophies converge at more or less the same place in my understanding. They can push me to the edge, the outermost limit of intellect but they can't take me any farther, and that is where I want to go. Beyond. Into what? Where? How?

Intimations of dreams and visions, are they analogies, approximations? Do they mislead, do they wilfully distort or merely conjure hope beyond repair? Who's in charge then, who runs the show? Don't find the language proffered by psychotherapy of much consequence, new names for old ideas or old names for new ideas lead to the same destinations. They can take you to their own limit, not beyond. I want to *know*.

More. One night casting about in the dark for something to hang onto, a glowing light, uncentered, all radiance, transforming the room and its darkness. A manifestation of unimaginable peace. No questions, no images, just light. After some time, with concentration, experience repeated on several occasions, never at predictable intervals. And once or twice most unexpectedly, that is nothing I was aware of doing seemed in any way responsible, the pure light itself just came. All comment unnecessary, undesirable.

Now you see it, now you don't. Is the curtain ever really pulled aside? Do we twitch at it ourselves, snatch a glimpse when we're not supposed to, or does someone lift it for us when we are consumed, exhausted by an endless search? Is it a sneak preview, are we like the member of some foreign chemical species in the prebiotic soup surveying all creation which has yet to come? If the reason we're here is to know the reason we're here, let me see, let me have more than an intimation, let me know.

And more. Someone comes, luminous, compassionate, as familiar and remote as an unremembered face smiling into the cradle. He comes again and again in the night, beckoning.

It was a long, slow springtime one bud unfolding at a time, shaking out yellowy green flowers and damp, curled leaves, the grass thickening in electric waves of lime green, tender and soft, the bird choir day by day more practised, more confident, augmented by recent arrivals and passing strangers, the air crisp and bright, amazingly bright with the memory of a dark, hooded winter still there. Then one day you looked down the street and saw all the trees in flower; the city bloomed with such unexpected loveliness it was impossible not to remember the starkness of winter you'd hardened yourself to all those months, and be grateful it was annulled once more. This was the last moment to look back. After that you climbed, you soared with the season to unthinking light, no past, no memory, each day flowering into the next from the beginning, each day swelling beneath the weight of those to come. On such a day Eddy collapsed in a slung canvas chair set out on the green oasis beside the workshop carved from the dusty compound behind Spohr's house. He sighed happily, unbuttoned his shirt to the waist and let his long arms and legs droop blissfully over the chair. The hot midday sun warmed his face, his arms, the wide vee of exposed skin on his body, and he groaned with relief, stripped by the sun's touch. He dozed, somnolent, a golden salamander in the sparkling sun, thoughts of Sally perforating his dream-like state. 'Can't imagine what they'd make of a girl like that at home. Thalia and Jack would adore her, she says such outlandish things, and my dear mamma has a weakness for exotic creatures, but the old man,

Henry, that would be rough waters all right. He'd prefer a call girl if her accent was right, the miserable old geezer. Can't imagine this coming up, what with the wife and child flourishing there. Forgotten about them somewhat, gives me the willies to think about that. What on earth will I do? Ah me, just an old stud horse down on the farm. Lord she's lovely though, the best yet. In bed. When's she due home? Take a girl like you down to New Orleans, that's the ticket, keep one here, one there, visit back and forth. Maybe I should take Sally home with me. O that'd straighten Rosalind out in a hurry, the silly bitch, hanging on like that across thousands of miles, across an ocean and half a bloody continent. What does she want from me, does she think Henry's going to die and she'll miss out on the loot? That mean old buzzard, he's so tough he'll live longer than I will. Hope not. It can't be my bodily charm, can it? Glad I stopped sleeping with her, that drove her away soon enough. Still, she insists the child's mine, and he is the dead spit of me in the photo, so I guess that's straight enough. Why can't they let you alone?' He opened his eyes and shifted around restlessly, peering down with annoyance at a few hard, pustulous spots on his chest. 'Damned acne, at least it's not on my face, thank the good lord for small mercies. They say the sun's good for it, pity you can't roll over in these damn chairs, cook the other side.' He went into the kitchen, took a cold bottle of beer from the fridge and sat down in the sun again, remaining upright this time, one leg crossed over the other, the crepe soled desert boots heavy in the heat. 'Must trot out those old Mexican huaraches, these are too hot now. God, what a place, freezing your ass off one minute and boiling the next.

211

Terrible town, just terrible, how did I ever land here? Really have to move on. What about that damn degree? Spohr and Monty both strong on my sticking it out, I don't know, I don't know. Maybe I should go out west, work on the boats for awhile. That might be awful. If I got a lump of money together it would be worth it though, and Sally? Well she can look after herself.' He squinted at Spohr who was passing through. 'Hey man, good to see you,' he murmured, 'What's happening?' He had picked up the jargon listening to the blues and during a few hectic cross-country runs by automobile from New York to the west coast or New Orleans. There he made it a point to consort with black women and honkytonk musicians, he loved the lingo. 'Nothing much,' said Spohr. 'Just trying to look busy so Nella won't get ideas, what about you?' 'Well if this christly town doesn't finish me those damn exams will. Do they do it just to scare you or do you suppose they actually have something in mind?' Spohr laughed, 'I never myself put much store in the ordeal by fire; so I can't really say. Just do what they expect of you and try not to be too excited. In the humanities you can always get away with charm or wit if you don't have anything else.' 'Lord I hope so, I can't tell you what twaddle I've committed to paper in the last weeks. Have a beer.' 'Can't now, catch me on the way back though,' as he disappeared through the garden gate on some private errand. Eddy slumped down in his canvas cradle lulled by the sun, 'My word that feels good. Suppose I ought to be contemplating modern European history. Imbeciles, where do they get their version of modern? Metternich and the German confederation, the king of Italy, Bonapartes and empires, ententes and triple alliances, what is history supposed to mean anyhow? His story. Whose, some damn king or unscrupulous politician no doubt, who perverts the facts to his own satisfaction. Nothing changes, cannibals the lot of them, feeding on each other. Ought to be a course in survival, empire survival, class survival and the individual, Sweeney. Poor damn Sweeney who's never going to make it anyhow, why would anyone want to make a revolution for Sweeney? He'd rather drink his beer and lie in the sun, like me. No, not like me, there are a few worth preserving though. Spohr, that's a good man, generous, free with his knowledge, withholds nothing, offers it around like drinks on the house. Still, he lacks caution, probably rushing off to score one with Brenda in the middle of the day. Sometimes he doesn't bother to cover his tracks. It's not as if he didn't care, then why is his camouflage so offhand? By God he's evasive, not one you can pin down. Sometimes he talks too much, tells too much, more than he needs to, is it bravado? Didn't care for the things he told Sally about me. Have to set him straight on that, what to keep her in the dark about. No secrets, just no need to talk. She wants someone to stay with her, I don't expect to start empires, can't even say whether we'll last out the year. Not now, it's still so good — why do these things always start well and end pathetically? Juice seems to run out, the feeling goes, the grip at the stomach goes, is this any different? She's got me now, but proper. Maybe it'll go on, maybe I'll take her home with me and set Henry back on his heels for a month. He howled when I married Rosalind, doesn't leave him much scope. Funny that, her father his best friend, until we got married. Now he won't speak to the man

213

because he ought to have had more sense, ought not to have let his daughter marry me. Our family better than theirs Henry says, is it? There her family sits in a huge house on the Embankment, tarnished by trade. Pompous old Henry, these things can't matter, can they? I guess if you want to live with them you have to notice their rules, if you want to live with them. Like savages I suppose, or empires for that matter. Really it's too much nonsense.' He fell into a superficial sleep, dimly aware of the sun, the bottle of beer in his hand, the chair he reclined in. A passing cloud woke him, he set the bottle down and dozed again. This time his sleep was peopled with figures tripping in and out like actors, bit players all of them, delivering a single line. A smile, a look and they made their exit from the other side of the stage, like Spohr going out the garden gate. Rosalind appeared picking mushrooms in a long dress covered with an apron, and there was Henry, his large belly tastefully concealed in a pinstriped suit. He laughed once, or did he snort, then strode offstage with a determined step. Thalia appeared with Jack, her misty blue eyes vague but encouraging, 'Sorry darling, I can't stay.' 'But mummy you never do.' 'Sorry darling, sorry.' It was pleasant, a springtime garden, a Watteau. 'What a fine dream,' he thought in the dream, 'How nice they are, why can't it stay this way?' Spohr came in looking like a bear as he chased two young girls across the stage, was one of them Sally? No, of course not, she was over there, in a corner of the garden sniffing what, lilacs, wisteria, some dazzling mauve and pink blossoms bursting from a tree which swelled in a corner of the set. *Cupid, as he lay among Roses, by a bee was stung.* She came towards him offering a bouquet. He caught their fragrance which he took to be hers, then she disappeared and he was left alone with a child he couldn't quite identify playing happily on the grass. A foot nudged his, 'Is this what you call study?' asked Spohr with amusement. 'What time is it, I've been having such a good dream I don't think I want to wake up. How long have I been here?' 'Couple of hours maybe,' and he continued into the house. Eddy moved his chair around so that he was facing the sun and slept again; this time all the friendly shadows eluded him, he felt the brooding presence of something unpleasant, a heaviness. He found himself in a court of law quite unprepared for the stern, unsympathetic judge who glowered without pity. His hand was in the air, the gavel raised, Eddy knew if he brought it down he would certainly be sentenced to prison. He tore himself from the dream and woke muttering, 'Bloody hell, we don't want any of that. Should have stayed awake when Spohr poked me. Damndest things, dreams, probably nothing more than neural spasms, I hope. Wonder where Sally is, maybe it's too early. Feel like it, O do I feel like it now!' He stared at the blemishes on his chest before buttoning his shirt again, annoyed they appeared so unchanged, startled by the citric smell drifting from the clotted mats of dark blonde hair in his armpits. The back gate opened noisily as Marguerite came through wearing the shortest dress Eddy had ever seen, her long pale stockingless legs wavering on high heeled shoes. She sailed a little self-consciously through Spohr's marvellous debris which spurted up like clumps of mechanical flowers. He looked at her in the short, short dress hardly longer than a shirt and stirred with the recollection of an old ache, a feeling like an itch at the base of his spine which spread and flamed and fanned itself as it grew louder, more insistent. *Sappie che tosto che l'anima trade come fec' io, il corpo suo l' è tolto.* He didn't say anything, he studied her from head to toe, up and down, down and up. She stopped in front of him, her eyes lowered, stimulated by the effect she had on him. 'How do you like my new dress, my English frock as Bollard calls it? He gave it to me, do you like it, isn't it unbelievably short?' He didn't answer as she turned to walk away, 'Now you just bring that pretty ass of yours over here,' he said laughing; when she spun towards him he reached up under her dress to run his hand across her dark, secret places. They were both so startled by the sudden rush of desire, a rampant weed snaking across their bodies, joining them, binding them, they looked at each other with shock. Eddy's brain began a whirling computation of how to consummate the brazen moment, 'My place, her place, now, later?' She spoke quietly as she backed slightly away from him, beyond the reach of his curious, probing hand, 'Someone's watching from the kitchen window.' She stood back and laughed, 'To be continued.' In the kitchen Spohr said to Sally, 'Come now Sally my dear, did you think he would never look at another woman?' 'I don't know,' she said, 'I really don't know what I thought, it doesn't matter now. *Ya rabb, com vivireye con este 'l-halaq?* It won't ever be the same again.'

They are undeterred.

216

Untitled Section

The world was shifting into a new era, hurled on a different course in a different age, greeted with violence, revolution, insurrection, the politics of blood, the economics of deprivation, volcanoes, earthquakes, floods, torture, murder, wars, race against race, religion against religion, family against family, gender against gender, famine, destruction, every imaginable degradation, all the subtleties a tireless appetite for terror and a matching taste for horror could produce. The west dispatched their miracles of science and technology to the east which in turn, released a flood of secrets they had nursed for thousands of years. They bowed to each other with varying politeness and rapacity, surveyed their markets and grabbed each other by the throat, exchanging charlatan for charlatan, truth for technique. The north continued to look coldly upon the south, the darker continents which raged in useless counterpoint against the east-west fury. Mad by any known human standard they butchered, slaughtered, tortured, dismembered, maimed, disfigured, disemboweled, murdered, violated, mutilated and killed each other in a thrilling attempt to ennoble themselves, emulating their more enlightened kinfolk in the northern hemisphere. Jointly they entered upon treaties, alliances, commitments, alignments, spheres of influence, tariff agreements, trade associations, arms races, disarmament talks, crises, unions, federations, peace talks, border squirmishes, ultimata and negotiations. Death was their constant companion, fear was their constant ally, treachery their constant friend. The world was busily casting off what it could no longer use, discarding its junk and its treasures with an equal eye, littering the universe with the wreckage, odds and ends it could no longer accommodate. And whose fault was it? You can't blame the politicians, you can't blame the generals, the businessmen, the multinational corporations, and you can't blame their advisors, their governments, their bankers, their executives, and you can't blame the housewives, the workers, the unions or the police, you can't blame the psychiatrists, the doctors, the social workers, the philosphers, the bookies, the bartenders, the bomb, the pill, the weed, the dope, the acid, the junk or the learned journals. Well whose fault was it? While the world convened conferences to preside over its own dissolution, to launch the eclipse of the world on a rocket ship to the moon and a satellite to Mars, pockets of dissent massed their rebellion against war, injustice, brutality, inhumanity, and became powers themselves, putting their faith in demonstrations and protests, in a private, parallel system unified by communal music, by illuminating drugs. They put their faith in a style of dress, in a distribution of music by decibel, declarations of subsistence and self-reliance, proclamations of universal love and peace inspired by a few seductive leaders, counterrevolutionaries or false prophets, expecting for a shining moment to save the planet, as they liked to call it, until these saviors themselves were grabbed by the throat and sacrificed for pure profit. For what is a new era but an old one realigned, and what is revolution but a turn of the wheel, a point at which you see what is rejected falling away and what you hope for as the rising curve of the future, without noticing that the future also drops away beneath itself merging behind the present with the past. What do we in fact see, what do we in fact know?

Thomas Archer (Steele) lay chained to a bed while the world turned around and away from him, his revolutionary fervor crushed by the judicious administration of chemical depressants and electrical stimulants, his perspective split, his genius and talent nullified. He capitulated to the fear of fear and permitted himself to be manipulated, programmed, charted. Undone. For awhile he was reduced to plain Thomas Steele, the leaping, soaring Archer hamstrung by a meticulous therapeutic process which laid claim to a compassion it did not possess, which released the thief and held the artist. The artist however, rose again, liberated by his own capacity to soar, but with wings damaged now, ruined for flight. He lost the ability to consort with his gods; all that remained was an aging, down at heels urchin deprived of his secrets, resembling the homeless loiterers in the streets, their brains blown out by furious private woes. During the years of Thomas Archer's eclipse his friends would try to find him, or at least they would discuss some careful plan to search for him, save him if they could. When they met by chance they asked each other for news, calling upon Sevcik for information, but even Sevcik who had eagerly undertaken to rescue his old comrade, his adversary, seemed incapable of action. It was as though Tom's misfortune had been contagious and his friends were infected too. There was a collective paralysis, they didn't know what to do and floundered in a wash of confusing alternatives, as ignorant of remedying a sore on the social body as they were incapable of healing themselves. Nella understood what it was but not why, and in any case, she was considered merely eccentric when she talked about the need to understand your own well-being without invoking a socio-pharmacological machine which crushes while it cures. She recognized that most people had traded in the responsibility for their own condition in exchange for guarantees to wipe out disease, only the guarantees didn't save Spohr, they didn't save Sally and they didn't save Archer. As the years passed a toxic inertia settled over Spohr, it became more and more apparent that the great champion of intellect, the master of reason, the sword poised for the thrust against ignorance had been blunted. Why this happened was difficult to say, his work had always been slow, demanding repetitive experiments inspired by occasional clairvoyance. Perhaps he was bored with these endless requirements, certainly he was annoyed by the nonacceptance, the failure of the world to invite him to the feast, the banquet table of their respect. He had expected at the very least to teach in some distinguished university, he was galled by his inability to finance a decent laboratory, by the lack of money to live as his reputable colleagues did in houses which did not crumble, who drove automobiles which did not falter, fathered bright, talented children, went to the south of France on vacation, to conferences in California, received titles, awards and honors, deferred to each other in public and exploited each other in private. He would have been the sun in that universe, obscuring the stars if he had come out, but it was not to be. He worked less and less, there were days when he locked himself in his room, would not open for anyone, all that was known had to be deduced from the sounds on his side of the door. And what could be heard? The Edge Of Night, As The World Turns, definitions of conflict and despair prescribed by small scale infidelity, by large scale ignorance. The master was nailed to his bed in numb acquiescence to the wounds of trivia, bored with his work, bored with his life, bored with himself, but he never admitted to that at all, he said he was working if anyone inquired. When Nella suspected he was doing nothing more than watching television day after day, she was amused and said nothing, thinking how funny it was that the impervious, impenetrable Spohr should be humbled this way. At first she even thought it might be good for him, thought it might soften that unyielding epidermal toughness, make life easier for him, more accessible. It did no such thing. He told Nella he used the recorded sounds and images as variables in certain theorems he was propounding, that the inventory of human activity provided samples for specific processes he was classifying and encoding. Some days he left early in the morning, as if he were going to a job with the rest of the world, not returning until dinnertime. Reports came to Nella that on such days he sat at Union Station watching the passengers arrive and depart, train after train, doing nothing, sitting, watching. Was he aware of what he was doing? If anyone approached him he spoke

223

normally, cheerfully, explaining he was busy when they tried to lure him from his post. He talked so convincingly, so reasonably to Nella who came to see for herself one day, it was impossible to find anything wrong with what he was doing, except that he was doing nothing. He accounted for himself without difficulty, improvising the tests and samples he claimed to be conducting, and since he had always been guarded about his projects, Nella sighed, hoping he was telling the truth. If he was not telling the truth she hoped he was not merely lying, if he was not lying she hoped he might not be deluded, if he was not deluded she hoped he might not be mad, because if he was mad she abandoned hope. He continued to do just enough, making it impossible for her to establish he was doing nothing. A certain quantity of papers, covered with fine writing, equations or calculations would be exposed to view upon occasion, and this contradictory evidence dispelled her inquiry. Their life together continued unchanged, superficially at any rate, but Nella's impatience increased as the grounds for her dissatisfaction were carefully excluded. Over the years Spohr had practised deception and his round cheerful face behind the steel rimmed glasses revealed nothing, his blue eyes bright when he knew she was looking at him, a lassitude clouded them when she looked away. These were critical years and his weapons, those instruments of reason he had polished, none of them could do anything for him. If he was troubled nothing he said betrayed him, only once in a moment of irritability he spoke almost vindictively about Thomas Archer. Nella did not discuss Spohr's difficulties with anyone. Her respect for him, the conviction that she would in some way betray him by suggesting his mind, his balance, might have shifted or tipped precluded that. Years later when Spohr had been dead for more than ten years, she told Sevcik her husband had been subject to recurring visions of Tom during this period, visions which immobilized him and convinced her Tom was dead. Sevcik had by that time become a prosperous business consultant, his stock market predictions eagerly if surreptitiously sought. He was to stand as an independent candidate in a forthcoming provincial election, his wife Birgitte as tightlipped and supportive as ever, pleased that her faith in Sevcik was about to be validated. She had never for a moment doubted his moral ascendancy, and now the time was coming when the rest of the world would share her trust. He was of course, defeated. Spohr would have enjoyed the spectacle. In the years when he and Nella were moving away from each other across open rivers of time or indifference, she spoke to no one as Spohr's peculiar behavior separated him from his friends.

People had once flowed through their diverting home, a quiet stream of actors, painters, students, philosophers, musicians, journalists, scholars, businessmen — they all admired him, consulted him and took his advice. From the moment Archer disappeared the stream gradually diminished; the tide flows in and the tide flows out. It made little difference to Spohr, at least if it did he never said so, when he met his old friends he was cordial and relaxed, offering advice if they asked as he always had, without surprise, with a painstaking attentiveness to the smallest details. However, when Eddy returned after a year and a half on the west coast where he worked on a tanker and bootlegged for the Indians, he felt that Spohr had lost his grip, had lost all caution: when he spoke, no matter how smoothly, how persuasively, he failed to assimilate the consequences of what he said. He was like a lawyer so sure of his ability to win he played all the cards openly, without regard for any incidental damage he might inflict. His clients became his victims, unwilling to dispense with so gifted an advocate but devastated by the cost. Then later, when Eddy's estranged wife arrived in search of her roaming husband, Spohr had befriended Rosalind at once. Although she talked incessantly she was quite beautiful; Spohr made love to her without hesitation. 'Didn't you want me to?' he asked Eddy, surprised that some objection was offered, 'Don't you see how untenable her position became as soon as she went to bed with me?' burying his complicity in an avalanche of innocence. 'I don't like to think of myself as a cuckold, no matter how old-fashioned that sounds,' Eddy replied with discomfort. 'Look old man, I'm terribly sorry if I've offended you,' said Spohr ingenuously. 'Well it's quite all right of course, just as long as you understand me on this point, I admit there were no reproaches by the time she caught up with me.' Spohr saw to it that Rosalind, properly counseled, found Edwin soon enough for him to assume paternity of the child he had inadvertently fathered upon his friend's wife. Rosalind was sent back to England again for the birth of her second child who, in later years, bore a striking resemblance to her natural father. Edwin felt that Spohr had gone too far, and this was characteristic, he pushed things beyond the limit not merely because he was curious to observe what happens outside normal relations, normal values, something else seemed to motivate him. It was this slight aberration, this not quite rational edge which Eddy couldn't put his finger on. Spohr accounted for the things he had said or done so plausibly, 'Didn't you want me to?' actually surprised, it was hard to maintain the suspicion that some aspect of his behavior was not exactly right. Since it was impossible to get the better of him in any discussion, the most you could hope for was a draw granted by tolerance on Spohr's part, Eddy thought it unlikely he would ever penetrate his defenses. Then later, much later, after he had received word that Spohr was dead Eddy wrote two harsh letters to Sally, berating his dead friend's lack of discretion, his apparent incapacity for ordinary life. Sally was shocked by the brutal, insensitive language, but attributed much of it to Edwin's grief at Spohr's abrupt departure from life. Hers followed soon after. Of those who had been close to Spohr, Sally was the only one who did not believe he had changed significantly before his death. She recognized a sadness in him, especially after Nella left, for the rest she found nothing unusual, he was solid, her friend, helpful, considerate, affectionate. They had an understanding of each other, a warm and rare thing. Sally trusted him absolutely, would have done anything for him, anything to save him from the boredom which growled at his heels like an angry dog, the sickness which reached into his chest, squeezing his heart with a single, powerful spasm until he died. They talked and laughed together about the verdict of their friends who found him wanting in some way. Were they perhaps disappointed, frustrated because his immense gift, the dazzling intellect seemed, as his life unfolded, not to mean so much? They studied their friends' expectations and were amused, comforted even, by the spectacle of feelings that could not be concealed. When he realized the money he needed for his larger, more important projects would probably not be forthcoming he put that work aside, reluctantly but without rancor, turning to smaller, trifling assignments he set himself from time to time when his interest was aroused. Quite happy to leave the city for days by himself on the farm, if the hunger for town life and its bustle overtook him he fell naturally back into the strange life he had established there. As Nella grew farther and farther away from Spohr she was unaware that his life remained more or less unchanged. His mood was different, the dark side which had filtered through occasionally in the early years of their marriage now cast a somber shadow about him. There was however, a faint outline, the projection of a new, a milder man to come, a man whose roughness had been eroded by the waves of his life as they broke upon him, one by one. So even the shadow he cast was ambiguous, like the formless shadow in Archer's painting; Spohr became incomprehensible to his wife. As he changed he became more like her, but this she was unable to see because Nella herself was more like the old Spohr she had married, the old Spohr who was the younger man. He was never truly honored except by Sally whose death followed closely on his. His life was a meteoric shower, a brilliant stream which exploded for the smallest breath of time on the galactic clock, then fizzled abruptly, vanishing without a trace. Nella became more and more like cool water before Spohr's death, she was calm, undisturbed, flowing quietly away from him downstream to a life which was easier, more manageable, away from the upcountry wastes where every rock was a dangerous problem, every current a magnetic pull to be resisted, where comfort could only be sought at the small fires of logic.

When Eddy left for the west coast he promised Sally they would be separated for three or four months at most — he would earn some money and they would go to England together, to his home. He phoned a week later, Marguerite's house a few doors away from Spohr's where Sally had taken refuge. As he described the cross-country drive in his little red MG which expired in the mountains, was replaced by the cheapest blue Chevrolet he could buy, he was a bit drunk, affectionate and misrepresenting when he claimed to have stayed with 'a nigger family' in Chicago. He meant that a black girl had taken him in for a couple of nights of whiskey and casual love, but Sally only understood that much later. She had come to live at Marguerite's house when Eddy went away. They had been obliged to leave Spohr's the previous autumn when Mrs. Hurst, tightly corseted and already protected against the cold by her grey Persian lamb coat, ejected them. 'Mr. Spohr,' she said in her even, heavily accented way, 'I rented my house to you and your wife, one couple, not two. Either your unmarried friends leave or I shall consider you to have broken the terms of our agreement.' None of Spohr's blandishments had the slightest effect upon her, she was insistent, unmovable. Edwin and Sally left quickly to avoid embarrassing their friends; they found an old farmhouse beyond the northeast edge of town and settled in happily, commuting in and out every day, a full hour's drive each way. They deduced Mrs. Hurst's real displeasure lay in their unmarried state, shrugging without concern that her tolerance stopped just short of unhallowed love. Spohr discovered by chance during the following year that it was something Nella had said which made the old lady notice them at all, wondering whether his wife might not have preferred the irritation of rent day to the inconvenience of never being alone. She might have put Mrs. Hurst up to it but he deferred his investigation, planning to save that for some unpredictable skirmish in the future. The battlements of indifference and deceit are long in preparation.

When Edwin on his well-deliberated impulse decided to go west for the summer, Sally left their house at the back of town and returned to the city. Looking back sadly during the slow months of their separation she could distinguish four phases in their year together, each one bringing her closer to the inevitability which the incident in the garden clearly harbingered. At first in the early days, for a month or two, Edwin had craved her like a drug and she willingly dispensed everything, holding nothing in reserve, letting him glut his appetite; in doing so she awakened her own, completely. *Ich schau' dich an.* She cared for him, thought his charming ways were innocent rather than calculating, was touched by the

230

fervor he brought to whatever he did, his studies, his work, and especially the drinking which became the imperative, the motivating force. She found this recklessness something she understood, joining him at once, never doubting the gaiety or powers the alcohol released were genuine. She drank exclusively to attain a giddy pinnacle from which she could survey all she had ever wanted, knowing she need only stoop to retrieve the prizes, but Eddy drank to clarify something for himself. He was full of fun, considered everything amusing, became briefly more articulate, then as the ability to speak coherently deserted him, what remained was a giggling which might last for some time, a condition he never tried to explain, and finally he would collapse glumly, grimly, sometimes becoming abruptly sick, more often than not passing out immediately afterwards. Hangovers, the shakes, the willies he called it, followed invariably but with good humor and a resumption of the drinking which surged forward in a slow crescendo as the day progressed, abating at intervals, certain plateaus of rest, with the climax in the evening. That was the style of so many days, the pattern Sally automatically adopted. There was briefly a quality of ecstasy between them, a frenzy she took for the purest, most exquisite feeling she had ever known. During this short-lived time there was no self-examination, there was no questioning the passion, the intensity they inhabited. It was the landscape of their paradise, a purely sensory bliss which flared, brilliant with light, a fire which could not be approached and could not be expected to burn that way again. *Ich schau' dich an.* A perpetual springtime flowered until she saw his hand exploring another secret that day in the garden. The humiliating agony, the treachery sent her sobbing to their room, away from Spohr's cool compassion, 'Did you think he would never look at another woman?' She had not thought about that, it had not occurred to her such bliss would end. This marked the end of the first phase and the beginning of the second which continued until his trial late in the summer. During that time they had a sense of interlocking futures; in many ways little had changed between them, but once in awhile the shadow of his hand, groping and curious, came between them; the shadow lengthened across their delight as summer advanced. Sally knew what she hadn't known before, there was an end to this, it was finite and human, what happened before would happen again. She was caught in a net she had cast herself, no one could cut the filaments which bound her, no one could rewrite the lines, he as enmeshed in his part as she in hers. She loved him sadly and forgivingly knowing he was bound to betray her. *Ich schau' dich an.* What else could he do? The trial for his offenses committed at the time of the accident was a weight hovering over them, binding them together. Fearing the consequences deeply, he hired an expensive lawyer to plead for him and was readily acquitted. They celebrated his victory over the August holiday weekend, touring the countryside, stopping at drab, inglorious local hotels still to be found in little hamlets, all untouched by the crust spreading like a sore around the more populous areas. Obliged to choose between a place to sleep and the drink which was, after all, the object of the journey, they slept two nights in the car, Sally cramped and curled around the steering wheel, Edwin stretched out behind, his long legs dangling over the side of the car. The first night they parked in a shady laneway under the maple trees and went wading in a stream when they woke up. The second night was rather dark as Sally drove right into the middle of an unenclosed pasture. In the morning they found themselves surrounded by dozens of mooing, lumbering Holsteins who looked upon their invasion with scant tolerance. Eddy retreated carefully, expecting the noisy, backfiring red car to provoke a stampede at any moment. Excited by their absurd situation they roared off down a country road in dense clouds of dust and uncontrolled laughter. Sally had him stop farther along the way, running back to an orchard, picking a few greenish apples for their breakfast. The outraged farmer who had suffered more losses in that way than he could tolerate was waiting with a loaded shotgun, he took aim and missed. Sally ran, laughing so hard she tripped and stumbled as she looked over her shoulder to find him in hot pursuit on his tractor, a young boy driving, the distraught farmer standing behind him taking wild shots. When Sally got back to the car quite incapable of speech, she could only mime instructions to Eddy, sobbing, gurgling sounds all that could be produced. Finally he understood and put his foot down on the accelerator, mercifully the car responded, then off they sped. Eddy looked rather displeased, finding her hilarity incomprehensible. 'Don't you see how ridiculous, how totally improbable it was for me, for Sally Reger to be shot at by a farmer from an ancient tractor? It was like being someone else, like finding myself in another time period or like waking up in the wrong play, it was too funny, it was the funniest thing that's ever happened in my life, don't you see?' Loosed from the ties which bound them before the trial, the sense of inevitability began to dissipate, Sally noticed a change, a shift in his attitude. Nothing happened, nothing she could identify made the third stage very different from what came before, yet the separation had begun, his desire was adrift like a raft at sea. As the summer came quietly to its end and autumn's cool fingers touched the days, winding them down, tightening them, making them respond to the stroke of the wind and the rain, she felt him quite casually slip away. *I, too, was fair, and that was my undoing.* The abortion, necessarily illegal, was not without its comic side. Sally was horrified when she discovered she was pregnant, thinking she would never bring another creature into the world, a child who, like herself, might not give thanks for the favor, who might some day spend her time listening for the crack of oblivion in the brain. And then she dreamt sadly about going away by herself to rear the child, a companion, a remembrance of their brief, perfect love. She realized this was a hopeless fantasy and began to search for someone to do the thing. Everyone had a friend who had undergone that barbarous procedure at one time or another, but the practitioners moved around frequently, making themselves hard to find. She eventually confessed her difficulty to Edwin who groaned with rage. Later she could never decide which of them his anger was directed against. 'Am I some damn kind of stud?' he ground out between his teeth, not without pride. It so happened that one of his former coworkers, a truck driver for the national television service, had a wife, a 'nurse' who helped ladies in trouble, and the matter was soon arranged. For one hundred and fifty dollars, a decent although not a bargain rate the job was done, a working class district over in the east end near Jones Avenue. Eddy was invited downstairs to the basement for beer and a game of darts while Sally hopped up on the kitchen table, 'Well,' she said nervously making conversation, 'I suppose this is preferable to childbirth.' The 'nurse' paused, a mysterious implement poised in midair, 'Don't you know what I'm going to do?' she asked. 'Why no, I haven't the slightest idea.' The technique was explained, friendly advice offered, the solution introduced. She finished by saying, 'Well I hope it takes the first time so you won't have to come back. Don't forget if you have to go to the hospital, say you did something yourself. Bye now, here's Eddy to take you home.' It was Spohr who stood by her during the gruesome ordeal the next day, Nella mysteriously away from home, Eddy at work. Perhaps there had been some prearrangement, perhaps Spohr was the only one who assessed the danger correctly. None of them spoke about it afterwards. Then the days grew colder and shorter, the sun drained away from the land. When Sally and Edwin moved from Spohr's house she recognized another change, this one marking the last phase before they were to separate forever. It was a cold winter and they spent most of their free time in town, often sleeping overnight in their old room at Spohr's. They were invited to parties at which Edwin would dance with another woman, not a succession of women, just one, all evening. Quite often it was Marguerite if Bollard was not there, once the faithful Lisa succumbed to his charm while Schradieck drove his cab; Sally would sit in a dark corner, contorted with grief, incapable of leaving, incapable of reproaching him, incapable even of tears. Her mouth twitched, she did not speak to anyone, she did not drink, she could only tremble like a stricken deer. Once on the long drive home she asked, 'Do you do it to torment me?' He replied, 'O you know how it is.' She did, there was nothing more to be said. When he left she rented the empty room at Marguerite's house to be close to Spohr and Annie March. Nella who had been her friend seemed distant. Possibly her delight in Sally had not been strong enough to survive the alliance which emerged beside her, or to endure the hectic duet played with such passion in their living room every day. Although she was not unkind, she had retracted the clause of pure friendship during the sonorous summer days and nights as her husband with his two allies laughed and drank and talked. It was probably the talk which drove her away, the haggling, speculative talk which ground each word to fine powder while they examined its meaning. She saw no point in it, what they said did not deepen her understanding, change her feelings or affect the way she lived. Nella might have given the impression she was indecisive or vague, actually she was practical, committed to living in explicit accordance with what she believed, not studious, far from it, but firm about the things she was prepared to encompass and resolute in what was rejected. It did not occur to her to comfort Sally when Eddy went west.

He telephoned from Vancouver more than a week after his departure. At one o'clock in the morning Sally stood barefoot in the unlit hallway beside the telephone, a crystal laugh in her throat at the sound of his voice. They both laughed and cried, she offered to come at once, he said it would better to wait, if he found a ship she would be happier there among friends. She told him no matter what happened to her, no matter what happened to him, she would love him as long as there was life in her body and beyond. That was the last time they ever spoke to each other. When she hung the receiver up Bollard suddenly appeared in the dark, 'I'm sorry, I know I shouldn't have listened, I couldn't help overhearing you at first and then I couldn't bear to miss the rest. What you said touched me, no one has ever spoken to me like that, I've never spoken to anyone like that.' He took her hand gently, possibly intending only friendliness, but they had both felt a key turn in a lock as Sally withdrew quickly.

When I left Spohr I wanted to be alone, uninfluenced, neutral, responsible only to myself like a green plant in the sun. I needed to establish my equilibrium, find a sense of balance apart from the weights and measures Spohr had assigned me over the years we spent together. He had infected my perception, the mode of perception and my capacity to perceive. He had effectively circumscribed everything I experienced, grounding intuition with a quiet derision which did not consist so much of mockery, he was too polite, too civilized ever to be rude or condescending, but of a continuing invitation to reexamine the things I valued. The request was invariably so pleasant, so liberal, so fair and magnanimous it was unthinkable not to comply, and even when he wasn't able to eradicate an idea, the shadow of doubt, not to mention his displeasure, inevitably eroded something I could never quite recover. I couldn't take anything for granted, not my preference for wearing white or gold, not my taste for spicy Italian food, not my belief in astrological influences, homeopathic remedies and certain esoteric matters which are better undiscussed, undisclosed. A concept, a word, sensations, feelings which had not been scoured by his scrutiny could not be claimed until they passed that ordeal, until they had been made acceptable at the tables of his truth. Quite often a thing was no longer any use to me once it had been scrubbed to his specifications. He didn't intend to be repressive, this however, was the result. Everyone was subject to the same polite, scrupulous examination, that was his way and most of the people we knew found it helpful, almost flatteringly indulgent, like the attentions of a perceptive analyst, to have their thoughts scanned and rebuilt. They were not obliged to live with his constant scrutiny. I had not expected him to die, just like that, pouf and he was gone. How could I have known? If I had imagined him dead in one year, or five or even ten for that matter, I would never have left him. The truth is I loved him, was devoted to him, admired him, respected him, only I was afraid he might wear me out, not with his infidelity, I was not myself restrained in that way, but with the pressure, the weight of his presence, his intellectual minuteness, the scientific absolutes. That was the theatre of our war, our rational battleground, and he was winning without any doubt. O I won the odd skirmish, it was hard though because we always played his game, with his rules. When I first came to Spohr as a bride

238

I accepted that, wanted it, wanted his understanding, the imposition of his values. He used to look somewhat forbidding, a smiling face dominated by cold blue eyes which looked askance above the spectacles, his hard, round body slightly overweight, the rather outmoded style of dress often garish. I had a simple advantage however, he loved me. It irritated him but he did love me, not in the way he was successively infatuated with several women over the years of our marriage, that was the romantic side he kept concealed. He loved me in a solid enduring way, classically, as his wife, an adjunct to himself. In becoming that, by embodying his abstractions it was necessary to put away certain aspects of myself, and the only way I could reclaim this submerged territory was to cut myself away from him, my refuge which had become a prison. I did it, cast myself on open waters hoping to float in time back to my own country, making good the defection which brought me there in the first place. The marriage had seemed like a fair bargain at the time, except I had no way of knowing what the transaction would entail. In pursuit of knowledge I acted in ignorance, even though I might have chosen what was right for myself. Let me declare openly that my choice was dictated by good intentions and bad reasons, that it took many years until my uneasiness at relinquishing one kind of treasure for another which didn't look particularly bright or valuable as the years passed, until my uneasiness grew so heavy I could no longer bear the weight of it. I hadn't planned to move in with Sandy Burns, that just happened. Sandy was an attractive young man, sympathetic, an ardent admirer of Spohr's in fact, but I found him drifting in the waters where I launched myself when I cut loose. We did no more than drift together side by side until we made a decision which ended our aimless contiguity, we moved to New York together. Oddly enough his passion seemed to emanate from what amounted to a deep love of himself, his talent, his own body. He was so in love with that he had no need for a companion; in a way I thought his absorption in himself would leave me free. Spohr was distressed to think I went from being his wife straight to Sandy's bed, as he with modified righteousness put it. He would not have been so offended or mystified if I had remained alone. He knew what I thought of Sandy and this made no sense to him, running to such a man. There you are, that's the way it is, the things we do are occasionally unintelligible, even to ourselves. Still, I would do anything now to pull the thorn from his wound. When I look back through my own wrinkled mortality I feel his pain as if it had been mine, as if it had been a disease I never recovered from. Now that I am old myself I wonder what Spohr would have looked like, might have become. Sometimes I pass a man on the street, in a crowd or in a store, and I stop, thinking yes, he would have aged like that, his hair would have turned grey then white, a little thin on top, his fat cheeks would have kept their resilience until at last they might have drooped, gracefully. What made him somewhat formidable as a younger man would have become his advancing years, would have enhanced his figure in old age, and whenever I recognize that quality in a passing stranger I am pierced by the thorn I left, almost casually, on his path, certainly without the rancor some friends attributed to me. Poor Spohr, who would ever have thought I would live to say poor Spohr? He was such a strong man, so deliberate in every act, he never did anything in haste, was never impulsive, never impetuous. Perhaps he was right, perhaps I would have come back to him in the end, who can say? He knew me better than I knew myself in some ways, but he was squeezing the life from me, drop by drop. He had my heart in his heavy fist, squeezing the secrets from it one by one.

I don't go out much now, in the city I guess I never did. I stay at home, look out the window or watch the televised world go past. It rocks me, comforts me much as my mother's old rocker used to soothe her, and then there is the pleasure in being alone, my own master, my own servant. Am I like her now? How indifferent we were to each other, right till the end. Neither of us ever pretended any emotion we didn't feel, and she kept silent until her death; if she rocked to the tune of some unspoken sorrow or joy she rocked it to her grave. Sally who was my friend . . . we understood each other perfectly from the moment we met. It's hard to believe all this happened in the same lifetime, so long ago a mist like memory has dimmed the shape of time, the dotted row of events clinging like beads to a curve in space. My dear Sally who was beautiful, who was my friend, they broke her heart, literally. First they wrung her dry, the faith and love, those liquids pressed out like wine, her body tossed on a desolate shore where she lay gasping, unable to breathe. All she wanted was to love, to be faithful, to trust in God, only it didn't suit them, they took that away from her and she perished, she died of it, her heart cracked with longing. When we met she was so riddled with grief for her brother I thought she might not survive. She seemed to be waiting, listening and waiting for the bullet which flew through his brain, pasting the ghastly particles to the pillow, the wall, the chest of drawers, waiting for the same bullet to penetrate her skull with the long clear whistle that would blow her to eternity. She walked around, tears once in awhile pouring down her face like Cecily Turnbull, poor thing, marching up and down Avenue Road moaning O dear, O dear, at nothing in particular. Sally's eyes were unfixed, bound by no horizon we could see, but her heart was visibly bound with grief. What exploded instead was a bullet of love in that springtime long ago, the bullet which spattered her brain, tore her heart and sped the ghostly body in search of a grave. What could I do, what could I do? I watched an alliance emerge — she was happy for awhile in their mad pursuit of pleasure, only they drained her of love and faith. I have to keep reminding myself Spohr was not an evil man, Edwin was merely foolish. He didn't reject what was offered, he merely ran out of the need for it. They thought between them to save her; if only they had known she could have saved them, she could have saved them but they finished her off, crushed her, broke her like an egg. Sometimes I miss Sally more than I've ever missed Spohr, and I was the one who sent her away. Twice, to save her if I could. It didn't work, her death is a monument, a tower of darkness which fills me with sorrow. *O weep for Adonais,* she was so bloody young. I got them out of our house thinking she would hold him off, defend herself, protect what was precious. They were so dependent on Spohr by then it was too late, she didn't see, she didn't know. She rejoiced in her own dismemberment, the slow interring of the purity which had saved her again and again. I thought something might be coaxed up again, might filter through if there were just the two of them, alone, away from us, away from Spohr. I hadn't counted on so rapid a disaffection from Eddy. He had always wandered from woman to woman, like Spohr even through the seams of his marriage. Tom used to talk about Sally, he had admired her fire and her beauty. She was such a remarkable woman I could hardly believe Eddy put her aside casually, just like that, done, thank you very much, that's it for now, I'm off. All she needed was a little looking after, with time she might have risen above their scruples, might have understood their hollow truth had no power, that she was right and they were wrong. O God, the pity of it. Well what's done is done, I can't hold it against Edwin any more than I can hold it aginst Spohr.

During the year and a half Eddy was on the west coast he wrote occasionally to Spohr. Brief, witty airmail letters would arrive regaling us with his adventures, first on a tanker off the coast and then in Fort St. James where he took up residence as bootlegger to the native population. Life on the tanker was hard but he enjoyed the physical release and earned enough to accommodate his almost regal need for dissipation. If Spohr noticed Eddy's insistence upon being a gentleman on the one hand and his random capitulation to varieties of degradation on the other, he never commented. I always found the contrast between his attitudes and his actions oddly attractive. In some ways he was like a magnetic needle pulled from direction to direction as circumstances dictated, he had no fixity, no point

which was solidly his own. When he said farewell to life on the
tanker he went on a spectacular binge, the details remaining
obscure even to himself. In a letter he described with
amusement how he woke days later in the bunk of a seaman he
barely knew, with that sailor sprawled naked alongside him.
'Who knows,' he wrote, 'The fellow might even have
deflowered me.' That seemed funny to him. The next word we
had, months later, was from Fort St. James, a village up in the
northwest, a Hudson's Bay fort where he settled for a year in
the company of a woman, an Indian whom I have no doubt he
treated badly. I think she had his child although he was never
explicit about that. All this time he did not once write to Sally;
she never stopped expecting him to return, not for a moment.
Ah sorrow, ah sweet sorrow. That period in her life was dark, a
black flower blossoming at the tip of an ever lengthening stem.
I have never seen anyone so wretched, except Tom when he
was going mad and trying to hang on. She spent her time alone,
weeping by herself, not caring for company, not caring for any
alleviation of her sorrow, it was all she had. She stayed at
Marguerite's house down the street from us, and except for
Annie March there were times when I don't think she spoke to
anyone for days, possibly weeks at a time. She came once in
awhile to visit us, never asking about Eddy, although Spohr
quietly let her know when he had word from him, treating his
communications lightly. Once with abrupt lewdness he said,
'We musn't be surprised if he comes out of the wilderness with
his member,' he used an obscene word, 'Chopped and trimmed
in accordance with some obscure ritual of anthropological
interest alone.' Another time he sketched in a few revealing

244

episodes and turned to me when she went out to the kitchen saying, 'I don't think we went too far that time, do you?' She overheard him and answered for me, 'No my dear Spohr, you didn't, not this time.' She left in tears, her tall slender form a broken stalk in the wind. *Have mercy upon her, there are enough women in hell.* I don't know what happened to Eddy, we lost track of each other after Spohr's death. Some years later I heard that he had come into his inheritance at last, a fortune sadly diminished by the world's economic woes, that he spent his short remaining time travelling around drunkenly with a woman some years his senior, a rather sinister woman by all accounts, with whom he seems to have formed a more or less permanent liaison. But Spohr, I wonder what he would think now. Sometimes I suspect I might never have been free if he hadn't died, just leaving him wouldn't have been enough; his shadow was always there casting its disbelief across my intentions. Sandy was intimidated too in a way. I think he must have regretted the forfeit of Spohr's friendship, although Spohr himself was too diplomatic to let us make a complete break. He kept trying to maintain normal relations among the three of us, even insisting on visiting New York on weekends occasionally. Sandy and I stewed with discomfort while Spohr enjoyed himself, or at least pretended to, particularly when I made them sleep together in one bed while I slept alone in the other. He made lascivious comments all night, chuckling to himself between swallows of bourbon. I had to admire him, he was a brilliant strategist granting the illusion of separation, not quite letting go. 'Nella,' he said, 'Of course you are free, I would be the last person in the world to detain you. Decide how you want to live, if you find me an impediment my dear, then naturally you must be on your own, for awhile at least. When you tire of this please do come home, I am rather accustomed to you. And you, don't you find yourself turning to me automatically, for little things, as you always did?' That was the point, he had set the controls on a course which followed his. This was the force I somehow had to break away from, and I did in the end, after he died. The other day I saw someone who reminded me of the man Spohr might have become if his destiny had not played wanton tricks with his life. This man is younger than Spohr would be now, his hair is white, his face immobile, and he is rationally impeccable in spite of the atrocities he has been subject to. I heard Spohr's voice when he spoke, the words flowing without hesitation, calmly, unemphatically and yet with conviction, flowing from the round, unsmiling face set in a colored void. He had been tortured, more or less arbitrarily by political and military opponents in his native land, although torture, I suppose, is always arbitrary. He identified what had happened as his particular experience held up to be examined, to sicken us with its existence, held up like a jewel, a stunning refraction, illuminating coolly, facet by individual facet, imperturbably. A man of extraordinary dignity, he described how his life for a time had been nothing more than a predictable howl attached to an electrode, how he was teaching himself, training himself to remember the agony, the disbelief in another prisoner's naked eye as he lay bound and moaning on the concrete floor of an adjacent cell, how that eye had become his secret, his own perpetual memorial. Spohr was a man of such reasoned dignity too. For a time he seemed to hold us in the palm of his hand, in the light of his eye, and yet he too went down at the polls, the general, the custodian who wrested knowledge from its source. Perhaps that's just what we do, each of us, if we don't cheat, if we honor our commitments. Is it enough, did Spohr strike a bad bargain? At first he knew and then he did not; I was his wife and then I was not; we were young and then we were not. I cannot say, I do not know.

Monty Wells, aseptically drunk in the company of Marten Bender pressed the doorbell at number 18 Bellair Street. *'Dixhuit malheur'* he pronounced. 'Ah,' as Annie March opened the door, 'Madam, we seek refuge from the Women's Christian Temperance Union, may we come in?' 'Granted,' she replied laughing, 'You've come on serious business I see, welcome.' Both Bender and Wells were a little in awe of Annie, they admired her apparent solitude and respected her cheerfulness. Neither had any way of knowing she spent two evenings a week befriending and encouraging the sorriest specimens of humankind at an obscure downtown mission where they congregated. In those days the lonely, the abused, the desperate came there when they had no place to go, when even the street rejected them. Some were foul, filthy, others were incapacitated by cheap wine and Aqua Velva. To all these Annie offered coffee and normal conversation devoid of blame or preaching. She lost at cards, sometimes she beat them at checkers or dominoes, laughing with pleasure when she won. There were a few whose voices were so eroded they could only growl, a gurgle at the back of the throat, and they hardly knew her from week to week. Most were attracted by her warmth. She tolerated no misbehavior, yet there was no presumption of authority, only a declaration of the possible, always with humor, with compassion. She gave little thought to changing them, even those who preserved distant recollections of family or job or home. All she could do was put a pillow between their broken bodies and the pavement which drew them down, the appalling human refuse of the city. Most of them were men; a few bleak, foulmouthed women called her Miss Annie when they were sober and abusive epithets when they were not. Little enough could be done beyond sending them to a hospital if necessary, inviting them to use their limited bathing facilities if they would, giving them coffee and something other than the depravity of the street which had long since depleted their bones and destroyed their nerves. There was one old man whose eye had been put out in his nameless past, all that remained was a dirty yellow mark on the eyeball crisscrossed with a scar. Among the filthy he was conspicuous; like most others he lived in his clothing, the garments now a crusty carapace standing stiffly away from his stooped, snarling form. He spoke to no one, it never occurred to anyone to speak to him. He'd appear glowering in a corner of the room, standing out even in that company. There was a pair, a man and woman who preserved some remote matrimonial bond, the woman signifying this connection with a few obscene gestures. They spoke to each other in loud, mucilaginous voices incomprehensible to the rest of the world. Others who merely suffered the extremity of their lives survived mutely or with gusto as the mood took them. Annie had been coming here regularly for a couple of years, attaching little to what she did, quite clear about the hopelessness in that corner of the world. She was moved but not repelled, as if she had to hold the worst there was to her nose, her eyes, her ears, to learn the debauchery of the senses. Unmotivated by thoughts of serving the poor or a humbling charity, when Annie first stumbled across the mission she saw something was needed which it did not seem right to withhold.

Now she invited Bender and Wells in, happily diverted from her writing for once. The experiments in prose left her baffled, she never entirely knew what it came from, while the poetry she felt, was embedded at the root of her sanity, just where it branched off into uncharted wilderness, a wild garden which bloomed according to its own unpredictable seasons. 'Please Annie,' said Bender sucking on his pipe, 'Can you lend me a cigarette?' 'I don't smoke, Marguerite does, I'll get you some.' He was embarrassed to ask, but not quite so embarrassed as not to ask at all. Years later when he had established a moderate reputation he would still, when meeting a friend, importune from habit, 'Please, can you lend me a cigarette?' Annie returned to the dining room, the communal household room, with Marguerite and the cigarettes. Monty was delighted, she was the object of his visit. He was now passing through an apparently lucid interval, having drawn himself in from that borderless state, that climate with no perimeter occupied earlier, the change primarily inspired by respect for Annie March and an accurate surmise of how much she would tolerate. A plan formed somewhere behind his confusion gave him the semblence of rationality, a secret winding through like a bright thread thoughtfully concealed. 'I don't know why,' said Marguerite neither approving nor disapproving, 'Everyone seems to be drunk all the time these days.' 'Who could otherwise endure it my dear?' asked Wells. 'Endure what?' 'This,' he said pointing to his own body, 'This, this.' 'Ah, a tragic note,' commented Bender, 'Prince Hamlet in disguise.' 'I have no disguise, this is it, me, incarnate, in person. Why should some royal malcontent have my best lines? I'll play it myself damn you, without an understudy.' Capering around the room his tall, prematurely bent figure opened and closed like a knife, its point barbed and murderous. 'I adore you,' he declared dropping a bow at Marguerite's feet. She laughed in a lascivious way. Monty sat down at the old upright piano beside the doorway leading to the hall, but as soon as his fingers touched the keys he stopped, immobilized by the sound which rose to his ears. He struck the keys again, played several bars and turned to Annie with a bewildered, almost hurt look. Then he turned to the keyboard once more in disbelief as a loose, clattering tumult responded to his touch. 'What is it?' he asked recoiling from the piano. Marguerite and Annie laughed together. 'A friend of Nella's,' explained Annie, 'Dropped by with her last week, played the piano awhile, decided it was a poor old thing and made a few home improvements, as he called it. The thumbtacks on the hammers give it a metallic twang, like a harpsichord, don't you care for it? He thought it was much better.' 'My God,' moaned Wells, 'How crass, how can I play Chopin with thumbtacks on the hammers?' 'Forget Chopin,' advised Bender, 'Play Bach instead.' 'Do you expect me to seduce Marguerite with that mineralized thumping? I need passion, I need crescendos, I need rolling arpeggios to woo this lady, not a handful of broken, tinkly sounds.' Everyone was laughing except Wells who seemed to be serious, quite stricken, as though his secret had been ripped from him and torn to shreds before his eyes. 'You're awfully sweet Monty, but never mind, don't feel bad about the piano.' They laughed again as Wells joined in with a false, ringing staccato which rode unnaturally high above theirs, making them laugh even harder. Bender recovered, 'My dear Wells you are a great teacher, a fine musician and a complete ignoramus. Now you play something or I'll play Scriabin, thumbtacks or no thumbtacks.' Monty uttered some indecency and turned back to the keyboard. Once the ear was accustomed to the sound it wasn't unpleasant. 'I have it,' said Monty, 'It's a lute, I'll win this creature like a troubadour of old, improvising on my love, a boogie woogie balladeer.' Everyone was amused as he began to shout out his song in a strident, tuneless falsetto. While they applauded Jan appeared grimacing and sour in the doorway, startling everyone with his unexpected appearance. Bender went to shake his hand, but Jan shoved him away with uncharacteristic roughness as he stormed upstairs. They froze in uncomfortable silence. The hot, moody light of an August afternoon filtered through the open doorway and tall narrow window, folding them in a mothy chiaroscuro, uniting their dumb discomfort,

251

orchestrating the silence in rising, ringing planes. They looked at one another, their surprise paragraphed in a single breath. Bender spoke, 'Marguerite, perhaps you should . . .' 'No, no, it's all right, he's been like that lately, it's nothing, he's worried about things. There's no point talking to him now, this will blow over.' Monty leaped up knocking over his chair, running around the room to apologize in a voice which came thinly from his throat, sounding insincere. He often spoke that way, perhaps it was an ironic inflection adopted for lecturing, perhaps something else, nevertheless it rang flat and hollow. 'Look I'm terribly sorry, this is all my fault, what a disruption I've caused. Marguerite, if I've offended you or Jan I'll never forgive myself, I'm such a fool. Please forgive me, I'm so clumsy, now see what I've done. You'll never invite me here again, this is awful, terrible, I'm sorry. Annie, will you pardon my imbecility just this once, please?' 'Monty yes, now stop, there's nothing to forgive, surely you understand it had not that much to do with you.' They all began to speak at once like chirping sparrows, laughing as the tension dissolved. Bender sucked noisily on his pipe until Marguerite offered a cigarette, then turning to Sally as she walked in, 'Don't you agree my dear Miss Reger, when it's a question of sorrow, a question of grief or sadness, it is essential to take the century eye view?' Sally smiled, 'Why Marten, that's true, one of the few sensible things I've heard anyone say about human misery. Then I guess if we actually manage the century there's always the millenium.' She laughed adding quietly to him alone, 'You can't imagine how wearing, how exhausting it is to be miserable all the time, like being at the bottom of a huge mountain you have climb again and again. No fun, believe me.' 'Then don't do it my dear, don't do it.' 'O well, there doesn't seem to be any choice, you know.' A stranger appeared in the open doorway. He was a slight man of medium height in rumpled light blue trousers which were a little too short, a white tee shirt, dark loafers and white socks. His brown hair was long and combed straight back off his face, the beard short and casually trimmed. His face was red, burned by the sun and an inner fire which shone from intense blue eyes which were slightly bloodshot, excessively bright. When he spoke the whites of his eyes were visible all the way around the blue. 'Hello folks,' he said, 'My name is James, I'm a street evangelist. I was looking for Jan, but are you interested in spiritual matters? Have you heard the voice of our Lord, have you been saved, have you been born again?' 'Good grief,' sighed Monty to Bender, 'A religious maniac, my day is complete.' Marguerite spoke quickly, 'Why don't you come in, what do you want to talk about?'

- It's simple really, I used to be a sinner like you, but the Lord took pity on me. Jesus directed me to be baptized and forgiven of my sins, that's what I'm offering you. Baptism, escape the wrath to come, wash away your sins and be free. Look at me, gentle as a lamb and total peace. This can be yours, would you like me to set you free?
- That's interesting James, said Monty, Forgiveness, peace, interesting indeed. Tell me, what do you do, how do you live, do you work?
- I'm engaged in the work of the Lord.

- How do you pay the rent?

- I've given up all that, the Lord provides.

- And where do you sleep at night?

- Wherever they take me in, can I stay here?

- Well that might be difficult, we don't have any room.

- Jesus always made room for one more. Let me tell you about my baptism, even Jesus had to be baptized to be freed of his sins, you know. This'll probably sound strange to you — I was fully immersed right here in Lake Ontario. If you would like to come down to the lake with me now I'll baptize you, set you free. You can't have your miracle if you don't accept that plunge. What do you have to lose? You're all wretched, lost and unhappy anyway.

- How long have you been doing this?

- It's six or seven years now since the Lord relieved my life of torment.

- Well James, I don't know why we should accept a word you say. Frankly, I don't find you convincing, said Monty.

- My friend, first you have to accept the baptism, then you'll know. Until then it's only talk. So come with me and find out, I've changed the life of many people in these few years.

- Do you have a church, an organization?

- No, we meet in the streets, out in the open, that's where God sent me to do His work.

- Do you read any other scriptures, do you know the teachings of anyone besides Jesus? What about the other prophets?

- Jesus is more than a prophet, he is God's only son, our savior, our Lord. God so loves us He sent His only son.

- Aren't we all God's children?

- Not in that way, Jesus died for us, for you and me. His blood alone can save us from the wrath to come.

- Now look, said Monty, Does your God have a form?

- He is a formless God.

- Then how on earth could He have produced a son?

- You'll understand this if you abandon your rebellious, disobedient ways. The truth will be clear to you.

- Do you think if I jump into Lake Ontario in the company of the dead fish, the rusty cans, the algae and the excrement I'm going to have some revelation?

- Yes my friend, I know it sounds hard to believe, but that's the truth, that's the long and the short of it. Well my goodness, my spirit raged within me until a few years ago, I know the torment you're in, I see your disobedience. Just look at me now and remember I was exactly like you. My peace will be yours, I have that power. I will heal you.

- James, asked Bender agreeably, Isn't that an awful responsibility you have vested in you? How do you handle it?

- I have no ego, I've overcome my sins and I have no ego, that's why I'm so free. Now come, why hesitate? All of you, come with me down to the lake, let me set you free.

- It's a nice offer, I'm afraid I can't take you up on it though.

- No one? Not one among you?

- James, I have the feeling we are wasting your time.

- No, no, don't give it a thought, this is my work. All you have to do is listen, submit and come with me. I'll change your life, I'll set you free of sin, save you from the terrible wrath to come. Give up your disobedience, leave your rebellious ways, listen to God's command. Do what He says, come, be baptized now.

- James, I'm sorry, said Annie, For your own sake don't say any more, we are not interested and we will not come with you. We don't want to hurt your feelings, it would probably be better if you left.
- Of course I'll leave if you don't want me to stay, but you're making a mistake, all of you. Repent before it's too late.

They stared at each other as he left. 'Annie,' said Monty, 'Why did you send him away, it might have been entertaining.' 'That's the reason, there is the breath of truth in his cuckoo talk, and that's nothing to be frivolous about, we could hurt him, we could hurt ourselves.' 'What bothers me,' said Marguerite, 'Is the way he proclaims everything by rote, as if he doesn't even hear what he's saying. He just goes on pouring out his little number without emphasis, and as far as I can tell without thought. The words are terrible, only he doesn't get excited, he isn't worked up, he just keeps repeating the same thing over and over again.' 'Crazy as a jaybird,' said Monty, 'Without a doubt. I know what Marguerite means though, I kept expecting him to wave his arms, to rant or just raise his voice a little, but he kept on in that conversational, matter-of-fact way — his eyes were edgy though. There's a tiger raging in there all right, and when it comes out, whew, look out! Did you know Marguerite, there are tigers everywhere, striped and loping the laneways of our lives, flaming faces, glittering slit-like eyes. They lie hidden at intersections, stalking their prey, intense. There are beasts who prowl the night, beasts of ecstatic slaughter; a carnivorous beauty pervades their lust. They seek us out Marguerite, they visit our private niches, our sanctuaries, and strip us down for pleasure. We retreat when they invade, my pretty, we hide in some crumbling fortress built against obsolete terrors, long since dissipated, supplanted by new and fragrant fears. Look out for tigers Marguerite, a deadly species nourished on sullen flesh who sip thin blood, lurking around the shadows of every indecency we commit. Ah yes, we do invite them in, look at this splendid, glowing beast, I'll take him in, tame him. Nice kitty, he'll be my pet, I'll stroke him, feed him, play with him and he'll be mine. Here kitty, kitty, kitty! Tigers unfortunately, do not make good pets, they're too big, too savage, and they eat you in the end, yet who will admit to that? Few, very few.' The light began to change while he was speaking, a sudden dark gold filled the room followed by a rushing, accelerated twilight. Trumpets of thunder split the skies with a roar. 'He speaks but don't listen, don't be seduced by the power, the terror, the fear, don't press against him, don't offer your body for his feast.' The stacked clouds were purple and rimmed with gold, then grey, then black as a burst of warm, white water fell from the sky, pounding the roof, the trees, the pavement. They crowded together at the doorway watching the water build in twisting rivers, rampaging through the gutter to the sewer where it crashed and slammed, then down to the waters of the lake. A brief frenzy and it was gone, the rain stopped, the leaves were magnetically green, all but translucent, darkness parted as the light returned. Marguerite began to dance around the room wagging her rump like a dog, almost barking with pleasure; the damp smell of charged earth rose in a mist they could taste. She stood behind Monty, touching him, saying in her silky accent, 'I know what you mean, I know what you mean.' He turned around quickly seizing her shoulders, 'Do you now, do you indeed?' He stared in a fixed, menacing way, then laughed as she danced her retreat, scampering across the room in mock terror. 'What's this, what's this?' asked Bender, 'What games are you playing now?' 'Only the voracious, deadly kind, so watch if you want but don't say a word.' Bender smiled, there was an elasticity in his disposition which tolerated what others might have construed as abuse. In any case, he liked to watch. Sally took Annie to the kitchen to make tea while Marguerite and Wells circled around each other, sniffing under the careful scrutiny of Marten Bender, a man who had great convictions and no scruples whatsoever. Spohr walked in unexpectedly, swaying in the cool light for a moment, sitting down at the dining room table. Bender laughed, 'Welcome to the zoo Spohr, we have a ferocious tiger on the loose, a prowling bitch, I hope Marguerite will forgive me for that, and yours truly,' counterfeiting a bow. 'You I take it, must be lord of the beasts, your servant sir.' Spohr glanced up following his nimble movements around the room. When Sally and Annie came back he began his little fable quickly, without preamble.

Once upon a time a dog, a tiger and a monkey set off on their travels. They made an ideal team, the dog with his nose for an obscure scent, the monkey calculating from a safe distance, and the tiger who prowled the limits of their terrain as guardian. They were adventurers, their journey had no object, they came and went pretty much like tourists, scavengers at the world's feast gorging on scraps, considering the spectacle but never quite taking in the point. They travelled light and they travelled fast expecting their perceptions to balance the speed times the distance covered. In the early years they toured the great north-south axis through the western hemisphere, starting from the glittering wastes in the Arctic where they found only ice, isolation and the thin ribbon of civilized settlements spread across a border thousands of miles long. City states they were, controlled by an ambivalent central authority. Life was pleasant but unspectacular, bland, too careful for the youth and vigor of their appetites.

They descended with pleasure into the open, central corridor of power with its vast corrupted cities ready to explode like poisoned fruit. 'There is something filthy, fecal and delicious here,' announced the dog to his companions, 'We might even settle down in this place. There are no secrets and they have almost miraculous technical competence, I could live in one of those bedrock dreams they fabricate, completely furnished, terribly comfortable. What do you think?' 'Well,' said the tiger, 'I think I know rapacity when I see it, seems to me like heavy competition.' Restless as ever the monkey picked at a flea on his chest, 'Look friends, we didn't say anything about settling down before, just forget your dream of aperitifs and aphrodisiacs, follow me.' They swung off down a multilane highway heading due south, not stopping until they crossed the next border, squeezing in through the Central American funnel. The language changed, the dreams remained beneath the pressure from above. They travelled a two lane road, a single lane highway, sometimes a dry riverbed, but small, naked children with swollen bellies lined both sides of their route wherever they went. They could look neither to the left nor to the right. 'Let's not stay for the revolution,' said the monkey, 'Go man, go!' They passed through the perilous isthmus pouring forth on the great southern plains and mountains which had been carved into national enclaves over the years. Within the self-destructive boundaries of each state some committed fratricide, matricide, patricide, infanticide, others dedicated themselves to homicide or suicide, developing as well a proficiency in lies, theft, cruelty, barbarism, depravity and torture.

In one of those countries, one with a considerable reputation for such exploits, the dog and the tiger fell in love with the same woman, spending months avoiding each other while they pursued their mutually exclusive aims. The monkey was seriously thinking of leaving his companions, of continuing on alone when the two were arrested by rival factions, each prisoner charged with spying for the K.G.B., the C.I.A. and assorted paraethnic organizations. In despair, the beautiful young woman who loved them both dearly begged the monkey to help rescue them. Challenged by this dangerous enterprise, he responded with all the ingenuity his mind was heir to, producing a scheme whereby each side attacked the other as the monkey escaped with the dog, the tiger and the woman in a fast flying jet to distant, transatlantic parts.

Here began the east-west axis of their journey. Times had changed now, the companions were older if not any wiser, and they had the added responsibility of caring for a beautiful woman. The tiger prowled less, didn't seem to mind staying

260

home nights once in awhile. The dog whose joy it had been to spend his days and nights in amorous pursuits now refused to leave the girl's side. The tricky little monkey, observing these changes in his fellow travellers, fretted and worried that their days of glory might have ended. It took all his skill to lure them from one sagging empire to the next with talk of cultures and capitals their imagination could scarcely aspire to. 'Really,' said the tiger, 'It's true I might once have cared for all this, perhaps been inspired by it. What can I say? When you've seen one damn pillared place you've seen them all.' The dog however, who had learned to court desire for its own sake, was not so easily bored; the monkey soon rekindled his flagging appetite. Between them they dragged the grumbling tiger along, and the woman of course, went where they told her to.

Bypassing the dark continent they proceeded east, eventually leaving the world as they knew it far behind, voyaging forth with something like the old instinct for wandering, for self-indulgence, there in the bazaars and arcane marketplaces of the Middle East. Then a strange thing happened, the three friends began to tire of the curious, the novel, the wonderful, hankering for home, wherever that was, familiarity, anything ordinary, predictable. Now the beautiful young woman encouraged them to keep going, 'You have come so far, seen so much, learned so little. Isn't it time to give point to this endless wandering, this senseless voyage? If there's one thing the east abounds in it's wise men, let's see what happens.' They were sceptical, also reluctant to take a woman's advice, but they were so bored they agreed without protest, touring the shrines and holy places with about as much enthusiasm as they had mustered lately for the marketplace. They visited ashrams, joined sacred pilgrimages, listened to the discourses of men reputed to wise and noticed only that the pickpockets worked these crowds a little more energetically. When the wise men spoke the tiger loped aimlessly through the crowd, yawning noisily or studying the audience for victims and rivals. The dog curled himself up in a circle, his nose under his tail, and went to sleep. The monkey, whose interest was occasionally aroused, seemed content to observe that none of them were half as clever as he was.

The beautiful young woman had led them now from the Middle East to the Far East; a comfortable but disquieting middle age settled upon the three companions. They came to the ends of the earth and nothing had changed. 'Well my dear friends,' said the woman who remained both young and beautiful, 'I won't abandon you now, but I don't mind saying I am disappointed at the way things turned out. Do you want to go home, wherever that may be?' 'Do we!' they shouted in unison, 'What a great idea!' So they travelled back in an unhurried way to a civilized city state adjacent to the great corridor of power, bought a house on a quiet street at the back of town where they settled down.

There they remain to this day. The rapacious tiger sometimes hears the old alarms although he is generally happy to lie about the house, and the dog has been known to stay out all night pursuing an old love, yet he too, more often than not, can be found on the sofa in front of the fire. The clever little monkey still plots and schemes even though his scope is purely local. What became of the beautiful woman? That's hard to say, some think she stayed on as their housekeeper, others insist she returned to her native land where she was imprisoned, others are equally certain she found new travelling companions.

'The real enigma Spohr,' remarked Bender, 'Is that you tell these stories at all.' Monty looked black, Marguerite was frowning. 'I know you didn't intend to be unkind,' said Annie, 'But Spohr, don't you think you've invited the possibility of a personal response?' 'There was a time,' said Monty, 'When your stories were ethical, instructive, now I think you've become a little barbarous, vicious perhaps. What do you say old man?' 'Whoa, hold on a minute. Let me see, let me see — you think I'm being nasty? I just make these things up as I go along, on the spur of the moment, they mean nothing. It's a habit I got into, a way of talking, nothing more, a little fanciful to be sure, intended as entertainment however, nothing other than entertainment.' 'Ah yes,' said Marguerite, 'And yet if you hurt anything, even a single thread attached to the root of a feeling, it may never recover, it may be shocked, there may be some kind of available pain which will echo whenever the root is touched. You have to think about that too. It's like our piano, someone we'd barely recognize again stopped in for a visit, but he makes himself known every time a key on the piano is pressed, however lightly. The key unlocks that man, turns him loose among us, there's no avoiding him. He's there like your story and that's that, something will weep all the days of our life. You can't cancel it, you can't undo it, you can't unsay it, what's said is said.' 'Now Marguerite,' said Spohr, 'It's the easiest thing in the world to fix that piano, look.' He walked across the room, removed the front panel, bent over the action and started pulling the tacks from the hammers one by one, working systematically from the top end of the keyboard. 'Somehow you can't extract the thorns you've scattered quite as easily.' 'That story was not directed at anyone, take it or leave it, what difference can it make to me?' 'Well, well,' said Monty with asperity, 'That puts you in good company, a pity you came too late for James, the neighborhood evangelist. He wanted to wash away our sins in the blessed waters of Lake Ontario, and he didn't seem to mind much whether we came with him or not as long as he got to make his speech, admonish the congregation. Now you listen to me, here's the good news for you Spohr,' all his drunkenness seemed to uncoil within him, 'I've had it with your sanctimonious claptrap, your methods are not only vile, they reek, do you hear me, they reek. Everyone knows there's something despicable about you Spohr, you live on the charity of your wife's family, you are routinely unfaithful to her, you're lazy and you don't work. So leave your trash somewhere else, I have my own garbage to dispose of, in my own good time, in my own way.' He stormed out of the house to the nearest bar, conveniently only a few steps down the road. 'I didn't realize how drunk he was,' said Sally. 'Don't worry,' offered Marguerite, 'He'll be back.' 'I think I'll toddle along after him,' Spohr said softly, 'Just in case.' 'You see,' Sally whispered quietly to Bender, 'He really is concerned, he's gone after Monty to keep an eye on him.' 'Don't be too sure he hasn't gone home instead,' laughed Marten. 'I think you are all very hard on him,' countered Sally, 'Do you think he wants to hurt anyone's feelings? He's not like

264

that, it would never occur to him anyone would be upset by a little fable.' 'Well,' observed Bender, 'Perhaps that's the point.' 'I don't know why everyone likes to think he doesn't have feelings, the same as the rest of us. He does you know, he just handles them differently.' 'You're probably right Sally, you're probably right,' replied Bender imitating Spohr's manner. Everyone laughed.

As evening approached, the clouds which had lingered at the horizon began to cruise across the sky again, higher up, flattened out. Two darknesses collided and spread a soothing balm over the earth. The leaves on the trees turned black, there was quiet except for the single, raucous note of a bird which heralded the coming of night. 'I've heard that bird for years on summer nights,' said Bender, 'I have no idea what it is, does anyone know?' No one did. They did not speak for a long time letting the darkness gather, unwilling to relinquish the peace which enveloped them. 'It's funny,' said Marguerite sighing, 'Usually I feel enclosed, trapped by my life, then there are moments of absolute respite when the walls crumble and fall away leaving a space too beautiful to comprehend. I wish I could understand, I've never known how to reconcile the extremes, the purity and the pain. When I was a child my mother left me alone quite often and that frightened me, only I could never tell her, it didn't seem honorable, fear of being alone, fear of the dark. Odd, isn't it? We were so poor, you know, we had only a tiny apartment, a room actually, in someone else's house. One night, I was seven or eight, I heard a crash like a plate being smashed, then a kind of yell or scream. It was our landlord's daughter, a girl about my own age, and I knew something unimaginable, not to be thought of must have happened. Her father had a heart attack, fell off his chair in the kitchen where he sat and was dead before he reached the floor. Later she cried, "If only I had caught him, if only I had caught him before he fell." They sent for doctors, an ambulance, their hope, their single hope pinned on the doctors although they knew it was no use, he was dead, beyond help. I wanted to go downstairs, wanted to look at the dead body, the corpse, but I was so terrified I sat frozen to the edge of my bed. Finally, shaking furiously, I tried to go into their kitchen, tried to look at him from the doorway, only my eyes refused to move to the spot where he lay. The idea that he had been alive and now he was dead was more than I could bear, I was horrified by his deadness, his not aliveness. The family was crying, circling, wandering around in confusion. An aunt in a bright green suit took long swallows of whiskey from a flask moaning, "O my God, O my God," it was like a movie. No one noticed me and I went back upstairs to wait for my mother. "Poor Marguerite," she said, "I'm sorry you had to face this alone." "That's all right," I answered, "That's all right." I find the courage to look when the walls are blown away. Peace, I don't know how it comes, I don't know why it goes. You'd think we'd be able to summon it, yet it comes and goes on its own. Who can find peace by wishing, willing or even by praying? Do you suppose it comes from God, that is assuming of course, He's still there.' 'Shocking my dear Marguerite, is that in your catechism?' asked Bender. 'I'm afraid so, in a way I have the feeling nobody's home while we all still fool around thinking somebody is.' Annie said nothing, Sally was lost at a point beyond belief or disbelief. Bender turned abruptly to Annie, 'Have you thought of having your poems set to music?' 'No I can't say I have, they sound complete in my own ears, I can't imagine where the music would go or how it would fit, if you see what I mean.' 'That's only because you can't hear it. Would you let me try?' 'Why yes if you'd like, why not? How about a series of connected short poems?' 'Perfect, a song cycle, I can start immediately. May I see them?' 'They're still in longhand, I'd have to type it out.' 'Never mind, just show me what you have now.' She hesitated. 'Don't you want to?' 'Yes I do, very much, I'm just a little nervous.' Bender was puffing excitedly on one of Marguerite's cigarettes, 'Read them out loud,' he said as she came back, 'Everyone wants to hear.' 'All right then, here goes, the title is The Boatman's Holiday.' She began to read, simply but emphatically, letting her voice follow the lines as they broke across the page.

The Boatman's Holiday

Spain

From the Notebooks of Annie March (1968)

Found these two letters among Sally's things.

Devonshire,
15 March 1968.

Darling Sally,

Thank you my sweetest for your touching letter. It must be a great shock but please don't grieve for him, his life was so screwed up it's just as well the poor shit is dead. This must sound awful, but I had the feeling he died on us a couple of years ago. No tears then, it's better this way. I don't know what happened to him these last few years, I don't suppose anyone knows. For a man like that to have come unstrung is more than I'm prepared to contemplate. Will write again when more coherent. Rosalind and I, in somewhat less than marital bliss, down here for extended stay with the two brats.

All my love,
Eddy.

Ilfracombe,
25 March 1968.

Dearest Sally,

Hope the letter I sent last week or whenever did not cut too deep, was more affected than I cared to admit, then and now. The truth is I felt so disappointed by his life I hardly knew what to make of his death; still don't. I cannot imagine him dead, do you know what I mean? There was a time when he was the most important man in the world to me, I looked up to him, learned from him, modeled my intellectual life on his, and yet I still mean every word in that letter. Don't weep for him, it's better this way. We'll never know what happened to him, why he ran out of steam.

I keep trying to remember the last time I saw him, the very last time, and I can't. Odd that it should be frustrating not to recall whether it was at his place, in a bar, most likely, or somewhere else. When I came back from the west coast Spohr seemed to have fallen apart, you know, and he gave me the impression it was somehow connected to Thomas Archer; I could never put my finger on it. His name came up frequently for no reason, as though Spohr was somehow preoccupied with him. I hardly knew Archer myself, was certainly no admirer of his, yet he does seem to have had a certain hold on his friends. Spohr, needless to say, had never been impressed by any of that, he treated Archer as he treated everyone in those days, with friendliness of course, also with reserve, a distance. How he was finally gripped

272

by him I can't say, I do however, associate Archer with that cloud which hovered over him last year. What was he like when you got back from Spain? It wasn't as if he didn't behave as he always had, when we talked he was in command, in control of himself, the situation, everyone. Perhaps that was the delusion because everything had gone haywire. I mean Nella had left him, after all those years she walked away and he treated the whole thing as if she had gone on vacation. He even said, 'The silly bitch, she'll come back soon enough.' And there was the thing with Rosalind, he told her everything, I mean everything, then sent her off to find me. When I finally managed to ship her back here, I felt obliged to confront him with what I considered to have been a disservice to me, but his reaction, his totally ingenuous reaction was, 'Well didn't you want me to?' What can I say, he stopped me with that, believe me. It doesn't seem to matter much now, he talked and plotted and schemed as always, only there was no point to his schemes. He had become hopelessly unrealistic, out of touch, all his plans had what I have to describe as an unworldly quality, they were somewhere else, out there. On the one hand what he said made sense, hung together, on the other it made none because the things he said were connected logically but not to anything else. Within his own understanding he was coherent; unfortunately his world and ours no longer coincided — I don't know how that disjunction occurred or why. For me a light had been extinguished, I felt lost, the compass I relied on no longer registered true north, it veered off on some wild course of its own. So I mourned his passing then. Don't grieve for him my dear sweet Sally, he had run his race, he was finished.

What do you do with the promises of a dead man?

Spohr did not die too soon, there is nothing to pity here. Hard words you'll say, very hard. The fact is, something disagreeable already clung to him when I came back east, and I've made little effort to keep in touch from here.

Try not to think unkindly about me for this, I would not want to deceive you. Thalia and Jack asked me to send fond remembrances, you must have made a hit with them. Poor Jack has been driven into bankruptcy and my dear mamma is mistier than ever. Have picked up my studies again; expecting to be admitted soon to some reputable institute or other.

All my love,
Eddy.

Spohr's father, the tears falling down his face, told me he received a letter from Edwin Knight consisting of one line scrawled across the page, 'Think I miss him as much as you do.'

Sally said, 'I've never been afraid of dying, I've only been afraid of living.'

Have less and less to say now, perhaps that's why a taste for solitude is growing, for an aloneness fully peopled with thoughts, recollections, contemplation. Job necessitates only minimal contact with others; possible therefore, to maintain an unbroken contour, the whole fabric. Prefer this, by far. The arrogance, the assertiveness seem diminished, even though this seems to have nothing to do with humility. In any case, either there's nothing to say or I've been worn down by conflicting pressures, or the circumstances are different now. All this about arrogance and humility sounds stupid, childish, perhaps it's not the point, perhaps it's not what I mean, perhaps I have become, always was, merely stupid. Underneath, a nagging, biting voice: all affectation, all.

Secrecy, the need to be secret grows. Contain everything, reveal nothing, hide. Especially the private, the inner things. Be still, be very still.

About Spohr, so preoccupied with Sally's death attention to his overshadowed. Cared deeply for him, respected him, always felt his affection for me in spite of, even because of, widely divergent attitudes. Think he was interested in the mechanism belief entails without caring much about the object; he totally lacking in awareness of God. Yet he was tolerant, a good man with an appetite for the truth, an explicit sense of justice, both meticulous and generous. A powerful influence on those around him. Who can mourn the death of a friend?

Aspects of life and death — the thing which is the source of strength may also be the thing which destroys. In his case, the intellect. And Sally? The line between strength and weakness seems to be a fine, frail one involving skill, profundity and grace. Find it hard to accept that Schradieck, a man apparently petty and vicious, should be so devastated by Spohr's death while Sevcik and Birgitte, both oddly, unnervingly cool. Indifferent? Is it possible their generosity, their friendliness is grounded in nothing more than opportunism? Discard what you cannot enlist, when it's done, it's done. Spohr would have been amused. Feel certain the connection between Sally's death and Spohr's went beyond grief. Sally's death flowed from the opening made by her brother's death, her own life trickled from the gap, the wound which had been cauterized but would not heal, not in the place where the cells have their genesis. She faded and withered, a delicate flower who will not bloom again. Sally, dear Sally, Spohr, dear friend, may God protect you both.

Sally dead, Spohr dead. My God, my God.

The secrets of the night transform the day. Let the hiding place be concealed, let the comfort remain a mystery, let the night begin with dying.

Cannot say why I haven't thought much about death, we all die, the thought of death doesn't trouble me, not especially attached to life in the body. And after? When the time comes, return. Nevertheless we are encouraged to live a long time, but the trick is to live correctly; a tiny flaw spoils the jewel, a single drop of poison corrupts a well of sweetness.

There are things which need to be affirmed about Alfred Spohr and Sally Reger. That fine, separating line is a fulcrum which tips us one way or the other. And yet they say Spohr died of a heart attack; in that case Sally did too. Her body was like white wax, the look on her face, that sadness draped across an open desert, that look imprinted on her face can never be erased. Sorrow sprang from the heart of each bereaved cell, sorrow followed her to the grave and beyond. I saw her laid on the stretcher, a white candle, melting, melting beyond death. I saw the fire extinguished, the soft pale body lingering behind. She made no dent in the stretcher, her body was no more than a crease, a fold in the blankets. No weight, only sorrow, her body usurped. I can't mourn the death of Sally Reger, I grieve for her life which tapered to a waxy filament, a thing so light it was blown away, scarcely leaving a mark on the earth, not even a dent, just a loose fold, a crease. I grieve for the life carried away on a breath of wind, she was consumed, blown away. Her heart gave out, unable to support the tiny flame which guttered and died in liquid wax. They carried her away beneath a fold in the blankets, nothing left but her sorrow.

Old Miss Turnbull appeared from nowhere, standing there in the street, shopping bags in both hands, eyes wide with horror, murmuring distractedly, 'O dear, O dear, how terrible, what a dreadful, what a perfectly dreadful thing. Poor Sally, she was my friend. It was like this with mother, O dear, O dear.' There was no one to comfort her as the tears rolled down her cheeks, and she continued up the street muttering sadly to herself.

Sorrow you perpetual companion, give us time to grieve, give us a moment to wash away the pain and a place for our tears of remembrance. We thought she would recover, we thought there would be an end to the blood pouring from her brother's head. They were like Siamese twins she said, joined at the heart. It wasn't just that, she was tossed like a leaf through her unforgiving life, nothing was easy, every step along the way had to be proved, had to be fought, claimed and won. Nothing was gratuitous or casual, her playground was a battlefield, going to school was like going on maneuvers, even her bed became an instrument for triumph or defeat. I don't believe she gave up, it was her heart that gave out. She died I think, of heart failure, like Spohr. The heart that failed. And him, they drove a nail through his heart and marveled when it ceased to work. What did they expect, what do we expect, any of us, what can we hope for? More than a waxy body going up in flame, more than a mind blowing out the limits of its intellect. But why didn't that occur to Spohr and Sally? Why didn't they see it too?

Spohr told me a bitter secret, something he had not told Nella, when I asked why not he replied, 'Not relevant.' He had been a precocious child raised with affection in a climate of intellectual curiosity which valued questions as much as answers. But he was restless, eager not so much for friendship as leadership, an opportunity to control, to sway, deter, influence, affect, alter, manipulate, he needed that even then. He was a personable child, a little awkward perhaps, the intellectual dominance abundantly, and for some, intimidatingly evident. He did not care to look for companions, kept pretty

278

much to himself, staying with his family for the most part until he was twelve or thirteen, then the opportunity to acquire a ready-made following presented itself. There were six or eight boys, older, a little rougher, none particularly bright. Spohr became indispensable to them, planning their escapades, harmless enough at first, childish adventures, halloween pranks. He showed them how to share their school work, get passing grades with minimal effort, he had them recruit a network of older brothers and sisters to buy cigarettes or alcohol, he counseled their first delicate negotiations with the young girls they pursued. Eventually he began introducing financial stratagems to accommodate their maturing appetites. All this was innocent enough for awhile as he quietly but persistently began to advance their affairs, putting them together, inconspicuous, well-behaved groups of two or three for pilfering expeditions to the bakery, Woolworth's, the delicatessen, variety stores, hardware stores, wherever they could practise their skills. They never went out alone and never without specific instructions, they learned how to dispose of their merchandise, began to show a profit. Inspired by something more than bravado, never for a moment thinking they were doing anything wrong, Spohr decided they were ready for more sophisticated enterprises. They invaded the school one night, removing a quantity of sporting equipment which was sold in a nearby city without arousing suspicion. They stole tools, looted their neighbors' houses, finally had to rent a falling down shack (for a club house they told the farmer) to store the accumulating goods. Spohr never accompanied them, he merely planned or directed each operation, like a general from a safe place. When they were caught the boys candidly informed the authorities he was their leader. They did this coolly and without malice in exchange for dismissal of the charges against them. Just in advance of his fifteenth birthday Spohr came before an iron faced judge who considered the boy with distaste, informing him he brought shame and disgrace to himself and his grieving parents, to his friends and his community. Shocked that a child could lead older boys astray systematically, skillfully, the judge decided he would be made an example for other bright boys, reminding them they must never set themselves above society. He was sentenced to eighteen months in a training school. Spohr vowed no one would ever judge him again. *No one? No one?* He had no regrets for that early calamitous experiment, but after the time in jail he was never the same again.

The present, the past, the future, three separate, interlocking worlds bound at both ends by eternity, human history, all of time, a drop in the infinite ocean. Why do we think we are important, unique even? History, the alternation of life and death, why seems it so particular with thee? Turning to the place they no longer occupy, that empty place, wanting automatically to tell Sally, to ask Spohr. They remain in the heart, there in a space they will always occupy.

So much needs to be affirmed. With the exception of S., that was different, I have never cared for anyone as much as I did for Sally and for Spohr. No one in my family, no friend, no one has ever meant more to me than they did.

280

Once, when Sally was living at Spohr's she said to him, 'I think I am completely amoral.' 'Why do you say that?' he asked, 'I've never known anyone as acutely conscious of right and wrong as you are.' It surprised her, she had not seen that. We miss the obvious about ourselves, things we easily observe in others. Some people found Sally difficult — what she saw and felt bubbled spontaneously from her without restraint. When she thought about God she talked about God, when she noticed something silly she said, 'How silly,' when she was bored she walked away, when she was happy she was ecstatic, when she was filled with sorrow it was unendurable. She had none of the mechanisms for suppressing what she felt. She was vocal, very vocal; people thought she talked too much, that her voice was too loud, too penetrating. She read too much, was too acquisitive of facts which she treasured abstractly. She was a rare, precious thing lost to her own worth.

I cannot weep because life is so short, so sweet, I weep because it is bitter for some, intolerably difficult, and there is nothing we can do about it.

By chance a few days after Spohr died I met Jock Carogna's wife, I thought she and Jock would not have heard. She was standing outside Isaac's Gallery when I came up to her, introducing myself, uncertain if she recognized me. 'Hello, I'm Annie March, do you remember me?' 'O? Yes, how are you?' 'Look, I've got terrible news for you and Jock about Spohr. I think you should know he had a heart attack and died, Nella would want you to know.' Her brown eyes with puffy lids set in a round, fat face opened wide as the flat voice which made her sound stupid leached out, 'I'll tell Jock, the boys will dedicate a set to him, I know they will.' She had nothing more to say. I walked away angry that I had spoken to her, hurt that grief could be so routinely circumscribed, in a sentence proffered to strangers.

And more. Marguerite came for me when she found Sally. We stood together beside her bed looking down at the faint, waxy image caught in a fold of the blankets. She was so still, so drained, as wretched in death as she had been in life. I felt nothing, a little queasy, afraid to touch her. Marguerite called an ambulance, I phoned Sally's sister. 'She was already dead, you know,' she said painfully, 'I don't know what this will do to my parents.' She slipped through our fingers like sand, her life passing through ours, the grains of her time sifting through ours, mingling the sorrow of her world with ours. Weeks before when Spohr died Nella called me at work, it had taken his family two days to find her in New York. She had come at once. Calm to begin with, she started crying when I did, then neither of us could speak. Someone who passed my desk said later she thought I was laughing, it didn't sound like crying, it sounded like laughing. Nella told me Spohr would be buried at the cemetery near Luther. His family had no objection and that was her wish.

Let us then do what we have to, learn what we have to learn, be what we resolve to be. I have seen them put courage and determination into lives of such limited aspiration, I have seen them put so little, almost nothing, into a great dream, so much done for the wrong reasons, so little for the right, so much nobility poured into futile purposes, so many gods worshiped, so many idols fashioned from the ignorant clay of desire, greed, ambition. The petty gods Thomas Archer resurrected, were they so different from the gods I wallowed in? The arts, I worshiped the arts as the purest expression of beauty and wisdom, as everything we could aspire to. Then for a time the seeking was appeased, the only thing I had to do was write with absolute purity. That was my way to confer value on existence, make it deliverable. Eventually I began to recognize, apprehensively because no alternatives were in sight, this left vast plains of searching and longing unacknowledged, unaccounted for. The process was slow, at first I thought certain forms, the novel, the sonata, had been used up, had died, and I awaited the birth of something new. Instead I observed my belief in art as the perfect mode of human expression diminish, fade, not just a single form, an isolated rock in the stream, the entire river itself was halted, the tremendous flood with all that power stopped dead in its tracks as the dissatisfaction took root and flowered. To trace it back: there was the recognition that the focus, the subject was no different from anything else, not only philosophically but practically too, and therefore the mink lined urinals of our Dada forbears, the *objets trouvés,* the *musique concrète* which now shelve the history of imagination. Branching out on a parallel limb was the recognition that the activity itself was no different, you could bring the same intensity, the same clarity, dedication, purity and exactness to science, gardening, cooking, arc welding, whatever, and experience the same exhilaration, the same consequence. When art and business merged it meant the artist was up for redevelopment or his option would be dropped, something like that. This left the goal, the point, the purpose, the object, the motive, what I was searching for; this, art itself couldn't deliver. I wanted the meaning and it wasn't there. Art is form, a succession of forms and what I sought is formless, before and beyond concept, uncreated, without beginning or end. Archer wasn't looking for that, he wanted the power to manipulate form, any magic which would bend the universe into an arc of his own.

And there is more, much more, no end to it I suppose. Once linked in life, can death dissolve the bonds which tied us each to each? If death is a transition to another state, for want of better description, what mysteries does it solve, what does it leave unclaimed, untouched, what work remains, what suffering begun here is carried on there? And then how does it end, or does it? Does mystery persist? O God, protect my two dear friends who drift in the mercy of Your being.

When Nella was certain Eddy was not coming back she persuaded Sally to go to Spain, hoping the change in climate and scenery would help her. She left for London at the end of January in the dead of winter, moved as much by the repeated cries from Roger Niemann, her ex-husband, as by her own turmoil. The plane was a lumbering turboprop whose undercarriage froze in the thirty degree below zero temperature at Dorval; the scheduled half hour stop was extended by several hours. She sat strapped in her seat, immobilized with so many others, wondering whether she ought to save herself, escape the icy flight to hell. 'A turning point,' she thought, 'Clearly a turning point and I can't face the turn, wherever I look a great, gaping hole, *le néant,* less formidable in French but just as desolate, the same black inner hole. There was something else, wasn't there? Death, the desirable option, it was easy enough. I wanted a bottle of sleeping pills so that I could say at least here in my hand is an alternative, I don't have to face fifty years of staring into the void, nothing to value, nothing to alleviate the empty day, the dark night and sad morning. The doctor at the first clinic said, "I don't think anyone should be able to waltz in here to get sleeping pills, don't you have a family doctor, don't you have someone who knows you?" How righteous, preventing something, just a shadow, a possibility at the back of his mind. Why shouldn't I have them in my hand — like the aspirins in my purse for a headache — or even if it comes to that, to swallow them one by one, those little white hills of oblivion?' Misleading activity centered in the tail of the plane distracted her; when immobility was reestablished her thoughts broke loose. 'It is possible to be sane about this, I am clear, completely clear about the alternatives. They are what they are, what they always were, it is merely cruel to perpetuate a condition which makes me so wretched. I hold death a prize, a reward for putting up with all the rest, how can it be harmful? Death would be a comfort, release from torment, and who would be hurt, who would grieve? There was someone, but that's done, isn't it? My fantasy, my illusion, a private joke that he's coming back, no one believes it, not even me. As for the others, family, they are not real family, we hardly know each other, and friends, they will recover. So I only have to think about myself and I look upon it as reprieve, no harm to me, little pain for anyone else. I think it's right to consider myself in this, right to act on my own behalf. In any case, freed by the sanctity of self-annhilation. The decision is easy, why is it so hard to do, why am I on this plane? Nella expects me to find the articles of survival in a different place, to dislodge the painful experience and replace it. With what, another painful experience? She doesn't know, she hasn't seen it, the pattern, the repetition, the inevitable cycle. And when you're up you're up, and when you're down you're down. It's not that I'm afraid of being mistaken, I'm not, or that I'm looking around for a possibility I might not have seen, something that would change me fundamentally. Why the delay? I ought to have done it, anything other than this meaningless flight. No comfort here, nothing to shake off the nightmare that begins with waking and ends with dying. Here is the alternative, I carry it with me everywhere, death in a handbag. What nonsense, I was right though, the need has lessened now that I have the remedy, now that I have it wherever I go the need to die has abated.' The undercarriage was thawed out at last, the famished passengers were served coffee as the great plane soared away, carrying Sally and her dreams of damnation into the freezing night. Her seat was next to the window where she sat staring through the hole cut in the darkness. Midway across the Atlantic as her fellow passengers lapsed into vertical sleep she felt the pressure which had tied her down suddenly float free. Smiling out the window she relaxed, breathing the physical release from a crushing burden, she felt weightless, almost transparent, as if her body were a line drawing, no substance and no mass. 'Spontaneous remission,' she laughed, 'An interlude of bliss in my fatal disease, God is gracious to me again. The therapy of being nowhere, not here, not there, not in time or out of it, beside it, occupying the empty seat next to mine. I haven't booked it but there it is, unoccupied for awhile, *libre,* vacant. I'll sit there instead of here, who will mind? I wonder if you can outwit fate, even for a moment, a little breathing space. I guess the contract must be written up in full, the whole thing, the large bold type as well as the fine print, but there has to be a little maneuvering space, doesn't there? Here I am on both sides of the fence and sitting on it too, how bizarre, how funny. O it's going to work, I know it's going to work, it has to.' She drank a cup of tea and fished out the copy of *The White Pony* she had put in her purse at the last minute. The glued binding was broken at Po Chu-i's poem, The Sand And The Waves; what disturbs me, it said, is that you are not so faithful as the waves, that my love abandons me here. The smoke of her unending chain of cigarettes drifted up comfortingly, 'I was so depressed, then those long hours while we sat there, no smoking, no food. My irritation and my hunger must have overtaken the depression, and the fear this plane might blow up. Fussy about the way I die. Schradieck said three planes crashed in the last few weeks, I am safe according to him, they always crash in threes. Nella says he won't fly, he's never been up. If they'd have let me off at Dorval I might have gone back. Couldn't have though, not just because of Roger waiting at bloody Heathrow, I can't go back, not to Bellair Street, not to Marguerite's or to Spohr's. Whether I like it or not I can never go back, there has been a natural division in time.'

She spent some weeks in London offering Roger what comfort she could. The city Sally had once loved now seemed grey, undesirable, even squalid. 'Perhaps I can't come back here either.' She wondered how it had been possible to efface the memory of a cold English corridor, how you wake up freezing and walk the unforgiving hallway to the rigorous English bath. 'Has the city lost its beauty or have I lost the ability to see it?' Roger hated London with a quiet, bland paranoia, had no idea why he stayed on after Sally went home. Ostensibly preparing a manuscript, a collection of minor eighteenth-century verse written by certain obscure poets approximately two hundred years ago, some unknown then and ever after, others enjoying a moment of recognition or notoriety before joining their colleagues in obscurity, he worked on alone in the Rare Books room at the British Museum. Day after day he sifted the volumes, searching for poems which his unsung poets had produced once or twice in a lifetime, poems which had a sweet, authentic ring because an accidental rhythm or metaphor reached across the years speaking directly to the place in the heart it addressed, or because said Roger in his deliberately uninflected voice, 'If you keep grinding it out sooner or later you get a winner.' Sally was curious about the thoughtfulness which a recital of their names would elicit from him. 'Let me tell you some of the names: William Bagshaw Stephens, James Grainger, James Beattie, Bonnell Thornton and his friends George Colman and Robert Lloyd, James Hurdis, William Falconer, that's right, Cuthbert Shaw, nice name that, John Langhorne, Christopher Anstey, William Combe, William Dodd, Charles Jenner, Hugh Downman, Thomas Bridges, John Armstrong, Erasmus Darwin, Henry Needler, the antiquarian Bishop Thomas Percy, William Lisle Bowles, Michael Bruce, James Macpherson, Christopher Wagstaff, poor young Thomas Chatterton, Thomas Russell, Joanna Baillie, Mark Akenside, William Shenstone, Hugh Blair. Shall I go on, doesn't it make you sad, all that talent, all that ambition squeezed into one volume which announces here, this is what remains, this is what lives.' His sensitive, unnaturally florid face looked serious as he pushed his fingers through the long, dark brown hair while Sally thought without regret of their interrupted marriage. 'Does ambition move anyone to write poetry? It seems hard to believe.' 'You know nothing about that awful state, do you? Yes, I would say sometimes the most transparently pure motives are generated by nothing more than this little worm's nibbling, a sore tooth in the night, the desperately private need to be set apart, acknowledged. But you are so without that, aren't you Sally? It's part of your charm, your unworldliness. Still, you have to be careful or you'll be blown away, you do know that, don't you?' She noticed how often he ended his statements with a question, adding this to her nearly complete catalogue of things about Roger which irritated her. He seemed so foreign, so dislocated she found it difficult to keep her attention on him, even when he made love to her. She did indeed, offer everything to make amends for her indifference. His first tardy declaration of love, wholly delinquent during the bleak married intervals, arrived on the same day as John Adolph's abusive visit. For several months his letters came frequently, daily at times, begging her to come to London for a few days, even a few hours. He said he would return to Canada, to Vancouver, Toronto, Montreal, wherever she would meet him, he said so many things uncharacteristic of his normally phlegmatic manner Sally began to think he might have strayed across the line into some mania. Roger the calm, the unmoved, admitted to having been in love once before, with a young girl who died when she was fifteen, entombed ever after in his memory. When he talked about her, too often to suit Sally, he spoke in a voice which was unctuous and an accent appropriate to neither side of the Atlantic. She was continually frustrated by an impossible comparison, a difficulty which persisted through the short unhappy episodes of marriage, along with his inability to say he loved her, in spite of the evident affection. A light greenish colored suit he invariably wore, lapels somewhat wider than enjoined by fashion, looked almost appropriate as he waved his large hands covered with dark hair and spoke about the dead girl, as though she had been a perfect work of art whose fineness had survived the changing times. Sally would think to herself, 'Well that sure cooks my goose!' His niceness, his mannered language brought out the rakish in her disposition. When he had first discovered Sally was not absolutely virginal, a husband among others preceded him, he forgave her; then of course, after they were married it became clear that the soft voice and impossible green suit protected an appetite for a specific sexual digression Sally assured him she would never be competent or willing to gratify. When the declarations she had once wanted more than anything began pouring forth in letters, cables and phone calls she could hardly remember his face, so intense was her preoccupation with Edwin Knight. What he revealed in his wretchedness horrified her, he knew she found him repulsive, quite rightly so, he said. If they were to live in the same city he would never embarrass her, never try to see her, he would be content to communicate by letter. At other times he promised he would not write anymore if only she would just visit him, he would not expect her to sleep with him or even touch him. He subjected himself to the most debasing humiliation while he pleaded with her, sent cables saying he was dying, begging for an immediate answer. At last he phoned her at work where she could not refuse the call and asked, 'Is there someone else?' She did not reply, unwilling to cause the pain her answer would bring. He was so insistent, in the end she said, 'Yes, there is.' 'O God,' he moaned, 'I was afraid of that, I've always known the day I told you how much I love you would be the last, why do you think I kept silent for so long?' He hung up as a transatlantic finality settled between them for months. He began to write again but not so often, and in one letter he sent an open ticket quietly urging her to use it when she could. Sally understood how helpless he felt, only by then she also knew that limits would be imposed on her own limitless love.

There vere two women Nella was close to, her connection with Lisa was silent and telepathic. She knew she was needed, appearing at Schradieck's house to find her friend lost among the disorderly children. 'Did Schradieck tell you to come?' Lisa might ask. 'No, you needed me; so you see, I came.' Once, much later, when Nella did not arrive in answer to the unspoken summons Lisa said, 'You didn't come, you knew I needed you and you didn't come.' 'I'm sorry, I was sick, forgive me.' With Sally however, things were open, verbal. As Eddy referred to the same girl more than once in his sporadic letters, Nella realized she had to do something for Sally, she sent her away. Slowly but carefully she edged along the same ground again and again, 'Why don't you use that ticket, you know Roger needs to see you, then go on to Spain. You've wanted to do that, just take a vacation. If Eddy turns up I'll cable or phone, you could be back in a day. Why stay in this place, there's nothing for you here and you seem so unhappy. Go away for a few months, a few weeks, whatever, just make this waiting bearable.' She was too tactful to mention he had not written to her, not once in all the months since he had gone out west. 'You know those restless Sagittarians, they can never keep still, stay in one place for long. I'll look after your books, throw some clothes in a suitcase and go. You love to travel and I think it may be the perfect antidote for an absent, wandering love. Go, see Roger, visit Spain, it's so cold here now. Just think, you can step off a plane into warmth, into sunshine —

there's nothing to hold you here.' Sally sank deeper and deeper into some private desolation that could not be altered, she clung to it. If she abandoned her sorrow she abandoned her hope, what could she do? Spohr watched from a distance, almost with kindness, then engaged her in lengthy discussions on those rare days when she visited. Although his conversation was immediately distracting and entertaining, over a period of time it distressed her. While they examined a range of natural phenomena so analytically, with such linguistic precision, she became absorbed in the conviction there was no other route to understanding; at the same time she came to think it irrelevant to consider whether her own life might have some meaning. 'Sally, go,' said Nella encouragingly, 'You hate your job, you live like a recluse, the money is there, why not take off?' And so she landed on that day late in January at Heathrow, the sun a mere image of itself traced through the heavy air, the grey sky a gloomy canopy stretched across the mute, frozen spheres. Roger whose passion had quieted but deepened knew at once when he kissed her that her feelings had not changed, that hadn't happened. He shook slightly as he drew back and lit her cigarette. Sally found him different, he was affectionate, even playful. Once he knew without question the game was lost he was graceful in defeat. He put his arm around her almost casually while the taxi drove them into London, pointing out landmarks she might have forgotten, telling witty stories about his neighbors' bemused search for bottles of milk lost in the snow. Several inches had fallen a few days earlier concealing the miniature bottles left on doorsteps, and the congested traffic, the confusion, the disbelief of the unprepared populace all diminished before the prospect of no milk for their tea. They drove to his small flat in Oakley Street, near the Albert Bridge and Embankment. He didn't ask how long she would stay, she didn't volunteer much except she was on her way to Spain. After a few days Roger returned to his routine, working at the Museum all day, returning for supper and the evening with Sally. They talked, went to the local pubs, concerts at Festival Hall, Peter Grimes at Sadlers Wells, *La Dialogue Des Carmelites* at Covent Garden, plays in the West End, Sloane Square and Hammersmith. During the day Sally rode the cold buses to her favorite parts of town like a tourist, taking the 39 from the Embankment or a 19 from the King's Road, and Nella was right, she felt better. She did not want Roger to know more than he had to and masked her feelings quite well, she thought. But he was more perceptive than she gave him credit for, he knew how matters stood. Her deep desolation was put away for awhile, except when nightmares stalked in dreams, trampling her with visions of cruelty.

One day she saw Rosalind and her child shopping in the King's Road, she recognized them from photographs Edwin had shown her, trailing after them like a lost child herself. Rosalind pushed the pram slowly from shop to shop accompanied by two longhaired dachshunds, one a young black and tan male attached to the baby carriage by a leash, the other a reddish, overweight, wheezing female padding slowly after her, needing constant exhortation, 'Come on now Patsy, there's a good girl, come on sweetie, don't keep mummy waiting, come on now.' The words of encouragement rang out in a sibilant, high-pitched voice which never paused for breath. Sally could scarcely breathe herself she was so moved at the sight of Edwin's wife and child. She wanted to talk to them, wanted to run up to Rosalind whose long black hair streamed down her back and say, 'Look, this is who I am,' but she couldn't, she knew it would be wrong, completely wrong. She could hardly say, 'You don't know me, I am your husband, your never to be ex-husband's cast off *amie*. I have loved him, now I'm waiting to die.' She studied the child sitting up straight in his pram, serious, never laughing or smiling, why was that child so serious? Loitering a more or less discreet distance behind them Sally half hoped she might be noticed and questioned, but even when she turned down Tite Street to follow them Rosalind was absorbed in her world of parcels, dogs, child, pram, and never glanced back once. Sally found a bench across from their house on the Embankment, sitting there for an hour trying to decipher some message, some meaning from the tall, grey house she would never enter. Finally numb as the cold mingled with her mounting hopelessness, with the penetrating damp, she returned to the flat in Oakley Street, pumping sixpences or shillings into meters for the stove and gas heater, a futile attempt to warm herself. 'God curse me, curse my madness, I'm sick of it, sick of it.' When Roger came in she was taciturn, withdrawn. They went out for dinner to the Kenya, a pleasant coffee shop along the King's Road near Sloane Square, had tomato soup with cream on top, egg Florentine and frothy capuccinos. Sally felt warm again and became abruptly talkative, chatting about friends in a great rush of words, some known to Roger, most however, strangers. 'I've known Thomas

Archer for such a long time, we picked each other up in the Art Gallery one day and became good friends. I trusted the prophetic quality he emanated, was fascinated by the interplanetary conversation, the ancient deities. He's a wonderful mixture of science fiction, neurosis and art. His paintings are imperfect in some ways, I mean he has limited technical resources, he's not much of a draftsman, yet there is an extraordinary residual power which attracts you, something like posthypnotic suggestion. I don't know where it comes from, he more than dabbles in magic, the occult. There was a time when he was fond of Nietzsche and Wagner, that whole transcendental German *crapule,* I beg your pardon, you know what I mean. Everyone's attention was riveted on him when I was home, do you know why? He wasn't there, he had disappeared, vanished. There was a great outcry but no one could find a trace of him, foul play was suggested, mystery, strange happenings. Schradieck, one of our seamier friends had some tall tales, although he was probably telling the truth for once. Shall I go on, are you interested? The thing about Tom is that he is mad, certifiable, yet he has an inspiring genius which makes people want to be near him. It's exciting to play his games, act out his fantasies, exhilarating to listen to him, so moved he stutters as he speaks about the deities he fancies protect him. He's filthy, you know, unclean, I can't imagine . . . but Nella used to live with him, isn't that amazing? And how he adored, worshiped her I think, never gave her up, never relinquished a particle of their life together, not when she left him, not when she married Spohr, not ever. I have a confession, I have to tell you something I've never told anyone. It happened when Tom was

296

quite unhinged and I invited him to stay with me for a few days, thinking my own madness was a match for his. O he was very bad then, he should have gone to the hospital. I remember him sitting in a corner with bare feet, it was winter, dipping his feet into saucers of tea, rolling oranges along the floor; someone had told him oranges would be good for him. He would hurl lighted matches across the room, in ones and twos at first, then whole books of them. He would watch them curl and burn, laughing, sinister, snapping his fingers in circles around his head. All this made me nervous as I recognized he was beyond my ability to cope with, to reach. God he was a mess, I came home from work one day, found he had burned some unspeakable concoction in the coffee pot and I blew up, I was outraged, told him he was disgusting, filthy. He didn't say a word, not a word in his own defense or in protest, he just left. I had incurred his wrath and nothing could change that. For days I felt his hatred follow me, seek me out. I've never stopped feeling guilty about it and needless to say, our friendship was never the same again. O I apologized, we made up, we were still friends, only he held me off slightly, there were limits. Every once in awhile he would change his mind about something he was going to tell me or he'd look away, I've regretted that too. Sometimes it seems I became a bit crazier myself after that. Do you think it was because I yelled at him? I'm fond of him you know, he stood for so much once, still does in a way. Let me explain if I can. Another time, this was in the early days, I walked him back to the hospital where he was a patient, he talked at great length, quietly, hesitantly, describing an experience he'd had many times. He would find himself in something like a cave, a shadow filled cavern, apparently underground. It was so dark he could barely make out the walls, but if he kept searching he could see, dimly, through a dense mist, exquisite colors and forms, frescos painted by the master of some remote age. With intense concentration he could isolate small sections, catch fragmentary glimpses of the life they conveyed, guess at the secrets partially revealed and partially withheld. The figures gestured deliberately and women stared hard at him through lidless, almond shaped eyes. Sometimes they seemed almost Roman, superbly detailed, realistic, like the shadowy beings at Pompeii, other times they seemed Egyptian, hieroglyphic, suggesting remote cults, reminding him of old mysteries to be enacted again and again. He also felt the master's presence, strongly from time to time, urging him on through the darkness. He described patterns he had seen on beautifully wrought urns, explicit about glazes, designs, symmetry, shapes, textures. Sometimes he saw ornamental figures, real or sculpted he could never quite be sure, locked in different postures or strolling through gardens, surrounded by tall grasses, flowers, birds, trees, bees, butterflies, frogs, grasshoppers, all wrapped in the damp cool smell of the earth. He seemed to attract their attention, but only briefly, they would look at him seductively, with recognition he felt, then dissolve in the mist or amorphous walls. He longed to be part of their world, learn the master's secrets and know what they knew. Once he thought he caught sight of open blue sky, pale light and drifting clouds. A break in the roof he speculated, until he observed the edge and realized it had been painted in

298

too. He never questioned how he got there or why, there was no doubt this shadowy cave filled with the resonating beauty of another era was a clue to some unleashed power he could not control. He would simply discover himself there, often not recognizing where he was until he became aware of the floor beneath his feet, rising and falling like the earth itself, covered with a gilt tile mosaic forming a patternless pattern in whorls and circles. Here and there the earth broke through the tiles as though part of the ancient floor had worn away, had decomposed. The golden color could be seen as light reflected from some source he never identified. When he walked across rolling open fields in the country, the roughness, the unevenness of the earth beneath his feet felt like that floor. It was a complete, beautiful world, filled with everything he would ever want, yet inaccessible, denied to him because of his fear, his paralyzing fear. When I talked about this with Nella a few years later she said, "You have to understand when he found himself there he was wrung with fear, throughout his body, tormented. Nothing could equal that terror, nothing could account for it." I can't say whether fear saved him or destroyed his only chance to study the secrets he hungered for. Curious, I'm surprised now that I think about it, the extent to which Tom has influenced my life, and Nella's too, although I'm not sure she'd admit it. Spohr wouldn't be happy with an idea like that. You know Spohr and Archer have an interesting connection which only seems improbable on the surface, once you start noticing things they have in common it doesn't seem so farfetched. Nella is the obvious link, but that's difficult to account for, what would bind two such opposite men to the same woman? Of course Nella herself is pretty interesting — that uncompromising rock she's built on, she doesn't know her own strength at all. Do you know she thinks of herself as fragile, inconsequential, yet she has a profound self-reliance which I think she must have acquired during childhood. I met her father once, he's a strange enough character, over sixty years old but not a grey hair on his head. Nella says he's been interested in raw food and theosophy for as long as she remembers. Seems he used to drag her off to meetings of every esoteric society he could find when she was a little girl, and that made her an outcast, a pariah is the word she used, at school. To be seen talking to her she said, was social suicide. It made her wretchedly unhappy but she had her father's gift for examining the unconventional, the unacceptable, she knew she was right, they were wrong. She never lost that conviction, that certainty. At any rate, Tom used to mention her once in awhile, she was not just a woman to him, she was woman, the emblem, no, more than that, like an ikon, not outwardly but abstractly, the inspiration, the drawing in of the breath, a pure flame, the work of art itself. I think that's why he can't relinquish her, and Spohr too. Even though he takes her for granted, he is so casually unfaithful to her, they are attached at the center, umbilicus to umbilicus, she feeds him a quality, an energy which is indispensable. She may not realize it but he is far more dependent on her than she is on him, I doubt if he could actually survive without her. All very interesting, isn't it? You know, Spohr doesn't believe in God, not at all, not even a little remotely buried, just not at all. And his scepticism has somehow cut my faith loose, O I still believe in Him, but it's a complicated thing now. It used to be so simple, there was a direct line, heart to heart, nothing in between. Now the pain of the whole world stands between my God and me, He keeps receding and I just let Him go. It's not Spohr's fault, his thinking, his way of analyzing is a separating process, extracting cream from milk. In some ways I look at the world through his eyes now, everything is held up for inspection, even God Himself is subject to Spohr's scrutiny. Sometimes I think I will lose Him altogether, do you suppose it's possible?' 'It makes you sad, doesn't it, I've never heard you talk this way before. You seem terribly unhappy, if I may be permitted to make that observation.' Sally smiled, 'Well that's been true enough, not now though, I felt awful for awhile, I'm actually okay thank you. You'd like Spohr's stories, he tells these ambiguous little *contes* which you can't quite make up your mind about, it's hard to say whether they're really deep or somehow inane. Often they make you twitch, they drive you round the bend, as you say in this country. I think what I meant about the connection between Spohr and Archer is they're both looking for ways to glimpse beyond the present, they both yearn for prophethood, O on a quiet enough scale, a few trusted disciples, not a cast of thousands; they know that hunger in each other and it seems to have engendered not rivalry but respect. Nella is very fond of Archer too, even if the earth has swallowed him up, although, you know, I think she's enslaved to Spohr. It's a curious ambivalence, that apparent self-reliance on one hand and abject dependence on the other. Some people are like that.' 'Not you though.' 'No, not me.' 'When you cabled Sally, I kept hoping you were coming to stay. I knew as soon as I kissed you at the airport it wouldn't happen, I felt you withdraw, back away, and that made me tremble because it was the final blow. In a way it was a relief, deliverance at last. I still feel unhappy but at least I'm free, do you know what I mean?' 'Yes.' Sally smoked cigarette after cigarette into the dark silence which grew all around, clinging to them, making them invisible. They left the restaurant, walking along the King's Road enveloped in a heavy mist which had risen while they talked. They were reminded of the walk years before when they had been engulfed by fog in an unfamiliar place. 'You said, "Don't worry, I know this place like the back of my hand." Did you?' 'Actually no, but I thought you might be frightened, and I felt responsible. It wouldn't have been dangerous, it might have been uncomfortable, no, that was just bravado. We did walk right out though, didn't we, as if I had actually known, then I was so overawed I couldn't admit it was just luck.' 'Do you suppose it was luck?' 'What else do you think it could have been?' 'I used to feel I was watched over, protected, I would never have been afraid, not then.' 'And now?' 'Now is now, that was before.' *Before my brother and the whole world blew up.*

Sally went to visit Thalia and Jack one day. Thalia was a pretty woman who wore soft wools and sipped brandy in milk all day. Her hair had already begun to turn grey, her face was composed beneath the slightly bewildered expression which accepted the passing of time and beauty with resignation, even good humor, in spite of a certain incredulousness. She hated wearing glasses, something which kept her at a distance from the world. She studied the tall, ardent girl and liked her at once. 'I must say my son's wives get more and more beautiful.' Jack was a pudgy, engaging fellow with a vestigial stammer. He reminded Sally of a large bird whose ruffled feathers perpetually needed smoothing, his arms flapped up and down while he talked with innocent frailty about the disarray in his personal affairs. He felt crushed, betrayed in a gentlemanly way by certain conflicts and pressures, describing a few friends' loyalty as the only thing keeping him from total ruin. They had a helplessness about them, not at all her idea of anybody's parents. She found it hard to believe Thalia was Edwin's mother and said so. She laughed, 'I haven't been much of a mother I'm afraid, we were separated so often when he was a child, either by school or his father's whims. He hated that I think, then the moment he was able to, he ran off and I hated that. Now this handsome boy who is my son seems a little mysterious to me. You're here and he's away off there in the wilderness you say. I never hear from him, he's a hopeless correspondent, I guess you've found that out, or does he write to you?' 'No, he doesn't, to a friend of ours once or twice, but not to me, no. He promised he would, but he hasn't.' 'My dear, I don't understand young people at all, why on earth did you leave him, why did you let him go?' *One parting but ten thousand regrets.* Sally was touched, 'I didn't have much choice, sometimes you are overreached, powerless to do anything except yield. It was like that, I couldn't have changed it then, I can't now, that's just the way it is, you cannot choose.' Thalia put her arms around her and said, 'I wish you really were my daughter.' Sally left for Spain the next morning.

The BOAC plane to Málaga was almost empty, Sally removed the armrests beside her, lying across the seats to dream her way south, unaware of the mountains, the plateaus and plains rolling below, those somber landscapes etched in blood, beauty stretched like skin on a dry corpse. Sally had never been to Spain before, had declined to make her peace with the tyrant, the icy Generalissimo, el Caudillo, el Jefe, and wondered whether going there even some thirty years later did not in a way condone his treason, his murders. She had declined the peace, now however, she was prepared for a ceasefire, perhaps a truce, a time to inspect the battleground and weep for the war that had been lost and won. She went, a pilgrim disguised as a tourist. For her it had been a holy war, a succession of holy wars, the forces of good and evil lined up against each other over the centuries, one blood crazed general leading his troops into battle chanting *viva la muerte.* What bony bride led them to the angel of death, what dream in the charnel house gave dignity to their ambition for death? And the generals' frenzy was a match for the mad ideals burning the hearts of their adversaries. The generals at least were recognizable, familiar figures of destruction, compelled by recognizable, familiar methods designed to control the world. Some of those however, whom history ought to have cast as the good men in this struggle were betrayed by their shallow virtue, were exposed in time as rapacious idealists soaked in their comrades' blood, quite ready to slit a throat for a good idea. The only possible reparation, all the dreamers said to the world, arms for the people of Spain, but the world did not care, ignoring the truth. The ultimate political paradox flowered here, a mixed garden of treachery, deceit, betrayal and lies; it turned out that neither an idea nor a concept was enough, the politics of democracy died in Spain impaled on thorns that flank the sweetest flower. Necessity was not fussy, it used good to subvert good as readily as bad. The betrayal of generations who waited for mankind's redemption though generosity, tolerance and equality was enacted here while the whole world watched, misled by issues, misled by methods, misled by intentions. Sally had been nurtured on emotional, heroic stories about good men who longed to plant truth in the hearts of the ignorant, there to be watered by time, fertilized with a wakening sense of justice and brought to fruition through the efforts of a decent, humane populace. The liberal egalitarian myth was brought abruptly to bed in Spain where, in the presence of every species of midwife, it bore a monstrous child whose advent was concealed by the war that baby's birth proclaimed. What clung to Sally was an emotion, the possible, a reckless dream burned to ashes and revived by the heat in its own embers, the need for good on a universal scale. She came to Spain to weep for her own betrayal and lament the politics of the possible, she came to distract herself, to deaden the sound of one bullet whistling in her brain, one among how many thousands which reached their target, detonating worlds within worlds within worlds.

An unsympathetic steward nudged her as the aircraft prepared for descent, and she woke to find herself plunging suddenly towards the exquisite cerulean waters of the Mediterranean. The wing pointing down to the sea leveled off at the last moment, swinging the gigantic craft in a heavy circle, sweeping them back to land. They came in from the sea, unimaginable sunlight drenching the tiny airport. Her lungs still full of stale English fog, Sally got off the plane. She looked around in disbelief, first at the palm trees, then the soldiers, then at the airport guards dressed in comic opera tunics, their wide leather belts girded about fat waists and clownish pantaloons. The Napoleonic patent leather hats on the heads of the Guardia Civil completed her astonishment. For a moment or two she wondered whether it was a circus, but the austere grey uniforms of the Guardia, their correct, penciled mustaches sour with explicit comprehension, soon made her understand they were actors in a solemn drama, not to be taken lightly. The sun bleached the first glimpse of their world, a personal and entirely blissful warmth. The trappings in this military society blurred under the forgiving light never to reemerge with such clarity again. Sally looked down at her own incongruous costume, black tights, a heavy pale blue woollen skirt, bright yellow sweater, also a checkered maroon and black winter coat over her arm. A mysterious balm the sun alone can dispense to northerners in the freezing winter of many lifetimes fell upon her then, dissolving the ice in her heart with a directness which was both matter-of-fact and irresistible. She capitulated at once, here was nothing to fear, nothing to despise, here was only the composure, the literalness of the Spaniard, replete, at perfect equilibrium wherever he happened to be, driving a taxi, working in a shop, in a bar, grinding a living from the sea or soil. He was the least reflective and most philosophic of men, the least emotional and

306

most passionate, the least secret and most covert, an abstract of mystery, a perfect materialist measuring his feelings in pesetas. Sally responded at once to the dignity without arrogance, the intuitive respect for others, the poor man sitting down comfortably beside the rich, calling him *señor* or *don,* but rhythmically, naturally, reserving what he needed for himself. Spanish generosity touched her deeply, an openhandedness among the poor with food or cigarettes or wine the mark of a common, shared understanding. Many people had little, there was imbalance, but no poverty or deprivation in spirit, none. Sally fretted along the dismal airport route to Málaga, speculating why airport roads are ugly, feeling apprehensive until the bus drove into the city itself, a rare flower touching the lips of the sea. Even at winter's end it was bright, greenery grew recklessly over long low walls, bougainvillea, jasmine, orange groves glowing in the clear, dazzling light. *0 nimms, pflücks das keinblautige Heilkraut.* The buildings were all yellow, soft brown or ochre, a few people sat outside cafés, the police wore white and made balletic signals to the traffic. The city was quiet, uncrowded, the great tourist influx not expected for several months; it buzzed happily with optimism. Times were good and getting better, they had work, and although they knew Franco was not personally responsible for the well-being which amounted to something like prosperity for a growing number, no one wanted to be rid of him just then. The Falange was there looking more like a social club than a military or political instrument, the *obreros* had their carefully controlled, ostensibly harmless societies too. Sally stood in the boulevard they had named after that mad general Queipo de

Llano, looking out at the ships in the harbor, hearing other voices sing from the bottom of the sea. She walked through the Alameda Gardens waiting for the bus which travelled east along the coast to Almería, reflecting on the martyrs as she walked, those commemorated by the Plaza de los Mártiros, hoping they had died their savage deaths hundreds of years ago murdered by religious fanatics, not recently by political fanatics and arbitrary firing squads. The bus driver was a round sweating fellow with a big black mustache, fortifying himself for the work ahead with *salchichón,* a loaf of bread and a litre of white wine. Sally considered his meal with amusement, believing her fate was in any case sealed in God's great book. Later it occurred to her the only drunks she saw were foreigners. Eventually the bus was full: women in somber black dresses with small gold crosses and enormous backsides, the triple legacy of a Spanish woman's life; men in soft, sagging grey suits and berets; a few brightly dressed children, noisy, running up and down the center aisle of the bus screaming their husky, unrestrained messages to each other in voices which had not yet dipped or settled in the Andalusían rasp; some chickens more or less tucked inside baskets on the arms of a few passengers, clucking noisily, knowing too well their ultimate destination. The driver was in no hurry to leave. Fifteen or twenty minutes after their scheduled departure time, the sun low in the sky, late afternoon light a dark yellow glow, the bus pulled slowly away, slipping from the city past the bullring to the sea where the road had been carved along its shore. Sally's destination was a little town, more like a village than a town, fifty kilometres down the coast, past Rincón de la

Victoria, beyond Torre del Mar, past the winding road to Frigliana and a few scattered white villages clinging to the face of the mountain, a slow, winding journey. The bus was a local not the express, stopping frequently to let people off, occasionally to pick up new passengers. The route wound perilously along the coast, sheer rock face on the left decorated with flowers which burst from the heart of the rock itself, on the right the sea, very still, shining, slate blue, the golden tracery of the sun laid delicately upon it. Sally remembered the thousands of desperate, fleeing victims strafed by machine gun fire from planes overhead, homeless, doomed. *Federico was denounced, dragged away with ignominy, and condemned to death.* She felt their presence among the passengers as the darkness settled slowly upon them. 'No more,' she thought, 'I'll go no more, this is the last visit, the last venture forth. Death waits everywhere, why not meet him at home on common ground, why go in search of a remedy we have already waiting on the shelf at home?'

Nerja. It is early March, midday, a wrought iron balcony infested with light. Remote from neighboring rooftops, projected above flowering rocks which guard the sea, Sally sits in the sun thinking nothing, feeling only the heat, penetrating, comforting, all abuses wiped clean. Beneath her nothing but crumpled brown rock hung with spring flowers and crushed silver nests of leaves. Over her right shoulder, between the sea and the vertical bony peaks high up the Sierra de Almijara, here lie rows of tiled red roofs, inert in the sun, blotched with a green or yellow fungus painted in by the careless hand of time. The topmost peak of the mountains like the curved beak of an eagle soaring to the sun is white with a ring of snow, while down below they say snow never falls. The austerity at those distant peaks aloof in the silence is new, breaking open imperishable places in the heart until now sealed tight like the halves of a walnut. The shells lie scattered about, the afterbirth of awareness when the earth comes home. Understanding which strains towards those peaks opens in spiraling breaths, spurting uncontrollably on a dazzling plain, unencumbered by past, by recollection, by comparison. What will happen next is history, and in between each passage through the heart bubbles, chaotically here, slowly, gently there. The landscape is bombarded, altered by wave after wave of blows to the heart. And the mystery does not end with mountains, beyond Sally lies the sea, the flat blue surface unchanging, a constant flux, moving in and out with her breathing, lungs, her own, a mirror. It is more than she can resist. The mountains and sea fuse somewhere beyond perception, beyond understanding, her body loses weight, substance, an outline alone persisting, expanding until the dimension resembles the towering mountain and bottomless sea. At the centre a translucent bubble captures the whole, annihilating the separation between out and in. Confronted now by the outline of the universe in her limitless body she begins to ascend, to disappear, conscious only that the corporeal disintegration must not be interrupted. 'Please don't make me come back, let this be without end, let me go.' The bubble rises, rises, drifting endlessly and away, carrying her from the latitudes of longing and the fixities of earth, desire and death. At a point which comprehension negates the purity is transformed, light descends in a refined shower carrying her back, returning. She must descend. The horizon shrinks and glows, the sea whispers sweetly offering its peace, its comfort. Far away two black spots, toy ships of the microcosm, play out some nameless drama in the blazing noon. 'Like us,' she thinks, 'Two strangers who pass back to back in this disquieting light.'

After a time in solitude she emerged from the cocoon, the web of days she had wound around herself, restless, curious at last about the little town sitting like a jewel on the cliffs above the sea. She stood at the end of the *paseo* which was laid out on top of a high, very narrow fortress jutting into the bay, and listened to the slap, slap, slap of the water slamming beneath her feet on the rock wilderness below. A voice whose thin English twang surprised her as it drifted closer came within hearing, 'The Phoenician traders made that fortification down there I'm told, three thousand years ago, then stayed on for five hundred years until the Greeks and Carthaginians drove them out. When the Romans came they finished off the Carthaginians and what was left of the Greeks. The Romans themselves lasted hundreds of years until barbarians in the fifth century, Visigoths, pushed them out. The greatest, the most civilized invaders were the Islamic people who came from North Africa in the eighth century, remaining on the peninsula for centuries, spreading light and the glory of a golden age wherever they stayed. Their very Christian majesties, Ferdinand and Isabella, had the ferocious satisfaction of driving these distinguished inhabitants from Granada, the last stronghold, in the same year their hireling Christopher Columbus made his way to the new world.' Grateful for the information Sally glanced sideways at the historian, observing a stooped and white haired woman whose stabbing gestures with a heavy cane seemed as inappropriate as the moldering blue polka dot dress. The lady smiled politely at Sally, sweeping her guest up the *paseo* towards the kiosk. She found out later the Englishwoman had lived there for years, somehow surviving on a meagre pension and the occasional sale of sketches and miniatures. Sally sat down at the Marisol, a café on the *paseo* west of the kiosk which was a marker dividing any rare traffic venturing onto the promenade. The sun had not yet emerged from the heavy dark sky that day, a damp cold wind made Sally shrink deep into her coat. If you sat directly in the sun you were warm, too warm, but without it you were treated to the remnants of semitropical winter. There were few people about at that hour, before ten in the morning, and Sally's first excursions into her new life were carried out in the cold obscurity of these early strolls. She ordered *café con leche* which had a slightly randy taste, the flavor of goat's milk. Studying the snow speckled mountain surging up behind the town, north of the *carretera,* north of the *campiña,* Sally was not lonely, she had brought a suitcase full of books, hadn't the slightest desire to speak to anyone. When she realized the polite voice with the clipped accent was addressing its amused comments to her she was startled. 'Good day to you, thought you might like to know this café charges exhorbitant prices compared with the more modest but thoroughly decent Bar Alhambra down there,' pointing to the café closer to the sea with his neatly pointed beard, 'And Miguel who's a decent chap would put a chair out for you if you prefer to brave the out-of-doors. A *coñac* by the way, with your coffee, will take the chill from the Spanish wind. There now, two invaluable pieces of advice, must not burden you any further.' With that he nodded as he set off on a quick trot across the *paseo*. He walked right around it twice then leaned against the railing at the end, looking out to sea. Sally had seen him before, but this was the first time he had spoken to her. She was relieved by his tactfulness and attracted by the humor close to the edge of his brisk manner. While he remained with his back conveniently turned to her across the *paseo* as he contemplated the Mediterranean, she speculated on the English speaking residents in Nerja. The man who had spoken to her looked occasionally over his shoulder towards Calle Pintada, it was still called this locally despite the plaque renaming it Calle Generalissimo Franco, he looked to the place where that cobbled, winding street spread into the waiting arms of the *paseo* and the sea. 'Is he expecting someone?' she wondered, 'For a little place which is supposed to be unknown in distant lands they seem to have a lot of non-Spanish residents.' Now she realized she wouldn't mind talking to someone, if only to map out the society she found herself at the fringe of. Reluctant to risk anything, she took solace in the mountains and impenetrable sea, washing her asleep by night, lulling her restlessness by day. Still, still, something about this town affected her, touched her as never before. Although several thousand inhabitants moved unobtrusively by each day the proximity of mountains and sea offered a sense of open countryside. Far below on the shore to the east the cries and shouts of children mingled with fishermen's voices as they mended their nets, as they overhauled the small fishing craft beached by the heavy sea. Women called to them from houses carved into the rock, below at the mouth of the sea. 'There is something here, there is something which is different, something I've not known before.' A young woman with bronze colored skin, a long Byzantine nose rising high on her face and a thick braid of honey colored hair walked onto the *paseo,* stopped at the kiosk for cigarettes which she dropped into a large straw shopping basket, then continued somewhat aimlessly until she joined the man with the beard looking out to sea. They stood side by side. Sally couldn't decide whether or not their shoulders touched. 'Is she his wife, are they friends, are they lovers? Is one of them, are they both married to someone else? No, I don't want to know, I really can't cope with a whole new cast of characters. How can I look at the seamy little dramas played out by one *dramatis personae* or another, what can it mean to me now?' And yet she was as curious about them as she was about the flowers blooming precariously down the cliff, curious enough to lean over, catch their sweet fragrance, touch the soft petals and thorny leaves. How could she let them go unnoticed? After awhile the woman with the bronze colored skin and honey colored hair walked up to her smiling, 'Hi, my name is Roberta West.' A sunny smell of New York or the Bronx emanated from her accent and manner. 'Are you just passing through or do you plan to stay awhile?' Smiling, 'Aren't we all just passing through?' 'A good point,' laughing, 'What I meant was my husband and I have been here nearly two years, we pretty well know our way around. If you need any help let me know, I can bargain like a Spaniard and I've found a few edible goods in the impossible stores of this town.' 'That's awfully kind, I might just have to take you up on it, there are a few galling difficulties in my little *apartamento*. I don't know what to do with the *brasero* and I'm terrified of the *bombonas*. The concierge, if that's what you call him, explained it all to me, but I didn't understand more than two syllables in twenty, in spite of the glorious pantomime.' 'Where are you staying? You're not at Antonio Tercero's, are you?' 'Where's that? No, I don't think so, I'm just over the road here.' 'Ah, at Pepe Rico's. Antonio Tercero is not his real name, there are so many Antonios, Josés and Miguels we've sometimes had to resort to numbers to distinguish them. Pepe Rico's is really a nice place, hope they're not overcharging you, it's still way off-season.' She chatted on happily and cheerfully, something pleasantly vulgar in an immensely sophisticated way lacing her talk, as if she had been raised on gangster movies. Who could resist her charm, her confidence, the cheerfulness which seemed to spring spontaneously from the earth she walked upon, the unfeigned optimism which swept her universe with a broad beam of light. She said there was no time to sit down, she had to get to the market before the fish, the oranges and greens were sold out, yet she remained leaning over the chair across from Sally, her back bent at nearly a right angle to the ground, the thick blonde braid hanging down in front of her, moving when she did. 'I'll come later today or tomorrow with someone to help you master the Spanish niceties of your place. It's no joke, you can de-oxygenate yourself over the *brasero* and people blow off limbs with those darn *bombonas*. Not my husband though, he's hopeless at that kind of thing, writers are notoriously incompetent to do anything except write and that's what my husband does, or at any rate what he says he's doing.' In a frank, open way Roberta continued to scrutinize Sally as she chatted on and on, 'There is a bunch of *extranjeros* here if you're looking for company, you know.' 'Actually, I haven't spoken to anyone, I've needed to be alone for awhile.' 'Do you like it here?' 'I love it, I've never been anywhere like this before. I want to spend the rest of my life here or up there perhaps, on the mountain. Does everyone fall in love with it at first sight?' 'No, not everyone. Look, I must do the shopping. We live at number twenty-four on Calle Pintada, why don't you drop by this evening and I'll introduce you to a few people. Would you like that?' 'I think so, but I'll have to brace myself for it, being with people again.' She smiled, 'I'm not sure how much I can stand.' Roberta looked at her with an inquiring light in her eye, repeating the invitation, 'Well come then, it might do you good.' Sally laughed for the first time, 'How kind of you, for some reason I've always been blessed with friends who get me to do things which are good for me, thank you for the invitation. I don't feel like such a stranger in town now, and maybe that's good.' Roberta walked off, hair swinging behind her like a metronome as her feet landed sharply and squarely, like a dancer, on each step. Sally ordered

316

another coffee and a little warmth from the hidden sun began to invade the *paseo. Solitary wave whose gradual sea I am.* The man with the beard remained staring out to sea. A youngish man, short, wearing jeans and a denim jacket, quite evidently American, sauntered slowly onto the *paseo,* hands shoved deeply into his pockets, head down. He noticed the other man when he was halfway across the *paseo* and walked towards him. They talked for awhile, turned in her direction once or twice and eventually came over. 'Now,' she thought, 'Now if I'm going to escape, this is the moment.' But she hadn't paid her bill, it would have been impolitely obvious to run. 'How do you do,' said the man who had spoken to her earlier, 'My name is Seamus Lynch and this is my friend whose closely guarded name is alleged to be Jacob von Hahn, we call him Jake.' Her solitude quietly began to dissipate. Both men held themselves slightly in check, just in case their combined boisterousness should be unacceptable. She introduced herself, invited them to join her and said to Lynch, 'Then Roberta is not your wife.' 'That has not been my good fortune, I'm afraid the lady is married to a friend, Jason West by name. Do you believe we attach too great importance to names?' Lynch was without question the most clinically Irish specimen she had ever met, including as he did, Dublin, Trinity College, insufferable reverence for James Joyce, an accutely lapsed state of Catholicism, an alienated wife and child, a terrible thirst for alcohol, exhuberant scholarship, compassion for others but no mercy for himself. Jake said little, content for the moment to wrap himself in the outpouring of Lynch's wit. Lynch respected his friend's solemn capacity to keep silent. It should be mentioned that Sally discovered when the urge to speak came, as it did once in awhile to Jake, nothing could halt the flow. Now the three engaged in an amiable interlude of first acquaintance, during which they interrogated each other about the things they considered important, and for Lynch and Jake nothing was more important than their love of books. They were both writers, Jake who was a novice in fiction had retired from journalism to write something more lasting, Lynch was a published author held in high esteem by a few loyal connoisseurs. They shared, among other things, acquiescence in a slightly absurd poverty and ambition merged with purposefulness in pursuit of their craft. Very quickly it was a meeting of old friends trading off titles, authors, opinions, eager to recommend a favorite unknown to the others, to announce some hitherto obscure truth. Sally's blunt tongue soon absolved her companions of the restraint they had imposed upon themselves. 'Jake my good man, honest friend, speak the solemn truth now, don't we deserve a drop of something to keep off that chill, unnatural wind?' 'Couldn't agree more, nothing better than a few hits of *coñac* to keep the *levante* at bay. The prevailing wind you see, comes from the west, but when this nasty one blows out of the east, well as you might have noticed, rainy weather is the result.' 'Did you know that 'east wind — rain' was the Japanese code for the attack on Pearl Harbor?' 'No, extraordinary intelligence, do please in honor of that, permit me to buy what I take will be your first drink of *coñac*. Fundador,' Lynch said ordering, '*Tres* Fundador, *por favor.* I must warn you that it is not normally wise to drink this stuff before the sun begins to decline late in

318

the afternoon or you may find yourself subject to visions. That wind is the devil though, and this the holy water to purge him.' They drank from small glasses, the white saucers placed beneath each glass accumulating in neat little stacks to facilitate the reckoning. The harsh liquid had a round oily edge and the pungence of apples. They took their warmth not from the reluctant sun but the small fire ignited in the pit of the stomach, fanning and spreading itself up to the lungs, the breath and the brain, down to the knees. The *tapas,* savory tidbits that came with every round, Sally found unidentifiable. 'What is it?' she asked finally after consuming several. 'Goat's meat,' replied Lynch watching her closely. Jake sat upright in his chair, one arm flung over the back, no longer slouching to keep warm. 'When I first arrived, in winter as luck would have it, I was cold and wet, the house I rented was so damp I was ready to call it quits and leave. Roberta came to my rescue, she found my sunny *apartamento* at the top of Calle Granada, which I have no doubt, saved my life.' How else she might have helped him Sally could only speculate, there was something attractive about this intense, quiet man. His face unfolded in peaks, the nose craggy and slightly spatulate, the chin needle pointed, both the gift of nature; the minor displacement of the jaw however, was a surgeon's endowment following an automobile accident. He came from a small fishing community, much smaller than this little town, an island off the coast of Massachusetts. One of his principal pleasures he took by recalling the boyhood exploits in that rural paradise, telling his stories slowly, with careful attention to detail, ornaments under no circumstances to be omitted. 'Knocking over outhouses was routine, and greasing a pig, well you did that for halloween. One time there was this mean son of a bitch name of Josiah Johnstone, everyone hated him. Didn't have kids of his own, maybe that's what made him ornery and hard to git along with.' He would pause deliberately over the country way of saying *git* instead of *get,* making sure his auditors caught the inflection. 'Now we had been aiming to pay him back for his unfriendliness; so one night, it was a Saturday and some of us was hangin' out back of the general store with a bottle of likker passin' among us fast and furious until we emptied it, clean and shiny as a whistle,' he rolled his eyes slowly in mock appreciation, 'When big Jim Scranton ups and says, "I got me a plan!" It was a few miles down the road to old man Johnstone's farm, a freezing mid-winter night. The sky was incredibly lit up with stars and a half full moon, the ground was white, crunchy under hard packed snow. It was as cold as it needs to be, only we weren't feeling a thing. We crept up to Johnstone's barn and I could hear the cattle moving, shifting about inside. He kept a big dog in the barn but we didn't see hide nor hair of him. We put his wagon on top of the barn that night. I would like to have seen his face in the morning, standing out there to have a stretch or two, his glance suddenly falling on the wagon straddling the roof.' Jake chuckled happily to himself lost in those days of wonder. 'I'm sorry,' interrupted Sally, 'I don't quite understand, how did you get it up there?' 'Easy, took it apart, passed it up, put it back together up there,' and he laughed hard and long. Lynch and Sally laughed as much at his amusement as at the story. He exhaled deeply, satisfied with the past, with his account of it.

320

Sally caught the stale smell of Celtas which he smoked at the rate of two packs a day; she always associated that not unpleasant smell and a residue of dampness with this droll, kind man. 'You want to be careful what you say when Lynch is around,' he said to Sally with a smile. 'He's a dangerous man, don't repeat anything you wouldn't want to find in print one day. He writes down everything we say, I've seen his notebooks, nothing escapes him. That story I told has already been recorded, this fellow had the audacity to show it to me, insisting I correct a few trifling details. Talk about nerve, he thinks he's some kind of painter and we sit for him whether we like it or not.' This was high praise from Jake. Lynch maintained strict discipline where his work was concerned, rising now to leave. 'Well Sally, I can't help but be grateful for your arrival among us,' he glanced at Jake, 'You are the missing link. Your humble servant,' and he strode away, his shoulders hunching involuntarily against the *levante.* 'How long does that wind blow?' 'Sometimes for several days in a row. I think Seamus was indulging in a little matchmaking, I hope you won't take it unkindly.' 'O of course not, can he really work after four or five glasses of *coñac?'* 'He seems to, marvellous isn't it?' She nodded, suddenly uncertain about what to do next, 'I guess I should be going, can you point me towards the market?' 'Sure, be glad to. Walk past my place with me and I can point out the post office if you haven't found it yet.' They swerved left from the *paseo* pausing to look at the simple, clean white lines of the church in Plaza de los Mártiros, 'Does every town in Spain have a Martyr's Square?' asked Sally with a rush of remembrance. 'I don't know, why?' 'I keep

thinking about political murders, assassinations, firing squads.'
'Don't have any use for politics, even less for politicians.' 'You
might not feel that way if it was you lined up against the wall,'
'A good point,' said Jake politely, closing the subject. Sally
remembered having heard the phrase earlier that morning. The
plane trees lining the square looked naked, the small bells of
fruit hanging like decorations on a Christmas tree, the polished
bark peeling back in soft shadows, green, grey and yellow.
'Strange,' she said, 'How aware I am of the violence, yet at the
same time, how strongly I feel the peace.' 'Ah, the mystery of
Epaña,' he pronounced it in the Andalusían way, eliding the *s*.
They parted company at number eighty-eight on Calle
Granada, the location of his *apartamento* with its large
whitewashed balcony on the third floor. He was building a
fireplace in the central room at his own expense, firm in the
conviction that wood heat alone would keep the cold Spanish
winter nights warm. He went upstairs to work on it now,
pointing out the route to the market for Sally. 'There won't be
much left,' he commented. 'That's okay, at least I'll know
where it is for tomorrow and the days to come.'

Late that afternoon, about six o'clock, Jake and Roberta
arrived together, noisily, at her *apartmento*. 'Here's the man for
you,' she said to Sally, 'He knows how to open the shutters,
light the *brasero,* hook up the *bombona,* everything I
assure you.' There was no doubt some conspiracy had been

322

undertaken to put Jake and Sally together. 'Now as soon as you get all fixed up here, you are both to come and have dinner with us. You should meet Jason before the crowd arrives tonight.' Sally was about to object, but she was grateful to these people who took her in and treated her kindly, she did not refuse. 'What's he like, Jason?' Sally asked Jake. 'Old Jas? As nice a fellow as you could ask for, a bit neurotic, secretive about his work, like me. Won't show a word to anyone, except he seems farther down the road than I am. He's a hypochondriac too, damn cheerful though, even when he feels the imminence of death. Poor fellow, he lived in terror last winter when several *extranjeros* caught hepatitis. It's no joke, raging fever, totally debilitating, leaves you too weak to move. Roberta brought me food every day for three weeks, might have died otherwise. A good woman, a very good woman. Anyhow, I think you'll like Jas, he doesn't have the wit that Lynch has — can't decide whether it's a curse or a blessing Lynch says — but he's an amusing man, mostly I think because he finds himself so funny.' He paused, 'That makes him tolerant, very forgiving.' 'Are all the foreigners writers then?' 'No, not all,' he laughed, 'But darn near all. Jas's work will come to something, he's huddled himself away from the world up against it. You won't see him hanging around like the others, he's miserable when he's working and miserable when he's not, a sure symptom. Some of the others, you'll meet them tonight I guess, one or two are serious, one's an academic, well you'll see for yourself, and time alone will tell. It's one thing to want, another to do it, let alone bring it off. At any rate, a good excuse for a sabbatical, leave of absence, "Gentlemen, please consider my application for a year's leave with/without pay. I'm off to Spain to write exalted prose." Aside from the dedicated wives who read, type and sit it out, there are a few painters up in Torrox.' 'What happened to Lynch's wife?' 'That's a bit complicated, they've had a falling out but she'll come back, I'm sure she will. Enough, you'll see it all unfold before your eyes this evening.' Jason called his wife Bert, no one else did. 'Bert,' he moaned during the pleasant dinner, 'Why did you lay this on me, you know my nerves will take weeks to recover.' 'Never mind Jas darling, we have to invite everyone once in awhile, it's only polite.' Smiling at Sally, 'Forgive my barbarian, he's lost whatever social grace or tact he might have had, and it was, I assure you, little enough to begin with. I must be gregarious enough for two or no one would ever speak to us, and what a desolate life we'd lead. You see my dear, it's all very well for these gentlemen who have their talent to keep them company, the rest of us find little to do except get together for cosy chats, our principal entertainment, and people are so disobligingly dull most of the time. You're a new girl in town, I'm counting on you to stir us up, you won't let me down, will you?' 'God Bert, you're a staunch little trooper.' 'You'd be lost without me and you know it.' They laughed at each other good naturedly. The dinner was *muy típico* and delicious, garlic fried *mariscos* in sauce, potato omlette with Swiss chard, tomato and garbanzo salad, as well as a litre or two of a pleasant white wine. Sally had brought a bottle of *champán* which they consumed first. She had expected to drink a glass with Lynch, but he bypassed supper altogether, didn't appear until later in the evening. He disliked large numbers of people, finding himself incapacitated by more than a few at a time. He did not want to be the center of attention, did not want to be noticed, unlike Roberta who had a confident sexuality which she threw out, casually almost, like bait. She calculated the effect of every posture, every remark, that was her style yet nothing about it was offensive. Jas knew how complicated, how restrictive his devotion seemed to her and disguised his jealousy; this was perhaps the reason he gave her a lot of leg room, as he put it. He was a tall, gangly man, a little too thin, although that was well-concealed by several heavy layers of clothing. Sally joined in the laughter as they examined, article by article, the garments Jas had wrapped around himself like swaddling clothes. Having consumed a good share of wine against the night's entertainment now about to begin, he was giggling as they rolled him on the floor, counting sweaters, vest, a long scarf twisted around his neck, the ends trailing behind him, flannel shirt, undershirt and a thermal vest. It was too much. Roberta was insisting that he show Sally and Jake the matching drawers when he was saved by the appearance of the first guests. As more and more people arrived, about twenty-five at one time or another, Sally was quite pleased to sip her wine with Jake, sitting close to the end of the long narrow room, a gallery occupying the entire second floor. At the bottom of the staircase which rose in two easy stages was the dark, roughly tiled and spacious room that, along with the kitchen and pantry at the back, made up the first floor of the handsome little house. 'Spanish architecture is comprehensible in summertime, which is after all, most of the year,' Jake explained. 'I think they're afraid of the sun, not just of being too warm, but afraid the rays generate some evil. You won't see a Spaniard sitting in the sun if he can avoid it. That dark cold room downstairs is cool in summertime, that's why the windows are so heavily shuttered, to keep out the light, they won't even open them in winter. Now take my flat, the Commandante, that's my landlord, he wasn't able to rent it till I came along, it's got so much light it's uninhabitable for a Spaniard. Come and visit me, you're welcome any time. Roberta likes to sunbathe there, she'd be pleased with company I'm sure.' Whatever it had been, if it ever had, was clearly terminated. 'Thanks, the little balcony I have gets the sun until well after midday, but I'd like to come anyhow. Is everyone received this cordially?' Jake laughed, 'No, in fact we have a hands off policy that can last for weeks, that's mostly to keep from getting involved with tourists who might be passing through or spending a week or two in the summer. We are working against the government to keep this place secret for another couple of years, then it will yield to the inevitable. Torremolinos is not far behind, that new hotel they're building, the Balcón de Europa, will be heaving with tourists of every kind and number in a year or two, then it'll be game over,' he concluded pessimistically. 'You can always go up the mountain,' said Sally. 'It wouldn't be the same, just wouldn't be the same.' They turned their attention again to the room full of people. 'Somebody is smoking dope, they do at home too of course, but not openly like this. I don't care for it myself, or more truthfully, perhaps I might like it too much and I'd be lost altogether. I'm a compulsive type, when I started to smoke

326

cigarettes it was pack a day, when I started to drink, an instant alcoholic. Just not safe with the pleasures of the senses. Do you smoke grass too?' 'I have been known to.' 'Well I don't like it, don't approve, I'm sure all the horror stories are true.' 'There are some disadvantages no doubt, but look at him, that older chap over there. Name's Parker Stubbs, a scholar by trade, writing some abominable book on American history which will probably earn him a pension for the rest of his life. Notice how quiet he is, even peaceful you might say.' 'I don't know, he's just sitting there, bolt upright with a dopey smile on his face, I haven't seen him talk to anyone.' 'That is the miracle of grass.' 'I guess it's not my kind of miracle.' 'The man is a terrible drinker, an alcoholic, I've seen him mean, loud-mouthed, foul, making trouble for everyone. Heard that folks even called out the Guardia he behaved so badly, especially to her, that little girl sitting beside him, Emma, his wife, a child bride. She was his student, he divorced his wife and married her. That's why they came here for a year, to let the waves die down. It's been rough on her and she's scarcely more than a child. He must look different to her now.' 'You can't be sure, love endures terrible storms.' 'That's fantasy.' 'That's truth.' They considered each other. *The tears I shed were drops of blood, falling, falling to the waiting earth.* 'The fellow over there with the handlebar mustache is Jack Traherne, and Anne, the tall bony woman talking to Jas, she's his wife. She just had a baby, the first American woman brave enough to concede babies may be born in countries other than the U.S.A. Lynch and I went to visit her after the blessed event. He bent over the cradle, examined the child and murmured *tapas.*' Sally laughed, 'We are all destined for the butcher's shop.' 'While Anne endured the final difficult months of the pregnancy, her husband found comfort with a lady from Torrox who will be here accompanied by her husband this evening, it's a tight little community. Ah yes, we do occasionally enjoy some social contact with the natives, the man behind the bristly mustache and glasses is the doctor. He speaks a little English, a fine fellow. He's been trying to lure Roberta to his office for an intimate examination, at least that's her version. Let me fill your glass.' He moved slowly through the room stopping to chat here and there. Sally had by now met all the permanent residents, she had spoken to Mitsi, the German-American with a soft accent and tic-like grimace, a woman of ambiguous sexuality who was supposed to have had a liaison with a lady from one of the richest families in America. Her husband, a painter like herself, was a small and polite man with simple, direct manners. They were both painting to music, seeking their inspiration in the meticulous forms of Johann Sebastian Bach. 'You must come to Torrox,' she invited Sally, 'I like to be close to nature, this place is too big, too populated.' She had spoken also to a Danish couple, to a startling Jewish-American beauty in her mid-twenties whose husband had been briefly employed by the *Saturday Evening Post,* to another American couple who had weathered six rough months and were going home to get a job, raise a family. She had talked briefly to Helena Eckler and Con Richards, an American entrepreneur of the flesh whose principal support was the lady at whose side he had made himself indispensable. There he was to remain until a few petty indiscretions and the fortuitous appearance of a younger, handsome rival vanquished him from her life. Helena, of uncertain age and talents, owned a small business in the States which she managed from her comfortable Spanish villa and frequent trips to New York. Here a surprising link in Sally's fate was wrought and beaten at the forge. In a time which was to come, after her own life had flickered and died, this singular lady whose curving nose and shadow of hair laid along the upper lip made her somewhat but not altogether unattractive, whose capricious, unchecked manners sought to make servants of her friends, whose taste was flawed by poor judgment, whose greed was superseded only by her possessiveness, this dark lady was to become the life's companion of Edwin Knight. When Sally died soon after Spohr, Edwin was overwhelmed and fled south, plunging directly into the serpentine embrace of Helena, the keeper of his final unhappy days on earth.

Sally made no move to find Jake, she felt glutted, exhaling deeply with something like despair to find herself drowning once again in the sea of mortal misery. 'It's not that I don't care about these people, it's not that I'm unmoved by their dilemmas, it's just that I have so little time. Because I have no future. It's selfish and practical, put the house in order, bind up what needs binding up, cut loose what cannot be tied off. But why a whole new cast of characters at the end? Is this the way the world ends, is this the final *invitación* you cannot decline?' Lynch appeared with Jake at his elbow. 'Sneak out with us for a quick turn on the *paseo,* it's crowded here,' offered Lynch. 'Thanks, yes I will, I was just feeling it's a little too much.' They stepped into the damp cold night and found a heavy mist binding the palm trees on the *paseo*. 'Let's stop in at Pepe Gómez,' suggested the resourceful Lynch, 'We can wait out the worst of the crush there, Roberta won't miss us for awhile.' They sat down in the large empty room on the far side of the bar at La Molina, a *taverna* which stayed quiet except for Sundays, ordered *cerveza* and smiled comfortably at each other. 'Tell me, how did you find our Jason of the West?' Sally paused, 'I think he is a good man who will win his wife in the end.' Lynch listened to her answer carefully and frowned, 'Do you believe, do you really believe that is his purpose?' 'For the moment, yes, don't you?' 'I cannot say, that is something I cannot say.' 'Do you, as Jake insists, write down everything we talk about?' 'Sometimes, yes I do, doesn't everyone?' They laughed. Sally persisted, 'Tell me why you do this.' 'To remember, to get it right.' 'It?' 'Ah, that is the question.' 'I've given up on the question, what I'm looking for now is the answer.' 'Heavy stuff girl, heavy stuff.' 'Why don't you two stop talking in riddles,' said Jake, 'And order another round.' José, the waiter of an age impossible to determine, somewhere in his middle years well beyond youth and well before old age, José who had worked in a bar seven days a week since he was a boy of eight, shuffled slowly back with his tray held up, but not too high. '*Invitación* Pepe Gómez,' he announced as the smiling face of the *patrón* appeared through the serving hatch at the bar, waving, nodding, wishing them *salud, suerte y pesetas*. 'He won the money to buy this *taverna* in the lottery, must be the most generous man in Spain,' said Jake. 'I have an idea,' added Lynch, 'That when he ascends to his celestial *taverna* they will inscribe a marker, a memorial here on earth

with the words *Invitación* Pepe Gómez.' By an unspoken
agreement they decided not to return to the party on Calle
Pintada. Jas found them there an hour later, 'Thought I might
run into you here,' he grinned, 'Can only stay for a quick one
or there'll be hell to pay.' They talked with gusto about
literature which Lynch knew more systematically, more
intimately than any of them. Jas, obliged to teach at a small
college for a living, consulted him, deferred to his authority
and respected those opinions which didn't coincide with his
own. Jake who was awed by the Irishman's erudition was in a
determined way plugging the gaps in his reading, directed
quite often by Lynch's recommendations, while he, Lynch, was
unaffectedly grateful to the two for their friendship. Sally had
a feeling Roberta united these men in some way they preferred
not to acknowledge. As the only woman among three men who
were so close, she evoked an aspect of common property which
might have been construed as insulting if she had not clearly
enjoyed the arrangement. When Jas left, the other two
accompanied Lynch back along the winding Calle Carabeo to
his home where, true to his origins, he grew a large potato
patch in the garden at the back. The bottom of the garden
beyond its fence dropped clear away to the sea below. 'A little
dangerous for the boy perhaps, but good for my soul, the
imminence of destruction,' he said pointing out features of the
terrain utterly concealed by the dense white mist. 'Where is
your wife then?' asked Sally directly. 'Gone, banished,
defeated, driven off, ha!' 'Basically,' explained Jake
diplomatically, 'It was what you might call a literary
difference.' 'By God, you're right Jake, it wasn't myself, it was

331

my life cursing book, my ruin for sure. The wife you see, became convinced, whether rightly or wrongly is not the point, that certain aspects of my private life were laid bare in the manuscript she's typing. I can't type, I've never typed, she's always done the typing. One day, in tears mind you, a genuine flood, she burst out, "I'll not type this, not one syllable more you bastard," she used that word, she actually used that word, "It was bad enough to live through your vile experiment but I'll absolutely not type it for you." Can you imagine that?' He seemed quite serious and Sally didn't dare answer, knowing she'd be overcome by laughter. A gifted man's folly seems perhaps more acute in the context of his gifts. 'Never mind Lynch,' offered Jake comfortingly, 'A few more weeks in your soggy native land and she'll come scurrying back, you'll see, she'll have to, just to warm her bones.' 'Do you think so, do you really think so? She's a brave, resourceful woman.' Lynch became quiet, saying less and less during the following hour. Finally Jake announced he would escort Sally home, she agreed and they departed, leaving their friend in a dark mood. 'Will he be all right?' she asked. 'O don't give it a thought, he's not that unhappy about their separation, it gives him a little scope for certain adventures, maneuvers which tend to be complicated under the nose of a loving wife, especially in a small town with everyone looking on, nothing else to do except wait and see, watch and wait. He'll be fine.' Sally got into her narrow bed doubling the blankets for warmth, throwing her heavy winter coat on top of them. She kept very much to herself again for days.

SALLY REGER'S PERSONAL MONOLOGUE
(III)

The days and nights pass quickly erecting monuments in time, hallowing the seas of separation, and I cannot believe we shall meet again. I cannot banish what may only be superstition, or is it experience, a pendulum, the accentless weight of the coded message: what happened before must happen again. The cycle once set in motion, however casually or accidentally, is perpetuated. Will it ever end? The truth, the irreversible truth is I cannot speak without your voice, I cannot touch without your hands or even believe without your faith. Yet I cannot abandon what I cannot accept, nor be forgiven with lies in my mouth, and I cannot be deceived in desire. Is this retribution? I know and you know, but we remain ignorant of each other. I would rather know than be tormented like this, not knowing. I am sick of silence, sick of distance and chronic solitude, only I would rather be alone forever than live in hope. I prefer death to the fantasy which becomes a nightmare crossing the boundaries of time. Now the last drops are draining from me, one by one. What is compassion, what is loyalty? Do they exist, these inventions, these chimeras bred by strangled desire? What continues is a hopeless mixture of mistakes, passion without culmination, betrayal without remorse, all this time without end, knowledge without wisdom. How do I outwit my sanity? Rescue me, save me from time, from distance and destruction. Why have you deserted me, why have you left me alone? I can see the future as a mere weight on my conscience, dragging me to the depths of the seas, beyond despair. Save me, save me from my own death and yours. Where is goodness, where is love, where is kindness? Gone, all gone, vanquished. They never were, I deny the joy, the exultation, they never were. Time and distance alone remain, and the hot white sun, blinding, implacable. What then is beyond the sea, what is that dim shadow I barely discern lying athwart the opposite shore, do I really see it or do I imagine some dubious African horizon, the last temptation? It no longer matters whether anything remains to be given, taken or denied; I am so depleted love or the lack of it is irrelevant. The feeling that my life is finished gets stronger every day, becomes more pervasive, the awareness of death permeates what I think, what I say, what I do. I don't even have to die, I am dead already, just fasten the tie around the green plastic bag and throw it away. Well where does that leave me? Left over, a nightmare that hasn't expired by morning. I don't know what to do, I need not to be yet every day I encounter the stupidity of being here, again and again, minute by minute. Ah but time itself would be the willing assassin if I could wait long enough. I can't, it won't. The oath has been taken, the affirmation given, not to partake of anything less than perfect. Without that, I want not. Let's get this straight once and for all, even if you still want me, I'm out of it.

Bellair Street,
24 August 1966.

Dear Sally,

Your epistolary talent, scorched I have no doubt and dried in the heat of the sun, we are obliged to reconcile ourselves to a few tantalizing postcards: wish you were here indeed. Does Antonio really bring in the mail by burro or is that just a figure of speech? Nella and I, each from our separate empires, miss you and find life quiet and rather dull these days. Everyone seems to have disappeared or gone his own way. The result is I find time on my hands, my work has not been particularly exciting lately. I did put together a collection of games and puzzles to be played on the computer, something I had started before you left and it didn't take long to finish. Foolishly, I offered the project to the Science Centre thinking it's the sort of thing they might have some interest in. This unfortunately, delivered me up to the warring, internecine bureaucrats who run that show. The upshot was they put me on contract for two months, and failing anything better I've been trying to manipulate a sinecure of one kind or another. No luck so far; I arrived a bit late on the scene. The politics of science dominates everything and I'm not entirely sure who plays on whose team, an entertaining enough puzzle in itself. Schradieck, standing at my elbow this very moment, sends you his love. Birgitte and Sevcik who were quite surprised to hear you had left town asked to be remembered. There's no news of Archer — Marten Bender still convinced he languishes

335

somewhere against his will. Nella, as I think you may know, has never written a letter in her adult life, but she insisted I write to let you know we've received a short, incomprehensible note from Eddy. He remains in the far west bootlegging for the natives, engaged in heaven knows what other reprehensible practices as well. If he returns to us dismembered in accordance with some outlandish custom we will welcome him back anyway, won't we? Life is a charade my dear, so don't attach much importance to the specifics. Stick to general principles and don't get bogged down.

Love to you,
Spohr.

Late afternoon. They sat in a golden stream outside the Bar Alhambra transformed by light into gilded statues, their garments and faces painted on, three canticles of mutability, Roberta, Lynch and Jake. Glistening like some vestal offering Roberta sat on the edge of the seat inclined towards Lynch, her lips open as if she was about to whistle or sing, her toes pressed against the pavement, heels braced on the bottom rung of the chair. Was she offering or refusing the point which glowed between them like a heated sword? Lynch was still, trapped in the silence before a question or after the answer, while Jake sat turned away from the other two as though indifferent to the outcome. They were caught like a gold frieze in high relief,

336

wreathed about with palm trees, behind them the distant disk of the sun, a dark blue sea and clusters of purple shadows like grapes in the silence. Ornamenting the *paseo* as if they were a continuation of the rocks below, they flowered in the Andalusían mystery impregnating the soil, the sea, the air. Think of García Lorca impaled on the futile ignorance of his people, think of Ibn 'Arabi, think of al-Ghazali and Ibn Rushd alive in the holy fire, the vision of God, all the saints whose purity clarified the dust they walked upon, think of the Carthaginian generals, their emblems blazing from the backs of elephants, and think of ancient Phoenician traders bringing blue and purple cloth along with their lettered secret, that was the rock they sprang from, a cluster of gold and light and death. From a kiosk on the *paseo* where she paused to study this refraction, this prismatic flash, Sally felt drawn to the mystery, drawn to the fire, ready to brush wings with the angel of death for what burned on that rock high above the sea. She approached them slowly as the light shifted, reddening like blood, as the sun steadied itself for the final drop into its silken bed, the sea. When she stopped at the table they waved and laughed normally, offhand, ignorant of their divine descent. Breathing the air deeply she searched for some intimation, some vestige of the secret she had nearly touched and looked into her friends' eyes as if they had usurped the bodies of waiting strangers. The gilt, carved chiaroscuro dissolved upon them as the light became pale and thin, a few birds hovered nervously above the shore, and somewhere down below a mother called, *'Eh niño, niño venga, venga aquí,'* again and again. They were served glasses of *vino tinto* by Miguel, the discreet, aging, ex-anarchist warrior who held a tray aloft with blazing dignity in his rumpled white, high collared waiter's jacket, the uniform of office he occupied now, dispassionately, without comment. He was pleased to down a glass which they offered from time to time, standing close to the table, saluting them with indulgent gravity, head bent at a slight angle, the hoarse, rough voice filtering through gaps in his broken teeth. Lynch admired him, studying the correctness and polite, careful manners, noticing how he observed them, surprised continually he was able to pry their secrets loose without speaking any English. Language for him was neither essential nor primary, and this startled Lynch. 'The Spaniard,' he said launching a favorite theme of the *extranjero,* 'Is a truly remarkable man, there are so many contradictions. Just look at this peninsula, surrounded by the sea on three sides and high mountains on the fourth, ostensibly cut off from civilization, European civilization,' he qualified nodding at the others, 'But in fact, a transmission center, the unacknowledged archive, a secret passageway between the east and the west. There is so much that is the opposite, so much which contradicts the appearance alone. Now take Miguel here, what do you make of him Sally?' 'What should I make of him, I've hardly spoken to him, my Spanish being what it is. Why do you ask?' 'Because I guarantee that he by now knows a great deal about you, he could probably give you details of your last love affair which would be revealing to you and the lover himself. Don't be uneasy, he is a man whose discretion is his valor.' 'How can you say what he knows?' asked Jake a little acidly, 'Your Spanish doesn't spread much farther than the occasional *por favor* and *gracias.'* 'It's all in the set of his shoulders, the angle of his head. I've watched him watch us, I've seen what he takes in, we have no secrets from this man, he knows everything,' glancing at Roberta. 'Hogwash,' said Jake, 'I have no doubt he is a smart man, a good man, but what you say is hogwash.' Lynch smiled appreciatively, 'Well then, look at it this way,' he went on stroking his beard with the obligatory movement of his index finger, 'Now you've been to the bullfights in Málaga, you've felt that erotic preoccupation with death.' 'Why erotic?' interrupted Sally, 'The arms of Eros it seems, are everywhere these days.' Lynch turned, trying to fathom her remark, 'The Hindus I believe, among others, identify and classify the arts as sensual, sexual — music, poetry, dancing, sculpture, everything. The bullfight could hardly be excluded, especially here where the *duende* is mistress. And what is the *duende?* Not some aloof classical muse I promise, she inhabits you, possesses you, a loving demon who enslaves the beloved, rides him to death unless he masters her, learns to command what he wills, not what she wills. It's a remarkable duet, a duel, that's the bullfight, an invitation to death. Come says the matador, let us ride out this fantasy together, let us perform the *pas de deux,* life intermingled with death. No, you come taunts death in reply, you come and caress my deadly horns if you dare. They play together until one mounts the other and drives him out, the survivor wins everything.' 'I don't see things in such unyielding opposites,' said Roberta almost frowning. 'No, I didn't think you did, but it may be that way. And death should be a poor untidy thing, though it's a queen that dies.' 'You're very Irish today Lynch,' Jake laughed, 'There must be a sympathetic chord in there vibrating with all this Hispanic mysticism.' 'The god of lust is a popular god,' said Sally, 'He has dominion over most lives at one time or another, and as you noticed Lynch, in one form or another.' 'You're right Sally,' said Jake, 'Look up in the sky, you'll find confirmation, an act of celestial penetration at this very moment.' Five or so miles straight up, two almost transparent, insect-like creatures were locked in tandem flight, barely visible at the end of a long double vapor trail, an arrow across the western sky. 'The refueling,' continued Jake ironically, the submerged adventurer, 'Our jets keeping the west free, or whatever else Lyndon and his minions have in mind. Really a different kind of transmission Lynch, wouldn't you say?' Roberta interrupted, 'Now Jake, don't say another word against the president. You know, I think he's still in mourning for Kennedy.' She turned to Sally, 'Do you get so attached to your presidents?' 'Actually, we have a prime minister not a president, if you're interested.' Roberta inhaled the filter tipped Bisonte deeply, 'No, as a matter of fact, I don't think I am.' She was neither rude nor unfriendly but her indifference offended Sally, she felt saddened and didn't know how to hide the embarrassment which brought her suddenly close to tears. 'An American savage, remarkable beast,' commented Lynch disarmingly. They all laughed, even so Sally couldn't shake herself free. Echoes of that offhand dismissal would trouble her for days, yet Roberta never once considered anything amiss. Now as it began to grow dark she jumped up, 'Well I guess Jas isn't coming after all, I'd better make supper. See you tomorrow,' she called back to no one in particular, hurrying across the *paseo,* her bronze colored beauty a bubble exploding all around as she walked. They stared after her while the darkness began to settle beside them in bushy clumps like trees. 'I'll never get used to such beauty, does it diminish when you've been here so long, do you become insensitive after a time or does it stay like this, wrenching and new each day?' 'You are inquiring about the view then, and not the lady?' Jake put in. 'I never tire of it or find it less in any way,' said Lynch, 'There is as you say, something which renews itself every day, a spring of pure water always running clear.' *Nemt, frowe, disen kranz.* 'Who can tell where the source may be?' Sally spoke softly, 'Who can even contemplate the beginning? There is something which touches you so deeply you will never perceive it again except through the lens of that knowing. We are comforted like eagles, soaring alone. I was in Italy several years ago,' she continued, 'And saw the Tuscan landscape for the first time, it astonished me. Earlier, when I used to look at reproductions of paintings or frescos I couldn't help but be struck by the hard edged realism which captured the tiniest curls, the warts, the wens, the hook of a nose, and I wondered why they set those figures against landscapes which were so fanciful, so precarious they seemed almost surreal. I was bothered by that, why do they see the figure one way and the ground another? When I got there I was dumbfounded, I discovered the landscape had been set down as literally as the figure. I couldn't imagine it or take it in from photographs or paintings, but when I was actually there, standing on the terraced hills, studying the castellations of miniature silver trees, my ability to perceive was revolutionized. The same thing happened to me with García Lorca. He was always the most disturbing, the most surreal poet for me, he still is, only now that I'm here living in his landscape I find him more literal, more straightforward than I could have believed. Yesterday I walked east out of town, along a road high up, I don't know its name, past the Guardia Civil barracks where the houses are farther apart, there are a few small farms, and I passed a house with a woman singing inside. She was doing her housework, singing while she washed a rough, tiled floor with cold water and a rag. I had never heard that before, spontaneous singing which springs from a place always free to sing, which knows only singing, does nothing but sing, and that changed me. It was the fact of singing, the song itself, the thing inside her which sang and the woman on her knees, her labor melting through the song, flowing from her life. There is something here you know, peacefulness, some uncomplicated but genuine bliss, I don't know what it is, I don't know how you preserve it. That thing, whatever it is, apparently has laws too. Just when you think you understand, something happens, a word, an attitude, and it comes apart in all directons. O well, at least there is always something else to be grateful for. Maybe I just like being warm,' one hand floated deprecatingly as she concluded. They said good evening to each other, politely, seriously, and returned to their separate homes in the dark.

Early afternoon, hot, still, the sky a solitary note struck by the sun; the zenith scorched and shrill, a fissure, pure silence at the crest of the hill. Tall and slender she stands there, one hand cupped over her eyes against the brightness, down below on the sands of Burriana Beach lies a taut pink carcass tossed up by the sea. A small calf, perhaps a young colt, rejected by life, rejected in death, its skin pink and slick. Not yet too stinking, not yet too disgusting. Running down the difficult slope with the merest implication of a path to guide her feet, she stops where the animal lies, studies it holding her breath lest the smell enter her body and take possession. She considers the dead creature, troubled by her inability to identify it, know how it came there. 'My God, it is so dead I can't even tell what it is, poor beast. And when we die? Why is it so nude, is it unborn or did the sea wash away the hair from its skin? Will the flesh melt on our bones and turn us into shining corpses when we die? Suppose we are not dead when we die, suppose some horror crushes us beyond the grave, some terror persists in the bones too deep, too subtle for death, then what? Suppose we do not die, then what of the remedy?' Walking farther down the coast she watches two fishermen take their siesta in the shadow of a heavy fishing craft beached on the painted shore, their sleep a drug taken at high noon, hallucinating the sea, the hill, the dead beast, Salvador Dalí dreamt by the sun. Keep me safe from the Sleeper in Darkness. 'What if some grief persists in the bones beyond the grave? No, this is just a poor creature coughed up by the sea on a shining day, why should I look beyond the grave for its meaning, what does it signify to me? Those fishermen take their siesta in tranquility, their sleep is not disturbed by phantasms, why should I awake to messages which come snatching the remedy from my hand? God protect me, it is the truth, it is the truth.' Immediate solace from the sun is unmistakable, clothing her with the heat of its body on hers, washing the undiluted brightness into each pore, balm on a broken wound, an unearned blessing. She laughs and laughs, 'I have to start all over again, before it was *Sin al-habib no vivirey,* now I do not think the dead lie easy, their mysteries burned away. Death is irrelevant, now what? I suppose I should feel terrible but I don't, what does it mean you silly old cow lying there in death's solitary splendor? Whose game is it after all, mine or yours?' She climbs slowly back to the top of the hill, this time up across terraced levels carved into reluctant soil. At the top once more she finds a place in the silver shade looking down at the sea which flutters on a breath of wind. 'What's done is done, what remains are the waves, the wind and the sea. The larger truth does not obliterate the smaller; it is confirmed.' She moves into the sun again, sitting with head back and legs stretched out in front of her.

Shoes in their hands they ran barefoot over the hot white sand, spreading a soft blanket beneath the terraced hill. They stepped from their outer clothes and lay side by side, not touching but intertwined by what coursed between them. A bright blue bathing suit clung to the bronze and honey colored beauty of her flesh. His pale nondescript trunks matched his pale skin. In a little while they stood up, she tucked the beautiful hair into a white rubber cap molded to the shape of her head, held tightly in place by a strap buckled under the chin. He reached out to take her hand as they walked together into the cool waters of the sea. They walked and walked and finally swam, two briny creatures slipping out between the waves. 'Too far,' thought Sally watching them from above, 'Too far.' Way beyond the shore in the arms of the ceaseless sea they stopped and turned to each other. Did they speak, did they talk suspended in their unnamed liquid of love, or did they merely hold each other by the hand there beyond caution, beyond the shore? Two faultless creatures of the sea played out their longing to slip inside a parallel fold in time, fall into love's golden crease, satiate their passion then reenter, lives unaltered, intact. *Est il paradis, amis, est il paradis qu'amer?* Farther and farther they swam. 'O surely too far,' said Sally from above hugging her knees to her chest, 'They have swum too far from the shore.' She jumped up to watch them, 'Please let them turn back now, now, turn them back.' Did they stop once more or did they only seem to stop? *I have no boatman, I cannot row, waiting for my love.* They turned at last like toys tossed on the waves, bouncing back to shore. Sally retreated unnoticed to the seclusion of a shady tree. When they had first come running across the beach she stood up and waved, was just about to call out when she hesitated, thinking perhaps they had not met by chance, perhaps they had planned this, to be alone, unguarded in their looks and thoughts. While she watched them swimming in the sea she had no doubt of their need and withdrew to assure their privacy. They lay close together on the scorched white sand as Sally turned back to town.

Helena Eckler had invited her for a drink of muscatel, and she made her way to the handsome but exposed villa that enigmatic lady had built for herself. 'Do come in my dear, yes we are alone, Con had some business in Málaga. Let's sit here, it's dark and cool, wonderful to keep still on these long hot afternoons, don't you think so?' Sally, feeling a little haunted, wondered why she had come. Helena spoke softly with traces of an imaginary European accent laid over the east coast vocal flats, producing a languid, penetrating whisper which infiltrated somewhat beyond Sally's endurance. Her nose, elongated but close to her face, swept down above the darkened upper lip like a bat in flight. Her eyes which might have been soft were narrowed by calculation when she spoke, 'So you like my pretty house, do you? So do I, enchanting, I find it enchanting. You've been here long enough now, tell me, have you seen any other so tastefully furnished? A few are more centrally situated, inside however, they are merely Spanish. I make my life here my dear, so it must reflect me, totally, don't you agree?' The muscatel was strong with a wild and grapey ring. Sally let herself drift in a distant, silent pool while Helena's low-pitched murmuring continued its abandoned cascade, equally confident and intimate about her clothes, the stock market, Spanish politics, her furniture, American foreign policy, local gossip. 'When Franco dies they will turn to Juan Carlos, who else can offer any government, whether colonels or politicians, some symbol of legitimacy? They must have that to be secure in their own eyes and the eyes of the world. The Falange is not as dormant as it appears to be, I've spoken to people, Spaniards, they assure me the Falange will never tolerate anything less than a strongly militarist, right wing regime. And they're right, it is best for Spain, best for us, strong ties with America.' Sally filled her glass from the heavy crystal decanter with an expression of noncommittal seriousness which could have meant anything. She felt quite drunk, determined not to interrupt the precarious tranquility wrested from the day's events. 'Yes, the decanter is lovely, isn't it? Quite old I think, I bought it in Seville last year. Con picked it out, he has good taste, a flair for discovering old treasures at bargain prices. He earns his keep.' She laughed, 'I was at Torrox the other day with Mitsi and her husband. They are both clever, although I think I prefer the toughness, the determination to pull the truth from the paint in Mitsi's work. Do you find him sad, just a little unhappy these days? Strange isn't it, with their powerful connections, I think they are in even worse straits than they were last winter. Mitsi said they were living on tomatoes and oranges they picked when no one was looking. I find that hard to believe, some people find it necessary to feign poverty.' 'Others needless to say, come by it honestly,' Sally added. Helena laughed, 'I've always had money, my father made a fortune during the war and then I married well, very well.' 'What happened to him?' Sally wondered if she had swallowed him whole or a little at a time, piece by piece. 'Who?' 'Your husband.' 'He died, tragically. It was difficult for me at first, it still is, life isn't easy, not even for me.' She was drinking methodically setting a solid, steady pace, watching her guest carefully. She sat in a huge armchair directly opposite, her eyes fixed on Sally. 'You have a lovely face my dear, but you mustn't sit directly in the sun. You'll regret it when you're older, your skin will dry out; when a woman loses that luster, that bloom, nothing can ever really take its place.' 'The soul, I think, will never shrink.' 'What an extraordinary thing to say, you can't actually mean it, no one believes that kind of thing anymore. How quaint, you are a clever girl. Here, let me sit beside you.' Helena chatted on and on, her long nose bobbing close to Sally's face. She kept wanting to duck, involuntarily, as you do when a bat swoops near. Helena's hand paused in its explanatory flights occasionally to rest on Sally's knee, she was beginning to find herself a little hemmed in. 'What,' she thought dizzily to herself, 'Does this dotty lady want? I hardly escape from one deadly peril when I find myself in the lap so to speak, of another, I'd better get out.' She moved to the chair where Helena had been sitting, her throne. 'Now tell me, you know Lynch quite well, don't you? I think there's a little something going on with Roberta, if you know what I mean.' Sally was alert at once, invaded by something, a coldness, 'No, I don't.' 'Well I've seen them walking by themselves once or twice, and I've caught the way he looks at her. O it's discreet but there I assure you, odd you haven't noticed.' 'I think you're mistaken, Jason and Roberta love each other.' 'Don't be naïve, of course they do, that doesn't preclude a little fun on the side for Roberta, does it? Come sit beside me again, we need to sort out the facts of life together.' She opened her arms, an ambiguous invitation ending with a pat on the sofa beside her. Sally didn't know whether to scream for help or run or laugh. She chose laughter and a slow, dignified retreat, 'I must be on my way now Helena, that muscatel delivers a wallop though, I'm quite plastered.' She staggered a little more than was necessary to make her point, having declined what might or might not have been offered without taking or giving offense. The warm late

348

afternoon light wrapped around her as she walked back to her *apartamento,* wondering absentmindedly why she had been so protective of Roberta, or was it Lynch? The muscatel had left her giddy, but after awhile she strolled over to the *paseo.* Jake and Lynch were sitting in a grim although not unfriendly silence, Lynch was usually taciturn without a few drinks to oil his tongue, 'Mrs. Sally,' he greeted her with pleasure, 'How good of you to come, Jake and I have nothing to say, you must wind him up so he'll talk. What have you been doing?' 'What have you been doing?' she countered. 'Why nothing worth mentioning, the work is very slow, are you sure you can't type?' They laughed. 'I thought your wife was coming back.' 'She is, I think, soon.' 'And a good thing too,' said Jake, 'I've missed her.' 'Well I have something for you,' Sally offered, 'I went to drink muscatel with Helena this afternoon. Do you know, I'm not sure whether it was the wine or my imagination, I had the impression she propositioned me as it were, made an indecent proposal, not in words, you know, but I think that's what she had in mind.' Lynch lit up, he was interested. 'You don't say, how extraordinary, please, if it's not too much bother, could you divulge a few details.' 'Look out,' said Jake, 'You know he'll run home and write it all down.' He found Helena rather more appealing than the others did, perhaps it was her poise which interested the small town boy not far below the surface, 'Don't be a pervert Lynch.' 'Come now Mrs. Sally, look here, I'll buy you a drink, what'll you have?' Sally and Jake began to laugh, Lynch laughed too, only he was serious. They drank wine and ate the *tapas,* garbanzos in tomato sauce. Amid a lot of teasing Sally finally told Lynch what he wanted to know, not hesitating to embellish her narrative with certain exaggerations. Jason and Roberta appeared unexpectedly, Roberta demanding almost suspiciously to know what was so funny. Lynch looked at Jas announcing with ceremony, 'Some firstrate copy provided by our friend here, tell him Sally, but briefly I beg you, save the fine points for me.' Sally told them. Jason whistled coolly, 'Well now,' he said. 'Nuts!' exclaimed Roberta, 'I knew she was queer all along.' 'In the spirit of the occasion,' remarked Lynch sardonically, 'I must admit that I have also been, shall we say, approached by that lady?' Roberta avoided looking in his direction as Jas began to laugh, 'By God, she's insatiable then, she was coming onto me all last winter.' 'I guess I'm not her type,' said Jake, 'She's never uttered a word to me or I'd have planked her across town and back by now.' Laughter followed his guileless revelation; Jas declared him the winner, insisting he buy everyone a drink. 'We're going to the movie tonight, who wants to come?' asked Roberta. 'God preserve us from John Wayne and a dubbed in Spanish soundtrack,' muttered Lynch. The cinema, apparently without a name, was commonly referred to as *hoy*. This word, meaning today, was the commanding prefix in large letters on the placard at the head of the *paseo* announcing what was to be shown that day. 'Too close to the jail,' was Jake's opinion as he declined. Mr. and Mrs. Jason West therefore departed alone, Lynch staring glumly after them. 'Think I'll run along,' said Jake leaving generously more than his share of money for the drinks consumed. 'Let's take a quick spin around the *paseo* before we touch another drop,' suggested Lynch, 'Or I'll say something indecent.' 'Agreed,' replied Sally. He seized her arm vigorously, 'You are indeed tall,' he commented with admiration looking her straight in the eye. She wanted to tell him about the dead animal on the beach. 'I was at the beach this afternoon,' she began. 'Which?' 'The Burriana.' 'Then you saw us.' 'Yes, but that's not why I mentioned it.' 'You know then?' 'Well yes, I had guessed there was something.' Lynch stopped walking, 'God she's lovely, I'm glad you know, I've wanted to tell you. I don't know what to do, I really don't know what to do, I feel so utterly possessed by her, by the need for her. Sally, I don't know what to do.' 'You want to make love to her.' 'O we've done that, it's not enough, I want something else.' 'You want to be with her.' 'Yes, that's it, something like that.' 'What about Jas and your wife?' 'Well that's the hell of it, I don't know what to do.' *Lost, lost in the arms of Eros.* 'I think you should know that Helena has seen you and put it together, I told her she was mistaken.' 'Thank you, everything will be hard enough when my wife comes back, if she comes. That's why she left, you know.' 'I didn't realize it had been going on for so long.' 'It hasn't, most of this has been my longing for her, my hopeless, impossible craving for what I cannot have, can never possess. Even if we went away together, absurd illusion, I would never have her completely, she's that elusive kind of woman, a narcotic, a dream, that's why I find her so irresistible, so devastating, I can't have her.' Sally said nothing and Lynch took her silence for sympathy when in fact, it was irritation. 'I was dying,' she thought, 'I was dying and I've come back, there is no one, not one person I can tell.' 'Let's go to Pepe Gómez and have a drink.' 'An excellent idea.' Jake was sitting at a table by himself. 'Caught!' they laughed at him as they sat down. 'It wasn't the company,' he explained, a little embarrassed, 'It was myself, needed to be alone. I'm thinking of going back to the States.' 'That's a serious thought.' Antonio, the gypsy fisherman who sang flamenco laments in a strident voice, accompanying himself with flat thin rocks instead of castanets, sat down at their table. He was drinking *anis* with water, *'La nuestra leche,'* he explained to Sally holding up the glass of milky water, chuckling at his old joke. His body was tight and thin like the mustache on his upper lip. Sally had seen him fish from a rock close to shore with nothing but a hook and line. Jake had heard his sister was a whore in Málaga. Like most of the poor Spaniards he was friendly, dignified and filled with a sturdy respect for his world, undiminished by poverty. Both Lynch and Jake were fond of him, they liked his forthrightness, the toughness his life was honed to, his singing, his good humored, apparently limitless capacity to withstand the effects of alcohol, and his ability to convey much across the barricade erected by their limited Spanish. He sat half facing the table to address a comment to them once in awhile, and half facing the *taverna,* chatting with José when he came past, or one or two other quiet Spaniards scattered around the large, dark and rather empty room. His tact permitted them to carry on their conversation in English without excluding him, and to offer the few words in Spanish which imposed no strain. Antonio liked Sally, he liked all the *extranjeros* who had come to live in his little town for reasons which were never quite clear to him. He turned suddenly to Sally, announcing in his gutteral, lisping Andalusían which seemed to elide every

352

important *s* from the language, that on the following Saturday in a place on the other side of the *carretera,* out in the *campiña,* he would for that day be cook, waiter and entertainer to busloads of German tourists who were to stop there for several hours. Sally, he insisted, when they had finally understood the place he was referring to with gestures and improvised maps, must come with Jake and Lynch to eat the *paella* which he promised would be *típico, muy típico,* and to drink the wine which would be abundant and free. They accepted courteously understanding that this was his *invitación,* a return for the drinks they occasionally bought him. 'A command performance,' said Lynch, 'We shall do this properly.' 'In style,' agreed Jake. Antonio said *buenas noches* and took his leave. They sat quietly not saying much, feeling the dark, heavy mass of rain clouds forming on the horizon, building, pressing slowly but unfailingly in their direction pushed on by the quickening wind. 'What to do?' sighed Jake, 'The rain must fall.' 'The funny thing is,' said Sally, 'After I arrived here, for the first few days, although I was deeply moved by the place, I kept thinking this is all very well but I'm a city girl, what do mountains have to do with me? The sea is vast, inponderable, only it's not a city street. Do you know how quickly those feelings vanished? Almost overnight I became a country girl, when I went to Málaga for the first time after six or seven weeks I felt dizzy in the noise, overwhelmed by the crowd. My fear now is I'm unfit to live in the city again.' 'You're not thinking of leaving too, are you?' asked Lynch with surprise. 'No, just worrying. The fact is I'll run out of money soon enough, but I'll come back, I must, this is my home. I never imagined such a place could exist.' 'What about you Jake?' 'Can't say for sure, maybe just feeling restless. The work's no good, you know.' 'Why don't you let me read it?' 'No, absolutely not, there's no point, it's not right, I don't need someone else to tell me that.' 'Isn't there anything I can do?' 'No, you're very kind, I do appreciate it. Damn, I want this so much, only I can't have it, at least not now. I don't suppose you know how that feels.' 'But I do, I do.' 'Some wise man said the thing we want most is the thing that kills us in the end,' said Sally, 'And Proust was right too. Albertine was a bit disgusting up close, a fat frump with a mustache, yet if she seemed unattainable, if the thought occurred to him she might be unattainable, or if there were the merest possibility someone else might be savoring her delights she was immediately transformed into a liquid nymph, the exquisite darling of his bottomless passion. Desire, the real thing, the thing that eats and tears and claws, we feel that only in the presence of what we can't have. How quickly we become indifferent to what is available, how casually we put our treasures away. We have to disengage the hook when we find ourselves caught, we need to know whether we're the bait or the thing baited, which one is the fish, which the fisherman, or we'll dangle from that hook until we die. Unless we're snared by some even more devastating lure.' 'Is it the wine?' asked Jake, 'This doesn't sound like you.' 'No one,' thought Sally, 'Wants to know about that dead beast lying naked on the shore, all pink and slick and well beyond the grave.' 'What you say is doubtless true Mrs. Sally,' commented Lynch, sorrow and amusement both in his voice, 'However it's one thing to know and another to swallow it down, change your ways. A characteristic of slavery is lack of freedom,' he added somewhat wryly. 'When the slave loves his chains he is free,' replied Sally. 'I'm not sure whether or not that's a platitude,' said Jake irritably. Jason and Roberta came in smiling, looking pleased with each other. 'Worst damn western I've ever seen,' Jas remarked affably. 'The worst,' confirmed Roberta nodding, 'A pleasant evening.' 'Look here Lynch, you have to come to terms with our culture, that's modern art out there, you know. Musta learned more about a good tight plot from watchin' westerns than all the books ah evah read. Y'all oughta git in on this afore books go outa style.' Jas leaned back tilting the chair behind him, hooking his thumbs on his vest. The long thin frame and earnest face with a faded remnant of freckles made him the perfect cowboy. 'Cheerful, isn't he?' commented Jake. 'And why not? Today's my lucky day.' He pulled out three cigars, passing one to Jake, another to Lynch. 'Finished the major rewrite today, I'm a downhill racer. Yesiree, today's my lucky day.' Lynch watched him closely while at the same time offering unfeigned congratulations. 'There were days, weeks even, when I thought I wouldn't make it, afraid I wasn't going to put out enough juice in the crunch, in the tough parts where you have to pump it up to get it just right, just so. It came out good,' he lit the cigar which looked incongruous jutting from the innocent planes of his face, 'But it weren't easy, you know, it was Stravinsky and snarling trumpets all the way.' 'What now?' inquired Lynch. 'Still a piece to go, then it'll be look homeward angel for Bert and me.' Five of them on five blazing compass points, holding each to his own true north on the changing axis of the world: Jason puffing a cloud of triumph, Roberta rising up from the foaming sea, Jake the one who watched, Sally the one who knew, Lynch bound by chains forged with his own hand. *And yet the door of the King is never closed.* José came to their table smiling in his patient way at their solemnity. He pointed to the nodding jester's face peering through the hatch, '*Invitación* Pepe Gómez,' he said softly, bringing them back together again.

The Return

The Boatman's Holiday

Harry: Are you going to the funeral?

Sam: I can't face it. My father's was the worst day of my life. You?

Harry: Have to work.

Sam: It's hard to grasp, hard to believe. I mean he wasn't a close friend, I only knew him through Nella, and yet it cuts, it cuts deep.

Harry: Rough waters for all of us.

Sam: When I was in grade six there was a girl with long black hair and the reddest cheeks I'd ever seen. She stopped coming to school after Christmas, and by the time it was spring they said she was dead. Rheumatic fever. Seemed remote, impossible. She was the first person I ever knew who died. None of us went to the funeral.

Harry: That's just like you Sam, some girl dead and buried in your heart all these years.

Sam: What do you mean, just like me? I can't help it if the girl died, can I?

Harry: Well no, but you have a way of taking things personally, as though every time destiny strikes, the blow somehow glances off you.

Sam: I can't stand suffering, anyone's.

Harry: And especially not your own.

Sam: Look I don't need that.

Harry: Sorry old man, didn't mean to be insensitive, I just wanted to find out how you felt.

Sam: Funny how we always seem to end up in this bar. I hate it, I actually hate it.

Harry: Don't be pathological, it's convenient.

Sam: Every time I come back to this town the same thing happens, again and again.

Harry: O come on now, it's not like that at all.

Sam: That's what my old girl said too. Vicious optimists, all of you.

Harry: You know you're hopeless, don't you, absolutely hopeless. Look over there, it's Schradieck. My God he looks awful, he's gone down fast in the last few years.

[Enter Schradieck]

Schradieck: He was my friend, I'll never know why such a man would want to be my friend, but he was. And now he's gone, just like that. *[Crying]*

Sam: We all feel terrible.

Schradieck: What do you know about it? If only he hadn't been alone, if I had met him. I could have, I knew he needed a ride to the airport.

Harry: You couldn't have helped him, he had a heart attack, no one could have saved him.

Schradieck: Don't you believe it.

Harry: What do you mean?

Schradieck: Don't you believe he had a heart attack.

Sam: That's what the doctors said.

Schradieck: What do they know?

Sam: Why do you say that?

360

Schradieck: His shirt was spattered with blood, you don't spout a foam of blood with a heart attack, do you? O what's the use, he's dead, the only friend I ever had and he's dead.

[Exit Schradieck]

Harry: Nella's back, she was in New York with Sandy Burns, it took Spohr's family two days to find her.

Sam: I can't believe she left him, I didn't know.

Harry: No one did at first, not until recently.

Sam: It's always the way, the one who looks as if he's going to walk never does, it's the other one.

Harry: Did you think he was going to leave her?

Sam: He kept playing around, sometimes pretty seriously. Yeah, I thought he would leave her one day, find some gorgeous young thing and away he'd go.

Harry: Wonder what the women saw in him.

Sam: What indeed!

Harry: You mean . . .?

Sam: Precisely, fat lot of good it does him now.

Harry: Schradieck seems hit pretty hard.

Sam: What do you make of that, saying it wasn't a heart attack?

Harry: Hard to say, he seems to put the cause of death in some extramedical territory I don't understand. Then I've always found him erring along the subrational grain.

Sam: He's a rough customer, I like him, he's so twitchy he makes me feel normal. He really used to look up to Spohr.

Harry: Didn't we all, didn't we all.

[Exeunt]

He died on a cold intercalary day. A thin stream of blood erupting from the lungs spattered his shirt and congealed in a bubbling foam on his lips. His death came like an unscheduled eclipse plunging the world where he shone once, a light of pure reason, into darkness. Those who had known him when he commanded respect and admiration were stunned, but their sorrow, if such it was, passed quickly. As far as they could see his life had become trivial, he didn't work, his wife had left him, his friends had drifted away, the world no longer seemed to have any use for him or he for it. Everything had stopped, come to an end, he didn't know what to do next. It had been his time and it was ended. That year was a convulsive year, assassination, burning, revolution, looting, repression, war, reprisal, retaliation. That was the way it was, how the end began, his death falling clearly into the place held in readiness before the beginning of the beginning. Who can account for a single life? Ten years earlier he had seemed supremely, exceptionally equipped, fortune's child. The world changed, he did not. Years later his father said to Nella, 'He was never a man to bend his knee.' So what was left for him? Unless, unless. . . He was not without fault, but is he to be blamed for coming to the end of what he knew? The world did not grieve for Spohr, he came and went unknown, some interstellar event enacted light years away, his brief moment held in reserve, a secret kept by a few. He died on a dark, cold day, alone in a public place, no one to take his hand, on a day the calendar reckons only one year in four to balance the passage of time.

Death when it comes is very explicit, the day, the place, the time, the cause, the absence of cause, the convergence of natural events, politics, family, friend, passion, pain, pleasure, desire, they all disappear, count for nothing to the angel of death. He comes, takes what he needs then goes. He came for him one dark, cold day and that was the end of Spohr.

The first week in March was unrelenting. Winter was not prepared to relinquish its grip and would have to be pried loose, rolled back inch by inch, a deeply entrenched force unwilling to concede it must, in time, give up. Now this dominion appeared unchecked, the crusty snow on either side of the highway sentinals, guardians of a ferocity nothing had dared challenge. The sun was a sparkling light high on the pitch of noon, offering little comfort, only a glare that bounced off the unbroken snow lining their route. The wind in successive, icy gusts indifferently sucked the new fallen snow into deadly white funnels concealing the road, a curving wall of white with no beginning and no end. It blew continually from the northwest as Monty Wells negotiated each slow curve on the highway a good distance north of Guelph, his thin lips pressed so tightly together they disappeared in an undulating line. He squinted uncomfortably, his eyes squeezed to aching slits behind the rimless spectacles sitting high on the fine, thin nose. Between spasms of concentration the thought came again and again, 'This is the last time he'll do this to me, he'll never do it again, never.' Beside him sat his wife, her endless soft voice stilled for once by the serious occasion. She disliked Spohr, considered him in some ways her husband's evil genius, responsible for his drinking, his petty infidelity, and in an altogether indefinable way, responsible for the lack of academic success which he so evidently deserved. Yet she would never have failed to accompany him while Monty offered what respect he could to his old friend, his nemesis, now improbably, inscrutably dead. Annie March sat alone in the back seat, her white face folded in shock, the tightly pulled back hair making grief and fatigue stand out like ornaments on her lined face. S., unexpectedly in town, had refused to accompany her although she asked him twice. 'The boatman,' she thought sadly, 'Has certainly come again, the time of respite is over. Now we're out there right up against it; my God, what will become of us?' Farther back on the same road the bus rolled against the wind, the driver sweating but confident. Sally sat huddled in her heavy sheepskin coat at the back of the bus, blinded by the dazzling light and her tears. Both Monty and Sandy Burns had offered to drive her to Luther, but she declined, not caring to be polite. 'The journey to my friend's grave, to Spohr's grave, this I have to make alone. I want to go slowly, thinking about him, remembering him, weeping for him every inch of the way.' It never occurred to Sally the darkness which gathered him in was seeping now towards her, that her own light would be out in a matter of weeks. The few mourners came separately in ones and twos, Sandy drove up alone out of deference to Spohr's family, Nella and Marguerite having arrived the day before. From the moment Nella returned Marguerite took charge, she bought whiskey and procured a supply of Valium. These she administered in relentless doses like a well-starched nurse, solicitous and domineering. Nella became too confused to object. Spohr's parents drove the lonely miles to Luther alone, grieving with unbearable pain. Two grim faced uncles and a cousin came from a distant state, they drove all day and all night. John Adolph appeared briefly the day before the funeral, offered his condolences to Nella and to Spohr's parents whom he had never met, and returned to the city. The others, including Sevcik and Birgitte, Schradieck and Lisa, were to meet at the commercial hotel where rooms had been booked, then proceed to the funeral parlor together. As Sally got off the bus at the restaurant opposite the hotel, an icy wind froze her face still wet with tears. She put dark glasses on, looking up and down the barren street, a highway straddled by the town. If there had once been trees lining the road they had long since been removed to accommodate the streams of summer traffic bound for Georgian Bay. The shops seemed pointlessly ugly: a couple of clothing stores, two hardware stores, a mill, then a co-op, two small grocery stores, a variety store, a large furniture shop which owned and operated the funeral parlor, a down-at-heels restaurant, a shoe store, a small appliance store, a rundown tavern called a hotel, presumably the source of local shame, a bank, a post office, indeed the only building of any consequence before you came to the church which was farther along at a jog in the road. Here the street mercifully changed character, more trees and dormant shrubbery surrounding a hairdresser's, a doctor's office, a secondhand furniture store, a shop front indistinguishable from the others except that it announced library hours a few days each week, a laundromat, an Eaton's catalogue store, the land registry office, the Legion hall, a garage and two gas stations, everything in short, to sustain the village and surrounding farm community. Once off this bleak main street which Sally eyed fondly, remembering frequent visits and escapades with Eddy Knight in pursuit of these memorials to rural taste, the little village gave way to a restrained, very modest charm, amplified considerably in the summertime by its deep, shady maples. But now the wind and a circling snow squall undeterred by the parallel row of shops slammed against her. She crossed the road quickly, went into the hotel and asked for Nella. 'No such person here,' she was smoothly informed. Then Sandy Burns appeared, leading her down a dark concrete corridor which a thin carpet and careless coat of paint did nothing to disguise. 'Marguerite,' he explained, 'Booked the rooms in her own name. You must get her to stop pumping booze and pills into Nella, she brushes me aside insisting it's best for her that way. It's absurd,' he concluded somewhat less distractedly. Nella sat on one of the twin beds jutting across the narrow room, she looked up at Sally and smiled with difficulty. 'What did you do to your hair?' asked Sally. 'Marguerite has been trying to turn me into a respectable widow, what do you think?' Her long blonde hair was tied into a straggling bun at the back of her head exposing the small bony face. Sally had never noticed that Nella's ears stuck out; her sallow skin looked green, her eyes bulged. Marguerite had insisted she wear black, the only thing she could find was a taffeta dress with rhinestone buttons. Sally nodded ambiguously. Nella said, 'God, I thought so too.' Marguerite, also in black, a trim little dress which suited her square body, was persistently cheerful, smiling at nothing in particular, making jokes that fell into silence and indifference.

Nursemaid to Nella, she became hostess as well for the lugubrious situation she had taken over. 'Sally dear, let me get you a drink. Neat whiskey okay? There's ice and water if you prefer. Nella, I'd better fill your glass again, O and here, take this.' Nella held out her tumbler, a water glass provided by the hotel, and kept sipping automatically as if it had been a cup of tea. Tears poured from her eyes and ran down her face. Sally passed a wad of tissue which quickly became a soggy ball. Sandy reappeared, 'The others are leaving, I think we're supposed to go now.' Marguerite looked at her watch, 'Too early, it doesn't start till two and we only need a few minutes to get there, it's just outside the town. Sit down, let's have another drink.' She poured a small quantity of scotch into each glass, Sally began to feel as if she was floating, suspended in a net separating the past from the future. The present quietly slipped away until there was a knock at the door. Sandy discovered a small, dark figure, 'Preacher asked fer me to tell yuh they cain't start service withouten you be there. Folks all be waitin' on yuh and could youse please git there now.' They jumped up, Marguerite put on a black hat with a spidery veil, Sally wrapped the brown and white raw sheepskin coat around herself. She and Nella both put on dark glasses as Sandy aimed the car into disappearing clouds of snow, driving slowly, carefully. Five minutes beyond the outskirts of town he asked Nella, 'Which side of the road is it on?' 'The left.' 'Do you think we passed it?' 'I haven't been watching.' 'We'd better turn back then.' They drove back into town, carefully. 'Must have missed it, let's try again, everyone watch this time.' 'Did Spohr want this, to be buried out here?' asked Sally. 'It was my

idea,' said Nella, 'Can you imagine Spohr talking about his
own death?' 'Anyone see it yet?' 'Do you think we should turn
back?' 'Give it another minute.' They missed it and tried again,
then they found it, a bleak house with a circular driveway set
close to the road. The enlarged house might have been a solid
country home except for the sign which lit up at night,
McDonnell Mackie, Funeral Home. Sally took Nella's arm on
one side and Marguerite the other, Sandy followed behind.
They opened the door of the chapel and paused briefly in the
doorway while the few dozen people already there turned to
stare. The dark glasses, their late arrival, the huge coat which
made Sally look like a bear, the dramatic pause, it was too
theatrical for the assembled mourners. The silence became
tense, they held their breath as they waited, watching the three
women walk down the aisle to the front row where seats had
been kept for them. They sat down; someone sighed. It was too
hot yet they made no move to loosen their coats, certain that
any move would be the wrong one. The Reverend Allen
Norman, less shabby than usual, strode to the lectern at the
front of the chapel, looking over towards Nella affectionately.
When he had spoken to her the night before she requested only
that he try to limit references to the Father, the Son and Holy
Ghost. His capacious Anglican conscience was equipped for
the challenge as he began to speak, hesitatingly at first,
reaching up often to pat the strands of white hair back into
place across the shining bald head. *I come to pluck your berries
harsh and crude.* 'This is a difficult, sorrowful moment for us
all, to lose a husband, a cherished son, a trusted friend, this is
a terrible grief in our life. We must comfort each other, comfort

368

ourselves at such times, that is our duty, impossible as it may seem to find solace in this moment of suffering. We must look to the future, know that our pain will diminish, will be less as time passes. Time, it is true, does indeed heal all wounds.' He went on in a bland, soothing way, not saying much, wanting to say something decent, to offer something profound in memory of this man who had been his friend. He cast about for the comfortable images which he customarily applied like gauze dressings to a desperate injury, useless yet somehow better than nothing, but the restraints imposed on his rhetorical flow seemed to tie his tongue a little, he made no headway. Soon he began to sweat and unbuttoned his jacket revealing an old grey cardigan underneath. Seeking safer, surer ground he talked instead about Spohr whom they had gathered to lay to rest. Sally heard Nella sobbing deeply, the tears were pouring down her own face, anything to release the wrenching pain in her chest. Nella retched twice and Sally whispered, 'Do you want me to take you out?' She shook her head groping at the soaked tissue for a usable spot, made a convulsive effort and recovered. Sally slumped back in her chair. 'Alfred Spohr was a remarkable, an extraordinary man whose scientific genius, whose intellect we shall all remember and be grateful for. He was not a man of God, but I would offer God's comfort to those who can accept it,' he inserted tactfully. 'We are born, we live for a time, long or short, and we die, that is the way of it. In the midst of life we die, no one escapes, death comes for us all. During the time we are given we must seek the reason we're here. He would not I know, have put it that way, yet Alfred Spohr spent his time on earth examining the great questions, on

369

his own terms, in his own way. Whether he found the answers is not the point now, the questions themselves are barely communicable, let alone the answers. Jesus said, "Seek and ye shall find." No one sought more ardently, more durably than our departed friend.' He paused, remembering with sadness the long midnight disquisitions. 'Science itself may not be the appropriate basis for pursuing God's love, for knowledge of Him, but He bestowed the gift of science on us, and to develop or explore such gifts must in part respond to the search enjoined upon us. No matter what else he was doing, he fulfilled this obligation in his own way. We must consider that for millions and millions of people in the world today, for whatever reason, God does not exist; that is not to say they do not exist in His eyes. He sees their difficulties and with endless compassion, endless mercy He is moved, He protects us all, believers and nonbelievers alike. Alfred Spohr was not a man of God, yet how can we say he has not accomplished the things he was sent to do? Not one among us can profess to know how his life will be assessed, God Himself is the only judge, the ultimate judge.' He looked into the sad faces, most of them unknown to him, and prayed for help, 'To his parents,' he said studying their dazed faces shattered by incomprehensible pain, 'I can only say that I am a parent, that your son was like a son to me too, everything I ever wanted for my own boy. It seems insupportable to have the natural order reversed, to mourn the death of our own child who ought to have lived to mourn for us. I know he was a good son to you both, be comforted, he is remembered with great respect. But O the heavy charge, now thou art gone. To his wife,' he ignored the estrangement, 'I beg

370

you to seek what you can from the remainder of your life. To grieve for a time is necessary, only let comfort begin too, you are a young woman, very young. How soon hath Time the subtle theef of youth Stoln on his wing my three and twentith yeer! The great poet's view was limited only by his youth, if he had dreamt, if he had known what the future held, how might his song have rung from the crystal spheres. Let your life be full, use every precious moment as though it were the last. To his grieving friends and relatives, among whom I number myself, may we look for and find what peace we can in this trouble, each in his own way. God willingly comforts those who turn to Him, taste what He offers, remember your friend well.' He nodded to the man sitting at the electric organ in the corner, a dreadful sound filled the air. More pitiful than weeping, a tuneless, unrecognizable hymn staggered from its mechanical depths spreading a wash of sorrow. 'Let us conclude by reciting The Lord's Prayer.' They were spared the graveside ordeal, the earth would not receive his body until the ground thawed in the springtime, and meanwhile the refrigerated remains were kept on a shelf. The mourners returned briefly to the commercial hotel to offer their final, formal condolences. Marguerite, the spidery veil turned up over the rim of her neat black hat resumed her duty as hostess, producing apparently from nowhere, an urn of strong, hot tea and paper plates neatly piled with only slightly stale cakes. The grim faced uncles drank whiskey. The parents, incapable of speech sat side by side at the edge of a bed holding each other's hands, not moving, not weeping.

The subtle arc of time is never bound, it flies and flies and never touches down, trapped in flight, a bird on the wind soaring without destination, blown beyond circumstance, above the crests of pleasure and pain, beyond the living, the dying. Remote from good and evil it passes equally over everything human or frail, leaving only the marks, the pattern of flight. When I was a child I longed to fly with that bird, far away from the life that held me, arrive like a stranger in a new world where I would know and be known. And when finally it swooped in flight, obligingly as it always does, and seized me with sharp, fierce claws that would not let me go, whirling dizzily from one far peak to another, I begged for rest, one point that would not change, one point not measured by the flight itself. I longed for a place that did not curve out of being into nonbeing. The cities I visited were nothing more than prisons; I found no place for wisdom or certitude on time's endless arc, that must be sought elsewhere, at a point beyond seeking, with knowledge beyond knowing, and scarcely one among millions and millions I learned, finds his way home. In all the restless years after I left Spohr, the years of wandering across North America, *interstices of time, filled as it were, with sieveholes,* up and down the west coast, south as far as Central America, back to the maritimes then hurrying south again where they spoke slowly and hated strangers but at least you kept warm, then finally in the end, here at the farm, no more than ten miles from the grave where Spohr has been lying all these years, uninterrupted solitude at last. In all the decades which slipped between my fingers like white sand, which flew like a bird unanswerable there in the clouds, I have tried to put the pieces together, tried to find the shapes that interlock. I cannot say I've succeeded, yet it has not eluded me entirely, some areas remain dark while others are nearly complete. What is missing is the structure, the links joining part to part which would make the picture visible. There are moments when I seem to have a glimpse of it, an intimation which keeps me going, but will I ever get close enough to know? Now I find myself hovering like a hawk on the same spot, glancing back to study the trajectory. *Gibt es wirklich die Zeit, die zerstörende?* I watch the golden honeybees buzz from flower to flower, the green and blue dragonflies snatching food from the air, I see the twittering goldfinches zoom up and down, I hear the endless cricket chorus as my time falls away between these gilded moments, like rain back to earth, to oblivion. Dead and dying leaves of memory, I catch them one by one as they fall. The wind blows, the snow falls, each wet flake an intricate design, the mourning dove sits alone on the wire, the cold sun crosses quickly from east to west and my time drops slowly back to earth, the arc descending. Is there a destination? I haven't seen it, but I think it may be there even so, beyond the end. How Spohr would have laughed to hear me talk this way. I can hear him now, an oasis between derision and pity, somehow with interest enough to keep the conversation alive. After all the years of wandering it does not seem strange to be here, it helps, this looping back, like a dream vivid and shining, a dream of coming once more to a place you have loved. Outwardly it is not the same, nothing, no details match, yet where else could it be your heart keeps asking, where else did you find such light even though the streets run straight where they ought to curve and the river disappears where it ought to flow, what other place could touch you this way? Nowhere, nowhere but there the answer comes. The voyage out and the voyage back, do they amount to the same thing in the end? What can I say to that voice which sounds like my own, the voice which belongs to the girl I no longer am yet resembles what I have become? There was a time when I thought I knew, or at least would come to know. The summer after Spohr died, when I came up here with Sandy, the summer Thomas Archer came back, then I thought the answers would come, I thought if I closed my eyes, concentrated hard enough, clearly enough, I would discover everything. Perhaps that was so. Nothing ever happens the way we expect it to; I waited and waited, now I thought, now I will have the truth. I used to think about my mother rocking in her chair at the window. What did she know, why didn't she tell me? When that long, fruitless summer ended, when the anguished cry of the wild goose grew more intense day by day we left separately, and I began to wander. I never caught sight of it again until I came back here, exhausted, worn, finished with life, waiting for that lone, fragile bird to come to rest at last. My heart is a handful of dust, now I do nothing but remember, thinking things over, telling myself each story, a gold bead on a chain, passing the beads in succession through my fingers, pausing to search for a disappearing fragment, confused by the odd perspective, the selectivity of memory. Some scenes unreel willingly, almost seductive, others decline to come, the good times intermingled with the bad, and what does it matter whether they come or they go, what does it matter whether I remember or fail to remember? I've taken what I wanted and given back what I could.

Late summer, a long cool day in late summer. Rain. The clouds of Thursday and mid-afternoon. The old DeSoto edges cautiously up the hill, a dignified ascent. Overripe, uncut, the fields are hollow where the grain has fallen, flattened by its own weight. The maples lining the road are dark and quiet, the leaves not quite ready to change but thinner now, brittle, the green more static than vibrant. Two weeks of cold rain, insistent, unyielding, weeks which have dismissed the larks, the swallows, flickers, finches, killdeer, waxwings, even the robins have left, leaving only pairs of doves and the solitary, stalking hawk, *great Hawk that fliest with the flying Sun!* Down at the marsh the geese group and regroup, their jagged vees lacing the sky, their haunting cry splitting the silence like lightning at the heart of a storm. The curving nose on the dark blue sedan pauses as it crests the hill, champion and conqueror but aging critically. Nella shifts gears coasting down the gently sloping road to the bottom of the rise, then up towards the white stuccoed house standing in perfect symmetry against the grey, rolling sky, parking now in the pebbled laneway. The shining black and white cruiser, like some efficient, chromed scarob roaring out of a windstorm slams into place, rocking on its springs inches behind the DeSoto, a quick no exit maneuver. Nella slips from the driver's seat, turning slowly, gracefully, her hair a shower of unexpected gold, a windup doll turning on her pedestal. The uniformed constable observes impassively.

- Well hello there, not such a nice day then, is it?
- It's all right.
- You just stopping by?
- Duty ma'am, on duty.
- In that case, is there anything I can do for you?
- We've had reports
- Reports?
- A suspicious character in the neighborhood.
- Hm.
- Seems he frightened Janie Wardle half to death down there at the general store. Last seen sitting under a tree in your driveway. Seen him?
- What would you say he looks like?
- Weird, some kind of weird.
- Then I think it's my friend. Bleached blonde hair almost white, rather diabolical little black goatee?
- Sounds like him.
- Mauve trousers and possibly, just possibly a turban.
- Friend of yours, you say?
- Well yes, he's my guest, arrived day before yesterday. Look, I know he seems bizarre, but I assure you, we've been friends for years, he's quite harmless.
- What's his name?

- Thomas Archer, that's what he calls himself, his real name is Steele, Tom Steele.

- O Tom, is it?

- He's been in the hospital, the looney bin from time to time, but he wouldn't hurt a fly. I've known him a long time, I can guarantee he would never harm a living creature, except possibly himself. He's quite shy actually.

- Well he frightened a few around here, Mrs. Wardle thought she might get her throat slit.

- I'll go talk to her. He dresses strangely, and his hair, well he thinks that's a disguise. He's dreadfully paranoic, you know, he dresses that way to protect himself, not to frighten anyone. He tries, if you can believe it, to be inconspicuous, he doesn't want anyone to notice him.

- Tom, you say?

- Mnn.

- Well now, harmless you say?

- Absolutely, we've been close friends for many, many years. He likes to wander around the countryside but I keep an eye on him.

- Are you on your own here?

- No, I have another friend visiting. He's a brilliant man, you know, his brain is cracked, but he's still a very brilliant man. It's sad, terribly sad. He was an artist.

- Was?

- The hospitals, they must have given him every kind of shock treatment in the book, he can't do much any more. They took away his memory, destroyed it to save him. He was strange enough before, but now . . .

- Poor devil, well tell him to keep away from the village. How long will he be here?
- Probably not much longer, he doesn't like to stay in one place. I'll talk to Janie Wardle and ask her to let everyone know he's here. I should have done that sooner, but I'm used to him, I'd forgotten how strange he looks. Sorry you've had all this bother.
- Well if you'll keep an eye on him.
- O certainly, and I'll talk to the folks at the store.
- If you're sure he's okay.
- Quite sure.
- I guess it's all right then.

The cruiser backs slowly down the laneway to the road, shoots into first and screams off down the road, accelerating into each new gear with high-pitched frenzy, then disappears in a diminishing funnel of sound. Nella turns, watching a backward somersaulting figure approach with accuracy and agility.

- Where were you?
- Hiding in the woodshed.
- I thought so, I just lied and lied to the O.P.P.
- You're generous today.
- Why did you go to the store? Janie thought you were an assassin come to finish her off, poor old thing. You're visible in the wilderness, you know, the city offers more protection. Out here everyone notices everything, especially anything unusual, and you *are* unusual. Were you wearing the turban?
- Afraid so.
- Not such a good idea.

- What did they want?

- To know who you are and what you're up to.

- What did you say?

- I was diplomatic, said you were a visiting foreigner who had not relinquished his native dress.

- Very accurate, on our planet we all dress this way.

- Nevertheless, it would be a good idea to keep out of sight. At any rate, I'd avoid the village.

- One visit to Niflheim is sufficient. Armed conflict becomes tedious.

- Tom, please try to be discreet.

- Promise.

- Good. Where did you go today?

- In pursuit of the beauteous *ascweepia,* my queen.

- Of what?

- *Ascweepia,* the fecund, the fruitful. *Ascweepia* the green goddess, beneficent and demure. *Ascweepia dachia,* don't you know her?

- *Asclepia?*

His rotten stumps of teeth make the pronunciation of certain letters difficult.

- Right, haven't you ever eaten *ascweepia?* Delicious, a perfect food with a little oil and salt, but young, tender leaves only. The older ones get tough and stringy. I've actually found some, remarkable this time of year, I'll cook them for supper.

- No thanks, I've heard of eating milkweed but the leaves seem a little too fuzzy, too hairy.

- Nonsense, it's saintly food. Lived on it almost exclusively last summer, never felt better. You must try some.

\- How did you sleep last night?

\- Terrible, a huge rat, swoosh, swoosh, kept pacing the attic floor. He crawled past my ear, very close, very slow, swoosh, swoosh, a big one, mean and old and fat.

\- It's possible, you know, but I don't think there are any rats in the house.

\- I saw it, a big one, swoosh, swoosh with his tail, back and forth.

\- You'd better sleep downstairs tonight.

\- Impossible, slept there already. No, tonight I'll sleep outside on the ground.

\- But it's so wet and cold too, the nights have been getting colder again. There's a nice bed in the small room.

\- I don't sleep in beds.

\- Okay Tom, whatever.

\- Sorry, it's unsafe you see, since they deserted me, left me, one by one. There's no protection, any amateur can get at me now. The invincible reduced to dust. I saw the ancient bird this morning down at the marsh, the snake bird looking like a tree stump.

\- The heron?

\- The great blue heron.

\- It's grey.

\- Sh! That's a secret, names are cloaks to wrap around the dagger.

\- Who deserted you?

\- My gods, one by one, I will not say their names. I want you to know something Nella, remember the castles they built for you and me, towers of gold, rocks of crystal and shining walls crusted with mosaics. When they blew up the towers and split the crystal rocks they showed me the floors, all slime and filth. *But now I know that mercy teems in hell.* It was a monstrous deception, they took back the powers they granted, reduced me to this, a magician learning tricks like a child. They are not to be trusted, they accused me of betraying their secrets, yet they were the ones who abandoned me. I believed them but the truth is they are all fake, there is only one God and He won't have me now. Why do you keep this fellow Sandy around Nella? Are you still a bleak hearted witch?

- Sandy's all right, I'm leaving anyhow. Next month. Going to the Yucatan.

- I'm sorry about Spohr, I did all I could, tried to stop them and I couldn't you see, because they had stripped me of my powers.

- What do you mean?

- They killed him . . . spitefully.

- Who?

- They did.

- Tom, he had a heart attack.

- That's what they want you to think but they did it, I know how they operate. You know, you used to.

- And Sally?

- I don't know anything about Sally. Bender said she swallowed a bottle of pills.

- That's a lie. I mean she did take pills only it was an accident, too many, entirely accidental. She would never have done that, never. It's over for all of us, isn't it? I didn't think there would be so little time. Did you know how little time we would have?